# Season of the Dragonflies

# Season of the Dragonflies

SARAH CREECH

𝓌𝓂
WILLIAM MORROW
*An Imprint of* HarperCollins*Publishers*

P.S.™ is a trademark of HarperCollins Publishers.

HarperCollins books may be purchased for educational, business, or sales promotional use. For information please e-mail the Special Markets Department at SPsales@harpercollins.com.

A hardcover edition of this book was published in 2014 by William Morrow, an imprint of HarperCollins Publishers.

FIRST WILLIAM MORROW PAPERBACK EDITION PUBLISHED 2015.

Designed by Lisa Stokes

Library of Congress Cataloging-in-Publication Data has been applied for.

ISBN 978-0-06-230753-8

15  16  17  18  19  ov/rrd  10 9 8 7 6 5 4 3 2 1

FOR MY MOTHER, CHAREATHA

*I do not wish [women] to have power over men; but over themselves.*

—MARY WOLLSTONECRAFT

*A woman who doesn't wear perfume has no future.*

—COCO CHANEL

Season of the Dragonflies

## THE BEGINNING OF LENORE INCORPORATED:

# Serena's Story

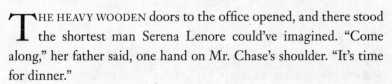

THE HEAVY WOODEN doors to the office opened, and there stood the shortest man Serena Lenore could've imagined. "Come along," her father said, one hand on Mr. Chase's shoulder. "It's time for dinner."

Mr. Chase smiled at Serena, his thin lips spread so wide they nearly disappeared. The sight of him made her thighs lock together. Those lips, and only those lips, would eventually find their way beneath all these layers of petticoat. His head was so long, like a horse's, and his eyes too small, like a doll's. How could her father do this to her? Did he have no feelings at all? Did he not remember what it meant to be in love? Mr. Chase was a banking heir. His family owned stock in rail, steel, and now oil and even grocery chains. They invested in small men with big dreams and made fortunes. Anyone who wanted to develop real estate in the city needed the Chase family, and her father needed Serena to sacrifice herself for his business expansion. "For your future and fortune, my darling," her father had reasoned.

"But what about love?" And to this her father had no answer. Could she say no? Serena dreamed about saying no; every night the same settee and the same tumbler of scotch in her father's hand appeared. But when she told him, he dissolved on the spot, her only living parent lost to her forever. The same dream every single night, just like the same dull days in the dull marriage she'd succumb to soon enough.

Undoubtedly, Mr. Chase would work as hard as her father and be home just as little, and this brought Serena her only comfort. Her bitterness bubbled like percolating coffee as she walked behind the two men down the mahogany hallway, which was as narrow as a coffin. She smelled vegetable broth boiling in the kitchen. She sat down at the dining room table set for sixteen, thankfully many seats away from her father and Mr. Chase. Serena recognized only a few faces at the table, like the decrepit Mrs. Barts, whose breath smelled like rotten meat. Serena's trust manager, Mr. Hart, arrived without a date, as usual, and he was seated next to Mrs. Barts. At least it wouldn't be Serena's charge to conduct close conversation with the old woman tonight. Otherwise, Serena's father had invited potential business partners to witness this momentous day in her life. She hardly knew any of them, though Mr. Chase seemed familiar with all of them. He shook their hands and they patted his shoulders, one by one, before taking their seats. Mr. Chase's mother was the only other woman in attendance.

A young man sat directly across from Serena, a man she hadn't seen before at her father's table. He'd slicked his dark blond hair into place with pomade, like waves in the ocean, and his eyes were so blue she had to look away for fear of being indecent. But he didn't look away from her. Indeed, he stared. His lips were not too thin, his skin not prematurely wrinkled.

Her father stood with a champagne flute in hand (none for Serena, of course) and said, "Tonight's very special. My daughter, Serena, is now engaged to Mr. Chase. Such a delightful match; I couldn't have asked for a better son-in-law." Everyone turned and smiled at Serena and raised their glasses. The man sitting across from her looked at Mr. Chase and back to Serena. He mimed a small gag, and for a moment Serena really thought he was choking, until he smiled and his leather shoe rubbed against her ankle. She immediately sat up straight.

The man leaned over and spoke to the mayor as if nothing had happened at all, but no one spoke to Serena, and she stirred her vegetable soup until it went cold. Occasionally she glanced to the end of the table where Mr. Chase and her father leaned close together and gaily conversed, like lovers. "You must do it for the family," her father had told her again and again to counter her very reasonable objections: *I don't know him. I'm not ready. I'm only eighteen.* "It's what your mother would've expected," her father had said, and this always silenced her.

Serena knew very little about her mother, except that she had been quite the beauty, a daughter of one of the wealthiest textile merchants in the city, and Serena's father had loved her very, very much. Her nanny insisted on this point. True love. However, her mother didn't return to the woman she'd been before her marriage—witty, charming, free. Only the birth of Serena had offered her temporary happiness. Throughout the years Serena had overheard the staff telling new hires the rumors about her mother, how her sadness brewed storms in the Atlantic, and the more she was confined to the home, the more her once-gleaming blue eyes turned the color of ashes, the more hair she shed, and the more weight she lost. Until a doctor promised Serena's heartbroken father that the only cure was temporary bed rest in Connecticut, and "temporary" became ten years. She died in her sleep when Serena was fourteen. Serena had never been allowed to visit. Her father had promised it would hurt her too much.

Wicked hurricanes would brew just for Serena. Her unhappiness would make lightning strike. Though her father had fallen madly in love with her mother, Serena wasn't convinced her mother would have wanted this kind of marriage for her, not if it felt like this.

During a main course of lamb medallions in a red wine and rosemary reduction, Serena's foot found its way into the pant cuff of the blond man. Their feet caressed for a brief moment before her father called upon him. "Dr. Alex Danner," her father said in his booming baritone voice, "please tell us of those wild adventures of yours."

Dr. Alex Danner cleared his throat, smoothed his tie with one hand, and then said, "In Southeast Asia there are remote islands with the world's oldest rain forests and an amazing range of biodiversity. Much like the Amazon, which most of you are familiar with, I assume." He had captured the full table's attention, especially Serena's.

"There's an English-speaking community in Borneo and Sumatra now, as those islands are referred to, and my company's offered to send me there to study the flora," he said. His cheeks reddened and his voice grew louder. "And to discover—at least we hope—cures for the maladies of our times. Tuberculosis and malaria, chiefly."

"Is it a dangerous place?" Mrs. Barts said.

"Yes, ma'am, I suppose it is." Alex smiled and added, "Tigers frighten me most."

"I should say so." Mrs. Barts fanned herself with a linen napkin.

"What do you most want to see there?" Mr. Chase said, and Serena cringed. He was the kind of man to ask others about the unknown world without any desire to experience it for himself.

Alex said, "Orangutans in their nests. They build them so high in the forest's canopy, they can be rather hard to spot. Dragonflies too. More species there than anywhere on earth. But I assure you, gentlemen, I will not go for sightseeing. I'm convinced those islands hold cures for human diseases, and that mystery is the only one I care about."

"Of course, of course," her father said. "Five years, is it?"

"I will make a return visit for an update then, sir," he said.

"Very well," her father said.

Five years. *Five years?* Serena glanced at Mr. Chase at the far end of the table, who dabbed at his mouth with his handkerchief like a woman might, and she swallowed hard. Five years from now she'd have two ankle-biters with that man and she'd be used and gray, just like her poor dead mother. She wrapped both of her ankles around Alex's leg and squeezed, and he pretended not to notice. With one elbow propped on the table Alex carried on about his research to the mayor, and with his free hand he lifted one of Serena's ankles and caressed her foot in the shadows of the tablecloth.

After dinner the men planned to sequester themselves in the library for scotch and cigars and to discuss investment in Alex's project. The women gathered for a game of bridge. Alex asked to be excused and the crowd of men moved ahead without him. As he neared the bathroom Serena took his hand from behind and led him to a room beneath the staircase, glancing over her shoulder just in case her father or Mr. Chase might inquire.

In the darkness of the closet she lit a candlestick, and here he discovered her romance novels and blankets and candies, this place she saved just for herself, a place where her father assumed the staff kept dry goods or utensils. And this is where she took Dr. Alex Danner into her arms, kissed him, and said, "Take me with you. Please, you must." He backed her against a wall and kissed her with such force she thought her corset might tear. She loved him immediately, and she knew he loved her just the same when he said, "Your eyes flicker with jungle fire." She wanted out of that corset, that closet, that brownstone, out of New York City. She was made for much more than she knew existed. Borneo. Sumatra. Plants unseen and unnamed. Exotic smells floating on warm night air. "Take me," she begged. "I can't stay here another moment longer."

SERENA PLANNED THEIR SECRET DEPARTURE as her father slumbered. She and Alex escaped from New York Harbor on the *Princess Anne* liner to the south. She'd left her father a brief note about her desire to travel without disclosing an exact location, and she prayed he might forgive her, though she doubted he ever would; there was much she couldn't forgive him for, and thus, they were even. They sailed beyond the Caribbean, South America, Cape Horn, places Serena had only read about in travel books. The ship stopped at seventeen ports, but she spent much of the time ill in their windowless berth, only partially from seasickness. Almost nine months later they docked on the north coast of Borneo, an area governed by British rule. Here she found medical assistance for the birth of her daughter, a girl whose first toys were palm fronds, rocks, and dirt sculptures of her making, not dolls. No one would force her daughter to wear a corset.

Serena and Alex grew more deeply in love and more infatuated with each other's company in the isolation of the jungle. Alex did not let a day pass without reminding Serena how happy she made him. Their conversation was restricted to each other and the children they raised together. They lived happily with their two daughters, the second one born in their mud-and-bark hut far inland from the coast of the South China Sea. Serena and Alex were more in love seven years later than either had imagined possible.

Serena's hips widened from childbirth, her breasts softened from feeding, and her back grew stronger from carrying her babies slung across it like the local Dayak women did. Serena had transformed in those seven years from a girl of eighteen to a woman of twenty-five with more firsthand knowledge of the world than any of the girls she had tutored with in New York. Serena missed many things about New York, like her bathroom and its running water; her father, whom she loved more now that she lived far away; and her brownstone, because her mother had decorated it. But the pristine rain forest, the uncultivated privacy of the world she'd grown to understand, had become her chosen reality. Her daughters wore loose-fitting clothes to ward off mosquitoes, but inside their dwelling they were as naked as the orangutans that loomed in their stick-and-leaf nests in the trees.

Stinking peels of durian fruit signaled a nearby ape, and Serena's children found playmates in the young ones and tasted those huge, spiked fruits that smelled of burned milk custard and onion. Serena loved her life. Most of all she cherished Alex, the only scientist daring enough to bring a woman to a place like Borneo.

Some families lived in more Western villages, but Alex and Serena did not often go to visit them, as it took a day's boat ride. With two young children it was only worth it if they needed supplies. They battled together as a team—fevers, bouts of malaria, strange carnivorous insects, bites so unusual only the local tinctures could heal them—and they survived together. Even prospered together. Only during the comparatively quiet nights in the jungle did Serena question whether she had a purpose other than raising her girls and supporting Alex's research, both of which she loved doing. Her daughters gave her laughter, and she enjoyed tagging plants and helping Alex organize his notes. Alex had discovered so many different species of plants with such promising possibilities that he believed they would be wealthier than Serena's father when he developed them in America.

News of America's financial collapse reached Borneo almost a year after the market crashed. Alex had been the one to share the news with Serena. She thought of her father and wondered how he had fared. Alex and Serena debated the severity of these events after sunset when the girls had fallen asleep and only the forest and its wild symphony were still hotly awake. He held her in the hammock they shared and said, "Investments are down; the company doesn't know how much longer they can support us." The company had postponed his return twice already.

"Maybe it's time," Serena said. She almost added "to go home," but the hut was home, and she had no idea what they'd find when they returned to the States. A few weeks later, the company requested Alex's return. His years of work had not been in vain. He had treated multiple local children for malaria in the past year with a formula based on an oil extraction from a small purple flower shaped like a honeysuckle that the Dayaks ritually rubbed on themselves for good health. He needed more advanced laboratories to develop his TB cure.

During their final days, Alex and Serena and the little girls sang sad songs about their hut and jungle and made jokes about a return to civilization. Serena told them, "It'll feel like a jungle of buildings." She knew it would feel as foreign as Borneo had the first moment she stepped from that godforsaken ship and stared at a wall of untamed trees so unlike any she'd seen in Central Park. Her girls would feel the same deep sense of fear at their first sight of a Model T.

On their last afternoon in Borneo, they cleaned up their hut for the next scientist and placed their few belongings by the curtained door in preparation for their boat the next day. But the girls worked slowly, and Alex continued to wrap a splintered bamboo shaft fifty different ways. Serena said, "Let's take a walk and do this later."

Serena led her family outside but stopped when she heard chanting. The voices lowered and heightened in waves. Alex pulled on her hand. "Shouldn't we go a different way? They're worshipping."

And even though their children trailed her and normally she would've avoided interrupting a local custom, she couldn't resist the sound of those voices. She felt compelled into the depths of the forest. The sounds grew louder until she saw a group of bare-breasted Dayak women hovering together over a single spot on the forest floor.

Serena advanced until she stood directly behind the circle of women and tried to peer inside, kneeling just as they did, as it was the only way to glimpse the small white flower barely visible amid the brush. One woman's dark hands gently pushed the woody leaves away from the plant, and each time her skin brushed the petals it looked as if the plant wilted on the spot. Each time the woman moved away, the plant grew healthy again and the group made noises of astonishment.

The women had never seen this particular gardenia flower before, that much was clear.

Serena needed to touch that plant. She pushed through the crowd. A velvety red dragonfly fluttered nearby, a much larger species than the ones she and the girls had chased during their stay. Without warning it dropped down near the plant and then disappeared into the surrounding trees. Serena closed in. The plant's white petals grew larger, and a woody branch appeared beneath it and reached in her direction. The Dayak women pulled away with small shouts of horror, and one woman tried to hold Serena's arm back. Alex and her daughters stood far away. Serena pulled herself forward and reached her small hands down to the plant as an invitation. The moment her finger touched its stem, the plant began to shake itself free from the ground, exposing its long white roots, and nearly leaped into her palms. A scent more heavenly than any she'd encountered in the forest invaded Serena's nostrils and filled her entire body with more glory than motherhood or love or sunlight could.

Her black hair fell loose from its bun and draped her shoulders. Serena placed the plant on top of her head and wrapped it up with her bundle of hair, the same pompadour style she had worn as a girl of eighteen. The Dayak women parted as she walked past, and a gentle rain followed them out of the forest. A perfumed wind surrounded Serena and her family with every step she took.

The plant she named *Gardenia potentiae* had chosen her, and it survived in her nest of hair for the voyage back to the States; it required only a splash of water in the mornings to keep its strength. With every day that passed on the liner, Alex vowed that Serena looked more regal than the day before. He wrapped his arms around her from behind, kissed her neck, and said, "Your skin's never smelled so good. This is your perfume." Other people on the ship destined for New York deferred to her in all matters, and the waiters offered her nothing but the best service. Exotic orchids arrived in their room each time the boat docked, and the staff reserved the richest of desserts and rarest of fruits for Serena's daughters. She was the most powerful woman on the boat. She swore *Gardenia potentiae* would be the last scent she ever wore.

The harsh northern winters of New York could not accommodate a plant that Alex deemed the most impressive species of flower he'd encountered in Borneo. They needed privacy for Serena's flower to flourish, lest people start questioning how and why the plant moved. So they decided to dock early in the Chesapeake Bay, the plant hidden safely in Serena's hair without raising a single suspicion from an inspector. The family journeyed three days to the fertile ground of Quartz Hollow in the Blue Ridge Mountains of Virginia, where Alex had been born. Serena wrote to her father upon settling in their cabin and notified him of her return, but he never responded. Alex turned in his research and gave up his post to take over his ailing father's farm, where Serena could graft and grow hundreds of acres of *Gardenia potentiae*. The flower moved only for her hands and the hands of her daughters, and it soon became the secret ingredient in the most enigmatic, expensive, and successful perfume in history. Serena appointed herself president of the perfumery and bestowed upon her business her name—Lenore Incorporated.

PART ONE

# DISTILLATION

## CHAPTER 1
### *Three Generations Later*

JONAH HAD LET his curly black hair grow out the way Lucia Lenore always liked it, maybe even to spite her, and his blue eyes seemed even brighter. He dropped down on their organic futon, sending her side up like a seesaw. This final piece of their shared furniture was destined for the landfill, and with good cause. At least Lucia would never sleep another night on a worn-out cushion.

Jonah said, "The sublet starts next month. I'll make sure the paperwork's straight."

"I'm out today," Lucia said, her thigh touching his knee by accident. She signed her name on the last page and handed Jonah his pen. He placed the stack of papers on the cardboard box she'd set up as a coffee table. A prenup and no children made this transaction easy, almost too simple—like it had been set up to fail. Overall, they'd met little resistance from friends, and as far as family, only Jonah's happily married parents knew, and they refrained from offering wisdom: "We'd better not weigh in on this" translated into "We agree this is best."

Jonah placed one long arm around her and squeezed. She let her head fall on his shoulder. Here was the moment he'd take it back, shred the papers, and finally apologize . . . and what was *wrong* with Lucia that deep down she wanted him to do exactly that?

He kissed the crown of her head before saying, "I'll always be here."

"I know," she said.

"Nina's?" he said quietly, perhaps to reduce how insulting it sounded that she would couch-surf at a friend's place, the very same friend who had introduced Lucia to Jonah at his MoMA opening eight years ago.

"Probably," Lucia said, but she didn't know; she hadn't even asked Nina yet. Silence settled between them.

Jonah squeezed her one more time and then stood up and said, "Can I go back to get a few things?" Lucia nodded, and Jonah retreated to their bedroom for the final time.

Lucia would never hear his hangers slide on the short metal rack again or see his beard trimmings in the sink or dropped toenail clippings beside the couch. When they were in love she thought those little memories might comfort her when he died. *If only I could see those obscenely hard toenail clippings stuck one more time in the low-pile rug.* But for the past year, maybe longer (if she forced herself to pinpoint), wicked arguments about such things had become another tenant in their small apartment. He couldn't stand fishing her long black hairs out of the tub drain. They felt genuine hate for each other, and that's all they needed to know.

What she never wanted to reveal to anyone was how many holes Jonah had punched in their drywall, hidden for so long by his over-priced canvases, and how many times she'd thrown shoes, keys, purses, and infomercial scripts at him. Jonah and Lucia and their marriage had crumbled together like buildings during an earthquake, but no single person or event deserved the blame.

She stood up from the futon and stumbled over the Persian rug they'd found at the flea market. Four years later it still smelled like dog. Lucia opened the clear five-gallon storage tub that held their liquor, all going to Jonah's new place. The gin and vodka and whiskey had acted like kerosene for their fires, a sure way to embolden a fight that could've been avoided or start a fight if one didn't exist. Yet they couldn't keep themselves from drinking together, like it was their only sport. She squeezed the last bottle in and then tried to snap the top into place. But it wouldn't go. She sat on it and hoped weight and gravity would do the rest.

Jonah returned from the bedroom and said, "Here, let me help." With her still seated on the top, he placed an arm on either side of her and closed the top with one forceful push down, his sinewy biceps bigger than she remembered—had he started working out? The sex had been hotter when they had separate apartments and no legal contract promising to be faithful, and suddenly this slight embrace on the storage tub made her horny for the first time in who knew how long. She wanted to tell him this, as if they could try again.

Jonah stared into her eyes. She let him kiss her, but she couldn't manage to relax her lips and she kept her eyes wide open. Too much had happened between them now to recover this element of their relationship.

A dart of indigo flashed by the windowpane; Lucia glanced in that direction and pulled away from Jonah. She saw nothing save concrete beyond the glass, but the moment to make this big mistake had already passed, and she ducked underneath his arms and stood up. "Not my best idea," she said.

Jonah traced the corners of his mouth with his thumb and pointer finger, the way he always did when he didn't agree with her.

Another bright streak of blue dashed outside the window. "Isn't that the strangest thing?" she said. Lucia moved toward the exposed brick wall in their apartment. "Are you seeing this?" She pointed to the window in the center, but by this time she didn't need to; so many blue dragonflies hovered right outside that she couldn't count them all, their collected mass blocking out the sunlight and darkening the room like a curtain. The insects tapped their jaws against the glass.

Jonah said, "It's like they want in."

Lucia closed her eyes and clasped her arms together. She couldn't suppress the smells of wild honeysuckle vining on fencerows and split trunks of cedar and tulip poplars and oaks ushering forth from her memory; the smells of wet leaf mulch on the forest floor and peeled peat moss along creek banks; the smells of girlhood, of her mother and her older sister and the Blue Ridge Mountains; acres upon acres of her family's flower planted on the hills above the cabin, blanketing the town of Quartz Hollow with a smell richer than jasmine.

She hadn't been home in so many years—fifteen, to be exact—and she knew these weren't random bugs coming down from Syracuse or Albany. These were Lucia's dragonflies. One dragonfly paused close enough to the glass for Lucia to gaze into its bulbous jade-green eyes, each with a black speck in the center. They appeared to gaze right back at Lucia. The yellow thorax tapered into a thin abdomen, the same color as the clear blue sky in the distance. Lucia bent down slightly, and the filament etching inside the wings turned metallic red in the sunlight. Adult dragonflies lived for only a month or so, but the symbol of infinity gave shape to their two sets of wings; they could control each set separately and had the freedom to change directions whenever they wished. Lucia envied them this trait. Then, just as quickly as they had arrived, they darted away; the dragonflies dropped below Lucia's window and vanished without a trace.

"I hate summer bugs," Jonah said, and backed away from the window. With both hands flat on the pane Lucia continued to stare, desperate to catch sight of them again. Jonah placed his hand on Lucia's shoulder and she turned around. He presented the only canvas of his that remained in the apartment, one she'd purposely quarantined in the bedroom; the real Lucia slept on the futon. It was a muse painting from when they had first started dating. He'd captured Lucia's bountiful hair, long eyelashes, pale skin, and alert blue eyes with an exaggerated lucidity. He had chosen not to sell it, though now she wished he had. How long had it been since he last painted anything connected to her? Two, three years? Why even count anymore?

"It's yours if you want it," he said. She stared at the painting but didn't recognize that girl. She'd never existed, not in all that confident glory. She shook her head.

"You're sure?" he said.

Lucia couldn't bear for him to recommend she sell the painting to the SoHo Corner Gallery, even though they both knew she could use the money. She said, "I'm sure," before he had the chance to suggest it.

Jonah placed the painting and a box of supplies on top of the storage bin of liquor and his jeans and sweaters on top of that, then crowned it all with his black-and-white-checkered Converse sneakers. Those sneakers had now become her emblem for Jonah: juvenile and on top of the world. He probably had an appointment with a buyer.

Jonah tucked the signed divorce agreement beneath his arm like an umbrella. "Call me in the next few days and let me know how you are," he said, and went to their door and looked back at her one last time before leaving.

The door clicked shut, and the brake-slamming sounds of the Upper East Side emanated from thirty stories below their small apartment. Those noises used to give Lucia comfort; when she moved to New York City on her eighteenth birthday they were auditory finish lines, a must-have soundtrack to her new life away from Quartz Hollow, but they had morphed into a recursive loop, and all she desired was an "off" button. Now she had another move before her. How had she let herself become so dependent on another person? Or how had *they* let it happen? Certainly Jonah had a part in it too. Lucia had so many questions for him that he would never answer. Such was the way of divorce.

Left alone in this apartment for the past few weeks, Lucia had made canned soup in the microwave and drunk Pinot Grigio from a box. Jonah could afford a one-bedroom apartment in SoHo, along with his studio on Eighth Avenue. Without Lucia to support, he had plenty of cash to spend on dating anorexic fashion designers. And only one recurring thought haunted her: *If I were as successful as Jonah Little, and on my own like him, then our relationship might've survived.*

Lucia Little. She wasn't comfortable using that name to sign checks or thank-you cards; she especially disliked using it at auditions and casting calls. Ms. Soon-Not-to-Be-Little plopped back down on the futon and opened the faded *Forbes* magazine she'd tucked underneath the cushion a week ago. Lucia stared at her maiden name on the "400" list, and she looped her mother's entry with the tip of her finger: *Number 27: Willow Lenore . . . Net Worth: $11.9 B . . . Age: 61 . . . Residence: Quartz Hollow, Virginia . . . Source: Diversified.* Why had she given up her maiden name? It sounded much better than Little. Lucia tossed the *Forbes* magazine in the black garbage bag she'd begun for all her soup cans and many boxes of Franzia. A poor effort on her part, considering how many splayed Progresso cans remained scattered on the floor.

Lucia couldn't stay in their empty apartment another night replaying the same bad marriage scenes in her head. With tomato soup as her only comfort. The dragonflies were headed home to Quartz Hollow, had to be. As much as Lucia hated to admit it, she had nowhere else to go. She could move into her friend Nina's place for a couple of weeks, but then what? Her funds were barely getting her by; she was just one nanny job away from eating nothing but one miso soup a day.

Lucia pulled well-worn yoga pants, one pair of jeans, and two T-shirts off the floor next to the futon and tossed them in a pink duffel bag. She promised herself it would only be a short visit home. A nip of her mother's moonshine and one of her extravagant picnics in the woods might go a long way toward restoring her, and maybe the quiet away from the city would help Lucia figure out her next move. She gathered her knockoff Coach purse and put on her black ballet flats to go to the airport and take the next flight to Richmond, the last charge on her Visa card before it imploded. Lucia locked the apartment door, headed down the hall toward the elevator, and refused to look behind her at a life she no longer called her own.

# CHAPTER 2
## Sex and Vision

Pinned beneath Mya Lenore's thighs, Luke rolled from side to side as if he couldn't lift her into the air and toss her onto the mattress like a sack of soil. She liked him just where he was, caught by choice beneath her. Mya released his arms, only to guide his hands up her bare abdomen so he could cup her breasts. His callused hands roamed the planes of her hips and ribs and collarbone before stopping at her chin. In his husky mountain accent, Luke said, "I never knew a woman like you."

"Tsk, tsk," Mya said like a preschool teacher, and locked his arms down beside him, then eyed the yellow silk scarves on her bedside table and walked two fingers over to snag them.

"You're bad," Luke said. Mya tied his wrists to one of the brass poles of her headboard and proceeded down from there.

Luke moaned and then said, "Get to it now."

"Patience," she said, and tickled his etched abdomen with her fingernails, dirt still visible beneath them. What she found appealing about a twenty-six-year-old at times also troubled Mya. Luke's youthful eagerness highlighted their ten-year age difference when she hadn't had enough rest, like today.

Luke pulled his wrists free and the scarves dropped to the floor. Mya let her long blond hair create a tent around his pelvis, and he stroked it at the roots. The flowers she'd gathered on her walk and inserted in her hair fell onto the bed. The sweet scent still lingered, but the limp and browning petals no longer looked like a white pinwheel. Luke spread Mya's hair all over his torso and said, "It's so fucking long and beautiful."

Mya said, "A family gift."

Luke pinched her nipple and said, "Don't bring up your mama. It's not a good time."

"True," she said, and rubbed her hand along his inner thigh where his thick, curly hair tapered.

Luke placed one arm behind his head so he could see her better, his biceps curved like a mountain slope. He said, "Your sunshine hair makes me crazy." He ran his fingers through it, and Mya continued to stroke his thigh and rested her cheek on his abdomen. Luke placed his hand at the back of her head and gently nudged it forward, and she gathered him in her mouth and let all her anxious thoughts drain away like water on a drought-blighted plot of earth.

Ten minutes later he shouted out, "Holy mother of good God!" Then he rolled over on the red poppy-print quilt and Mya slapped his pale behind before he got up to go to the bathroom.

Mya left the bedroom and went to the kitchen, where she poured a glass of water mixed with fine sea salt. Luke was still in the bathroom when she returned. What was he doing in there? Mya spread her body out on the hardwood floor and placed the glass of salt water between her feet. She stared at the exposed wooden beams on the ceiling and then called out to Luke, "I dyed my hair black one summer and it turned split-pea green for three months."

After a delay he finally answered, "That was dumb."

"It was," she said. "Lucia had such dark hair and I wanted mine like that." Her little sister had hair as smooth as an onyx stone, and it smelled of summer rain no matter how often she used shampoo. Hair like Great-Grandmother Serena's, a point their mother never failed to brag about, like Lucia's earning straight A's. So much of a normal life had always come easily to Lucia, but in all other ways she had nothing in common with Great-Grandmother. Lucia might have had her hair, but she had no gift for scent or visions.

Luke said, "She's still in New York?"

Mya said, "Married, acting, that's all I know," and she stood up and moved her operation to the bed. She stretched her long legs out on the lavender-scented sheets, balanced the glass of salt water on the bed, and clasped a pillow to her stomach. She stared at the room as a whole—the black rocking chair in the corner beneath an old net that held her stuffed animals, her clothes in a stinking pile desperate to be washed and hung on the line—and then she spotted a stray hair from Luke's head.

She caught it with her fingernails, lifted it up like the metal claw in the toy-vending machine at the grocery store, and secured it in her side-table drawer. A single strand of hair, dried chamomile flowers, seven drops of geranium oil, and a black ribbon secured with a safety pin always did the trick. Sometimes only this spell could break the irrational and impulsive bond of sex that so many people mistook for love.

Luke sauntered back into the room completely nude except for one stray flower pressed on his pelvis and stopped at the foot of the bed. He reached out for the glass, and Mya lunged for it and said, "It's salty." She moved the glass to her bedside table.

"What weird thing are you up to?" Luke said.

Mya tucked her knees to her chest and said, "My foot chakra's messed up."

"Your what?" he said, and he gathered his jean overalls and white undershirt.

"I made a mistake," Mya said.

He looked down at her like she was speaking French. "That got something to do with why we went out molly mooching so damn early?" he said.

She nodded.

Luke hooked his overalls and put his hands in his pockets. "Anything else?"

"That's all," Mya said.

He looked like he might protest but then gave her that sweet side smile. Luke bent down, kissed her on the neck, and tried to pull her closer for round two, but she said, "Can't. Don't you have fields to plow?"

"Ten," he said, and laced his work boots. When he stood back up he grimaced and grabbed his right shoulder.

"Your daddy's working you too hard," Mya said. She turned Luke around and massaged his smooth shoulders, then moved her hands down over his chest muscles.

He dropped his head down and groaned as she worked out his knots.

"When's your mom get back?" he said.

"Tomorrow," she said. She led him through the pale green linen curtains on the doorway. He reached for her hand as if to hold it, but Mya rubbed her hip instead. Not that close, she wanted to tell him. They entered the reading room—Mya's laundry spilled out from the bedroom and landed in this communal living space. Her mother had grown accustomed to it, and she didn't say anything about Mya's messes anymore. Not that tidiness came naturally to her mother. Mya couldn't remember the last time she'd seen the coffee table free of her office overflow.

Luke moved through the clutter without comment. Six months ago Mya had visited Luke's family farm to contract a year's worth of grass-fed beef. She'd expected to talk to his daddy, but he wasn't home. Luke had been restoring the barn's roof and came down the ladder to speak to her. He was shirtless and smooth and sweating and suspicious of why a Lenore woman had come to visit. Mya knew as soon as his boots landed on the earth that she had to have him. She asked him to deliver each week's portion in person, and on his first stop she asked him to stay for lunch. When Luke first entered the cabin, she wondered what he'd say about her messiness, if he might judge her for having bras and underwear strewn about, but all he said was "How long's it been since a man lived here?" And it had never occurred to Mya that a man's presence in the house might shape the array of items she left out. She told him, "Not since my granddaddy died when we were girls." That was the only time Luke mentioned the chaos. They could afford a maid, but her mother didn't like having strangers in the house.

Now they moved through the reading room, with every wall encased in books about perfumery, art, botany—so many books only her mother read. Mya's vegetable stock continued to simmer in the kitchen, filling the house with the earthy smells of onion, carrot, celery, and potatoes. She opened the red front door, where a dried bunch of eucalyptus and rosemary branches hung upside down on a hook. A family of wrens nested there, and each time Mya opened the door, one or more of the family members flew inside. Luke dodged them. They stepped onto the porch together and Mya said, "I'll make food for us tonight."

"Or we could go out," Luke said.

"That's not us, remember? I like us here," Mya said, and this had always been her response because she always felt the same way: she didn't like going to town unless it was for business. But he hated this answer. "You know I'm too old for you," she said, and she brought his mouth to her own and kissed him.

Luke patted Mya on the hip and said, "You're going on a date with me sometime, Mya Lenore. I mean it; I don't know when and I don't know where, but I want to take you out and buy you a drink and some food, and I don't give a damn who sees us." Then he crossed the threshold of the ivy-covered front porch; there was so much of it that the porch fans had been choked by the vines years ago. Long strands hung like a beaded curtain on all sides of the porch, and no one could see past the flora that led to their house. Not that anyone was around, not with a thousand and seventy-seven acres of buffer and the Blue Ridge Mountains just above like a fortress. He jogged down the slate front steps and walked to his Toyota pickup truck.

"There's always hoping," Mya called after him. Before he closed the driver's-side door she added, "Text me, if you're coming tonight," and he said, "Okay," and waved good-bye to her. Mya leaned against the wooden support beam on the porch and pulled her long hair over her bare breasts to shield them. Luke drove down the driveway with a thick cloud of Virginia red dust trailing behind his truck. Mya bent down and searched for buttercup flowers dotting the summer grass, and she wished she could rest there. But she couldn't, no matter how much her body insisted.

If she was going to fix her mistake, then Mya needed this time alone in her workshop with the musk pod she and Luke had collected at the waterfalls. Zoe's poor decision to cross industries jeopardized the business, but Mya had no intention of letting anything happen to Lenore Incorporated. The family business was Mya's only future. Without some convincing, her mother would never allow Mya to alter Great-Grandmother Serena's perfume formula to solve this problem, but the formula had to be changed, just this once, for this very special case. Willow would have no choice once she returned from her meeting with Zoe in L.A. Willow wasn't well, no matter how much she tried to cover it up. Mya respected her mother's privacy, but for the sake of the business, Willow needed to pass her title over to Mya soon, and then Mya could deal with the consequences alone.

Mya went back inside and turned to close the front door. Luke's cloud of dust dissipated, and in the green field that sloped down into a valley full of hay barrels, a thousand or more cobalt-blue dragonflies hovered like a standing army. With her blond hair rolling down to the small of her back, Mya pushed the door open again and ran down the steps, across the dirt driveway, and into the middle of the field. Lucia's dragonflies were amassed in a greater number than Mya had ever seen, and they parted as she approached. Mya grew nervous, and she looked up into heavy cumulus clouds, like giant peaks of meringue. In the center of a large billowing cloud, she saw her sister's face, so similar to Mya's with the high cheekbones and tiny chin and wide-set eyes. But it was most certainly Lucia.

Just as quickly as the image had arrived, the cloud broke in half, with the summer sun piercing through to Mya. She closed her eyes to feel the heat on her entire body. Why had the dragonflies returned? Lucia didn't have a place here anymore; there was no way she'd come home, not now, not after so many years away. But the dragonflies surrounded Mya until she felt cocooned, and Mya swatted at them and screamed, "Back off!" They spun all around her like a dust storm, and then they lifted upward and escaped into the surrounding trees.

Mya's stomach cramped. The dragonflies always favored Lucia. They had acted as an entourage for her during their games in the forest. They had guided Lucia to find Mya's hiding spots. The older Lucia had become, the less and less she had talked to Mya and their mother. If she wasn't with her boyfriend Ben, then Lucia was planning for the day she'd leave for New York City. The dragonflies had become the only way to know that Lucia was nearby. They hadn't congregated like this since she'd left. Mya had stayed in Quartz Hollow with her mother and devoted all these years to ensure she'd be the next president of Lenore Incorporated. She looked to the sky with its unmoving clouds and said, "Do not come home."

## CHAPTER 3
# Business in L.A.

A FIT YOUNG man stood up, his heavily gelled hair like fondant icing. He held a disc remote control between his palms in a prayer position and said, "I want to thank Ms. Lenore for making the long trip out here. It's such a rare pleasure to see you."

How many times had Willow accepted these platitudes? As many times as she had said, "Thank you, it's good to be here." Normally she'd add a name. She should have known his name. If he was present, he was important. But he sat down before Willow could recall who he was. Someone had hit the "flush" button in her brain; that's how it felt. She sent up a small plea to the language gods not to let her forget any words in this negotiation—*I need a free pass, just for today.*

The track lighting turned on by its own volition. The actresses removed their shawls and Jackie O sunglasses, Jennifer passing her items to an assistant and Zoe tossing hers in a lump on the table. In her signature pencil skirt, Jennifer Katz sat down first, beside Willow, and ran her long, elegant fingers through her much-coveted real hair—no platinum extensions for her. Zoe Bennett's red hair fell over one smoky eye, and then she tossed her head and both eyes were visible. Their entourages stood behind them and tapped away at the devices in their hands, arms tucked close to their chests like a T. rex's.

Zoe's manager held out her seat for her. After she sat down, she crossed her long legs and said, "You must think taking me on was a mistake, but cutting me off can't be the solution."

Jennifer said, "My manager thinks—"

Zoe said, "I think they all should go."

"Fine," Jennifer said, and waved a hand at her people, as did Zoe. Willow nodded to her driver and the man who had opened the meeting, then rested her laced fingers in her lap and tried to appear unconcerned about why they needed to be alone.

Once the door closed behind their entourages, Jennifer leaned onto the table and said, "We could flip a coin; the winner pays the other to fake her death."

Zoe gave an insincere smile, her mouth like a copperhead snake's, and said, "But you're so old. Why flip?"

Willow said, "Cool it." She'd said the same to her daughters when they were teenagers and fought like bobcats.

Jennifer no longer shared her Oscar-winning smile with Zoe. "I have other appointments today," Jennifer said, "and I want this resolved. *Arrow Heights* should've been my script; that was my second Oscar. I need to know what you'll do for me, Willow."

"For us," Zoe said, and straightened her back, her heavy cleavage nearly pouring out on the table, her black bra visible beneath the ripped and diamond-studded tank top that dropped off one petite shoulder. She leaned forward, and her breasts caved and slumped against her forearm. Time would permanently do that to both of those fantasized-about mounds. Maybe Willow could find some way to get Zoe on a show like *Fear X: Celebrity Edition*, and she'd be forced to eat buffalo gonads with hot chocolate syrup. And Willow could keep Jennifer where she deserved to be. At the top of Hollywood.

Willow had chosen Jennifer fifteen years ago, when she was just a teenager and struggling for gigs with Disney. She'd been brought to Willow's attention at a time when Willow needed her passion for the entertainment portion of their business to be reignited. Everyone had underestimated Jennifer's energy, her cobalt-blue eyes and long blond hair. Willow knew that with a small boost from their perfume, her talents would flourish. She'd come to think of Jennifer as another daughter and felt more invested in her career than in those of her other clients, Zoe especially. In the short time Zoe had had access to the perfume (about three years, wasn't that right?) she had landed bigger roles than Jennifer had booked at the same age. No one should have been competing with Jennifer for the best roles in Hollywood, like this highly anticipated film by director Nick Schol. They both knew that Jennifer might not have the chance to land another role like this one. She'd transition into directing or producing and do beautifully, but Willow wanted this script for her.

But then Schol had offered the role to Zoe and refused to explain why. Willow didn't need a direct answer from him, however. She knew he wasn't sleeping with her. Zoe was an energetic new talent who used too much of the Lenore family perfume too quickly. What director could resist her? Altogether, this situation had become a migraine.

Willow said, "What I want is for Zoe to go back to the music industry and give up this role to Jennifer. In fact, this wouldn't be a problem at all if you'd stayed in pop and honored your word." That last bit made Willow sound antique, but she didn't care anymore. It was how she felt.

Zoe tapped her cheek with her red fingernails and said, "My word is not my contract. Look, I can't help that Hollywood wanted me more. And I never agreed to stay in music. Just to start there. And I *did* honor that. Come on, Ms. Lenore, you're a businesswoman. This you can understand. Hollywood paid me for work I prefer."

"So then you flew all this way for nothing?" Jennifer said.

"No," Willow said, rather annoyed now. "I came all this way because you two refused a conference call."

Jennifer wrapped her arms around herself and said, "But you came with no real solution? You know Zoe won't quit. I know I'm right for this role and Zoe knows it too, she won't admit it but she knows it, and Schol picked her anyway. It's like the perfume's losing its power for me. Or maybe I'm just too old. I'm so sick of it, the same scent year after year. I don't even want the perfume anymore but—"

"Good," Zoe said. "Then it's settled."

"No," Jennifer said. "Stop being such a bitch, Zoe." Her perfume scent changed to musk so suddenly that Willow knew she was frightened.

Zoe said, "Mya has a solution."

"What?" Willow said, her throat suddenly dry.

"She asked me not to say anything, but you came all the way here and haven't mentioned it yet and I think we should discuss it," Zoe said, and now she held all the power in the room.

Willow was stunned and wished, as she sometimes did, that she could spank Mya again. How could she offer a solution to a client and not consult Willow? If Mya had all the solutions, she should have been the one in this seat, but instead Mya chose to go hunting for morel mushrooms with her new boyfriend in the middle of the night. That's what a teenager does to skirt an obligation like this one, not a thirty-six-year-old woman and not the only woman poised to take over Lenore Incorporated. And this mess was Mya's fault in the first place. She didn't add the clause to Zoe's contract to restrict her to the music industry. Though if what her daughter said was true, she'd left the contract for Willow to review on her desk and Willow had simply forgotten to check it.

Zoe pulled her long auburn hair over one shoulder and said, "Mya will make variants of the perfume's formula just for Jennifer and just for me, and I quote, 'to differentiate our strengths.'"

"And what are those exactly?" Jennifer said.

"Well, sensuality, obviously, for me. For you I didn't ask. Probably sweetness or something," Zoe said.

Jennifer's nose lifted like she smelled burned hair. Willow said, "Mya can't make decisions without my approval." She rested her right palm on the table, the wrinkles in her hands like pleats in a skirt compared to Jennifer's and Zoe's smooth skin.

"Then you'll lose us as clients and I'll expose your other clients and your entire business," Zoe said.

Willow looked over at Jennifer, who refused to make eye contact.

"Don't threaten me," Willow said.

Zoe leaned away from the table and braced her hands on the edge like it might break. She said, "My career's still young, so I don't care if I lose your perfume, just as long as no one else uses it."

"She's already contacted a few people," Jennifer finally said.

"Like who?" Willow said.

Zoe laughed and cast her head back to look at the ceiling, and then she stretched her thin little arms above her head and hugged them together.

Jennifer said, "Important people, just trust me on that. And she's threatening to expose us all, and you."

Willow pointed at Zoe and said, "The only solution I'm entertaining is cutting you off. That bright skin of yours will lose its glow within a few days. The ease with which you connect to a script and memorize lines will disappear as quickly as your wrinkles will start to appear, I promise you that. Give it a week, two at the most, and your career will be finished."

Zoe laughed again and said, "Just imagine the headlines if I go public, Ms. Lenore. Jennifer Katz, Hollywood's golden girl: a fraud, addicted to a substance for her success. And she'll just be the first; you'll drown in PR shit. I'm young. I'll play the naïve damsel. I've got plenty of time to remake my image without you."

Jennifer wrapped her arms around herself and said, "I'll expose myself before I ever let you do it." She turned to Willow. "I want this role, but if I can't have it and she stays in the business, then I don't want our careers to cross like this again or I'll give it up completely and agree to a tell-all, I swear. Just go back and talk to Mya. I don't want an altered formula. Only Zoe does. Would one alteration really hurt?"

Willow's jaw moved from side to side before she forced herself to lie. "I'll consider it."

"That's all we want," Zoe said before she stood up. She straightened her tight tank top and walked to the other end of the room to suit up in her disguise.

Jennifer waited for Zoe to leave before she said, "The both of us can't make it; we can't both be at the top."

Willow nodded and said, "I'll call you in the next few days. Try not to worry." Jennifer gave her a small, sad smile and then met the entourage awaiting her outside the door.

Willow leaned back in her chair and looked for her leather purse—the one Mya called beef jerky—but it wasn't beside her and her phone was inside it. She needed to call home but she couldn't remember where her stupid purse had gone. Willow wished that she could scream and scream and scream until her scream reached their cabin in Virginia and flattened Mya. She loved her daughter so much, but how dare she? Willow would've never crossed her mother, spoken with clients directly without telling her, and then sent her out here without so much as a warning. Not in a million years could she imagine doing a thing like that, and for the first time she felt grateful her mother wasn't alive. What would she say about this wrong turn in their company?

And those absolutely ungrateful actresses. What more could they possibly think they deserved? Neither woman could deny that her career had grown exponentially since her first application of the perfume. As with all of her clients no matter the industry, an aging starlet of the previous generation had guided each young woman to Willow. After just a few months of using the perfume, most of Willow's actress clients skipped the usual commercials, voice-overs, kid's shows, and indie films to land major supporting-actress roles in movies that just happened to go on to receive big Oscar nods.

Zoe's interview had been memorable because Willow had allowed Mya to control the proceedings and because Zoe didn't hesitate. Most women asked for time to think the proposition over, and Willow appreciated this quality, as it gave her time to consider whether the potential client had the most important trait for being selected: the self-discipline to never utter a word about Lenore Incorporated to anyone, not even her mother. But the promise of the right agent, simple financing for the product, and instant success had been enough for Zoe Bennett. She signed on the spot, and Willow remembered feeling wary at the time. But still she had agreed to sell to her. Mya had been convinced of Zoe's potential as a pop star, and Zoe did well at that for the first few years. She wasn't satisfied, however, and began contacting directors. When Willow found out, she hadn't considered this a threat to her existing client, as the perfume guaranteed success only for innate talent. But they had missed that Zoe's was acting, not singing and dancing, and now the public adored Zoe, which gave her bargaining power.

Willow's driver and an assistant returned to the room. The assistant, a waif of a girl with glittering sapphire eye shadow, leaned down and said, "More coffee, Ms. Lenore?" Her eyelashes were so long Willow thought they might reach out and touch her. Both of the girl's wrists clanked with a cadre of silver bracelets. "No, I'm fine," Willow said, and looked out through the glass panels at the dry and patchy mountains. They looked like they had a case of mange. The view of the Hollywood sign in the distance was tinged by smog.

The assistant brought Willow her purse. It had been hanging from a gold hook on the wall all this time, her cell phone peeping out of the side like a pocket square.

"Thank you," Willow said, and the girl swished her hips as she left the room, recycling a stack of papers on her way out.

"I'll be just a minute," Willow told her driver. She placed her chin in her hand and wondered how much longer she could continue this way, conducting business alone like this. Who'd be there? It could only be one of her two daughters, but both of Willow's girls existed far outside these glass walls. Lucia never called home. And how could Willow trust Mya to take over? Sometimes she felt like Mya and Lucia didn't love her. Irrational, maybe, but Willow couldn't help thinking that if her daughters loved her, they'd be here for her when she needed them most.

Willow tapped Mya's name on her phone. The line rang but she didn't answer. Of course not. Her daughter had better not do anything stupid before Willow had the chance to fly home.

Grandmother Serena had known what Willow knew, that there's no such thing as *one* alteration. Compromise yourself once, and you'll do it again. That's why Grandmother Serena had promised a curse on any variation of her formula. The potential for error and malice had existed from the perfume's inception, and Serena had always insisted the product be used for the empowerment of women and not for ill. Her formula was foolproof. Apparently, Mya didn't have sufficient fear of Grandmother Serena. She had also never witnessed how Serena's presence made the plants bend to her feet. Serena's power had terrified Willow when she was a little girl, just like the thought of a massive reveal scared her now.

What would happen if the public knew that Lenore Incorporated was responsible for the careers of the female entertainers they most adored, the politicians they voted for, the lawyers and judges who enforced the law, the doctors who cared for them, and, more often, the IT entrepreneurs who made their lives convenient? Never had there been more competition to be famous and wealthy in America, and Lenore Incorporated had simplified the process and immeasurably amplified women's talents for almost a century.

What viable option did she have? The company was Willow's entire life, and Zoe's threat against it was a threat against the Lenore family, past, present, and future.

CHAPTER 4

## The Musk Pod

THE VEGETABLE STOCK simmered all afternoon until the bouquet garni exited the pot looking like a drenched pile of compost. The flavors of rosemary and sage blended evenly with the carrots and onions and potatoes, and Mya had plenty of stock for that evening's dinner and a grand surplus to freeze. Cooking stock soothed her nerves.

From one glance at the kitchen an onlooker would have expected a dinner party of twelve to knock at the door, but it was a dinner for two—at least it would be if she decided to invite Luke. Despite his feverish texting, she hadn't yet responded. The crescent moon had risen before dusk—a waxing phase, a sure sign of developing events to come—and Mya decided to cook what she and Luke loved most: braised short ribs in a mustard sauce; quinoa with morel mushrooms picked that day in the forest and topped with fresh feta from their goats; and an arugula salad with local bacon from Blue Boone's farm, ripe summer tomatoes from the garden, and a vinaigrette with chopped cherries from the tree up near the fields. Mya left the kitchen smelling of beef drippings and retreated to the workshop in the back of the cabin to begin the real work.

She slid open the wooden door and walked down two steps into a dark room lit by seven white candles. Two red candles hung from brass fixtures on the ceiling—a fire hazard by anyone's standards. Sometimes the full moon provided enough light to navigate the cabin, but not this evening; the moon was the shape of a nail clipping. The left wall of the workshop contained different shelves with glass doors and locks, and behind those doors sat hundreds of amber-colored bottles: every base, middle, and top note a perfumer could want. Not that she'd admit it to anybody, but Mya considered herself a genius. She captured honey more perfectly than honey itself by submerging buckets of honeysuckles in the purest cow fat from a neighboring farm; she accidentally captured a note of summer rain by soaking sweet olive stalks in oak barrels before distillation. Her only pastime and her only passion, the workshop was her playground all grown up.

In the center of her workshop stood a large butcher's table, and Mya perched on her wooden stool and peered over the Bunsen burner glowing blue in the dim light. She placed a flat crystal as wide as a grapefruit on a plate above the flame. The rock warmed, and on it she centered the deer musk pod, a gift from one of her favorite animals in the forest. Mya had been tracking him since she was eight years old. This deer resembled the musk breed of Russia or China, except he had antlers *and* the long teeth in the front. And just yesterday she had found him dead in a meadow clearing inside the forest. This morning they had gone for him, and Luke draped a scarlet cloth on his body and Mya wrapped a ring of wild tea roses around his head before they removed the hairy pod from the shaft of the deer's penis. And then they buried his body underneath Mya's favorite weeping willow tree.

An hour later the musk pod had shriveled to the size of a kiwi. Mya slid the oven mitts onto her hands and removed the pod from the crystal. She tied the shrunken skin around the pod with a piece of hemp rope, walked over to the side of her workshop, and lifted the sheer white curtain that barricaded her collection of yarrow, bloodroot, and rosemary gathered from the landscape around the cabin. Mya hung the pod on the wall to dry next to a bundle of wild mint hanging upside down, and then she shielded the wall again with the curtains.

With this rarest of musks, she would make a perfume more potent than Zoe Bennett could've ever wanted. Mya had asked Zoe what she could do to fix this problem, and she promised Zoe that she would do anything for her. All Zoe desired was "more sex appeal, a respectable Marilyn Monroe kind," and Mya said, "That can be done."

But she wouldn't give Zoe exactly what she wanted. She had broken her contract, if not in letter, then certainly in spirit. The Lenores carefully timed and calculated whom they offered the perfume to, ensuring there would be only one or two superstars, depending on the industry. Zoe had abused her privilege, and Mya had no intention of letting anything happen to Lenore Incorporated. The business mattered more to her than anything else in her life. No, what Mya intended to make for Zoe was the ultimate in repulsion. Once Zoe used Mya's new formula, she'd be done in Hollywood. Forever.

The smell of her mustard sauce entered the workshop, and Mya tossed her gloves on the table and hustled into the kitchen, where the short ribs had already been removed and positioned on top of the stove. A duffel bag had been placed on the kitchen table. Mya froze and said, "Luke?"

She looked over her shoulder, her heart pounding, and repeated his name without reply. Then she walked over to the window above the kitchen sink to see if his truck was parked out there. And the only person she didn't want coming to dinner ascended the front steps. She wore all black and it didn't flatter her. Mya opened the door and said, "Lucia?"

"Someone's home, that's a relief," Lucia said, and stopped at the top porch step. "Still trying to burn down the house?"

"I was in the workshop," Mya said defensively. Neither Lucia nor Willow would ever let Mya live down the one time she started a grease fire by leaving olive oil in the cast-iron skillet. She'd been distracted by distilling irises. "The dragonflies," Mya said, and stood firmly in the center of the doorway.

"They were here too?" Lucia said. "Is Willow home?"

"Tomorrow."

A firefly crossed in front of Lucia's face, and she swatted like it might sting her. She took a deep breath and said, "The air's so clean. I've forgotten air like this even existed."

Mya said, "Why're you here? What happened?"

Lucia said, "Can we continue this interrogation tomorrow? I'm tired." She tilted her head to the side and said, "Aren't you going to let me in?"

Mya moved to the side to let her pass.

"Smells good," Lucia said. She picked up one short rib from the pan and made her way to the back of the cabin. Mya stood still and waited for Lucia to return to the kitchen, but instead she heard the flush of a toilet and the whoosh of the curtain on Lucia's old bedroom door-frame, then the sound of the springs retracting on her mattress. Mya waited a few minutes longer in case Lucia decided to come out, but she heard only the cicadas outside. The short ribs looked tender and juicy, not a degree overcooked, but Mya had officially lost her appetite.

## CHAPTER 5
# *Memory of an Attraction*

WILLOW WALKED SLOWLY out of the room, failing at first to notice a man with silver-flecked hair standing at the threshold. He crossed his arms in front of him, without a single piece of technology in his hand. All of his attention zeroed in on Willow. The pause between them lasted so long that she had enough time to convince herself he was looking for someone else. This man, with his wide jaw and solid chest and glowing black Oxford shoes, wouldn't be waiting for Willow.

Without meaning to, she let her eyes glance down to his left hand, just to check for a twinkle of gold. Not one piece of jewelry adorned him, not even a Rolex, a men's fashion statement she'd come to consider part of the uniform out here. He continued to stare at her, like he was expecting her to speak first, and then he moved away from the bamboo planting next to the door. He said, "Ms. Lenore."

She accepted his outstretched hand, his palm radiating more heat than she'd felt from someone's skin in many years. "How do you do?" she said, wishing she didn't always sound so formal when she was nervous.

"James Stein," he said like she should already know that name.

"Can I help you?" Willow said, a flush of warmth pooling in her cheeks.

He smiled and cast his eyes down to the floor before looking up at her again. He said, "I was hoping—well, now I'm hoping this won't sound strange to you. But I was hoping I might interest you in dinner tonight."

Strangers asking strangers out to dinner—that's how people operated out here now? Willow said, "Oh, thank you, but no. I'm exhausted." She continued walking.

He caught her elbow to slow her down and she stopped abruptly, with a look of outrage on her face that she couldn't prevent. He straightened his back, adjusted his shoulders, and said, "Now, hang on, I'm the new head of AGM Studios, and those two women and their careers are very much a concern of mine. And I'd like to talk it over at dinner."

Willow said, "But what business would you have with me?"

"I knew your mother," James said.

This startled Willow. Had she met him before? She must've, but she couldn't identify him. With a soft tone she said, "Oh, I didn't know. I apologize if I was rude just then. My assistant couldn't make the trip with me and my daughter canceled at the last minute . . . and of course you don't care to know any of this, I'm so sorry. I'm just travel weary. Would you consider a late lunch instead? I'm staying at the Beverly Hills Hilton."

James said, "I'll meet you in the lobby at two." He handed her his business card, a hard stock with bold black lettering.

"That's fine," Willow said. This was a business lunch, so she needed to stop wondering if he was divorced or dating anyone.

"Willow," James said, "don't you remember me?"

"Should I?" Willow said, taken aback, and she felt that same icy sense of encasement, like when she forgot words from time to time, or people's names. She stared at his face, the gold hue in his eyes and the lovely amber-colored rings around his brown irises, but no, she felt nothing like recognition.

"I hoped you might," he said. "We had dinner many, many years ago, on your first trip out here with your mother."

Willow continued to shake her head and squinted as if this might force a recall, wrinkles be damned. Still, she couldn't place him.

"A walk on Sunset Beach?" he said. "You wrestled me in the sand and won? No? Nothing?"

She wished he would stop. The more he remembered, the more her body numbed. Nothing made her feel as powerless as forgetting. "I'm sorry" was all she could say.

"A long time ago," James said. "I believe you were married not too long after."

Willow smiled. "That explains it, then," she said. "I excised all memories of that time in my life. Except for my daughters."

James said, "That I can understand. So I'll see you in a couple hours? Maybe I can jog your memory over sushi."

Willow said, "You can try."

"I'll take it as a personal challenge," he said, and ran his hand through the side of his thick hair.

She smiled and said, "Until then."


WILLOW SAT ON A CRANBERRY-COLORED chaise lounge in the Presidential Suite, hugging an orange cashmere pillow and staring out at bare mountains in the distance, wishing she could be home looking out at the lush Blue Ridge. She opted to stay inside rather than sit on the wrought-iron terrace to drink cappuccinos brought up by a handsome waiter from Saudi Arabia. Willow tried hard to imagine the lilt of her mother's southern accent. Was this normal to forget? A mother's voice? As normal as forgetting that dinner with James on her first trip out here? Would Mya and Lucia forget Willow like a to-do list they'd made and misplaced? Lucia already had, it seemed, as wrapped up as she was in her marriage and career and a "normal life" in New York City.

Small moments she still recalled, like her father's black boots flanking each side of the John Deere tractor; her mother's ironing board and the cinched-waist dresses she loved so much, the ones she always wore to meetings like the one Willow had today; her mother, who stayed up until three A.M. each night for business and woke up early to make her father scrambled eggs and bacon so he could spend all day taking care of the land; her mother's deep-set wrinkles, like the bend of a bow around her mouth, after he died.

How could Willow be sixty-one when she still felt like her mother's irresponsible little girl? A mistake like this one wouldn't have happened under her mother's care. Lily's time as president had been golden: she'd nurtured the pool of clients Serena had established in the entertainment world, but Lily spotted an outside opportunity and decided to branch out to college coeds who wanted more from their degree than just a husband. She visited elite universities, posing as a company interested in hiring talent for the summer; spoke to professors; and scouted the best of their students. From these endeavors she expanded into medicine, law, politics, science, and engineering. Willow admired this about her mother and added to her work by focusing on information technology and entrepreneurs. She used her mother's networking tactics and continued to manage the client pool that Lily and Serena had established. But Willow didn't care much for the entertainment world, especially pop music. This petty dislike had resulted in her foolishly letting Mya take charge on the Zoe Bennett deal.

A knock on the door ushered Willow out of her stasis, and a bellman handed her a small white box. She thanked him and carried the box to her bedroom. She opened the note on top. *Let's play fair. —James Stein.* A generous bottle of the newest perfume from the House of Chanel rested on a bed of red crepe de chine fabric. At first she thought it a joke, but then realized it was a polite suggestion. Don't disarm him; wear this instead. Let's play fair. Lenore women didn't need to wear their own perfume; they'd never had a reason to before.

It was one P.M. when she received his gift, and this prompted her to shower, freshen her makeup, and walk through a wall of the Chanel perfume. A decent product, though artificially powdery and not nearly as pure as the artisanal scents Coco Chanel herself oversaw many decades ago. So many companies now opted for cheaper, more efficient ingredients and methods, but Willow prided herself on her family's strict adherence to the original formula and growing methods created by Grandmother Serena. That quality was her sole responsibility to maintain.

Willow put on a black Dior dress and her size-seven Prada pumps and rode the elevator down at 1:50 P.M. James awaited her in the lobby. One bowl of steamed edamame and two dirty martinis later, Willow still didn't know why they were having lunch together. Seated next to a large aquarium with suckerfish glued to the sides and yellow-and-black-striped angelfish lazily swimming from one end to the other, Willow wondered at what moment during their swim the fish forgot they had made the same turn a million times before. The couple at the table next to Willow fed each other dragon rolls and salmon sashimi.

James had the tall, lean frame, wide shoulders, and tapered waist of a swimmer. She wished she could stop thinking he was so damn handsome, but so far, she'd failed. Her first thought when she stepped off the elevator and onto the marble floor of the lobby was *Oh, he's so good-looking,* and as they strolled side by side in the open-air lobby and he led her by the arm to their table next to the aquarium, her only thought was *I wonder what he looks like underneath that suit.*

James smiled at Willow, giving her a look more charming than a waltz, and said, "Let's order."

Willow forced herself to stop wondering what he'd do if she undressed him, and said, "Surprise me."

James's eyebrows lifted and he said, "My pleasure." He ordered fifteen different rolls with names like Sunshine Burst and California Dreaming, as well as miso soups and seaweed salads. More food than Willow could manage to eat for lunch, but James said, "A tasting," as if to reassure her.

The waiter brought two more dirty martinis and Willow decided to stop keeping track.

James drank his martini, and as casually as if he were complimenting the sesame flavor of their seaweed salad, he said, "You smell nice."

Willow said, "It's good to compare the market."

He swallowed a bite of seaweed and said, "How'd I do?"

"Decent," she said, not expecting him to be the kind of man to seek compliments. "There are so many outstanding perfumes, it's hard to say."

"And you're biased," he said, his chopsticks aimed in her direction like a pointer finger.

Willow thought for sure that his perfectly polished Oxford shoe was now touching the tip of her Prada pump. She shifted the position of her legs.

The waiter brought the miso soups and left just as quickly as he had arrived. James said, "I've got a detail for you." Willow slowly sipped her warm soup and James said, "Cold tequila shots out of a pair of goggles on a white surfboard," and Willow was already shaking her head no when he put his hand up and said, "Hold on, I'm not done." He continued: "Duke Ellington's 'Mood Indigo' right before a biker brawl erupted outside the Sandy Secret Bar at Sunset Beach."

She closed her eyes, and just as forcefully as a wave from the Pacific,

Willow saw James nearly forty years younger, his hair thick and curly and down past his ears like a band roadie's, his bare feet in the dark sand, his washed-out jeans rolled up at the ankle; he carried her out of that bar—she was too drunk to walk herself—to shield her from the flying beer bottles when the fight moved indoors. The sunset boasted a bright purple and orange at the horizon, and the white frothing ocean covered Willow's sandals. What a terrible and huge crush she'd had on James Stein that first visit, and how forcefully she had to forget him after she got married a few months later. He had a girlfriend too, if she recalled correctly. But those obligations had no longer mattered, at least for a moment, once James kissed her that night. A full moon was rising on the ocean's horizon. That's what Willow could remember now, and that nobody had ever kissed her like that before. This memory returned so effortlessly from the ether, she felt as giddy as she had the night she met James.

Willow placed her chin on her outstretched fingers, as if they were a small table, and said, "I can't believe my mother let me go out with you."

James wiped his lips with a napkin and said, "All I've ever had going for me is charm, and it worked on her."

"It sure did," Willow said, and remembering such a distant memory and the feeling of that night with James made her elated. She said, "Weren't you just an assistant then?"

"Not even," he said. "Mail boy."

"How did you rise?" she said, and continued with her soup.

"My mentor Donald Briggs, who was head of A-List Talent then, snatched me off the mail cart that day your mother came. His note-taker called in sick, and she approved of me. I moved up fast after that and ran the talent agency for a few years."

"I do remember that," Willow said. "But didn't you leave?"

"I went to New York with my wife for a long while," he said, "or ex-wife, I should say."

"That explains it," she said.

"Do I look much different though?" James said. "You didn't seem to recognize me."

Willow shook her head, though she'd be lying if she said he looked *exactly* the same. Boyishness hadn't fit him as well as this seasoned look. She said, "I had a difficult meeting today, that's all. I was distracted and not expecting to see you."

"Your mother liked me," James said.

"She did," Willow said. "She was so selective and revealed the perfume only to the people who needed to know about our business, and she chose to give you access that day." This move had confused Willow; she remembered feeling that at the time. And when she asked her mother why, she had told Willow that the boy had talent. She could see it in him, and he'd probably be a powerful force in the industry someday. A good ally.

"And Lily's opinion about the industry mattered to Donald and just about anyone important out here. I've got her to thank for a lot, that date included."

Willow smiled and placed her spoon on the table. "How long have you been with AGM?"

"Six months," James said. "My second ex-wife was a junior agent at an agency I ran in New York, and when we divorced I moved back."

Willow finished her martini. "A junior agent" translated into a younger wife, and a younger second wife at that. And recently. How silly for Willow to think he'd be interested in her. She glanced around the room. So many thin and big-busted women. For a brief moment Willow with her oyster-white hair and naturally aged skin felt as old and unattractive as that suckerfish in the tank. She reminded herself that she had more than enough money to afford any of those chemical peels and Botox injections and cheek implants. She chose to be wrinkled because no procedure truly reissued the vitality of youth.

"Can we talk about your meeting?" James said.

"I'd prefer to forget it," Willow immediately quipped. "And it was a private meeting, as I'm sure you know. I won't ask how you found out I was here."

James wiped his hands with his linen napkin and said, "Willow—"

"Lunch first," she said, and continued to enjoy her soup.

"We can make small talk, if that's what you'd prefer. The soup's good?" James said. He stopped eating and stared at her, and now the rest of their time together would be forced. "You have elegant hands," he added.

She sat back in her chair and said, "What's on your mind?"

"Zoe Bennett."

"Mine too," Willow said.

James leaned into the table with his strong hands clasped together. "The bigger she gets, the more toes she steps on," James said. "The public demands her and she knows it. I've never seen a career take off that fast, not even Jennifer's. *Arrow Heights* is a big one. One I specifically set up for Jennifer. She kindly auditioned for a roomful of studio execs and they all agreed she was the one. But Nick Schol gave it to Zoe for some reason only he knows, and no one's willing to fight him on it. But Zoe's not right for it. She's already threatened to drop it for some indie project with her boyfriend. I've got a lot of money wrapped up in this one, and it won't do what I think it can without a strong lead. And there's no way Jennifer will take the role now if Zoe quits."

Willow took a very long sip of her martini. She didn't know what to say.

James said, "Zoe's edging Jennifer out."

The waiter brought three oversize white plates and placed them on the table. "Enjoy," the waiter said, and James prepared a small saucer of wasabi and soy sauce for Willow.

Willow took one piece from each plate and James said, "Help yourself to more, please. I can't eat this much sushi alone."

She didn't have much of an appetite now, but she took another piece of yellowtail sashimi from the platter. "She was supposed to stay in music," Willow said. The pale fish landed flat on the plate.

James said, "But she didn't."

Willow waited for him to make the next move, but instead he began to eat and they sat in silence, minus the clink and clank of glasses and the soft, hurried talk of lovers and friends all around. Willow sighed. If only this could've been a date. Nothing more, nothing less.

James coughed once and then said, "Any way to get rid of her?"

"Excuse me?" Willow said, and put down her chopsticks. Had James Stein just asked her to commit murder?

"Like an antidote formula?" James said.

"Oh," Willow said. "Well, no."

"What's the point of the contract then?" James said, and continued to eat.

Willow folded her hands. Who was he to question her business practices? She said, "It's a formality, I suppose, an agreement that we can terminate the relationship at any point, as can the customer, and that there are terms, like use limits, that must be followed. Certain terms are always understood from the handshake, and it was no different with Zoe, but she broke the most essential of the agreements. You don't cross industries. Our formula is powerful enough to do what it does and without it—I mean, who would want to be without it once they have it? We've always had happy customers, never had to cut anyone off, and no one's ever threatened to expose our service. I don't think my mother or my grandmother ever imagined that someone would want to."

"Probably not," James said. "But all businesses experience setbacks."

Nearly a century had passed since Grandmother Serena launched the company, and not a single setback had hampered the business, not until Willow Lenore became president. "Setback" meant failure: another word Willow wouldn't mind forgetting. The rest of the meal would not taste quite as good as it did at the start, and she stopped eating and let him finish the last pieces. Willow turned down dessert and coffee and pleaded an overwhelming degree of exhaustion. He offered to take the elevator and escort her to her door, but she said, "I can find it."

"I hope I didn't upset you," James said.

"No," Willow said. "I have a lot to think about, that's all."

"If you need anything," he said, "call me." With his hand on the small of her back, James leaned down without a pause and kissed her. The longing she felt those many years ago to kiss him just like this returned with more immediacy than any memory she'd had at lunch. Then he hugged her and said in her ear, "I've wanted to do that for far too long."

She almost said, "Maybe you could walk me to my door," but he had already stepped away from her.

"I'll be on the East Coast next week. Could I drop down to Virginia and take you out for a proper dinner?" James said.

"I'd like that," Willow said, and the elevator doors chimed.

She stepped inside and he said, "Good-bye," and he remained there until the doors closed. When she arrived at her suite, a bouquet of white roses awaited her in the foyer. The note said: *Flowers almost as striking as your lovely hair. Until we see each other again, be well. —James Stein.*

He was too much. Like he'd done this more than a million times. Yet Willow couldn't stop smiling. She pressed the note against her chest and wondered if she would forget this date too. There in the suite flooded by afternoon sunlight, she admitted to herself that these slips could become permanent, along with her loneliness, and she might never experience deep love and romance again before forgetting those concepts altogether. She wished she could stay in L.A.

just one more day to share another meal with James. But work called her home; always work called her. Willow dialed the concierge desk and ordered a chamomile tea. She needed something to calm her down after that kiss.

A few minutes later the doorbell to her suite rang, and she assumed it was the waiter. She opened the door with the phrase "thank you" on her lips, but James Stein stood there instead, and she blinked a few times.

"One more kiss and then I'll go," he said, and leaned down and wrapped her in his arms.

"Why don't you just stay awhile?" Willow said, and gave him a knowing smile.

Without another word, James closed the door behind him.

## CHAPTER 6
### To Rue Her Return

THE CABBAGE PATCH-STYLE dolls her grandmother Lily had sewn for her when she was a little girl still sat on her white daybed as if they'd been waiting for Lucia to return. One cloth foot had lodged between Lucia's calves as she slept in the fetal position on the small twin mattress. She woke up in the cabin feeling almost hungover. The queasiness reminded her of nights of heavy drinking with a handsome stranger that led to the next morning's discovery that his eyes were a little too close together and his waistline a little too soft. Here she was in a bedroom she hadn't seen in fifteen years, and she had no clue why coming home had registered as a good idea. Divorce and despair were just as toxic as alcohol, and she had combined all three yesterday.

Mya didn't ask to come in. She never had, and Lucia wasn't sure why she'd expect anything more from her now that they were adults. The sound of her humming announced her. As the older one, Mya could do what she wanted—at least that's how she always rationalized her invasion of privacy. Lucia inched the smooth cotton covers down from her face just enough to see that Mya had sauntered into

Lucia's room completely naked except for a pair of fuzzy purple socks. Mya didn't seem to notice Lucia's presence in the room and instead inspected the closet. Slowly Lucia covered her entire head to make sure her sister didn't know she was awake. Mya pulled out a short yellow robe from the closet and then sat down in the rocking chair. The sound of the rocker falling forward and backward on the hardwood floor was almost unbearable. Lucia prayed her sister would just leave.

"That doesn't work," Mya finally said, and drew back the curtains to let in the sunlight.

Lucia sighed, and the cotton sheet billowed upward with her breath. She pulled down the covers and stared at her sister. And in the sunlight filling her room, to Lucia's dismay, Mya looked like the younger one now, her skin more radiant than Lucia's and her blond hair fuller and brighter. Her lips didn't look permanently dried out, and all the curves of her body were as perky as ever. Had it really come to this? Mya had told her it would, those many years ago right before Lucia took off. *The mountains won't take you back. The city will be hard on you.* The city *had* been hard on Lucia and her body—too much food and drink and exhaust. Not enough fresh air.

Mya lifted a nail file from the pocket of the robe that she kept in Lucia's closet for some odd reason. Or was that Lucia's robe from high school?

"Smells like liquor in here," Mya said, and worked her nails back and forth.

"I had a few drinks," Lucia said, and pressed down on her eyelids with her fingertips in an attempt to clear away the blurriness and the headache behind it.

Mya said, "Explains how you got here."

"I guess so," Lucia said.

Mya blew the dust from her nails.

Lucia squinted and tried to find a clock in the room. "What time is it?"

Mya stopped filing and peered out the window. "I don't know," she said, and then stood up for a better look at the sun. She stretched her arms above her head and the robe inched up, revealing her bare buttocks. "About ten thirty-five," she said. "Maybe ten forty."

The years of separation were already bearing down harder than Lucia had expected, and she didn't want to leave the bed. She just wanted the little things—a cup of black coffee would do just fine.

Mya said, "She'll be home soon, you know."

Lucia sat up slowly and placed her feet on the cool hardwood floor. The feel of it reminded her of being twelve years old and not wanting to leave the room to check the fields or go to the factory and distill oil. Mya loved it and woke up early; Lucia sighed and wanted to stay in bed.

"Where'd she go?" Lucia said.

"L.A."

"She finally accepted a premiere invite?" Lucia said. "That figures."

Mya said, "Just business."

Lucia hoisted the duffel bag she'd brought with her onto the day-bed and unzipped it. It did not smell fresh. Mya looked offended. That's what she got for having such a sensitive nose. Lucia's hair fell forward, creating a shield around her face. She'd brought home a suit-case full of filthy laundry just like a college student.

Mya said, "So what's the mystery?"

Lucia stood up in the jeans and T-shirt she'd worn on the plane, and the entire room smelled like sweat and gin. Was it possible her mother had kept her clothes from high school? She wished Mya wasn't in the room to witness her slide open those drawers. But she was, so Lucia did, and there inside the top drawer was fifteen-year-old underwear pressed and folded, and in the drawers below, overalls, leggings, midriff T-shirts, flannel shirts, and a wrinkled spaghetti-strap dress with a white flower print. Lucia's high school boyfriend had given her this dress for her seventeenth birthday. Ben chose it because the flowers in the pattern reminded him of the Lenore family flower. Lucia didn't care much for the style of the dress, but she still remembered his thoughtfulness, how proud he'd been to offer her the box over a dinner that he'd cooked and how quickly he conceded that he hadn't wrapped it himself.

Lucia unfolded the dress and held it up to her body like a child's dress-up piece, a wrinkled and shrunken relic. Many years had passed since she thought much about Ben White. A pang of guilt flashed through her body whenever she did, so she chose to ignore the idea of him completely. And this had been easy to do during the first years of her marriage. But later, during the aftermath of her worst fights with Jonah, her thoughts tended to drift toward Ben. Lucia had no idea what he was up to now. Mya probably knew, but there was no way she would ask her sister. She balled up the dress and stuffed it back in with the other clothes that would never fit her again. Why had her mother kept all this stuff? Did her nostalgia run so deep?

Mya flipped through Lucia's closet and then handed her a simple blue linen dress with high slits on both sides of the legs. It smelled like cedarwood. Her mother always kept fresh cuts in the closet.

"It's Jonah?" Mya said.

Lucia turned around to remove her clothes.

"Another woman?" Mya said quietly.

"What makes you say that?"

Mya said, "He always seemed like that kind of guy—at least that's how Mom described him. Looking for the better thing all the time."

What about Jonah could've possibly given Willow that impression? Willow and Mya did always see what Lucia couldn't; all these years, that's how it had been. Still, if it had been Mya's failed relationship Lucia wouldn't have said this to her face, even if she believed it. Lucia finished tying her dress, refusing to turn around. She said, "He cheated on me, so we filed for divorce." Mya let out a small sigh that mimicked boredom. Lucia wouldn't tell her or their mother the truth, that Jonah went to one of his friend's art openings alone because Lucia had stopped enjoying dates with him a long time ago—and sex, for that matter, the warming of her groin when he touched her a distant memory, as if she'd only seen it in a movie. She refused to go out to support his friend's bad high-end graffiti art. But then she felt guilty, and Lucia asked her friend Nina to go with her. They caught Jonah making out with a Calvin Klein designer ten years younger than Lucia and at least four jean sizes smaller. The sight of the two of them in such a passionate embrace actually relieved Lucia, since she hadn't had sex with Jonah in almost a year. She felt sure it was all her fault—she was too depressed about her career, and her life headed forward with no purpose or real momentum. She couldn't convince herself she was attractive enough to have sex with Jonah, whom the entire Manhattan art world masturbated over these days: "Our post-postmodern Duchamp delivered in a golden canvas." Lucia hated Marcel Duchamp's work, but that was the man her husband had become, and everyone loved him. Lucia wanted her response to his indiscretions to freeze with her feeling of relief, but inevitably the bile of bitterness settled and Lucia just felt old. Not that she'd dare tell Mya something so personal and humiliating, considering Mya somehow managed to look as young as that girl.

"The two of you can work that out," Mya said. "It's just sex. Turn it into some kind of fantasy or something."

Lucia stiffened. She'd arrived home only last night, and from the start Mya had acted like she wanted Lucia to turn around and go.

Mya said, "But I guess you should make him squirm for a day."

Lucia shook her head, too tired to respond. She and Jonah and their curdled marriage were done, but she didn't owe Mya an explanation.

Mya immediately followed up with, "And the acting? How's that going?" As if she wasn't satisfied with how uncomfortable she'd made Lucia already.

"Willow didn't tell you?" Lucia said, and she finally turned around but dodged Mya's stare. She pushed the dirty laundry she'd brought home to the floor and sat on her bed.

"Tell me what?" Mya said.

"I just thought she'd tell you first," Lucia said.

Mya lined up tacks on the empty message board above Lucia's dresser. "Sometimes she forgets things," Mya said.

Lucia tied her oily hair into a long braid down her back and said, "Last year I landed a role playing a mother in North Carolina who leases herself and her fifteen-year-old daughter to a pimp. Rehearsals were fine and preview nights were fine, and then opening night with the theater critic for the *New Yorker* sitting in the front row, I had a panic attack, and it made me blank out on the Acorn Theater stage. They fired me and gave the part to my understudy, but that didn't keep the critic from mentioning it in his review. And I just couldn't get past it, and then my voice-over contract for that teenage soap opera show wasn't renewed, and that had been my steady income. My agent hasn't sent me anything since. So, any other Band-Aids you'd like to rip off for now, or could we take a break from playing twenty questions?"

Mya stood to the side of Lucia like she might sit down, but Lucia crossed her arms. Mya said, "You need a facial. Something with strawberry and honey."

This was a kind way for her sister to tell her she looked like shit. Lucia said, "I'm fine."

Mya nodded, but for once, she didn't tell Lucia what she was thinking. For that Lucia felt grateful. "Is there coffee?"

"If you make it," Mya said, and turned to leave the room.

"And moonshine?"

"Same place it always was," Mya said.

Lucia massaged the base of her neck, then walked out of the room and instinctively went to close the door behind her. Still no doors, just curtains. Mya liked that no doors blocked her energy in the house, but for Lucia, it just meant less privacy. She walked into the open reading area and looked up at the loft. When they were little girls, Mya had spun tales of the men who would surely come into their futures, and she'd always led the way, just as she did now. Mya would crumble dried red rosebuds in their palms with three drops of lavender oil. She tied yellow ribbons around their fingers and described the men who would sweep them away. Mya's man lived for adventure— caving, biking, swimming, climbing, hunting. Lucia's man lived for enterprise—amassing wealth, building a home, and creating a family. Back then Mya and Lucia were friends and wanted to live next to each other and have husbands who would be like brothers. Together they blew away the pieces of petals from the loft above to the couch below and let the ribbons fall like confetti on their mother. "Watch out for my books," she'd say.

Books were still scattered about the room, along with mountains of overflow paper from Willow's office and dirty plates and cups from the kitchen. The space had never been tidier or messier than this. No matter how much time passed, the same thought still haunted Lucia: Why, if her family had so much wealth, did they live in such an outdated, cluttered, and small way? She had never understood her mother's need for simplicity. Willow invested in small businesses in the town of Quartz Hollow and in conservative bonds and concentrated on personal savings, just like Grandmother Lily and Great-Grandmother Serena. Willow kept investing in the fund Serena had chosen in the thirties with a reliable 30 percent return. But for what? Willow rarely spent money. She preferred to watch it grow, like the flowers.

"How's business?" Lucia said as she poured grounds into the coffeepot filter. She seated herself at the circular kitchen table and checked underneath for the wobbly leg. Still broken. She watched her sister float about the kitchen, pulling dishes from the refrigerator and placing them on the gas stove.

"Which business?" Mya said.

The coffeepot trickled, and Lucia said, "Is there another one I should know about?"

"I've got an herbal tea store in town now," Mya said.

"Willow didn't say. Good for you, but I meant the family business."

Mya shrugged and said, "Everything's okay."

"Number twenty-seven on the *Forbes* list," Lucia said, and helped herself to a cup of coffee and a generous drop of cinnamon moonshine from a Mason jar. She braced herself against the Formica countertop. "Better than just okay, right?" Mya frowned after Lucia said this, she was sure of it. Should they have been higher on the list? Being home always made Lucia feel like she was missing something.

Lucia took a sip. The coffee burned her tongue and the liquor warmed her body. Mya dropped a muffin pan on the wooden floor, and Lucia jumped, almost spilling her drink. There stood their mother in the doorway to the reading room, still holding on to her travel bag.

Willow's hair fell farther down her shoulders than Lucia recalled—it was shimmering white and thicker too. Her delicate features defied her age. How could she be sixty-one already? Why had her mother and sister seemed to stop aging while Lucia was away? She took this personally, as though her absence had helped them to remain beautiful. *Stop being irrational, say something to her,* Lucia told herself, but she couldn't find the words.

Before Lucia could open her mouth, a loud snap and a crash came from outside the kitchen window. Lucia and Mya both whipped around to find a large branch of an oak tree split from its trunk. Not a single cloud hung in the sky, and the sun shone as brightly as ever. Either the branch had just given up or their mother's anger had peaked. Her fury had a history of cracking tree limbs, like the time an FDA inspector came snooping around and a massive maple limb flattened his company car. Willow dropped her luggage on the hardwood floor. Her stare remained fixed on Mya. "I've called and called you."

"I didn't hear the phone."

Willow looked up to the ceiling and then said, "I'm sure you didn't. I need a shower but when I'm done, be in my office."

Was Lucia invisible? Willow turned around and headed for her side of the cabin.

Impulsively, Lucia said, "Um, hello?"

Willow stopped. She said, "You just show up? You could've called first."

Lucia's mouth fell open. Exactly what had she expected? On the plane ride and drive over she had imagined a hug at some point, but that had not yet happened with Mya or her mother. But protocol? Politeness? Remember your manners and call a day before you arrive?

"I didn't exactly know I was coming," Lucia said.

"I did," Willow said.

"What's that supposed to mean?" Lucia asked, charging after her mother. Within moments she was transported to her teenage years, fighting with Willow over comments she made about Lucia's desire to go to New York City.

"You; your career; the city; that husband, Jim—no, John—damn it, what's that boy's name?" Willow said, more to herself than to Lucia.

They'd all had lunch together a couple times in the city and Willow had visited Jonah's studio once. She liked his paintings—at least she said she did. And now she couldn't remember his name. Did she care so little? "Jonah," Lucia said. "His name is Jonah. And he's my ex-husband now."

"Well, I'm sorry for you and Jonah, I really am, but it was all coming to this. For years it has been, and it's taken you this long?" Willow massaged her forehead like she had a headache. Lucia remembered this gesture from the first time she introduced her mother to Jonah. After their dinner together, Lucia had hoped Willow would offer her approval for Lucia to tell Jonah about the family business. But Lucia had chided him about something small, like oversalting his food, and he'd walked out of the restaurant in front of Willow. Willow had massaged her forehead just like that for the entire hour they waited for Jonah to return, but he never did.

"You found me out, Mother," Lucia said. "I'm a total and utter naïve failure. And I came home—of all fucking places—thinking I might not be judged."

"Sometimes too much time passes," Willow said, and closed her eyes.

"Can't you be happy I'm here now?" Lucia said.

"You won't stay," Willow said. "What's the use?"

Lucia said, "How loving."

"You left us a long time ago and rarely call. Don't talk to me about loving." Willow frowned and retreated to her room.

Lucia walked outside through the front door and the damn birds flew inside, but she didn't care. She slammed the door behind her, hoping they'd poop all over the reading room and her mother's books. Lucia sat on the porch floor, next to the cast-iron bench, and surrounded by the hanging ivy she tucked her knees to her chest and put her face in her hands. She had absolutely no place to call her own, and she'd have to return to the city tomorrow and try to make her life work without Jonah, even if she wasn't ready. How did a person lose everything, including a mother's welcome? Not even the dragonflies seemed to notice she'd arrived. She hadn't thought of herself as a loser before, had always hated the slang silliness of that word, but right now she had no other term to describe how she felt.

Lucia heard a shuffle in the grass and lifted her head from her arms to see her sister standing out in the meadow, a herd of deer behind her, guarding her. Mya did not motion for Lucia, nor did she come to the porch to check on her. Instead, she walked off into the surrounding woods with the deer following her. Her mother might've held a grudge all these years about Lucia's leaving, but Mya certainly didn't.

Lucia's being gone ensured Mya would be the next president of the company. Lucia had never coveted the title anyway; Mya had made no other plans for her life. Even when they were little girls, Lucia had assumed the business was Mya's to inherit. All she ever wanted to do was make Willow proud the only way she thought she could, by succeeding on her own as an actress.

Lucia stared at the slivers of space between the wooden planks on the porch, convinced she could slip right through them, and she traced her fingers in the emptiness between. Willow wasn't the mother Lucia had expected to find—the exhaustion and bitterness, it all came as a surprise. This wasn't the woman who had marched her daughters on a weekly hike or into the tree house on a rainy day to have a picnic catered by a downtown French café, her mother's favorite— baguettes, brie, roast chicken, apple tarts and imported chocolates and cold sparkling grape juice. Far too much for the three of them to consume, but she did this each week without fail, as she refused to leave town on business for more than four days at a time. And in the woods her mother rolled on the ground with them and climbed young poplar trees and made cups from the leaves and scooped water from streams to drink. They buried treasure rocks together and they all promised to remember where they left them, but of course they never did. On the hikes back to the cabin they often stopped to say hello to the flowers, and if they were in bloom, Willow stood at the edge of the field, palms open and eyes closed, and Mya and Lucia held hands and their breath as they waited for the flowers to lean toward their mother, who looked so much like a superhero in those moments. Mya and Lucia tried, but the flowers only moved for Willow, Grandmother Lily, and Great-Grandmother Serena. Willow hugged them with a smothering intensity and seemed so young and vital. Lucia had believed Willow could do anything—so had Mya— and she wished she could rewind to just one of those days. But her mother was no longer that woman and Lucia no longer that girl.

A dragonfly crossed her vision, and she looked up but couldn't see where it went. And then it returned and landed on the tip of her nose, so close she went cross-eyed trying to focus. She shook her head because the tiny legs tickled her skin, and the dragonfly took off again, but this time slowly enough for Lucia to track its flight in Mya's direction.

## CHAPTER 7
### *To the Fields*

MYA STOOD ON top of the hill before the many acres of flowers in full bloom. The dark, glossy leaves relished the full sun, and the white flowers congregated like a crowd of summer-blond children, more beautiful than any stretch of sunflowers or Queen Anne's lace you might stumble upon in the Blue Ridge. The woody shrubs stood six feet tall in dense rows that stretched far back toward the forest line but stopped with just enough space to ensure there was no root competition between the trees and the *Gardenia potentiae* plants.

June reigned as Mya's favorite month and most anticipated time of year. She wished things were less chaotic so she could enjoy it before the workers cultivated all the flowers and transported them to the factory down the road to capture the scent for the family's perfume. But time still remained for Mya to inhale the warm summer winds saturated with the smell of these most unusual flowers, nothing like the scent of their cousin the common gardenia. No, *Gardenia potentiae* smelled like ocean gusts of lavender, vanilla, and cedar, and something much deeper and elusive, like the smell of lust or envy.

Mya lay down on a bed of clover and reached her palms out to the thick hedge of flowers, just to see if they'd move. They remained blithely unaware of her presence, just as they always had. She picked a bloom and held it in her hand. Mya touched the stamen, and the pollen from the anthers stuck to her fingertip like a stamp. The sepal encasing the pistil and ovary seemed overgrown compared to past years, she was sure of it. How strange. And the petals felt harder, less supple. Maybe they hadn't finished blooming. She'd inform her mother in case they needed to push back the harvest a week or two—another first for their company.

The herd of deer that had accompanied her on the walk circled around her, and one nudged her arm as if to ask when she'd be ready to go. The thick clouds above formed a walkway like a footbridge over a deep canyon, and Mya placed her hand over her eyebrows to shield her eyes from the sun. And then Lucia's face appeared above her. Mya squinted to make sure she wasn't hallucinating, then said, "You found me."

Lucia plopped down next to Mya, and her cheeks were red. "Sorry," she said, "I followed the path."

Mya and the deer left thin, winding paths in the tall grass. Her mother had never needed to concern herself about Mya's whereabouts, even when she was a little girl. The beaten meadow paths acted as her trail of bread crumbs. "How'd that go?" Mya said.

"Easy enough," Lucia said. "I'm here, aren't I?"

"I meant with Mom," Mya said.

"Not great," Lucia said, and picked a piece of wild wheatgrass and began to braid a crown. "She's clearly preoccupied about something."

"We made a mistake," Mya said, and she immediately wished she hadn't divulged this detail.

Lucia said, "Oh?" in a tone that Mya recognized—Lucia always spoke in a detached and cold way about family matters. She might've inherited Great-Grandmother Serena's beautiful black hair and skin as blemish free and fresh as the flowers around them, but growing up, Lucia always copied Mya's spell work because she had no intuition for such things. Lucia had excelled where Mya had not, with normal stuff like school and extracurricular activities and boyfriends, but she did so to compensate for not being gifted in the only way that mattered in the Lenore family.

"What'd you do?" Lucia said.

"Why do you just assume I fucked up?" Mya said, though the only answer to Lucia's question would reveal that she had, indeed, fucked up.

"Come on, Mya," Lucia said.

Mya covered her face with both hands. No reason to hide it now. She said, "I saturated a market."

"Which one?" Lucia said. She stopped braiding the grass.

"The worst one," Mya said, and then lifted her hands from her face to see her sister's reaction. If only she looked more surprised.

"Zoe Bennett, isn't it? She came out of nowhere," Lucia said. "I knew it, had to be when she got nominated for that small supporting role in *The Break Away* last year." She placed the finished crown on top of the soft tan head of one of Mya's favorite fawns, Little Spots. "Wasn't she in music?" Lucia continued. "I thought I remembered seeing her videos."

Something bit Mya from the grass below, a red ant probably, and she rubbed her elbow. "She was," Mya said. "She seemed right for it, but then she took the role in *The Break Away* and we had no idea she was even considered for it. She kept the audition hushed up, that's for sure."

"What about her contract?" Lucia said as she petted the fawn resting beside Mya.

Mya said, "I didn't add a clause to keep her from crossing over. I didn't know I needed to since we told her in her interview. It was made as clear as moonshine. Mom would've caught it, and I know I asked her to check it. She was at her desk and looked right at me and said she'd do it that afternoon, and I sent it off the next day." Lucia remained silent except for the sound of her breath. What could she really say in response? "Anyway," Mya said, "it wasn't a huge deal until she got *Arrow Heights* and Jennifer Katz confronted her and figured it out."

In an exact imitation of Jennifer Katz, Lucia said, "Excuse me, Zoe, but may I try a spritz of that perfume? Smells an awful lot like the one I use." She laughed and then returned to her normal voice and said, "I bet that was an awkward moment in the ladies' room."

Mya couldn't help herself and had to laugh too. "I never asked."

They were quiet for a few minutes before Lucia said, "Mom forgot Jonah's name."

"Not like they were close or anything," Mya said. She was always quick to defend their mother, even when Willow wasn't pleased with Mya. It was a response as automatic as blinking.

Lucia narrowed her eyes and said, "But she never forgot names. 'Good business starts with names.' Wasn't that what she always said?"

Mya scratched the ground with her fingernails and exposed the roots of the grass.

Lucia said, "She forgot to read that contract, you know she did. Is something going on?"

"I don't know," Mya said. "Feel free to ask her."

"No way," Lucia said. "You saw how she just acted. I'm just a weekend guest at the Lenore bed-and-breakfast; she made that very clear. The weekend might be too long of a stay even."

"Do what you have to do," Mya said, and wiped the dirt from her nails on her jeans. Lucia's leaving in the next day or two would be just fine with Mya, but she didn't want to seem too eager. Mya said, "She's in there waiting for me."

"You're stalling," Lucia said.

"Yep," Mya said, and rested her back against the ground again.

She lifted her long hair up and spread it over the grass. The feel of the earth on her bare neck centered her. Lucia didn't join her; instead she stared off into the distance like she'd dropped her keys somewhere but didn't have the energy to search for them.

Mya stared up at her little sister, so unlike the girl Mya had known, the girl who was so sure of what the future held for her. "I just don't get it."

"Get what?" Lucia said.

"Why you always refused." Every single time Mya sent Lucia a small vial of the family perfume, she always returned it in the original bubble wrap. If she'd used it, she'd have had an Oscar nomination by now and she wouldn't have been sitting here.

"I just . . ." Lucia paused. She glanced at Mya and then looked toward the woods again. "I wanted to know that it was my talent alone or I'd never think I deserved it, and that always seemed much worse than never getting it." Lucia laughed in a low and defeated way. "All I ever wanted was to be an actress, and I suppose I didn't want to find out that I was meant for something else."

A neon-blue dragonfly spiraled down like a falling leaf and made a delicate landing on Mya's fawn. The fawn rested its chin on Lucia's thigh. Lucia said, "Remember when I fell out of that weeping willow and broke my arm and that huge deer carried me back to the cabin? For the longest time I thought he was one of Santa's missing reindeer."

Mya laughed and then said, "I do remember that."

"Does he still come around?"

"He died a couple days ago."

"Oh," Lucia said. "Sorry."

"He was old." Mya sat up, stretched her arms, and looked back at the cabin. It was as still as their mother's anger. Mya said, "She'll come out here to find me."

Lucia said, "Should I go with you?"

"Why would you?" The last thing she needed was Lucia to be tangled in their affairs.

"What else is there to do? Sit out here? Go for a hike?"

That was exactly what Mya would have preferred to do.

Lucia finished the crown of dandelions she'd been working on and placed it on her head. "I'll be quiet," Lucia said.

Mya didn't want Lucia involved, especially not now, but she didn't know how to tell her. She said, "She might kick you out."

"If she does, then fine," Lucia said. "Let her. But you don't care, so why should she?" Lucia stood up and stared down at Mya.

"Now?" Mya said.

"Yes, now, let's get it over with," Lucia said. "You're sure you don't mind, right?" The way she said this suggested she knew how much Mya didn't want her in there.

"Why would I mind?" Mya said, and accepted Lucia's offered hand. "It's not a huge deal or anything."

"Exactly," Lucia said. "So no reason to keep me out."

Lucia led the way, and they left the deer and dragonflies in the meadow and hiked back through the cherry trees to the family cabin, where Willow awaited them.

## CHAPTER 8
# A Black Cloud

MYA WALKED INTO their mother's office first, Lucia trailing behind her into a room she had almost forgotten. It was more like a shrine to three generations of clients than a home office. Her mother kept gilt-framed photographs on the walls the way some people mounted the heads of deer: actresses and jazz singers from the "talkies" era in Hollywood, their hair short and curled with black ringlets popping out of cloche hats; models from the mod era of the 1960s with tiny legs and go-go boots and A-line paper dresses; pop stars with big hair and lots of glitter from the disco era in the 1970s; female politicians with shoulder pads and blunt haircuts from the 1980s and '90s.

The portrait of Great-Grandmother Serena hung above the fireplace directly behind the grand teak desk in the center of the room. Her wavy black hair and pale skin reminded Lucia of herself—or how she used to look before her wrinkles began to show. Next to Serena hung the photograph Lucia had adored since she was a little girl sitting across from Willow during business calls and playing tic-tac-toe with Mya. The black-and-white image caught a very happy Great-

Grandmother Serena with an arm around Marlene Lovett, a famous screen beauty from the 1930s and one of the first women to wear a smoking jacket on film. Androgynous with the sharp lines of her jaw and nose, yet glamorous with her waterfall of blond curls—she was a dream, and Willow had made sure to re-create her in the girls' imaginations.

After a long day of work, Willow had never failed to come to their room and rest in each of their beds for a little while to stroke their hair, ask about their day, and allow each girl to pose three questions. Then she'd tell one story before heading to her room to sleep, only to wake and do it all over again. Lucia would beg for her to tell the Marlene Lovett story; she asked to hear this story so many times that Mya often whined if Willow agreed. But both of the girls knew Willow secretly loved to tell it.

"The foundation of our business," Willow always began. Marlene had been tutored with Great-Grandmother Serena in New York and learned to play the piano with her, and Serena had comforted her after her mother died. She had been Serena's best friend.

After returning from Borneo, Serena had tried to contact her father, only to discover he had lost his entire fortune during the crash and jumped to his death from the Brooklyn Bridge. Serena thought her tie to her birthplace had been severed forever, until she received a handwritten letter from Marlene. The Depression had been especially hard on her dear friend's family, and her passion for the stage had led only to burlesque shows on the weekends. Marlene needed a lucky break, and Serena needed a subject for an experiment. She invited Marlene to Virginia to meet her new family, whom Marlene instantly loved, especially the bewitching little girls, and Serena offered a bottle of her hobby perfume to Marlene as a parting gift. "But do give a call in the next few weeks to let me know how you are," Serena had told her. (This was Lucia's favorite line of the story, one Willow always repeated verbatim and with a wink.)

Sure enough, Marlene Lovett landed one Broadway role after another, and not long after, she had taken over Hollywood. She had pink Cadillacs, many suitors, and a steady supply of dear Serena's unnamed perfume, which increased in price with each accolade bestowed upon Marlene Lovett. (Now the price of the perfume was fixed, adjusted only for inflation or major career advances.) Once Marlene established herself, she and Serena struck a deal: Marlene had to select a fledgling actress with potential, perhaps an extra from one of her movies, and direct her to Serena. And that's how the business continued to operate, as established during Serena's tenure: one woman tapped the shoulder of another woman for an amazing opportunity with a talent scout, but only when the president requested that she do so. And then the vetting and interview process began. Thus, each bedtime story turned into a business lesson for Lucia and Mya, quite like how this meeting would surely unfold, but far more pleasant.

Mya seated herself in a scarlet armchair in front of the desk, and Lucia sat in the matching one next to it. Willow moved into the room as quietly as a breeze, but the smell of freshly brewed coffee gave her away. She placed her ceramic mug on the desk and pulled out the chair. Her black linen dress did not have a single wrinkle. The house might be cluttered and old, but Willow's clothes were always neat. "First impressions happen outside the house," she sometimes used to say, as if this was reason enough not to clean or have someone else do it for her. Her skin, however, did have wrinkles, many more than it had fifteen years ago, though somehow she still looked youthful. She and Mya had maintained their life force while Lucia had given hers to a doomed marriage and a career moving swiftly into obscurity.

Lucia couldn't stop examining her mother as she might a stranger who refused to make eye contact. "I asked to come in," Lucia said, "but I'll go if it's a problem."

Willow directed her attention to Mya. "Is it okay with you?"

Mya looked startled to be asked. "I mean, only if it's okay with you, I guess."

"I'm sorry I was short with you," Willow said to Lucia.

Lucia looked down at her hands and at the pale circle of skin where her wedding band used to be. "I get it. And I'm sorry too." Certainly this apology could not heal fifteen years of estrangement, Lucia knew that, but the least she could do was finally apologize for so rarely calling to check on the family and the business, especially since they were in trouble and Lucia had had no idea.

Mya's mouth quivered.

Willow asked, "Does she know?"

Mya cleared her throat and then said, "Mostly."

Mostly? What *hadn't* she told Lucia? That was so like her sister.

Willow folded her hands together. Her fingernails were long and unpolished. She never missed a manicure, not that Lucia could remember.

Willow said, "You know I know, Mya."

Mya nodded. "I do."

"I wouldn't do that to you, not that I should even need to say it," Willow said, and then straightened her posture. "I've thought about what I'd say to you for an entire plane ride and I still don't know. Zoe Bennett knew more about our goings-on than I did as president. And you knew. How'd you expect me to handle that?"

The room pulsed with personal hurt, and Lucia felt embarrassed for inserting herself into this meeting. She glanced at Mya, who rubbed her cheeks with both palms and then covered her mouth with her hands.

"Nothing?" Willow said. "You've got nothing to say to me?" Lucia couldn't remember hearing her mother be so cross with Mya. With Lucia, yes, but not Mya, who had always planned to follow their mother's career path. Clearly their roommate situation had strained their relationship. Willow turned the chair away from Mya and did the absolutely unthinkable. How many times had she put hot-pepper lacquer on Lucia's nails to make her stop biting them? And there was Willow's pointer fingernail resting on her lips, her lower jaw working back and forth.

Without facing Mya again, Willow said, "She's contacting our other clients. How the hell she knows who they are and how to get in touch with them is beyond me at this point, but Jennifer said it's true. Zoe's blackmailing her too, so I believe her." Willow took a sip of her coffee and cradled the mug in her hands. "Jennifer seems so lost."

Mya raised her arm as if she sat in an elementary school classroom, but Willow put her hand up as if to shush her. "I've been informed of your little plan and you know we can't; it goes against everything I've ever told you about the business, not that you seem to give a damn about what I say anymore. But we don't change the formula. We haven't for a hundred years. My mother adhered to that, and I promised her I would as well. You *know* this. Why would I need to remind you?"

"You don't," Mya said, "but—"

Willow said, "There are no exceptions."

"There *must* be exceptions," Mya said. "Life doesn't operate without them."

"Maybe," Willow said, "but our business does. Don't you want the company? Don't you both want something to pass on?" And then Willow waved her hand in the air as if to brush away dust. "Well, not you, Lucia, I know, but, Mya, doesn't that matter to you? The decisions we make here matter for the future. Deciding to alter the formula without consulting me and then telling clients that was the decision we'd made—just irresponsible. I never thought you'd do something so low."

Mya shook her head and no one spoke.

"What about murder?" Lucia asked, and then smiled.

Her mother's mouth dropped open.

"Seems like the surest solution," Lucia said.

Willow pointed at Lucia and said, "Just stop. Or get out if you can't be helpful," and then she muttered something. All these years later and Lucia still knew how to fluster Willow. She couldn't help herself.

Mya narrowed her eyes at Lucia, then turned to their mother and said, "How do you know, and I mean with a hundred percent certainty, that they wouldn't have changed it if they *had* to, if they might lose the business altogether?"

Willow took a deep breath, her chest rising slowly. "No," she said.

"It's your fault you didn't read the damn contract! Now you won't compromise," Mya blurted, her voice raised high suddenly, as though she needed a witness in the room to have the courage to utter it. Lucia placed her hand on Mya's arm without realizing until Mya pulled away.

Willow turned her face away and placed her chin in her hand. This sign of contrition admitted all they needed to know. Mya settled back in her chair. In a soft voice Willow said, "You sent me out there alone so I'd have no other choice. Didn't you?"

Lucia felt like she'd arrived to a new family where the past didn't dictate who they were anymore.

"If it's both your faults, can't you just hear her out?" Lucia said to Willow, and braced herself by squeezing the armchair on both sides.

Mya's eyebrows lifted in anticipation, and she looked over at Lucia as if to say "thank you." Willow tucked flyaway hairs behind her ears and said, "Fine."

Mya said, "What do you mean 'fine'?"

Willow looked to the ceiling like she could make it collapse. "I mean fine, Mya, please don't test my patience."

"It's just that—"

"It's what?" Willow said.

Mya turned out her palms. "She comes home for a few hours and you agree to her suggestion even though I've been asking you to consider the possibility of a different formula for weeks?"

"Don't be childish."

"Agreed," Lucia added. Only Mya would quarrel when Lucia was pretty sure she'd just helped her out.

"Butt out," Mya said to Lucia. To Willow she said, "I'm glad you agree, I just don't know why it took her to get you to do it."

Willow placed a finger in the air. "I haven't agreed to any changes. Just to hear you out, that's all."

"Same thing," Mya said.

Their mother sighed. Willow finally said, "It's not Lucia."

"It's not?" Mya said.

"I meant to read it over."

"Thank you for finally saying that," Mya said, and slapped the arms of her chair before jumping up. "Let's go to my workshop, no time to waste." Mya ushered Lucia up from her chair and waved for Willow to stand also. Mya led the way out of the office, through the reading room, and to the back of the cabin. The workshop had always been Mya's sacred space, one she allowed Lucia to enter on select occasions, perhaps as a present for her birthday or for Valentine's Day. Lucia stepped down into the room and the smell of deep earth, like a freshly dug grave, overpowered her.

"Is that musk?" Willow said as she glanced around the room, her face lifted upward to catch the scent on the air. "Musk. That's what it is, but that's not synthetic."

"Nope," Mya said as she uncovered her wall of dried flowers, "but it's the solution."

This wall was where Mya had always come to gather supplies for the love spells they'd cast. When Mya unveiled the dried herbs Lucia felt nine years old again. Mya had promised it would take many, many years for those spells to come true, and Lucia had believed Mya because she could tame deer and see the future in the clouds. For a while Lucia had believed Jonah had come from those love spells. How very wrong she'd been. Many, many years had passed and Lucia and Mya were both still alone. Their mother too. Maybe something about Lenore women couldn't be sustained with a partner. Lucia wanted a healthy relationship—she didn't want to end up alone like her mother, with her career as her only companion.

Willow said, "Is that it?" and walked to the wall of flowers.

Lucia stood behind them. A tiny ball hung there: Was it a rock covered with dried moss, or a fig?

Mya removed it and said, "Watch this," and she took it to the butcher's block in the middle of the room. She sliced slowly down the middle and removed a dark and ruddy substance from the inside. It looked like dark sand from a faraway coast. Mya gently placed it into a small glass bowl. She took out a pastry brush and painstakingly wiped out the cavity to make sure nothing was left behind. Lucia wanted to know what she was looking at, but both her mother and Mya were concentrating so hard that Lucia couldn't step in with a question. She sensed she'd already have known the answer if she'd studied the business as well as they had.

Willow picked up the sliced-open pod and said, "The last time I held one of these I was in Paris with Mother."

Mya took it back from her and cradled it in her palm. "My musk deer died."

Mya finished working and put down her tools. "I'll wash the grains in water I got from the natural spring and let it sit overnight."

She pulled up a handle of Cold Creek Appalachian moonshine, made by men who probably still sat at the barbershop in Quartz Hollow all day long waiting for a local to place an order. The Lenore family had always been the largest buyer, as it was the best way to dilute the flower's essence. The boys kept a cold creek and a storage cave devoted to just their family's supply. Mya continued, "Tomorrow I'll dilute it with this. Then I'll have a musk base unlike anything you can get on the market. Zoe wants to focus on her sensuality, so I'll add the essence of *Gardenia potentiae*, orange blossom, patchouli, and Bulgarian rose."

"That's all?" Willow said.

Mya lifted a small amber bottle and said, "And a few drops of this."

Willow took the bottle from her.

"Don't smell it," Mya said, and reached out, but Willow deflected her pass.

"And why not?" Willow said, and began to remove the top.

"It's my hair."

Willow stopped and placed the glass bottle on the table. "Excuse me?"

Mya picked it up as if to guard it. "Well, not anymore. I used the enfleurage method we learned in Paris. Got beef fat from two farms over and spread it on those glass plates and pressed my hair. Took forever to capture, but I got it."

Lucia vaguely recalled the technique Mya had used, but those summer days in Paris were very long ago. Willow's head continued to shake from side to side, and Lucia wanted to command her to speak. Any time Mya involved hair she was up to no good; Lucia knew that all too well.

When Lucia was in the second grade and Mya was in the fifth, they'd begun a potion with the leftover rainwater from a spring storm that morning, and they'd spent almost all of recess perfecting it. With one more handful of honeysuckle blossoms, the healing potion for a dying robin would have been complete. Marta Mitchell and her group of friends from the fifth grade asked to play, and when Mya said, "Not right now," Marta pushed Lucia out of the way and took the stick Lucia was using to stir the potion.

Mya said, "Give it back, Marta, or I'll tell," and Marta said, "No," and drove the stick into the water and splashed it around until none of the potion remained. "Next time let us play," Marta said, and threw the stick back to Lucia, hitting her directly in the eye. It stung and she cried. Lucia held one hand over that left eye, but with her good eye she watched Mya ball her fists. She said, "Tell my little sister you're sorry."

Marta said, "Stupid little voodoo girls. Nobody even likes you."

Mya's face and neck turned red like a tomato. It was the first time Lucia had seen Mya's anger so visible on her body, and that was frightening enough, but then she walked straight up to Marta and a crowd of kids gathered around them and shouted for a fight.

Lucia was sure Mya would gift Marta two black eyes and a bloody lip. Instead she remained calm, slowly reached out to Marta's face, and plucked out a few of her hairs. Mya tucked the hair in her pocket and said, "Just you wait." Marta laughed all the way back to the swings. Mya never told Lucia what she did with those coarse brown hairs from Marta's head, but three days later Marta's beloved Jack Russell terrier jumped in a well and drowned, her parents lost their jobs at the factory, and the family moved out of town immediately.

As far as anyone on the playground was concerned, Mya had made Marta Mitchell disappear forever. Lucia and Mya were never again called voodoo girls, to their faces anyway. Lucia felt protected by Mya but afraid of her too. What would keep Mya from turning on Lucia? The bond of love? Lucia spent years thereafter offering to do Mya's chores just to stay in her good graces. Mya probably assumed Lucia liked to clean. Lucia didn't want to feel this nervous again, but she couldn't help it, not with returning to this place and seeing Mya's hair captured in that bottle, soon to be added to a perfume for a client who threatened the business.

Willow picked up Mya's bottle again, but timidly, like it might be hot. She said, "And your hair is necessary because . . . ?"

"Zoe lied to us," Mya said, "and now she wants to ruin us."

"But technically she wasn't contracted," Lucia said to add some reason to the conversation, since their mother wasn't objecting as much as Lucia had expected.

Both Willow and Mya turned around and shot her a terrible look, one that made Lucia glance to the door, looking for an escape route. Willow said, "Just so you know, Lucia, I was in those interviews with Mya and we made it clear to Zoe."

"But not in the contract," Lucia said.

Willow turned back around and ignored Lucia's statement. "What will it do?"

"I told you," Mya said. "Fix our problems."

"But how?" Willow persisted.

Mya said, "Zoe wanted more sensuality, right? So it's sexual, but to the point of madness. There'll be a huge backlash, one she won't be able to anticipate."

"Is that even remotely safe?" Lucia asked.

"Why wouldn't it be?"

Willow continued to stare at Mya like she didn't believe her. Mya said, "It *is*, I promise. She'll need a new career, that's all. Bartending or something."

"Could it be linked to us?" Willow asked.

Lucia turned away from them, walked to the wall of flowers, and covered them with the curtain. She couldn't believe where this conversation was headed.

Mya said, "She'll self-destruct. There'll be no one to blame but herself. And her PR person, I guess."

Willow made a long humming noise.

"As in yes?" Mya said, and Lucia turned around, just as shocked as Mya to see their mother nodding. Just like that. Lucia had never thought her mother would actually agree. She just figured that if Willow listened to Mya, at least Mya couldn't complain about being marginalized.

"I see no other option," Willow said. "She can't expose us."

"Exactly," Mya said.

"But swear to me that as soon as it's done you'll destroy this and stick to the original formula," Willow said, and touched the bottle of Mya's dissolved hair. "I think if we make this small adjustment just once, for the sake of the business's longevity, then the curse won't have a reason to come down on us."

Mya jumped up and down and then hugged Willow and said, "Thank you for letting me fix this. I'll never let it happen again, I swear."

She opened the jar of spring water and used the dropper to add the ingredient to the musk pod grains. Hunched over the glass bowl, Mya watched each drop fall, and then she began to swirl the mixture together. Directly above Mya's head, a dark, watery substance formed like a gathering tornado. Lucia closed and opened her eyes just to make sure she wasn't hallucinating. But it was still there. The dark substance lengthened and expanded, and Lucia caught her breath as she watched what no one else in the room seemed to notice. Mya hugged their mother tightly again, and the darkness moved with her and hovered over them both for a moment. Then Mya let go and moved back to her table, and the darkness followed her. As she handled her materials, the ethereal substance grew larger and took the shape of a single stormy cloud floating just a foot above the crown of Mya's head. In a flash within the cloud, Lucia saw her sister's bloody face. Lucia felt her own face go pale.

She shook her head. The earthy, animalistic smell that invaded the room during the musk wash had to be the reason Lucia was going crazy. She felt certain she might faint if she stayed any longer. She said, "I need to go to the bathroom."

"Are you okay?" Mya's brow furrowed.

"Fine," Lucia said, continuing to stare at the bruised cloud bobbing above Mya's head. It looked like thunder and lightning would issue forth at any moment. Lucia's entire body went cold, like she'd learned a damning family secret kept thirty-three years too long.

"You sure?" Willow said. "You look a little peaked." Lucia's face must've looked as drained as it felt. She stared at Mya, certain that if she walked toward her and reached out her hand she could insert it inside the cloud.

"I—I think I need to go outside," Lucia stammered, bracing herself on the doorframe of the workshop. "Just out for a bit, to get some stuff."

"Can you pick up sour cherries? Lots of them," Mya said, and smiled, the cloud bobbing up and down. "I have a craving for cherry pie and I used all the ripe ones from our trees."

Lucia nodded and tripped on the top step of the workshop stairs. She turned from the room and hurried out the back door of the cabin to their white truck, the keys already in the ignition, the engine running like it expected her. "What the hell?" Lucia leaned over the seat and took many deep breaths. She knew this feeling—it had happened on the Acorn Theater stage, and now she was experiencing the exact same panic attack for a very different reason. Lucia wanted that cloud to disappear; it made her feel so terrible, almost like she had the flu. She'd have to tell her sister about it and convince her, even though she had no proof and no history of visions. All she had was this burning, awful feeling.

Like spotting a cracked tree limb right before it fell.

Lucia hoped that by the time she came home, whatever hung over Mya's head would have vanished, and that the truck's being on was just a fluke. Maybe one of the land-maintenance workers had used it and forgot to shut it off. People did forgetful things like that sometimes, right? Her world couldn't shift so completely in an instant, could it?

## CHAPTER 9

### Choosing a Successor

WILLOW ADJUSTED THE wide-brimmed hat on her head, and the scent of her family's flower on the wind drew her closer to the blooming fields. She so rarely took walks now that her knees ached, but she couldn't stay another moment longer in the cabin. The smell of Mya's unadulterated musk had brought back so many memories of her days of training in Paris alongside her sister, Iris, and their mother. She missed them more today than she had in a long time. She could practically hear her mother's disappointed voice, southern accent and all: *No direction? No husbands? No babies? What are those daughters of yours doing?* Willow wasn't the least bit sure anymore. She'd done her part for the family business; she'd given birth to daughters and raised them by herself (minus the help she received from local women she'd loaned money to), and she couldn't keep thinking about the future of the business if neither of her daughters did the same.

Though Lucia had been away for so many years, Willow had at least hoped Lucia and Jonah would eventually send a granddaughter for Willow to train. The family business wasn't of interest to Lucia, but that didn't guarantee her daughter would feel the same way. Now both of Willow's daughters were single and in their thirties and no closer to a long-term relationship than Willow. Lucia reminded Willow of Iris—disconnected from the family business, working nine to five as a bank teller in Toledo, looking for a life she never found with a man she hardly loved, dying alone from a massive stroke without anyone finding her for days—all because she wanted nothing to do with the business. Willow worried Lucia would turn out the same way long after Willow left the world and had no power to help her.

She arrived at the top of the hill, where acres of *Gardenia potentiae* hedges stretched until the flowers at the farthest reaches looked like white dots of snow. She stopped and took an invigorating breath of the flower's scent, present only during these few weeks of the summer. A deep breath at this place always made Willow feel better.

But the scent was not as strong as she expected, and she lifted her hands into the air to feel for an east wind. The leaves on the surrounding trees did not move. She walked to the edge and the thick green foliage looked healthy, as did the blooms. Bending down to better smell the flowers, Willow touched a green bud, and it moved up and down as if it were nodding. Willow caressed it. The plants were blooming late this year. Perhaps that was all. She'd go in and call Robert over at the factory and make sure he knew.

Willow knelt down before the flowers and bowed her head, as if she needed to apologize to them for all that had happened. On the eve of retirement, Willow Lenore might have run the business into the ground. She'd be forever judged by this instead of by her strong history as president for thirty years without a glitch. Well, maybe one or two glitches. Too few ladybugs one year, if she remembered correctly. Or was it a white fungus? No need trying to recall what no longer mattered, a tenet she hadn't adhered to as a younger woman, but now she had no choice.

Willow decided to go to the pond down in the holler for a summer swim. She owned the pond, yet she rarely used it since the girls had grown up. Her bare feet crushed dandelions and wild onions as she descended the hill, and the air cooled as she came closer to the pond. In the pocket of her linen dress, her cell phone began to vibrate, and she stopped and debated whether she should check it. If only she could have ten minutes to herself. Was that so much to ask? But it could be Mya or Lucia or Jennifer Katz or, God forbid, Zoe Bennett. She lifted the device out of her pocket and James Stein's name scrolled across the bottom of the screen.

She smiled and let it ring for a minute, and by the time she was ready to answer she had missed the call. Willow didn't want to seem too available, so she placed her feet in the cool pond water and watched the minnows dance around in the algae murkiness she kicked up. Little nibbles on her toes and ankles tickled like a pedicure. Knee-deep in the water now and with her dress lifted, Willow tapped James's name on the screen.

After three rings he picked up, and his voice was smokier than she remembered. "I hoped you'd call back," he said. It sounded like he was smiling.

Willow eased herself out of the water and stretched her bare legs on the grassy edge of the pond. "How are you?"

"Between meetings. You?"

"About to go for a swim in our pond." Willow switched the phone to her other ear.

"It's hot here," James said, and then he told someone in the background to wait. "Willow, you there?"

"I am. Is everything okay?"

"Just an assistant," he said quickly. "So I'm calling because I'll be in DC next week and I was hoping I could come down and visit that pond of yours."

Willow's heart began to pound. Was that an innuendo? He flustered her, but she didn't want him to notice. She covered the speaker, took a deep breath, and then said, "I think that should be fine. It's harvest time, just so you know."

"I'll stay out of the way, I promise."

Willow laughed aloud and let a granddaddy longlegs spider walk across her palm. She said, "About Zoe."

"Bad transition," James said.

Willow laughed again. He had a knack for making her happy. "I just thought you'd want to know that I approved a new formula for her. She'll land sexier kinds of roles."

"She's okay with that?"

"It's what she desires."

"Good news then, right?"

"I think so."

"I can't wait to see you again."

"Me too."

"I'll send you my flight information soon. All I need is your address."

"I'll have my assistant e-mail you whatever you need," Willow said. "Should I arrange a car to pick you up?"

"No need. I'll take care of everything."

"Good."

"And, Willow?"

"Yes?" She pursed her lips in anticipation.

"I love your hair, always have," James said.

"Thank you," she said, and shifted her hair so it draped over one shoulder.

"But I need to go now, something's come up," he said.

"See you soon," Willow said, and then the line went silent.

Willow ran her hand over the back of her head and ended the call. She placed her phone on a bed of clover and stood up, removing her dress and standing completely naked before the pond. If only

James could see her now. She dove headfirst into the warm water and remained under the surface, testing how long she could hold her breath . . . Fifteen seconds . . . Thirty-three seconds . . . Forty-two seconds . . . She opened her eyes and it looked as though she were suspended in diluted ink. Sixty-two . . . Seventy-one seconds . . . Willow didn't want to die alone . . . Eighty-three seconds . . . Her breath gave out, and she stood up, drew in air, and peeled back the hair from her eyes. She climbed to the edge of the pond and rested there.

Clients and the factory and the flowers had always come first and her love life last. Her last relationship—how long ago had that been? Ten years? Eleven? It had become too hard to keep track of the years. She'd broken off her relationship with the governor of Virginia right before he was elected. Lenore Incorporated would have received too much scrutiny with Paul's advancing position. He couldn't understand her decision: *But imagine how your cosmetics business will grow, Willow.* That was the last thing Paul said to her, and she had to admit, it wasn't very romantic. Mya couldn't stand him. At least he'd been a very good governor. Eventually he'd married a Pilates instructor.

Willow had accepted that her love life had officially ended and she couldn't rely on the occasional business-trip fling to satisfy her like she had when she was a younger woman focused on running the business and raising her girls. Back then she'd refused to complicate her life by introducing someone to the family unit. Willow never revealed her business to any of her lovers, and she'd resigned herself to never finding a partner who understood her. Not even the girls' father knew. But Willow's mother had hand-selected James Stein for her, and all these years later he'd come calling again.

Willow wanted more, and she knew she could jeopardize her chance with James Stein if she remained as busy as she'd always been. She was starting to realize she just didn't have it in her anymore. Being forgetful did not serve a president well. But how would she ever give up her position? Her mother had only passed on the title to Willow when she was on her deathbed, and now Willow would be forced to give it up when her body was perfectly healthy, though her mind was not. Mya had found a solution to their Zoe problem, and now that Lucia was home, she could announce the next president of Lenore Incorporated and begin the transition process.

And who knew? Maybe this would be enough to convince her daughters to settle down. Perhaps Mya and Luke had a future together after all, one that Willow had underestimated. She couldn't give the business over to Lucia, since Lucia had long ago rejected the possibility, but Willow had always hoped her younger daughter would come home to witness Willow's decision. Lucia was here now and the time had come.

## CHAPTER 10
## *The First Date*

MYA CLEANED UP the workshop and locked the door to that room, then went to the bathroom, washed her face, and brushed her hair and tied it back into a bun. Her cell phone chimed just as she finished brushing her teeth. Luke texted, *C U shortly*. She closed her eyes and shook her head at what she was about to do. Had he finally won his public date with Mya? Surely that's how he'd see it, but it wasn't a date, not even close. If the tea store hadn't called about an inventory emergency, she wouldn't have needed him, but Lucia had one of the trucks and the other work vehicles were nowhere in sight. The crew must have been using them up at the fields to prepare for harvest. And Willow had the SUV. Anyhow, no matter her excuse, she'd called him, he was on the way, and there would be no convincing him this wasn't a real date.

Mya decided to wait out on the porch until Luke drove up, and she settled down on the steps and crossed her legs. From around the corner of the house, her beloved Little Spots came racing like she was being chased, her eyes wide with fear. Mya reached out her hand and said, "Easy there, what's the matter?" Mya went to the end of the porch and brought back deer corn for Spots, but the fawn refused to eat it. "Are you ill?" Mya said, and rubbed her little head. Spots backed away from Mya like she was the problem, and then she bolted away from her and back toward the tree line. Mya stood and followed the fawn's path around the cabin. She had just cleared the side of the house when she found two dead wrens beneath the willow tree. She didn't linger there; rather she raced back to the porch and checked the nesting wrens on the front door. She shook the eucalyptus bunch and two birds shot out from either side. Mya closed her eyes in relief but still felt sorrow for those other birds and wondered how they'd managed to die together. Had they killed each other?

She heard Luke's truck tires churn the gravel road, and she turned around and headed down the steps, all too eager to be away from the house for a little while, though she wasn't sure why she felt that way. But Lucia had gone to town and her mother had left to run errands, and Mya didn't want to be alone. And she'd missed Luke a little.

With one tan arm hanging from his truck window, Luke didn't turn off his ignition or step out to open her door; he just waved and said, "Hop in." He turned the truck around for her at least. She brushed away sawdust and soil from the passenger seat and then climbed inside. He immediately leaned over, held her cheek in his hand, and kissed her. "Glad you called," he said.

"Texted."

"You know what I mean."

"There's a difference," she said. "Anyway, thanks for coming to get me."

"My pleasure. So where to?"

"Herbs and Wellness. Orders are all mixed up."

"Want to catch a movie after?"

"Maybe," Mya said, and tried to conceal her discomfort. It could never be that simple, just a trip to town and back home. Why did people need so much from one another?

"Can we play some music?" she said. Luke put on a Gordon Lightfoot CD and an excruciating nostalgia filled the truck's cab. The town was a thirty-minute drive from the cabin, so Mya might be weeping by the time they arrived, for reasons not even she would be able to pinpoint. She made an effort not to listen.

The first half of the stretch was land owned by Mya's family. It had been owned by the Lenores since Great-Grandmother Serena first came here in the thirties to establish a factory and grow the flowers. It was Serena's idea to loan money to local businesses, and she turned what had been hill country into a bustling town with multiple stoplights on Main Street. Most of the families who had started businesses back then continued to run businesses many generations later. In turn, nobody asked questions about Lenore Incorporated. The kids at school had made jokes sometimes about Mya and Lucia. A few times they were called witches, and just once they were called voodoo girls.

At least Mya and Lucia were strange in a way no one else could be. Lucia spent all her time trying to fit in and Mya spent her time on the playground telling kids what she saw in the clouds. One time she told Jake Nelson, whose family owned the organic bakery in town, that she saw him burning his forearm as he pulled cranberry walnut muffins from the oven, and he told her she was stupid. A few days later he was in the hospital with a third-degree burn. And she remembered the time she saw Bridget Lanely's dog dead in the road, and sure enough, the next day Bridget skipped school to bury him. It wasn't all bad news. She did tell Lindsey Wright about the Barbie bicycle she'd get for Christmas, and after the break, Lindsey followed Mya around wherever she went on the playground and bugged her about the clouds. None of it had bothered Mya, not the way it bothered Lucia. But over the years even Mya started to avoid town. She was glad the herbal tea store ran smoothly on its own, for the most part. She'd only started it to give herself something to manage while she waited to be president.

Large, shading maple trees lined the streets of Quartz Hollow. Luke parked his truck in front of Blue Ridge Books, and Mya stepped out. Even here, so many miles away, she should have been able to smell the blooming *Gardenia potentiae* flowers. It had been this way for a hundred years. No one in town probably noticed anymore, just like the sweet olive hedge that bloomed in September and the honey-suckle vines in May, but today the scent of her family's flower did not linger in the air. The wind rustled the tree leaves, but it carried no scent with it. This puzzled Mya.

Outside Blue Ridge Books old Millie stocked the metal bargain bookshelves, her cane on the ground next to her. She'd always been one of the women Willow called to watch Lucia and Mya if she was tied up with business or had to leave town for a meeting. Millie struggled to stand up, and Mya trotted up to her and took one of her elbows. "Thank you, dear," Millie said, and then said, "Oh, that's you, Mya? So good to see you, it's been such a while, hasn't it?"

"It has," Mya said, and handed her the cane. "Glad to see you're well."

"You know me," Millie said, and winked. "I'll keep kicking as long as life keeps kicking me." She'd used this line ever since her husband died, and maybe that's why Mya had stopped coming around so much. Everything was aging, including herself, and nothing felt right about that.

Luke stood at Mya's side and greeted Millie, and Mya used his interruption as a good reason to move on down Main Street to the corner where Herbs and Wellness stood. "See you later," Mya said, and Millie waved good-bye, then returned to her seat outside the store. Not too long and her mother would be old like Millie. That was hard for Mya to imagine. But it was happening; she couldn't deny it.

Only Luke appeared safe from the grip of aging. He reached over to hold Mya's hand, and she playfully elbowed him in the side, but then he slung his arm around her shoulders and held on tight, and there wasn't much she could do to escape him.

The door chimed as she and Luke entered the tea shop, and Mya's store manager, Vista, came around the glass countertop in her earth-mother head scarf and broomstick skirt, with gold bangles on both arms, which were covered in squiggled henna art. She wrapped Mya in one of her patchouli-scented hugs. "Thanks for coming," Vista said.

Luke took a seat by the window while Mya went behind the counter and wiped away stray loose-leaf spearmint tea on the shelves. She'd had an old restaurant converted into her tea shop, but she'd kept the bar and the shelving behind it in place. People liked to come in for a pot of tea the way they might a cold IPA. Vista went into the manager's office, and Mya could see a mountain of cardboard boxes. Vista returned with an inventory slip for Mya. It was much longer than usual. "Just give me a second," Mya said, and she took it over to the table where Luke sat.

"Want anything?" Vista said.

"How about valerian with lemongrass?" Mya said. "Something to calm the nerves. Is that okay with you?" she asked Luke.

Luke shrugged. "As long as there's sweetener, I don't care."

"No problem," Vista said, and went behind the bar.

Mya squinted at the inventory list. It had been a few years since she'd had to look at one this closely. Vista ran the shop and the associated online store with a great deal of efficiency. Mya scanned the ten-page list and shook her head.

"What is it?" Luke said.

"It's like we ordered our entire inventory ten times over," Mya said. "How could this even happen?"

Vista returned with a yellow ceramic teapot and placed it on the table along with a honeypot. "Needs to steep."

"Can you sit?" Mya said, and Vista pulled up a chair from a neighboring table. "How could this happen? Who placed the order?"

Vista always smiled, no matter the circumstance. "I thought you did. I thought you'd made plans to expand without telling me or something. We don't have the cash reserve to cover it."

"Of course not," Mya said. "We don't need any of this."

"I know," Vista said.

"So return the order."

"I tried already."

"And?"

"No refunds."

"That's impossible," she said. "Try again."

"I mean, I will if you want me to," she said, "but the bags are already open."

"And why is that?"

"I thought you'd know," Vista said. "I didn't touch them."

Mya squeezed the bridge of her nose and closed her eyes. "This is ridiculous. I haven't been here in months. Did one of the part-time girls do it?"

"I don't know," Vista said. "Maybe, but I doubt it."

"Can we repackage them and sell it on eBay and recoup some cash?" Mya said, and Luke poured out the first cup of tea.

"I'll try," she said, "but it could take a few months."

"Fine."

Vista nodded in her slow hippie way.

"And thanks for the tea."

Her bracelets jangled as she walked back to the bar with the inventory slips.

Mya poured herself a cup while Luke dropped a large spoonful of honey in his tea. "Is it a big deal?" he finally said.

"I can't think about it right now," she said. Anytime money was tied up for no good reason, it was a big deal. And why had it happened? That mattered most to Mya. She should've been the one to hire the part-timers, but instead she had trusted Vista with the task.

Luke took a sip and grimaced. His muscular body didn't fit in the tea shop with its delicate wares. He reached underneath the table and squeezed her thigh. He said, "I can think of a couple ways to distract you. Let's go see a movie."

She brought the teacup to her lips so she wouldn't have to respond.

"Come on, Mya," he said. "I did your work thing, now go do something fun with me."

"I just don't—"

"Are you afraid or something?" he said. He removed his hand from her leg.

"Goodness no," she said.

"Is it our ages?" he said. "Because I don't care about that."

Vista turned on the small flat-screen TV mounted behind the bar. Mya had conceded and installed a television for Vista because the day-to-day business was so often slow—they did their best business online. Luke stared at the TV and broke from his questioning. Mya was relieved until she turned around to figure out what had captured his attention so fully. Jennifer Katz in a red couture gown filled the screen, and a headline scrolled by beneath: STAR TURNED HERMIT? WHERE HAS SHE GONE? COME BACK, JENNIFER!

Not good. So, so not good. Her perfume for Zoe needed to work and work fast, and though she believed in what she made, she was never 100 percent sure about anything. Not anymore. Not after what happened in the business deal with Zoe. If Jennifer refused to play her part as superstar in Hollywood, she might quit the perfume and expose herself before Zoe had the chance. What Mya wanted to do was go home immediately and send that perfume to Zoe, but the concoction had to rest a little longer to be effective.

Luke said, "She's still hot," and Mya glared at him. The TV cut to a commercial for men's hair-growth products and Luke lost interest. He was many years away from requiring products like those.

Mya rubbed her temples.

"It's a Saturday. Couples do things like go see movies," Luke said.

"Couples?" Mya said.

He finished his tea like he was taking a shot of tequila, and then his blue eyes brightened. He nodded and said, "Couples," as if she hadn't heard him correctly the first time.

Mya sighed. He was much too young for her and this proved it. He still had the gumption for romance. She no longer had the energy to hurt his feelings, not after the day she'd had. Plus, if she returned home now, all she'd do was hover over the formula. "Fine," Mya said, acquiescing. "I'll go see a movie with you." Luke clapped his hands together like he'd just won the lottery.

## CHAPTER 11
### The First Love

DISTRACTED, LUCIA DROVE for at least an hour before she finally remembered the correct route to town. Her hunger refused to subside. What was one more detour before the farmer's market? Lucia crossed the street without looking and headed for the bakery. Stress had often sent Lucia to some of the finest bakeries in New York City for French pastries and desserts. A fight with Jonah equaled a puff with rich, creamy filling, and a rejection from her agent for a dog food commercial or a lead in a B-rated play qualified her for two champagne glasses filled with chocolate mousse and homemade whipped cream, with a raspberry on top. She couldn't buy a classic strawberry tart at the Quartz Hollow Bakery, but she could at least find a homemade cinnamon roll and a cup of black coffee.

No one recognized her, so she ordered a half dozen cinnamon rolls and the largest coffee they had on the menu. Most people were out rafting, hiking, working the shops, or farming at this time of day, so Lucia was one of the few customers. The entire place smelled like vanilla and coffee beans, and a few other people sat around the shop reading tablets or the *Quartz Hollow Gazette* newspaper.

With her white bag of cinnamon-scented stress relief in one hand and black coffee in the other, Lucia left through the glass door, a small brass chime dinging on her way out. She took a left down the sun-drenched sidewalk. The Blue Ridge Mountains, with their deep periwinkle hue; smooth, rolling curves; and perfect visibility loomed in the far distance of Main Street. She understood for a moment why people born here rarely left and why people traveled from all over the world to hike these majestic mountains. Lucia remembered running errands around town as a little girl and encountering filthy, sweaty, hairy women and men who had just stepped off the Virginia highlands section of the Appalachian Trail. They came to Quartz Hollow to shower and eat and pick up packages in town, and if they arrived at just the right time, they swooned over a scent they didn't recognize from their journey. Hikers often asked locals to name it—a few had even asked Willow—but everyone answered with a shrug.

The local farmer's market awaited her at the end of the road, and it was bound to have local sour cherries. She took an enormous bite out of a warm cinnamon roll. As she chewed she tried to convince herself that the cloud above Mya was a result of sleep deprivation and a severe lack of coffee. Lucia couldn't see anything coming. Not a death, not the end of a career, not even the demise of her marriage. But the cloud had moved. Since it had appeared, Lucia couldn't shake the uneasy feeling it produced. Why now? The family gifts presented in childhood, not when you were thirty-three years old. But what if this was real? What if she'd finally had a vision? For the first time in her entire life Lucia no longer felt like the deformed one in the family.

Inside the open-air market, Lucia scanned the stalls. One table had baskets filled with local blushing cherries. Lucia picked up the taut fruits and gently pushed her thumb into the pink flesh to check their ripeness, then she popped one in her mouth just to be sure. Perfectly sour and juicy. Since Mya hadn't asked for a specific amount, Lucia filled the offered grocery bag to the maximum. How she would carry this bag plus her rolls and coffee, she didn't quite know, but she wasn't willing to sacrifice any of it. Just as she was about to double-bag the fruit, she heard a man's voice say, "Lucia Lenore?"

Her stomach dropped like an elevator. The familiar voice made her afraid to turn around, but she did. With one arm cradling the cherries like a newborn, Lucia said, "Ben?"

She couldn't quite believe that Ben White was standing there, back in Quartz Hollow, right in front of her after so many years. And Lucia hadn't taken a shower this morning. She also held an unusually large bag of cherries and an unnecessarily large bag of cinnamon rolls.

"Look at you," Ben said. He didn't even try the stock phrases like "You look great" or "Wow, you haven't changed a bit." Just "Look at you," like he might say "Look at that rhinoceros" at the zoo. If only she could say the same to him, but he *did* look great. His thin, lanky, and sinewy teenage body had filled out into a man's physique. Bigger muscles, broader shoulders. But his face had remained just as youthful as ever, framed now by a handsome beard. He had genial brown eyes, sandy blond hair, and skin that tanned easily and was already on its way to that cinnamon color. He had a strong and pronounced jaw that she had kissed many times. It was incredibly awkward. "I can't believe I'm seeing you," Lucia said, and immediately felt like an idiot.

"Me either." Ben took off his gloves and wiped the sweat from his brow. He pointed to a truck behind the market stalls and said, "I deliver here once a week, right around now. Good timing."

"Imagine that." Lucia took one step back. She hadn't seen him in fifteen years and now he was two feet away from her, the smell of him so familiar it shocked her. A salty smell mixed with soil.

"I see your mom sometimes. She didn't say anything about you coming to town," Ben said, smiling like he was happily misinformed.

"I'm not." Lucia swallowed. "I mean, I am obviously, but just for a short visit. Like a day or two." Lucia knew her mother had a lot going on with business matters, but a casual comment about Ben White's residence in Quartz Hollow would've been appreciated.

"You never did visit," Ben said. "Everything okay?"

Lucia nodded, not wanting to list the many things not okay in her world. "So you live here now?"

"A sabbatical. I've got an organic farm near my mom's."

"Sounds nice."

"You got married, right?" he asked timidly, perhaps taking notice of her bare ring finger displayed prominently on the grocery bag of cherries.

"I did," Lucia said. "But that ended. Recently."

"That's too bad," Ben said. "I'm sorry."

The pain in her chest refused to dissipate. She couldn't bring herself to use the word "divorce." She might as well have stapled the word "failure" to her back. Lucia glanced around for the stall owner. Ben whistled at a short man in overalls standing at a nearby stall with an elderly woman who sold canned relishes and goat's milk soaps. The man walked over and patted Ben on the back. Lucia placed a twenty on the table. He broke her change and thanked her.

Lucia said, "Thanks," to Ben.

"No problem. I better go," Ben said, and nodded at his truck. Why, of all days, would she see Ben White, and did he have to be so damn attractive?

"It was nice seeing you, good luck with your farm." Lucia picked up her coffee and forced a smile before she turned and walked back up Main Street. She hustled down the sidewalk until she heard a truck slowing down beside her.

Ben rolled down the window on his red Ford pickup and said, "You dropped some fruit."

Lucia stopped right before Blue Ridge Books and looked behind her at the trail of cherries. She lifted the bag above her head to find the hole in the bottom, and then the entire bag ripped open, raining cherries on the pavement. Ben parked his truck and hopped out with a potato sack. She bent down to scoop up the bruised fruit with him, and now their faces were only inches apart. Ben looked at her, his big eyes so happy to see her, and she felt sixteen again, just for a moment. He wiped his palms on his ripped jeans and they stood up together. He handed her the sack.

"Thanks," she said.

Ben's hand didn't let go of the bag; her face flushed like one of those cherries.

Ben said, "I want to hear all about New York, before you go back."

"There's not much to tell."

"Then I want to hear about that."

He wasn't giving her a choice in the matter. "I guess you could come by the cabin."

"Will Mya be there?" He sounded like he was hoping she'd say no.

Lucia refused to look him in the eye as she nodded. "You should come anyway. It's been a long time. I'll make dinner and maybe we can go for a hike." Already she was saying the wrong things to him. Lucia didn't know how to cook, and she couldn't remember the last time she went on a hike.

"Tomorrow's good for me."

"Five thirty?"

"Is six okay? Gives me time to shower."

"Sure." Lucia hoped he wasn't making a polite suggestion about her lack of hygiene today. She held the sack of cherries to her chest and watched him trot back to his truck. An azure dragonfly landed between his shoulder blades like the hand of a dear friend and traveled with him to the road. Ben had no idea. He turned once and waved good-bye to her. She worried he'd squish the bug against his seat, but then a second dragonfly swooped down and grazed Ben's shoulder, and the duo circled each other like they were dancing and flew across the road together before Ben had the chance to close his door. Lucia stood there and stared at this figment of her past, the boy he once was still present in the man he had become. She stared until Ben pulled out into the slow traffic of Main Street.

Lucia replayed her entire trip to town, almost minute by minute, on her drive home. She chastised herself for buying so many of those cinnamon rolls, for dropping the fruit, for not having showered, and for saying things like "That ended" instead of "I'm divorced." Why did she hide from him? He'd been her best friend at one point in her life, and more than a decade had passed between then and now, plenty of time to relieve the hurts. He'd forgiven her for breaking his heart—that seemed obvious to Lucia—and she had no reason to skirt the truth about her life. Yet she knew if the same situation recurred, she would hedge just the same.

Memories of young love materialize from the slightest provocations, and this alone had created tension between Lucia and Ben. Standing with him in the market had forced her to remember that he'd been the only boy she loved. He could name the world, every flower, every tree, every insect in their forests, and he obsessed over it. Lucia was attracted to his focus and spontaneity, and how he chronicled their hikes and camping trips in letters and dropped them in her purse from time to time. He was the kind of boy who stopped if he walked past two dandelion weeds in the field and picked them, entwined them, and presented them as a symbol of Lucia and Ben. Flowers were his specialty, and he loved to give her bouquets of wild roses after her high school theater performances, for which he never missed a rehearsal.

He first asked her on a date after the closing night of *Our Town*. She'd always known about Ben White, had watched him play soccer and heard what an ace he was at science, but she'd never spoken to him. Lucia could still picture him sitting in the first row of the empty auditorium after the final performance. She'd wondered if he was lost or waiting for one of her friends to come out from the dressing room. She was pretty certain she'd asked him both of those questions, but instead of answering, he stood up, presented her with a bouquet, and asked her to go on a hike with him the next afternoon. Apparently, he'd wanted to ask her out for an entire year but hadn't mustered the courage. He'd attended every performance of *Our Town* because he'd been struck by the beauty of her hair beneath the stage lights. She agreed to go on a hike with him, and he introduced her to the Cascades, the famed waterfalls in Quartz Hollow, which quickly became their favorite make-out spot. A beautiful place to visit, and Lucia promised herself she'd stop there for a hike before she returned to the city, if she could remember the directions.

Lucia pulled into the long, winding driveway canopied with tree-tops that led to the cabin. After being married for so many long years, she had completely forgotten what going on a first date felt like, or even a platonic dinner. Maybe it felt like being a child on the upswing of a seesaw or a final yellow maple leaf on an autumn branch. Her history with Ben had long since passed, and she was glad he wanted to catch up as old friends.

She walked through the front door of the cabin and found it silent. "Hello?" Lucia said, but no one answered. Her mother's assistant, Brenda, had placed the mail on the center island, and on the very top was an envelope addressed to Mya from Zoe Bennett. Lucia placed the bag of cherries on the table and removed her sunglasses. Lucia placed her pinkie finger in the small gap on the seal, too tempted to put it down. The sound of the screen door opening in the back of the cabin made Lucia drop the letter, and then her mother walked into the kitchen with a bouquet of wildflowers. Lucia held the letter up for her mother. "What's that?" Willow said.

Lucia didn't want to tell her. Willow looked more relaxed than she had since Lucia arrived.

Willow exchanged the flowers for the mail, and Lucia found a vase in the cabinet above the stove and filled it with tap water.

"Where's Mya?" her mother said.

"I'm not sure," Lucia said.

Willow secured Zoe's correspondence between her hands and left the kitchen without another word.

## CHAPTER 12

## *Detailed Plotting*

WILLOW NEEDED A manicure—her cuticles were as overgrown as the kudzu she noticed in the southwest section of the forest, about which she made a mental note to alert the groundskeepers. That greedy plant could not come near her flowers, not even close. She had forever been afraid of soil contamination by an invasive species, and kudzu was one of the worst offenders, though it did prefer to climb rather than spread. Still, if it had the chance, her hedges would be smothered in one season.

And she had to make an appointment at Joanne's Salon in town to take care of her dry hands and the cracked heels of her feet, along with a haircut and a cucumber facial. Willow put the letter down on the desk and covered Zoe's inked name with her hands. Her mind was so far away from business, the farthest it had ever been. Nails were her priority. And James Stein. He had specifically complimented her hands while they ate sushi, and now she noticed them with embarrassing admiration as she typed on her laptop or washed the dishes or shaved her legs. These were the types of distraction that had always made women less powerful than they should be.

Willow straightened her back and tapped her fingernails on the envelope. She had never taken Zoe Bennett for the handwritten-correspondence type. More like a texter—abbreviated and impersonal.

Willow had no clue when Mya would return home. She wasn't in the habit of leaving a note. Ever. Important information or requests could be inside, and as president of Lenore Incorporated, Willow had the right to access requests or complaints. But how could she prepare her daughter for the business if she didn't respect her correspondence with clients? Then again, Mya didn't deserve this consideration. Maybe in the future, but not right now.

Small beads of sweat formed on her upper lip, and she wiped them away with the envelope. Willow slid her silver letter opener into the envelope, opened it, and lifted out a gold-flecked piece of handmade paper. It smelled heavily of the perfume, as if Zoe had enough to waste on a letter to the very people who created it. She had never once worried that Willow would cut her off.

*Mya,*

*I received your letter and I absolutely love the idea of a perfume with more sex appeal. That's right for me. Go ahead and send your mother out here for a meeting anyway to make her feel a part of things. And I absolutely agree with you, she's done. She's too old now and she's lost her touch. Encourage her to retire, but no matter what she says, you need to make this happen. I already told Jennifer about your plan and I've contacted some of your biggest clients in case your mother resists. Call Justice Anne Reed of the Supreme Court and Jan Dorset at CNN and Lauren Dall at her investment house in New York if you don't believe me. They'll quit ordering as long as I promise not to expose them. But if the new formula works, all will be well. Contact me when it's ready.*

*Until then,*
*Zoe Bennett*

The girl didn't have enough sense to make sure this letter arrived before Willow's trip. And this whole time Mya had planned to set her up and urge her to retire, and worse, just like a middle school girl, she'd gossiped about Willow with Zoe.

Willow pinned the letter underneath the gold lion paperweight her mother had left behind, then stood up with both hands gripping the black leathertop desk and let out the longest, most deeply pent-up scream she'd ever screamed. She could feel all the trees and the flowers and the deer and the dragonflies pausing to let her have this moment. Not a single wingbeat, not a blade of grass bent to the wind. Lucia came running in with a face as deeply panicked as it had been when she was a toddler running to her mother's room during a thunderstorm. Willow grabbed her chest and collapsed in her chair.

"Oh no, Mom!" Lucia screamed. "No, no, no." She reached for the phone.

"Not a heart attack," Willow said, and waved her hand in the air. "A scream like that hurts the chest, that's all." But Lucia still came to her side, kneeled down, and placed her hands on Willow's shoulders. This was a comfort Willow had long since given up hoping for from Lucia.

"What in the hell just happened?"

Willow handed Lucia the note from Zoe.

Lucia crossed her legs on the ground next to Willow's chair and read it. When she finished, she offered it back to Willow and shook her head.

"She sent me out there and had already promised them something I hadn't agreed to. They all knew but me, and they were pandering to a wrinkled old out-of-touch has-been. Mya thinks I can't do my job anymore and she can do it better. Who will trust her when she pulls things like this? Zoe Bennett can rot as far as I'm concerned." Willow pushed the office chair into the back wall and knocked the paperweight off the desk.

Lucia retreated to the couch and braced herself on the armrest as Willow's voice grew even louder. "Let Zoe contact every fucking client we have and expose us. Tell everyone in the world about our flower and what it can do. Let the stupid FDA finally get in here for a sample and let Mya see what happens then. She'll have no business to take over whether she pushes me into retirement or not. I don't give a damn anymore. She's controlling things behind my back, and she can have the business and run it into the ground as far as I'm concerned."

A loud snap, and then a smack against the office roof: another branch downed. Lucia jumped up from the couch and said, "Get some control," and her voice outmatched Willow's.

Willow finally looked up at Lucia, who was standing across the desk from her, and was about to apologize to her when the office phone rang. Willow placed her hands on her abdomen, a move she'd instinctively developed while she was pregnant, a protective gesture, but the impulse never went away. Willow said, "That's probably Mya."

In a very calm voice and with her delicate hand already on the phone, Lucia said, "Let me handle this at least."

Willow nodded.

"Lenore Incorporated, this is Lucia," she said in a confident voice that Willow remembered her using on the stage or in her bedroom when she practiced lines from plays. Lucia switched the phone from one ear to the other, and Willow saw herself as a younger woman standing in that very same spot using the very same phone. "Hold on one second," Lucia said, her smile fading. She put the phone on hold and held it out for Willow. "It's Robert from the plant. He said he needs to see you right away."

Robert called for emergencies only. Willow could have collapsed like a house of cards, that's how little resolve she had to act like the president after that letter and reading what her daughter thought of her. She also had no choice but to go. She said, "Tell him we're on the way."

Lucia pursed her lips and raised her eyebrows like she wasn't sure what Willow meant by "we."

Lucia tapped a button on the phone and said, "Hello, Robert? Yes, we're on our way now."

# CHAPTER 13
## News at the Factory

*W*ILLOW SHOULD NEVER *drive when she's angry.* Lucia held on to the handle above the passenger-side window in the pickup and eyed the branches reaching across the road above them. The truck bed bounced on the smallest of bumps and often verged on fishtailing around the winding bends of Hickory Lane. When Willow was angry, she sped, and when she sped, the chances of the truck running off the road tripled. It had happened many times before, and Robert had always been the one to go rescue her.

Willow gripped the wheel as if her own strength kept it attached to the steering column. Her white hair whipped her face like tentacles, and instead of rolling up her window, she kept pushing the strands back, refusing to remedy the issue the easiest way she could. Lucia had witnessed her mother act calm under pressure, like the time Mya jumped from the crape myrtle tree because she assumed she could fly and fell on a boulder, breaking both arms. Her mother didn't shout or panic. She quickly made two splints from some broken barn planks and wrapped them with red handkerchiefs left by workers. But anger caused her mother to behave differently. Lucia would insist on driving home from the factory.

Hickory Lane snaked through the thick Blue Ridge forest with white Queen Anne's lace lining the roadway and bushy maples and oaks making a shaded canopy over them. Light barely penetrated the roof of leaves. Lucia knew she was close to the factory when the shade darkened the road. The sun beamed at the end of the tree tunnel, and a herd of young deer grazed in front of the gates.

Willow came to a sudden stop and waited for each one to pass, but one fawn remained stubbornly centered in front of their bumper. Willow leaned out the window and said, "Go on, now," and it still didn't budge. Lucia opened her door, stepped out, and clapped behind the deer, but it wouldn't go. She popped it on its behind and the fawn finally pranced away.

Lucia returned to the truck. Willow looked over at her for a long time, and then her blue eyes softened, her jaw relaxed, and she said, "Thanks," in a way that made Lucia feel like her mother was thanking her for much more than the deer.

"You're welcome," Lucia said.

Willow punched in the code to open the gates, which were covered in morning glory vines. They separated slowly, as if daring one to enter. "Get the tag out," Willow said, and Lucia assumed she still kept it in the glove box. She hung the white parking tag from the rearview mirror, and her mother drove down the gravel road lined by crape myrtle trees and headed toward the administrative building. Robert's main office was located there, and he also had a separate manager's office in the factory itself, which towered behind the small brick building where Willow parked.

The square factory with its flat, gravel-lined roof stood four stories tall, and on the top floor Lucia could see the heavy gold drapes that lined the windows of the loft where she had spent many afternoons as a young girl. It was a home away from home and the only part of the factory Lucia liked as a child. Sometimes her mother arranged a slumber party for the three of them in the loft if she needed to pull an all-night expense check or if a batch wasn't turning out just right. Mya and Lucia cuddled together in a king-size bed, drank cold Cokes, ate stale cookies from the vending machines, and watched animated movies on the broken VCR, rewinding the black tape manually and replaying it until they fell asleep. Those were the best nights—the comfort of knowing their mother was hard at work but never too far away to check on them. She'd slip into the bed between them, and they'd both curl up against her and toss arms and legs on her as they slept. Once Lucia and Mya started dating, most of their little rituals disappeared. Her mother probably hadn't stayed the night in many years.

Willow left the keys in the ignition with the windows rolled down and said, "Come on." She smoothed her dress and walked directly to the glass door in front of them. Lucia hurried behind her, just like she was nine years old again. Inside, the building was filled with a hyper mix of scents, high floral notes of jasmine and rose with the sweetness of vanilla and the earthiness of sandalwood. So many different products were manufactured in their factory, for which Lenore Incorporated acted as a middleman, moving organic soaps, body washes, shampoos, conditioners, and bubble baths from idea to store shelves. This brought in very little revenue compared to the perfume. As far as anyone working here knew, Lenore Incorporated also created small batches of high-end perfume that sold to obscenely wealthy clients in Europe. If a bottle ever broke, the entire factory evacuated immediately for cleanup by Robert only.

Lucia had overheard her mother's business affairs enough to know that this setup was the only way to manufacture the perfume for a few weeks each year while also keeping the factory running year-round like a legitimate business. The FDA had found out about their product a couple decades ago as a result of rumors, just before Lucia was born. The agency had attempted to obtain a sample to determine whether the perfume changed the chemical composition of a woman's body. If it did, then the perfume would fall under the FDA's cosmetic jurisdiction and require regulation. Willow had very good female friends in important political positions and, as a result, the FDA backed off and had yet to study it. The Lenore clients used the perfume at their own risk; that much was made very clear in the contract. No one had ever threatened to report them to the FDA.

The walls of the reception area were bare compared to her mother's office at home. They couldn't plaster the faces of famous clients on the wall, just in case the wrong people walked inside for a look around. The green walls did showcase the many different soaps and cleaning agents the factory produced for companies whose commercials graced the airways during prime time. Much had changed in fifteen years, and Lucia didn't recognize a single staff member's face, especially not that of Robert's male assistant, who looked closer to fourteen than adulthood with his pliant, rosy skin and happy demeanor. Genuine naïveté. He brought Willow a bottle of sparkling water. "Would your guest like anything?" he asked Willow, and she said, "This is my daughter. You can ask her."

Red-faced, he turned to Lucia and said, "I'm so sorry. Could I bring you a coffee or tea or soda?"

"No thanks," Lucia said, and she felt bad for him. Willow could be so blunt.

"Robert's waiting for you," the assistant said. He walked away with his head bowed like a child. Willow moved past his desk and knocked on Robert's office door twice before opening it. Lucia followed behind her, unsure if she should barge in with her mother. Willow looked over her shoulder as if to make sure Lucia was directly behind her.

Robert hurriedly ended his phone call and stood up from his desk. Lucia first noticed the soft roundness in his waist and then his balding head. Robert came around his desk with arms wide open. Before

Lucia could move, he'd wrapped her up in a two-hundred-pound bear hug and said, "I can't believe it. Look at you. You haven't changed a bit," and she loved him for that, because she knew it wasn't true. "I had no idea you were home," he said. "You'll have to tell me all about the Big Apple when we're done here." He brought a chair over from the far wall. Papers and wind-up toys cluttered his desk, as usual, and his office smelled faintly of macaroni and cheese. Of all the people in Quartz Hollow, Lucia had missed Robert the most.

Willow rubbed her cheek with one hand and waited for Robert to take his seat before she said, "You know I'm always worried when you call me directly."

"I wouldn't if I didn't need to," Robert said, "but this is serious."

"Well, come on already, Robert," Willow said, "what is it?"

He folded his large hands together and his shoulders settled. "I sampled the essence today and it's just not right."

"Not right?" Willow echoed.

"Yes," Robert said, and handed her the sample in a small vial. Willow uncorked it and waved it beneath her nose.

He continued, "The first two acres we harvested looked healthy in the field, but maybe they didn't handle the transport like they always have; that's all I can guess."

Willow nodded and Lucia's heart was pounding. Robert and Brenda were the only staff members who knew the truth about their perfume, and Robert appeared worried.

Willow said, "Have any procedures or equipment changed? Did a worker miss a step?"

"No, ma'am, I oversee it like a hawk," he said, "and if I wanted to change anything you know I'd run that by you first." Lucia loved this about Robert. He and her mother were the same age, yet he still deferred to her in this polite way.

Willow rested her back in the chair and tucked her ankles beneath it. She gripped the armrest like she was prepared for a bullet.

"What does that mean?" Lucia finally said.

Robert shifted in his seat. "Something's wrong with the flower. It's like it lost its scent once we got it here. And the whole harvest is probably contaminated. We've still got four hundred and five acres to bring in, and if it's anything like the first two we tested, then there won't *be* a yield this year."

Willow brought her hands to her lips and stared at Robert. "I went to the fields. They didn't look like they'd finished blooming maybe, like it's late this year. And I know it's not been late like this, but couldn't that be it? Just postpone the harvest for two weeks? I meant to call you and suggest it but I got distracted and forgot."

Robert shook his head. He said, "We wait two weeks and they'll die, I promise. I've known these flowers my entire life, you know I have, and two more weeks will promise us no yield this year. Maybe the flowers looked a little smaller, but they've finished blooming as much as they're going to; that's what I believe. But it's your company, so if you want me to postpone I will."

"Where's our botanist? What's his name?" Willow said. Lucia rubbed her lips with her fingertips and pressed in deeply with her nails, a nervous fidget she'd tried to conquer during the long wait of casting calls. Willow had forgotten to call about the flowers, she had forgotten to review the contract, and she had forgotten Jonah's name; it seemed like her mother's memory was failing. Had she seen a neurologist already and chosen not to tell Mya and Lucia?

"Dr. Phillips took off six months. Paid, remember? Went to collect plant samples in rural China or somewhere."

"Yes, I remember," Willow said defensively.

Robert gave a small cough, like he didn't believe her. Neither did Lucia. Robert said, "We could fly someone else in to test the plants, if that's what you're thinking."

Willow stared off at a point above Robert's head.

Something was clearly wrong with her mother. Lucia didn't

know where to begin or who to talk to first. She hoped the cloud over Mya's head would be gone whenever Mya finally returned to the cabin, because now they had a much bigger issue to deal with together: how to approach Willow about her memory loss. They'd have to confront her, and she'd insist nothing was wrong and that she was too busy to go to a doctor. Much had changed since Lucia last came home, but her mother's stubbornness surely hadn't. Her mother assumed Mya had gone behind her back with that letter to Zoe, but Lucia wondered if maybe Mya did it because Willow wouldn't admit her problem.

"There's not enough time to vet someone new, and I won't have just anybody come in here to work with the plants." Willow leaned forward in her chair and her voice lowered. "If I have to tell my existing clients I can't provide next year's perfume supply, that'll be it, won't it?"

"We have some in reserve," Robert said.

"But not enough," Willow replied. Robert nodded his head as if he knew she would say that. "I'd have to ration it, and what a nightmare that would be. We'd lose customer confidence in our product."

Lucia held her breath, expecting her mother to explode like she had at home, but instead Willow sat still.

"What happens now?" Lucia asked.

Robert said, "I can go ahead and test another few acres today. Or thin-wash what we have on reserve."

Willow said, "This isn't good." She repeated this phrase like she hadn't heard Robert, and Lucia grew even more concerned that her mother was losing her mind. "We can't waste any."

"Or maybe you can wait a few days," Lucia said.

"What for?" Willow said.

Lucia moved to the edge of her seat; she needed confidence for this one. "For someone else to check the plants, and I think—"

"No," Willow said, interrupting. "Absolutely not. No strangers."

"But he's been around them before," Lucia said, and the room became very quiet.

Her mother's face looked like a child's as she tried to guess the riddle. She said, "Ben?"

Lucia nodded.

"He's home now, that's true," Robert said.

"You saw him?" Willow asked her daughter.

"I ran into him earlier today at the market," Lucia told her.

"I should've told you," Willow said. "Didn't think you'd be here long enough to see him."

This wasn't the time to discuss why a warning would've been nice. "You know he's qualified."

"I could call him," Robert said. "I know he's busy with his farming and taking care of his mama, but it can't hurt to ask him."

"Mrs. White?" Lucia couldn't restrain the surprise and concern in her voice. He hadn't mentioned anything about his mother when she saw him.

"She's sick," Willow said, and Robert nodded.

"With what?"

"Lung cancer, I believe," Willow said. "I should know for sure but I don't."

"That's what it is," Robert agreed.

That explained why Ben was home. If Ben lost his mother, he'd have no one left. An orphan in his thirties. His father had died a few years back, and Willow had called to tell Lucia—one of the rare snippets of Quartz Hollow news that Lucia cared to hear about.

"Go ahead and call him, Robert, but be discreet," Willow said.

.  "He's coming over for dinner tomorrow night, and I'm sure he'd take a look then." The traits Lucia remembered most about Ben were his eagerness to take care of her family and his curiosity about the *Gardenia potentiae* plants. They were what had inspired him to study phytology in the first place.

Willow shot her a look.

"What?"

"You didn't mention it, that's all."

"It's just to catch up." The more Lucia tried to convince herself of the innocent nature of the dinner, the more her body tingled at the idea of him.

Willow raised one eyebrow. "Call Bennie for me, Robert."

"Will do."

"Mom."

"What?"

Poor Robert's head kept turning back and forth, like a referee's at a volleyball match.

"He's all grown up, remember?" Lucia said.

"I bet his mother still calls him Bennie."

With that, Lucia refused to look at her mother again. Willow had wanted Ben to be her son-in-law. She had even planned to finance his education and appoint him the resident plant pathologist in the family. She had wanted Lucia to stay in Quartz Hollow, birth daughters with Ben, and live happily ever after.

Willow stood and said, "Thank you, Robert. We'll see what *Ben* says and I'll let you know about the next step. Postpone the harvest for two days until further notice."

"I'm sorry to bother you about one more thing, Ms. Lenore," Robert said as he walked them out. "But do I still pay the extra guys for those days?"

"Of course. Please don't let them go just yet."

Her mother stepped out of the building, and Robert gently held Lucia's arm and whispered, "I'm so glad you're home," and gave her a quick hug before letting her go, just like a father might. Because Lucia couldn't remember her own father, who had left before she was born, she often imagined Robert—good, dependable Robert—as her father. He had a brood of five kids and a wife he clearly adored.

To be one of those five kids, with a dad who loved her—that's what Lucia had always wanted. Willow was a powerful woman and a good mother most of the time, and she deserved someone to love her like Robert loved his wife.

At the very least, Lucia thought her mother could afford a man like him. Lucia knew they were rich, though their wealth never looked like the ostentatious affluence she saw on television, and as a result she never felt uncomfortable using that term to describe her family. Her mother kept them rich, like her mother before her and Great-Grandmother Serena. Who wouldn't respect mothers like those? And it seemed natural for her mother to deserve a man like Robert with his huge, muscular forearms and buzz cut and smoothly shaven face—a man who opened the door, used his manners, and rescued your car when you ran it off the road; a man who didn't care if you couldn't drive very well. But a man like Robert never came for her mother. Lucia thought she'd found one for herself, but now she sat side by side with Willow in the small cab of this old truck, and they were both alone and dealing with a business matter.

As it always was, so it always would be. Except Lucia didn't want this to be her life, and her mother couldn't possibly want it either. Willow also didn't want a failing memory, but it had struck her. How could any woman control these maladies?

PART TWO

# A FIXATIVE

## CHAPTER 14
## *The Curse Manifests*

HAND HOLDING, CHECK. Popcorn munching, check. Coke sharing, check. Mya went to dinner and a movie, and for Luke that made it all feel official. Mya Lenore had a boyfriend. The theater in town only showed one movie at a time, and the movies were always a year old, sometimes older. Luke insisted on catching the nine P.M. showing of a film that featured one of Zoe Bennett's first cameos in a summer action movie. Not exactly original, but still, as much as Mya didn't want to admit it, Zoe and her red hair and plump lips demanded attention.

Without much effort or practice or many nights spent pining away for something to happen, Zoe had climbed the talent ladder until the people above her had no idea where she came from, including Lenore Incorporated. But Luke was oblivious. He was simply attracted to Zoe Bennett and had no real idea why. Mya had gifted Zoe this opportunity. A half-million-per-fluid-ounce gift, but a gift nonetheless. Mya had seen a spark in Zoe, and it reminded her of herself. That had been her first mistake.

At one point in the movie Zoe, who notoriously shot all her own action sequences, stood on a tightrope between two Colorado mountains with her enemy approaching from one side. A bullet zoomed toward her chest just as the rope, which she'd set on fire, burned through and sent them both falling. Mya wanted so badly for Zoe to plunge into the river below and perish. Even if it was a fictional moment, it would've made Mya feel better. Alas, her sidekick and soon-to-be lover sailed through the air and caught her before releasing his parachute at the last minute.

The movie dragged on for another hour and a half after that, and it was almost midnight before Mya checked for her phone, only to discover she'd left it at the cabin. Once she arrived home she discovered her voice mail and text message inboxes filled with commands from her mother to come home immediately. It didn't matter. By the time she found her phone, her mother and Lucia had already informed her about the plants. She never did get laid, which seemed like the only possible perk of a date. Not even a make-out session. Just a boyfriend, that's what she got, without the sex. Somehow that seemed exactly right for how her life was going.

Mya sat with her legs crossed on a tree stump the next morning and stared out at the field of flowers. Seven dragonflies sailed overhead, but the deer hadn't come all morning. Nothing seemed particularly wrong with the flowers. They were a little smaller but not drastically so. Maybe it was just a fluke, some misstep with the heat. They'd hired new people last month. From what she could see, she had no idea what else might've happened.

She looked to the pink morning clouds above, and they formed the shape of a giant hand reaching down with an open palm, fingers outstretched; she heard a rustle in the tall grass behind her and turned around. Lucia's black hair whipped in the wind, and she carried two white mugs of coffee. Mya took the mug from her hand and said, "Thanks." The sun had just begun to peek over the edge of the forest, a lilac hue from the sunrise beaming from behind the clouds.

"See anything?" Lucia said, staring at some point above Mya's head.

She glanced up but nothing was there. "No."

"But Robert's sure." Lucia approached a flower and touched a petal.

How could her mother not have an emergency plan for this kind of problem, one that could wipe out the entire business in one season? How many clients would they lose altogether? Would anything remain for Mya? She bit her lower lip. The one and only time she'd agreed to go on a date with Luke, this happened, and Willow had taken Lucia to an emergency meeting in her place.

Lucia stared at her, but just slightly above her head, as if static electricity had caused her hair to stand up straight. Mya looked up and still saw nothing. This tic of Lucia's annoyed her. Mya said, "What's your issue?" Instinctively she patted the top of her head, and then Lucia did the strangest thing: she placed her hand above Mya's head, waving it all around as if trying to catch a firefly. Mya jerked her head back and said, "What's wrong? Is it a dragonfly or something?"

"No," Lucia said with a tone that made Mya very uneasy, like she was mourning a dead kitten. "It's just . . ."

"What?" Mya looked up again.

Lucia scratched behind one ear and said, "Ever since we were in the workroom with that deer musk . . . ," and then Lucia took a deep breath and sped up. "Ever since then I see the darkest cloud just above your head, like a deep bruise, and it's freaking me out. I hoped it would be gone by the time I saw you this morning but it's still there."

"Right now?"

Lucia nodded and tucked her hair behind her tiny ears.

"Did you tell Mom?"

"No," Lucia said. "I thought maybe I was hallucinating. I hoped so anyway."

"But you've never had visions."

"Why would I make it up?" Lucia said. "I have a horrible feeling in my body every time I see it, like I could puke." She reached out again like she was trying to grip it, but she brought back her hand as empty as before.

Mya bit her fingernail. She wasn't a habitual nail biter, just a nervous chewer. She said, "You have to tell Mom."

"But she's asleep."

"It doesn't matter."

"I'll tell her when she wakes up."

"No, you'll tell her now," Mya said, and took Lucia by the hand. She jerked away. "Stop telling me what to do."

Lucia wanted to fight at a time like this? What was wrong with her? If some scary image only Mya could see hung above Lucia's head, she would've told her at first sight. Lucia had waited an *entire day* before mentioning it, and now Lucia wanted to complain about Mya's bossing her. Lucia had always had the most ridiculous expectations: acting, New York City, Jonah. Just look at how far those had gotten her. Mya wanted so badly to shout all of this at her, but it would only make matters worse. Instead, Mya took Lucia by the hand again and said, "Please."

"Please?" Lucia echoed as if she couldn't believe it.

Mya nodded.

"Fine," Lucia said. "Let's go."

It really was a magic word. If only Mya had employed it more when they were younger.


WILLOW'S HAIR WAS WRAPPED IN the white knitted cap she always wore at night, some relic of their grandmother's. Willow didn't *need* to wear it, but Mya believed she did it to be close to her mother. The morning sunlight filtering in through the curtains cut a triangle on Willow's cheek and she looked rather peaceful. Mya wondered how often Willow had gazed at them this very same way when they were babies. A few times Mya remembered waking up and seeing her mother standing in the doorframe gazing at her. Neither Mya nor Lucia wanted to be the first to disturb her. Mya poked her mother's shoulder and then looked for Lucia to do the same. Lucia blew her breath on Willow's face, and their mother grimaced and opened one eye like a cat. Mya looked over to Lucia and said, "Brush your teeth."

"Please," Willow said, and then the other eye opened in quick surprise. "What's this about?" She shot up in the bed. "Did Robert call?"

Mya shook her head, hoping her mother might see the cloud like Lucia did, but Willow gave no sign that she did. She propped herself up on her elbows and closed her eyes again like she'd fallen back to sleep.

Mya pointed at Lucia and said, "Tell her."

"I, um," Lucia began, and her mother stared at Lucia. "It's just that I see something."

"Not just something," Mya said, and she could hear the panic in her own voice.

Lucia continued. "I see a black cloud over Mya and it makes me nervous."

Willow sat all the way up in bed and massaged her eyebrows with one hand. She removed the cap, shook out her silver hair like a horse's mane, and stared above Mya's head. Mya decided then and there that she really hated people looking just past her all the time. Willow said, "I don't see anything."

Urgently, Lucia said, "Well, I do, it's right there." She pointed at nothingness. "It follows her around, and I know it's bad."

"Has anyone in the family seen things like this before?" Mya asked.

Willow took a sip of Mya's coffee and sat quietly for a moment. When she did begin to speak, she seemed to be talking to herself: "Grandmother Serena didn't, but her younger daughter saw visions in the clouds like Mya, and my sister did as well, but they drove Iris crazy. My dream visions have always directed my client selections, up until now anyway. But there's no history of anything stormy, and the visions never stuck around." She sipped the coffee again and finally looked up at Lucia. "You see it all the time?"

"I do."

"Just great." Mya gripped the foot of their mother's bed.

"Something's wrong," Lucia said.

"No shit."

Willow took a deep breath. "Between this, the flowers, and Zoe, I don't know what the hell's going on anymore. But they must be connected. When did it first appear?"

"In the workshop. When she told us about that new perfume. Right when she mixed that musk with water." Willow stared at Lucia for a long moment, and something intimate passed between them. Mya couldn't place it exactly but they seemed closer somehow, like partners.

"Have you finished?" Willow asked Mya.

"It'll be done today."

"What if the cloud and the flowers *don't* want Mya to do this? We weren't allowed to stray from the original formula," Lucia said.

"Look at you," Mya said sarcastically. "So invested in the family business all of a sudden."

"I just—"

"I'm making that perfume for her, Mom," Mya said. "You already agreed."

"But what if Lucia's right?"

Her mother deferred to Lucia now? The one who hadn't had a family gift for thirty-three years and now, poof, she swayed Willow's decisions? Zoe, the flowers, the cloud—all of these troubles would pass, but Lucia might stay. Above all else, this couldn't happen. Mya said, "You know we have no other choice. If anything, I need to get this out the door so we have one less problem today."

"We do have bigger problems," Willow said to Lucia, as though she felt obligated to convince her or receive her approval.

What had happened yesterday? *I should've never gone out with Luke,* Mya told herself. *Stupid, stupid girl.*

"Look, the cloud's only over me. And let's say it is Great-Grandmother's warning; why wouldn't it be over you and Lucia too? We were all in that room together. You agreed to it, Mother, so wouldn't you be cursed? And Lucia witnessed it, so why not her? It has to be the bad deal with Zoe; the new perfume will fix it."

"And if that's not it?" Lucia said.

"Then I'm willing to deal with whatever comes."

"You're sure?"

"Stop talking to me like I'm a child," Mya said. "Yes, I'm very sure." She was sure she didn't believe in that stupid curse or in her younger sister's right to act like this. One vision, so what?

"When will you ship it?" Willow asked.

"You're kidding," Lucia said.

"I can have it to her by this evening."

"Fix it," Willow said, and then stood up from the bed and exited to the bathroom. Her mother didn't seem too concerned about that cloud, and Mya should've been glad. So why did she still feel so uneasy? As silly as it sounded, her mother seemed mad at her, like a hurt friend, more so than she had yesterday. But what more had she done since then? Mya could *feel* Lucia staring at the cloud. Mya couldn't stand another minute of that concerned look on Lucia's face, so she walked past her sister without another word and went straight to the workshop, where she could lock herself away.

## CHAPTER 15
### *Business Matters*

WILLOW WAITED UNTIL Mya closed herself in the workshop before she sequestered herself in the office. Willow was doing everything she could to control herself for Mya's sake, but that stormy cloud scared her to death. Grandmother Serena had promised bad things would come if the formula was changed. Willow's mother had never strayed and insisted Willow agree to this one rule when the business changed hands. She'd promised her mother on her deathbed.

Neither her mother nor Serena could've foreseen a situation like this one. Only *her* daughter would be flighty enough to forget to add the most important clause in a contract. Why Mya hadn't simply copied the language from any number of contracts Willow had offered her, she'd never know, and that way Willow wouldn't have needed to check it over before she sent it out. Mya was strong-willed to a fault and had been that way since she was a toddler who refused to wear anything but tights and tutus, even to go swimming in the pond. How she missed those trivial conflicts. Willow was as angry with Mya now as she was scared for her, scared of what that cloud could mean.

Love for her daughter wrapped around all this frustration. Willow had long since experienced these conflicting emotions. Once the girls had matured and learned to talk back to her, the stress of young, single motherhood and ceaseless work created a withering exhaustion and resentment. She had done her best to quell these feelings.

And of all times for Lucia to finally have a vision, one unlike those of anyone else in the family . . . Willow believed her. One thing Lucia had never been was a liar. Her two daughters couldn't have been more different. With one exception: as babies they both loved to stroke Willow's long hair as they breast-fed, and those quiet moments still buoyed Willow during the troubling times with her girls. But beyond that quality during infancy, Mya and Lucia had little in common. Lucia believed she didn't have a place in the family because her skills with the flower and perfumery had failed to manifest; she might not admit it, but Willow knew this had been a compelling reason for her to follow a career in acting. Sometimes it had felt like she had one healthy daughter, born with all the Lenore family gifts, and one perfectly intelligent and lovely but mute daughter. Still, Willow didn't love Lucia any less. Early on Willow had sensed her daughter had the power to make people worship her, because the dragonflies congregated around her and rode into the cabin on her shoulders, and Willow had to promptly turn Lucia around and get her back out to the porch so she could send the dragonflies outside. Willow desired for Lucia to be successful, and the older she became, the more her talent with people appeared to be her magic—a perfect skill for the business. But Lucia didn't believe in it. Acting called her instead. At least today proved to Lucia that she wasn't a defective Lenore after all. So many years spent worrying about Lucia, and now Willow could finally relax, only to switch her concern to Mya. Such was the way of motherhood.

She didn't have the nerve to dial James Stein's number. She couldn't explain that she had to cancel because her younger daughter had a vision of a dark cloud hovering over her older daughter's head. To anyone outside the family, that would sound ludicrous. Willow would tell James some business issue had come up. It wasn't a total lie. Right now wasn't a good time, not with the flowers and the cloud. Would she ever live a life without interruptions?

Her girlhood had been the only time that flowed as one long, straight river, a time when she craved a bend to enliven her world. Any interruption had been welcome. She had most looked forward to her trips abroad. She remembered when her mother took Iris and Willow to France for the first time and they studied flower cultivation in Grasse in June and July, just when the jasmine had bloomed. Then they spent six months in Paris in the Eighth Arrondissement learning Parisian French from a college student attending the Sorbonne. During the day Willow and Iris were tutored while their mother visited the Louvre or the Musée d'Orsay or shopped on the rue de Rivoli, and in the afternoons she came back for them and they stopped at a *boulangerie* for a buttery baguette sandwich before taking the metro to 38 avenue Pierre 1er de Serbie. They walked to the House of Dubois storefront to study the art of perfumery under Henri Dubois.

Willow's mother respected the Dubois dynasty, which had been passed down from father to son for more than two hundred years, and avidly collected the variety of rare scents they produced. But it was Grandmother Serena whom Henri Dubois first contacted. Rumor had it that the finest, richest American actresses, who should've been the Dubois family's clientele, had a scent they adored but kept fiercely secret. The Dubois family was passionate about scent and traveled to Bulgaria and Turkey and Italy in search of the most luxurious rose, jasmine, and iris essences. The idea that a flower as powerful as *Gardenia potentiae* existed in secret nearly drove Henri Dubois mad. He was a wise businessman and a charming fellow, and Grandmother Serena relented and told him he could experience the flower if he allowed her dynasty of daughters to apprentice at the House of Dubois during the summer and study the time-honored techniques of infusion, maceration, and filtration for which his house was so famous. Serena's girls could study alongside the male heirs of that company, and perhaps a marriage or two would evolve from her deal. That hadn't happened, though. Lenore women seemed to prefer American men. To this day, the Dubois family master perfumers were the only perfumers in Paris to know of the existence of the *Gardenia potentiae* flower. Forever Willow would connect Paris with the smells of freshly baked bread and urine in the metro, and the absolute intensity of the rose and jasmine and tuberose and violet in the Dubois family perfumes. These scent memories, so easy to recall today but perhaps not tomorrow. Her entire life reduced to nothing but the present.

The phone rang in its cradle, making Willow jump like the smoke alarm had been triggered. When she answered the phone and said, "Willow Lenore speaking," the sound on the other line made her smile immediately.

James said, "I like when your voice sounds so professional."

"I was just thinking about you."

"All good things, I hope."

She sat back down. Nothing mattered now in the space between his phone connection and her own. "Absolutely." Willow couldn't keep the sadness out of her voice.

"Something's wrong." But before Willow could respond he said, "I've set up a meeting with Jennifer Katz and her manager and agent to find out what's going on. I hope that doesn't bother you, but I figure it's easier for me to do it from here than you flying out again. And it's a personal matter for me too."

She should know exactly what he was talking about. "About the perfume?" she asked.

He paused. "Jennifer's manager didn't call you?"

"I haven't seen my assistant today."

"Jennifer's convinced the perfume stopped working for her

because of Zoe. She's refusing to present at the Oscars now and her people are panicking. She won't leave her house for appointments. Her PR girl told the press she's vacationing in the South Pacific. I'm set to meet with them tomorrow but I doubt she'll show. You should call her," James said.

"I will, as soon as we're done here." Jennifer should've called Willow immediately if she believed the perfume wasn't working for her. Willow doubted that claim; she was probably just letting Zoe get to her, but with the way things were going, she couldn't rule out any possibility.

"Any update about Zoe?" he said.

"She'll have the new formula tonight. I'll let Jennifer know that also. I should've already."

"And we'll see each other next week."

"About that," Willow said. "I have to reschedule, although I really wish I didn't. Business matters."

"Now I'm disappointed. I had many plans to spoil you." Willow's thighs and abdomen grew warmer.

"Next time," Willow said, her voice breaking a little.

"You let me know when it's a good time," he said, "and I'll be there."

"I will." And then they said good-bye and hung up. She put the phone down. She needed to dial Jennifer's personal number; it was urgent and she had to do it, but she just couldn't force herself to pick up the phone again.

## CHAPTER 16
## *Prepping*

L UCIA HAD ABHORRED the nights in high school when Willow worked late and asked Lucia to make dinner. Maybe she assumed cooking would be Lucia's one useful skill to contribute to the family. Inevitably she'd forget to remove the organs of the chicken before she roasted it, and soon enough Mya took over those duties for her and became the family chef. Now that Mya had locked herself away in the workshop with a Do Not Disturb sign on the door handle, Lucia couldn't ask for some much-needed advice. She searched through a few recipe books in the kitchen, but the many suggestions overwhelmed her. What did Ben White like to eat? She forced herself to remember what he ate as a growing teenage boy, and the only memory she had was of pizza. He ate pizza almost every day for school lunch and still wanted his mother to order it on weekends. Few people develop a dislike for pizza, so Lucia found a recipe for homemade dough and went to the store for the essentials: all-purpose flour, yeast, olive oil, sauce, and toppings galore. He ate meat, so Lucia bought Virginia baked ham and local sausage, and to that she'd add green bell pepper, onions, olives. Maybe she'd surprise herself in the kitchen.

It wasn't until her hands were deep inside the sticky dough that Lucia began to doubt. Dough should be smooth and elastic, or so dictated the overly confident recipe, but Lucia's dough felt wet. She added more flour and then it felt too stiff, so she added more water and then worried about needing more yeast, and she wanted to give up and abandon this idea. Ben would never know, nor would he care, and why did she feel such a pressing need to make something home-made for him?

Willow walked into the kitchen and stopped at the entrance, probably impressed by the copious white dust caking the island and the floor around it. She said, "Can I help with anything?"

Her mother looked a bit haggard. Lucia rubbed her forehead with the back of her wrist to avoid getting flour on her face. She wasn't sure she succeeded. "Can you make pizza dough?"

"You don't remember?"

"I've never made it before," Lucia said.

"That's not what I mean," Willow said, and poured herself a glass of water. "Every Valentine's Day I made pizza for you girls. How have you forgotten?"

Lucia stared down at the gobs of dough clinging to her fingers. "Were they heart-shaped or something?"

"I'm not that good," Willow said. "You're too young to be forgetting those things. I, on the other hand, am old."

"You're fine, aren't you?" This lie made her mother smile.

"That dough doesn't look right." Willow plunged two fingers inside the overgrown ball on the counter.

"I know. What's wrong with it?"

"Everything."

"Thanks." Lucia stepped back to watch her mom sift the flour, remeasure all the ingredients, warm the yeast in water, and then knead it all together and roll it around the counter as effortlessly as she folded laundry. The joints of Willow's fingers looked swollen, and the sight of them jolted Lucia's memory of when her mother's fingers looked so slender and smooth as she prepared dough on the love holiday. "Because everyone needs comfort on this day," she remembered her mother saying, and it had never occurred to her then how lonely Willow must have been. So much about her mother had always felt like a mystery. But now that Lucia was alone too she could understand her better.

"Put a pan of hot water in the oven and the dough will rise before Ben gets here," Willow said. She placed the dough in a bowl and covered it with a damp dish towel.

Lucia followed her mother's directions, filling the teakettle with water and lighting the stovetop. Willow handed Lucia the bowl to place in the oven and then said, "I need your help."

Lucia became suddenly terrified that her mother might tell her she had terminal cancer and wanted her to break the news to Mya. Lucia closed the oven door and tentatively said, "Okay?"

"I need you to call Jennifer Katz for me."

Lucia laughed with relief. "What for?"

Willow braced herself with both arms on the island. "I should've followed up with her after my meeting in L.A. but I didn't, and I need to now. Something's going on with her and I'm worried, that's all."

"So you call her," Lucia said. "I wouldn't know the first thing to say. She'll think it's strange."

Willow smoothed her white hair falling all around her shoulders. "I don't think she wants to hear from me."

"Why would she want to hear from me then?"

"All you need to do is tell her the perfume is on the way and that it'll fix all of our problems."

Lucia wiped her sticky hands with a towel and couldn't believe what she was hearing. Her mother handing off business? She didn't want any part of it. "I'm not sure it *will* fix any problems," she said. "I didn't agree with any of this in the first place. I have no interest in managing the business; that hasn't changed. Have Mya call her."

Willow plucked a basil leaf from the bunch Lucia had gathered in the herb garden and ate it. "Mya's busy."

"Doesn't all of this seem like bad business?" Lucia said.

"Bad business is low customer confidence, and I can't afford for Jennifer to reject our product. And I think that's where she's headed. She needs our attention and I need you to try."

"Maybe the business *should* fold," Lucia said.

"You don't mean that," Willow said. "It's like wishing death on a family member."

"I've never liked the perfume," Lucia said. The teakettle whistled; Lucia lifted it off the stove with her bare hand and it burned her palm. "Damn it!" she shouted, and dropped it back down on the stove.

Willow used her handkerchief to lift it from the heat.

Lucia ran her palm under cold water and shook her head. "I won't do it."

"Why are you here then?" Willow said. "Shouldn't you be gone by now?"

With her hand wrapped in a towel, Lucia poured the steaming water into a pan and then placed it in the oven just as her mother had told her to do. She wanted to tell Willow that she'd leave tomorrow or the day after, but she wasn't confident she'd go. Her plans were so unstable: Would she return to New York and try acting again? Obviously, that was what she should do, but she had zero desire to try again.

"If you're here, you might as well help me," Willow said. "Consider it your room and board. When you leave I won't ask anything of you again."

Lucia placed the empty teakettle on the stove. "If it'll make you stop bugging me, just bring me the phone."

Returning moments later with her cell phone, Willow tapped

the screen a few times, then handed the phone to Lucia. "It's her direct line."

Lucia placed the phone to her ear and said, "What if she screens?"

Willow said, "Leave a message."

The line rang and rang and rang, and Lucia prepared herself to leave a message with a smile on her face, but then the ringing stopped and Lucia heard static. She waited for a voice on the other end but it didn't come. "Hello?" Lucia said softly.

"Who's this?" And it was the unmistakable voice of Jennifer Katz, a voice as charming as Marilyn Monroe's but not as meek.

Lucia's eyes grew wide because words had left her and she wasn't sure if they'd ever return. Across the island in the kitchen, Willow pushed her arms forward. She mouthed the word "talk," and Lucia said, "Hi, Jennifer, this is Lucia Lenore, the youngest daughter of Willow Lenore, and I'm calling to give you an update about some business you discussed with my mother."

"We didn't discuss anything," Jennifer said, and now Lucia was completely confused.

"About an alteration," Lucia said.

"She shot that down."

"She's had a change of heart, and it's already taken care of."

Jennifer said. "Zoe's right?"

"You spoke to her?"

"Briefly."

"We should've called sooner, and I'm sorry," Lucia explained. "No excuses."

"She's spreading rumors that I'm done. I could give a shit about other actresses, but directors and producers? It's so wrong."

This suddenly made Lucia furious, and with all the conviction she'd seen her mother use, she said, "I assure you that's not true. You're brilliant and America loves you. The new perfume will suit Zoe's strengths, but the original is, to be quite frank, tailored to a talent with integrity like yours. You're a very valuable client to us, and the perfume works best for a woman like you. Your career's a testament to that. You still have so much to accomplish."

Willow smiled as she held her hands to her lips.

"Thank you," Jennifer said, her voice rising like the full moon. "Your name's Lucia, is that right?"

"It is."

"I didn't know Willow had another daughter," Jennifer said.

This made Lucia go cold and she almost hung up the phone. "Well, I'm here now if you need anything. Please don't hesitate to call, and by all means continue to use our product. You have proven just how successful it can be."

"Confirm when Zoe receives it," Jennifer said. "I don't want to hear from her first."

"Trust me, you'll hear from me first." Then Lucia thought the line went dead. "Jennifer?"

"I'm here," she said. "Thanks, Lucia."

"You're welcome," Lucia said, and hung up. She hadn't noticed how heavily her heart was pounding until she handed the phone back to her mother. Her palms pulsed. Lucia said, "I think she's okay now."

Willow came around the island and hugged Lucia, and then she held her at arm's length and said, "I want to retire."

How much more could her mother sling at her today? This didn't seem like the ideal time for Mya to take over. Lucia said, "Why right now?"

"Because I need to and I want to," Willow said. "I know you know, don't pretend like you don't."

Lucia rolled a cherry tomato between her fingers. "Have you seen a doctor?"

"In time," Willow said.

Lucia said, "If you think Mya can handle it right now, then do it." She popped the tomato in her mouth and its juices coated her tongue.

"That's not exactly what I was thinking."

"Robert?" Lucia said immediately, though that didn't make any sense. No one outside the family had ever run the business. Willow looked directly at Lucia with a quizzical face, like Lucia was the one being foolish.

"Oh no," Lucia said. "No way, that's not how it was supposed to be."

"Things change," Willow said. She combined a piece of mozzarella, a cherry tomato, and a leaf of basil, popped the small tower in her mouth, and stared at Lucia while she chewed.

"But, Mom . . ." was all Lucia could say, but she blanked on how to follow it.

"I'm worried about you, Lucia," Willow said. "I don't want things to turn out for you like they did for my sister. I know you can do this. I always did."

The story of how her aunt had died alone and unnoticed haunted Lucia. She had promised herself never to be like her. She understood why Iris left the business behind, but she had settled for a life of mediocrity, and that was far from what Lucia desired. Lucia wrung a dishrag in her hands and said, "You don't ever have to worry about me like you did about Iris."

Mya's workshop door flung open and banged against the wall so hard that Lucia and Willow both jumped. Somehow Mya had overheard their conversation, Lucia was sure of it, and she braced herself for the yelling that would ensue. Her sister was the heir apparent and nothing could change that in her mind or Lucia's. What had Willow been thinking? Maybe she did need to retire if she was being so irrational. Mya came running into the kitchen with the black cloud above her like an obscene hat worn at a royal wedding. She said, "I'm leaving."

Lucia said, "Don't be so emotional. She didn't mean it and I'm not interested."

Willow and Mya both stared at Lucia with perplexed faces. Mya said, "Are you feeling okay?"

Willow motioned toward the perfume vial in Mya's hands. "You sure it's ready?" she asked. She took the small amber-colored bottle from Mya's hand and peered in as if she could see the new formula at work.

Mya nodded and looked as joyful as a child at the beach. Lucia didn't have the will to tell her that the cloud hadn't gone away just because she made the perfume. She couldn't continue looking at her, the way it sometimes made Lucia ache to see an amputee.

"I'm sending it out right now," Mya said.

"Hold on," Willow said.

"Smell it, if you must," Mya said. Carefully she removed the top of the bottle. She held it underneath Willow's nose and her mother's entire body seemed to glow red like an ember. She fanned herself, pulled away, and said, "Goodness, that's strong, Mya."

"I know," Mya said proudly.

Her mother adjusted her dress and wiped the sweat from her hairline. "It's unbelievable," Willow said, and she sounded out of breath, just like—well, just like she'd had passionate sex, as gross as that was for Lucia to think about. "Send it."

"I already told you, I am." Mya hurried toward the door and grabbed her purse off the entrance table.

Willow nodded, and they both watched Mya leave the cabin.

When Lucia turned around her mother was staring at her. She said, "Still above her, isn't it?"

Lucia nodded. "Still there."

"I need a shower before dinner," Willow said, and walked out of the kitchen, still fanning herself. "Think about what I said."

Her mother didn't wait around long enough to hear a response, even if Lucia'd had one. Alone once again, Lucia chopped vegetables for Ben's pizza, and with each slice of the knife she imagined untethering the cloud from her sister.

## CHAPTER 17
### *The Scent of Sex*

MYA BLASTED FLEETWOOD MAC for the thirty-minute ride away from town and back up the curving lanes to her land. Bright orange and luminous, the sun would sink behind the wall of mountains in an hour and twenty-two minutes, and Mya would have the pleasure of watching it set after a long day of hard and productive work. The rhododendron thickened as Mya approached the turnoff for their gravel driveway, lined this time of year with pink phlox, black-eyed Susan, and yarrow. It was perfection, just like the new formula. She couldn't keep herself from thinking about it.

When Mya had finished blending the musk with the alcohol solution in her workshop and added the essences of patchouli, orange blossom, and Bulgarian rose, she had stopped a moment, waved the small glass bottle beneath her nose, and inhaled as deeply as she could. The word "ecstasy" normally languished in her vocabulary, but the experience of completing Zoe's perfume left her with that single word in mind.

The scent alone could become a top-tier perfume competing

with the best of Parisian houses, but then Mya added the essence of *Gardenia potentiae*, and its notes of vanilla and cedar and salt water made the scent unstoppable. Mya could not keep the bottle beneath her nose for long. Just a few seconds of exposure and all she could imagine were naughty positions she'd ask Luke to try with her.

The final ingredient made Mya pause before she added it. If the drops of Mya's dissolved lock of hair failed—she'd only know that once Zoe received it—then Zoe's career could grow even more powerful, and Jennifer Katz would be finished. This new formula could be stronger than Great-Grandmother Serena's. Mya couldn't be totally sure that the perfume would have its intended effect, but she had to risk it.

Mya had held her breath as she used a long dropper to add the final drops to the vial. Normally she'd let a new perfume sit for a few months to meld, but one, she didn't have that kind of time, and two, she wasn't really sure how effective the final ingredient would be after a long wait.

She gave it one hour to rest before she smelled her experiment again. At first when she brought the bottle to her nose, it smelled exactly like it had before she added a few drops of her dissolved hair. She desired Luke and wanted to tie up his wrists and play with him for hours. But nothing more. Mya set the bottle down on her worktable and lowered her head, convinced she had failed. All of her confidence left her body at that moment, and she gripped the edge of the table until her fingertips pulsed.

The feeling crept over her body so slowly that she didn't notice it for the first twenty minutes, but then she fixed her stare on the wall of dried flowers and her thoughts began to oscillate without her control. *They're lovely*, she told herself, *for plain meadow flowers*. She tried to look away but couldn't, and her thoughts became more negative. *Stupid flowers*. And then they became dark. *Douse the wall in alcohol to rid the room of the ugliness parading there, let the whole house burn*. Mya took the bottle of moonshine out of the cabinet, walked to the wall slowly, and almost soaked the dried herbs and flowers and the curtain too, until the scent finally escaped from her nose and she rushed to the sink to wash her face, her hands, and any part of her that had come into contact with it.

The perfume was well beyond sensual—it was controlling. And that's what Zoe needed. That's what Mya wanted to give her. No more capricious, malicious decisions for Zoe Bennett. The scent would work on her inner circle first, her entourage and leading man, her agent, manager, public relations specialist, and stylist, and then outward with the directors and investors and executives, and finally the public. They'd all despise her; it could be that swift.

Mya sealed the perfume and then printed instructions and signed it: *So sorry for the mix-up. Hope this helps. With love and admiration. Yours sincerely, Mya Lenore.* She sped to the factory and commissioned her mother's pilot and his assistant to deliver the package today, ecstasy filling her heart to capacity. Nothing else gave her a feeling like this. Only an experiment proven successful had this kind of pull.

Now that one problem had been resolved, Mya worried about the plants. She tried to convince herself that whatever was going on was a one-time fluke, a result of poor hydration or sensitivity to the frost, but she just didn't believe it. The plant didn't operate that way. It was the most resilient plant she'd ever known.

Mya drove up the driveway and crested the hill at dusk to see a Ford truck parked in front of the cabin with a sign plastered on the back. With her headlights on, she squinted to read the words WHITE FARM ORGANIC PRODUCE. Instead of paying attention to the road, Mya was thinking, *What's Ben White doing here?* and then she felt a small thud underneath her tires. She parked the truck right there, assuming she had run over an Adirondack chair or weed whacker. She hopped out and her red cowgirl boot landed on the delicate leg of a young fawn pinned beneath her front left tire.

Mya screamed without thinking, and her mother came out of the cabin first, followed by Lucia and Ben. The legs twitched, but she couldn't see the little one's head, and her entire body froze: it was Spots. No matter how badly she wanted to move the truck or not move the truck or do whatever was best, she couldn't motivate her body.

Willow ran to Mya and stopped short as soon as she saw the blood on the grass.

Lucia followed behind her and said, "What is it?"

"Nowhere," Mya said. "I didn't see her. Just out of nowhere. I don't know."

Lucia looked at Willow as if Mya had lost her mind, and maybe she had. In all the years she'd lived in the mountains, she had never hit a deer. She'd come across many dead animals on her hikes, but a fawn was the one animal she never wanted to watch suffer, much less kill. Willow walked over to Mya and wrapped an arm around her, and Lucia followed. Ben dropped down on his knees to look under the truck, and the fawn's legs began to jump like it wanted to dash away.

Ben put the truck in neutral and then pushed it backward to free the fawn. Once the weight lifted, Spots jumped off the ground and then collapsed and let out grunt after miserable grunt. Quickly, Ben put his hands around the fawn's neck and broke it. Lucia let out a whimper. Ben scooped the deer up and turned toward the forest without asking what to do with the body. Mya watched him go as if viewing a play, and then suddenly her breath returned and she shouted, "No!"

Ben stopped. She ran to him and he refused to look her in the eyes. Mya outstretched her arms and said, "Give her to me, it's my fault."

Ben finally looked up, and his eyes told her that he definitely agreed. She'd seen that look from him before. "Here," he said.

She took the fawn's dead body from Ben and held the deer close to her chest as if it were an infant. Its little body was still warm, and behind her she heard Lucia say, "Hang on a minute." Ben quickly walked away, like he couldn't be around Mya and Lucia at the same time.

Mya just wanted to be alone, and she moved forward. A dragonfly landed on Mya's shoulder and she flicked it away, then Lucia's hand touched down in its place. Mya stopped walking. "I'm fine," she said.

"It's not that," Lucia said. "I thought you'd want to know the cloud's gone."

Mya turned around quickly. "It is?" she said. "Like *gone* gone? Disappeared?"

Lucia nodded.

So that's what it took to make the cloud go away: she had to sacrifice her favorite fawn. Zoe wasn't worth it. "Forever?" Mya said.

"I guess," Lucia said.

"Thanks for telling me," Mya said. Lucia returned to Ben and Willow.

She didn't need to see Ben. Why had that happened? Why hadn't Lucia warned her that he was coming over? It was all so long ago, but it still made her feel guilty, especially with Lucia so near. Mya clutched Spots tighter as she walked away into the faint golden light of the setting sun, and she wondered if she'd ever be forgiven for the many bad choices she'd made in her life thus far.

## CHAPTER 18

# Dinner with Ben

B EFORE BEN ARRIVED, Lucia had stood over the sink and washed the last of the pans she had used to lightly sauté mushrooms, green peppers, and red onions for the homemade supreme pizza. She'd left her phone on the island in the kitchen just in case Ben got lost on the way and needed directions. Lucia hoped that he hadn't forgotten his way back to her. Washing dishes and cooking for Ben made her momentarily forget she was divorced. She felt independent and twenty-one with a host of possibilities before her. Nothing set. Nothing determined yet about who Lucia would become.

Until Jonah called, as if he knew she had a semi-date. The phone vibrated on the island, and Lucia drained the dirty sink water. She stood over the phone with wet hands and watched as his name disappeared on the screen, his call sent to voice mail. She heard Ben's truck pull up and shut off just when a small chime from her phone signaled that Jonah had recorded a message. She could forget that until tomorrow, at least, and she tucked the phone into her pocket.

Lucia met Ben at the front door. He'd dressed up in jeans and a collared shirt rolled to a three-quarter cuff to show off muscular forearms that he hadn't had when they were teenagers. Dragonflies of every size swarmed the porch, and Lucia cracked the door just enough to let Ben inside. "Thanks," he said. "Wasn't sure I'd get through."

"Every day there's more," Lucia said. "I guess it's that season."

"They like it here, if I remember right," Ben said. In one hand he carried a six-pack of Quartz Hollow beer from the local brewery and in the other, a tub of homemade herbed goat cheese. "I know you ladies go nuts for this stuff." He handed it over.

"It's been so long," Lucia said. "Thank you." She stood to the side so he could pass. He smelled like fresh cedar mulch. Ben's father had always made the best goat cheese in town, the secret for an inoculation against poison ivy. The goats ate those wicked three-leaf plants, digested them, and left small traces in their milk, which built up the body's defenses in all who consumed their famous cheese. Though poison ivy grew all over their land and throughout the Blue Ridge, Lucia had never had a rash during her childhood, thanks to the White family.

Ben had only been in the house long enough to offer Lucia one of his craft beers when they heard Mya shriek in the driveway. Her mother came running through the kitchen, and Lucia followed her. She had never expected to see a fawn pinned beneath the truck. Mya had always been so careful, always hyperaware of the deer during this season. The trail of blood trickling from the fawn's head distracted Lucia so much that she didn't at first notice that the black cloud had disappeared. Something about it didn't make sense to Lucia. Why would it leave Mya now, in a moment of despair, when she'd accidentally killed something she loved? She stood beside her mother and Ben and watched Mya walk into the meadow to bury her deer with only a wash of sunlight accompanying her.

Lucia turned to Willow and said, "The cloud's gone." Ben instantly looked to the sky.

"For good?" Willow said.

"I think so," Lucia said. Ben was too polite to interrupt, but he scraped the ground with his boot heel and Lucia could tell he was confused.

Willow said, "I didn't even have a chance to say hello to you." She opened her arms to Ben and wrapped him in a hug.

Lucia said, "The beers are getting warm."

Ignoring Lucia, her mother said, "Robert called you, I hope?"

"He did," Ben confirmed. "Would it bother you if I went to the fields while it's still light?"

Willow said, "I wish you would."

"I'll go with you," Lucia said.

"Me too," Willow said, and Lucia controlled her face like a good actress so he wouldn't notice her frustration. They didn't need a chaperone.

"Lead the way. I just need a bag out of the back." He jumped onto the side of his truck bed and pulled out a leather bag. "After you."

Willow smiled. "It's nice to see you around again, Bennie."

Ben's cheeks turned red and Lucia wanted to shake her mother. She'd specifically asked her *not* to call him that, and that's exactly why she did. He said, "It's good to be here," and he checked out Lucia from the corner of his eye. She tried to suppress her smile but with Ben here it made the place not so oppressive. He always did love the land much more than she did.

Lucia and Ben hiked through the tall meadow grass and up the hill, remaining a few feet behind Willow. They didn't talk at first. Had they been alone, the process of catching up would've begun, but no matter how old you are, talking to a boy in front of your mother always feels strained. Lucia's hair came out of its bun and fell down her back. Ben looked away like he'd been caught. He used to stroke her hair and drape it over his face and inhale. Remembering this gave Lucia tingles. He caught her eye again and she smiled.

Her mother led them past the gnarled weeping willow tree she was named after, and the fields became visible on the hill. She turned to Ben. "Thank you for doing this."

"No problem," Ben said. "I can't promise anything."

"I understand." They crested the hill, the grass brushing against their knees, and then the ground leveled off and they stepped into a well-manicured field many acres deep. The white flowers looked succulent and healthy. Their saturated scent normally floated on the wind, but despite the movement in the air, Lucia smelled only a hint, like the trace of perfume left on an evening gown.

Ben dropped his bag in the cut grass and bent down to open it. He removed multiple containers and small spoons. "I'll sample every part of the plant, if it's okay with you to take it off-site," Ben said. "I need to culture them on nutrient plates, and I can do that in my home lab."

"That's fine, whatever you need to do," Willow said.

He looked up at Willow and Lucia. "And when I'm done?"

Willow straightened her skirt. "Return it all here, if you don't mind."

"Not at all." He proceeded to gather what he needed from the hedges closest to them, and then he walked through the rows to the far end of the fields. Lucia watched his strong back as he leaned over the tall hedges. That's when Lucia thought one of the flowers straightened its petals to try to reach out and brush against his leg. She shielded her eyes with her hand and continued to watch, but she didn't see it happen again. She was so sure of what she had seen, though, that she approached the edge of the field and offered her hand to a blossom.

"What're you doing?" Willow said.

The flowers did not budge. "Nothing, I guess," she said.

Her mother joined her at her side and said, "You want them to move?" She too reached out her hand and the flowers remained still.

"They used to." Willow pushed her hands deeper into the beds of flowers with no luck. "It's like they don't know me anymore."

"What if he can't figure it out?" Lucia said. "What if no one can help us?"

Willow moved away from the flowers and placed her hands in the pockets of her linen dress. "My accountant will know the exact hit we'll take. I e-mailed her. Big. Very big. That's not my concern."

"How's that?" Lucia said. The loss of an entire year's profit had to be more devastating than her mother suggested. It should be her only concern. Ben pulled a shrub out of the soil, the white roots dangling above the ground. He wrapped it in a cloth and cradled it in his arms as he walked out of the field.

Willow watched Ben also, and then she said, "What if they never bloom again?"

"Is that even possible?" Lucia said.

"I don't know; I never thought so, but I never imagined this either."

"That can't happen."

Willow frowned. "I think it could."

All the years Lucia hadn't concerned herself with the family business, she had still depended on the business's being there for her to ignore. But those flowers mattered, and everything Great-Grandmother Serena had worked for mattered—she'd always known that, but it was especially clear now with her mother's retirement looming. Their family was the business, the business their family. If the roots failed, the fields would never grow again and Lenore Incorporated would have no product to sell. They could keep the factory open, probably, but they'd be a middleman business forever, and that's not what Great-Grandmother Serena intended. The profits from that new business model would be significantly lower. Any fool could foresee that.

Ben came out of the field, sweat dripping from his forehead and cheekbones. He held a flower in his hand. "Willow," he said. "Will you look at this?"

Willow stepped closer to Ben.

"When I went in deeper, I saw this. You see here? These yellowing leaves indicate chlorosis."

Lucia wanted a better view, but Ben and Willow hunched over the plant like a shield.

"There's something wrong with the chlorophyll?" Willow said.

"There isn't enough, otherwise the leaves would be green. They aren't producing any carbohydrates."

"Will that spread? Kill the entire crop?"

"I should know something by tomorrow afternoon, Tuesday at the latest." Ben shook his shaggy brown hair to the side to move the strands out of his eyes.

"And the roots?" Willow said.

"I'll test it all."

"So then that's it?"

"For now."

"I think I need to go rest." Willow turned to go by herself before they could respond. Ben and Lucia walked back to the cabin together in silence, close enough to keep an eye on Willow, and they all stopped at the back of the house.

"I'm not too hungry," Willow said before stepping into the house. "I hope you two don't mind if I skip dinner."

"More for me," Ben said, and rubbed Willow's shoulder.

Willow smiled, and Lucia could have hugged Ben just for that. Her mother had looked so hopeless back there. Willow said, "You used to eat an entire one of my pizzas. Remember that?"

"I do," he said. "Let's hope Lucia makes a pizza half as good as yours."

"Suck-up," Lucia said. He poked her in the ribs, and she wasn't sure what to do about that.

"Let me drop this off in the truck and I'll be in."

Lucia walked through the back door with her mother, who said, "He's such a sweetheart," and stared at Lucia with that knowing look, like she should've never let him go in the first place. Willow went to her bedroom, and in the kitchen Lucia turned on the oven to its highest setting and placed the pizza stone inside to warm, then she pulled out the rolling pin to flatten her raised dough.

Ben returned and picked a beer off the counter, then opened one for her.

"Want to help me sauce this?" Lucia said. She pushed her fingertips into the sides to form a crust on the pizza. At least this part was easy.

Ben came around the island to stand next to her. "I've never sauced anything before."

"Me either." Lucia laughed and handed him a large spoon to get started. "Just use the back to spread it around, like this," she said, and then placed his spoon in the glass bowl.

"Got it."

Lucia gathered all the toppings and the mozzarella cheese from the refrigerator and peered past the door to watch Ben as he worked hard to make sure the sauce was even. No matter the task, he'd always been a meticulous worker, and that look of hooded concentration was one she hadn't forgotten. Jonah had it too, when he painted.

Ben had vowed to move to New York with her if that was what she wanted, but Lucia knew it wasn't the place for him and didn't want him to follow her for no other reason than to be with her. Ben needed trees and flowers and quiet, not traffic and concrete and stacked housing, and by that point nothing was the same between them, not after what happened with Mya. Then she met that first guy, and then another, and the city was so fast and the possibilities endless, or so it seemed, and she sped up and the idea of Ben faded away. It hurt him. He made that known in many handwritten letters. She was young.

Maybe he should've come with her. Maybe that's what people did for each other when they were in love, followed and were supportive, even if it seemed like the wrong choice at the time. Jonah had been serious and brooding and everything she thought an artist should be, and perhaps she thought that to be an artist she needed to be in love with one as well.

Ben glanced up like he could feel her stare. "Ready," he said. Lucia brought over her armload of ingredients and handed Ben a ball of fresh mozzarella cheese to grate. She removed the stone from the oven and placed the dough on it. Together they topped the pizza. Ben made a circle of pepperoni and sausage while Lucia dropped peppers, onions, and black olives from above. His forearm rubbed against hers, and she smiled. Ben carried the warm pizza stone to the oven, and Lucia held open the door. Ben said, "Done." He high-fived her.

Despite the years apart and the relationship they once had, he still felt like a good friend. Back then he'd been her only close friend. "Another beer?" Lucia asked.

"I'll get it," he said, and went to the refrigerator.

Lucia sat down at the round kitchen table, and Ben joined her with two beers in hand. "Cheers."

"To old times." She clinked his beer's neck with hers.

"You know, we never cooked together."

"No?" Lucia said. "I guess not."

He nodded and glanced down the hallway. "Think she's okay?"

Lucia shrugged and said, "Which one?" Mya could retreat for days or weeks at a time and Willow was like a poker player. Though these days she wasn't as impenetrable as Lucia remembered. Mya and Willow always isolated themselves when things went wrong, while Lucia sought company to work through her problems. "There's been a lot going on here lately," Lucia said.

Ben drank his beer and said, "My mom's ill."

"Oh," Lucia said, taken back by his non sequitur.

"Lung cancer." He said it like he needed her to know.

"Is that why you came back?"

He nodded. "She didn't have anybody."

"That's sad, Ben," Lucia said. "I'm sorry."

"I just got tenured." He shredded a paper napkin from the holder on the table.

Lucia said, "Not surprising."

"I couldn't do both," Ben said. "Worked out okay. They gave me a semester sabbatical for fall and I came back this summer. Spending the summer farming instead of writing papers."

"Always your first love."

"One of them," Ben said with a small smile, not looking up from the table. Lucia blushed and stood up to check on the pizza.

He piled the shreds of napkin and placed his beer on top. "What about you? I heard your voice on Animal Planet one time. It was so strange, like you were in the room."

"Really?" she said, and returned to the table. "I figured no one heard those announcements, they're so short."

"I did," he said. "I wanted to contact you but I didn't know how, and you were married and everything, so I didn't want to bother you, but I wanted to tell you congratulations."

"That's sweet. The support would've been nice, actually."

"Better late than never," he said. "So congratulations."

"I'll drink to that," Lucia said, and took another sip. When she finished she added, "But it's all done now, so that feels a little weird."

"You're not going back?"

Lucia smelled the baked crust. "Hold on," she said, and stood up and turned on the oven light again. The mozzarella cheese bubbled into small brown mountains. She put on oven mitts and pulled out the pizza.

"Can I help?" Ben said.

"I can handle it, but thanks," Lucia said, and placed the pizza stone on a wooden board and carried it to the table. She sliced the pizza and they waited a few minutes for it to cool. She said, "I don't know what I'll do next. I just don't think acting will be that next thing, you know? I gave it a good shot."

"You did," Ben said, and removed a slice from the stone. "I can't wait, sorry."

"Go ahead," Lucia said, and followed him.

Ben took a bite and his eyes rolled back. "It's the best."

Lucia smiled as she took a bite. "Better than Willow's?"

He took another bite and nodded.

"Liar," she said, but the bite she took was amazing, she couldn't deny it.

He said, "It's not for nothing you know. There's a reason you went; you experienced a lot, right? Did cool things, met cool people."

"It's true."

"And there's a reason you're back too." He used his thumb to wipe pizza sauce from his lips.

Lucia paused and put her pizza down. Ben always did have a penchant for fatalism. She almost told him about her mother's decision to retire. When they had dated, any time she needed to make a decision about a school project, quitting her job at the clothing store in town to take acting classes, or how to handle Mya, she had consulted Ben. He took time to think ideas through and never hurried his decision, but when he did decide, they both knew it was best.

"Think you'd like to check out the farm sometime before you go?" he said, and helped himself to another slice.

"I'd love that."

"No city wear though. I'll put you to work."

"Stilettos at least?" She faked a pout.

"Only if you're on composting detail."

"I might have some old boots in my closet. My room looks exactly the same. It's weird."

"I don't think I remember."

"Oh yeah?" Lucia said. She hadn't had sex in more than eight months now, and drinking beer with the guy who took her virginity was a dangerous combination. It would be too easy to invite Ben back to take a look and then sit on the bed and flip through an old photo album, and soon they'd kiss once and then again, deeply and fully, until he leaned her back on the pillows and she wouldn't be able to control herself. Just like teenagers. That is, if he'd even want to. "It's as confining as I remember."

They finished half the pizza. "Save some for Mya," Ben said. "And your mom."

"Good idea," Lucia said, and stood from the table. She wrapped the rest of the pizza in aluminum foil and put it away in the fridge.

"I wish I could stay longer," Ben said, his hands in his pockets. "The farm wakes up early."

"That's fine," Lucia said, but she couldn't help wondering if that was the real reason he had to go or if he had somebody else waiting for him.

He walked to her with confidence, wrapped her in a big hug, and said, "Let's do this again before you go."

"Sounds good," she said, her body folding into his like warm clay.

"Tell your mom I'll call her tomorrow."

"Will do," she said, and walked him to the door. They paused in the frame and waited for the dragonflies to part. Lucia wanted him to kiss her, on the cheek even, but he smiled and turned to go. She shut the door and leaned against it with one hand resting over her breastbone; she hadn't experienced desire of this kind in far too long.

## CHAPTER 19
### Shredding the Numbers

WILLOW HAD FALLEN asleep on the sectional sofa in her office, her stomach aching from hunger and aggravated by the smell of baked crust, but she hadn't wanted to interrupt Lucia and Ben. Their voices rose and fell, and laughter punctuated the conversation, reminding Willow of the time when Ben was the only one who could put Lucia in a good mood. He'd been Willow's last hope for keeping Lucia in Quartz Hollow all those years ago, but her daughter had a stubborn streak Willow couldn't blame her for. If anything, she'd inherited it. Willow had underestimated Lucia's desire to get away. Willow admired what a valiant effort she'd made, considering how miserable she had been for much of that time away. Lucia couldn't deny it; Willow knew, the way mothers always do. Last night was the happiest Lucia had sounded since she'd arrived home.

Mya had stayed in the woods and probably spent the night in her lean-to. Willow sat up from the couch and her feet landed on the reading material that had put her to sleep last night. She gathered the accounting report and placed it on her desk. Normally she read the annual report as soon as she received it, but she hadn't been as punctual this time around, figuring it hadn't changed much since last year. In fact this past year the profits were higher, since they'd signed a few new clients, and she'd increased the price on a few of her top clients, Zoe included, a systematic adjustment made when clients experienced significant strides in their careers. Other than equipment replacement, building repair, new hires, insurance hikes, and other day-to-day costs, Willow hardly worried about major losses, not like the loss of an entire crop. She stared at the bottom line on her accounting report and subtracted three-quarters of the seventeen million they'd made last year to project next year's potential loss if the new formula for Zoe didn't work and she blackmailed major clients. Willow worried that was a conservative estimate, but it was a prettier scenario than going into the negative, which would inevitably happen if the crop failed to produce again. How had this become her life, and so suddenly?

Willow's office phone rang and she looked down first to screen the call. Grateful it was her assistant and not Robert, she picked up. "Brenda?"

"How are you?"

"I'm fine, and you?"

"Great," she said. "I've got next year's orders squared away and I'm dropping by with those receipts this afternoon, along with two new client profiles. Did you know Leya Miner was a ballerina before she began modeling? I didn't know that."

Willow did know that. Leya had already appeared as a contestant on a modeling reality show when Willow interviewed her, an example of a model in progress. The industry had matured, the superstar models had aged, and Willow believed the time had come for a new face that would secure book deals, clothing lines, cheap perfumes, major catwalks during fashion week, and perhaps a talk show or two. All signs pointed to Leya's being ready, but now her ascending career might be stopped short. What would happen if Willow no longer had a product to sell to these women? Would they just drop off and never fully actualize their talents?

"You there?" Brenda said.

"Sorry. What time were you coming by?"

"When's best for you?"

"Late afternoon," Willow said. If anyone anywhere in the great wide universe loved her at all, then Ben would be in touch beforehand.

"How's six? Too late? I'll stop by the factory for an evening check-in too, if you want."

"Sounds fine," Willow said. "Thanks."

"No problem." Brenda hung up.

What else could she say without raising Brenda's suspicion? She wasn't ready to confide in her, and knowing Brenda she'd go into a doomsday scenario—she loved apocalypse theories, said they gave her comfort. Willow never quite understood it, but she wasn't against comfort. She could have used some at the moment. She placed the phone on the floor and let the operator act as her bodyguard against possible interruption. She could tolerate the sound of a prerecorded voice but not the sound of a live human being in need of something from her.

Willow collapsed into the chair at her desk. If she sold the company and the factory, she could avoid the total destruction of Lenore Incorporated. Ben might discover that the plants couldn't reproduce ever again, and it wasn't like Willow could order new ones from a catalog. Grandmother Serena had turned a single plant into acres of a thriving business, and Willow might be the one to destroy it all. She could liquidate. They could all travel the world for years at a time. Go to Borneo again. Travel to Iceland for the first time. The girls had loved Scandinavia when they were little, so they could go for an extended stay there. And Paris. Who ever tired of Paris?

But a person can't travel forever. What would they come home to if not the business? What would become of the Lenore women after them who would never know the flower or the fortune? Wealth could be wiped out in a single generation without a source to replenish it. Willow's chest buzzed like a beehive. She massaged her breastbone to calm down. She couldn't leave her girls with nothing. And her future grandchildren and great-grands. A multibillion-dollar business split three ways meant nothing to Willow, not after a lifetime of building that number, but it would mean something to Lucia and Mya. If they knew how much *Forbes* had underestimated her holdings and how much they'd inherit, they might urge her to liquidate. But Willow didn't have it in her to kill the family business. She wanted to retire and look on as her daughters ran Lenore Incorporated successfully.

Willow searched under her desk for the black trash-can-looking device that Brenda had so expertly used all these years. Now she couldn't remember what the hell it was for. Why was she looking under her desk in the first place? She tried to sit up too fast and hit the back of her head on the bottom of the desk. She balled her fists to keep herself from shouting. She looked on the other side of her desk, and apparently that was where Brenda kept it. The black thing was what she needed to get rid of these papers and it was already plugged in, thank goodness. She straightened the edges of the accounting report and fed it into the slot on the black trash can—that was what she'd call it for now, until she remembered the name for what she was doing. It was exactly what she should do, just in case her daughters came looking.

## CHAPTER 20
## *Snakebite*

SLEEPING BY THE creek was the only way Mya could nod off last night after her accident. Without the trickling sound of the water navigating smooth stones, she would've stared at the snaking crack on her bedroom ceiling until the first light of dawn. At least out here no one could come knocking to see how she was doing. No one would bring her coffee and breakfast. She didn't want pity. She just wished it hadn't happened. At least the black cloud was gone, no longer an albatross above her. If that thing never showed up again for the rest of her time on earth, Mya'd be grateful.

The sun hung low in the tree line and Mya couldn't get a clear view, but it felt like a quarter to nine, maybe later. She walked out of the lean-to she had built many summers ago, surprised by how sturdy it remained. The throw rug on the ground needed a beating, so she dragged it out, hung it over the branch of a short locust tree, and found a sturdy stick to swing. Puffs of earth rose each time she connected, covering her naked body in brown dust like a powdered Parisian courtesan. The main purpose of perfume from its inception had always been to mask the unpleasant smells of life happening, especially urine, feces, and death, all of which Mya had smelled at close range as she buried Spots in the ground. But the scent of detritus and vanillin from split and rotting trunks could not be captured in a bottle; despite Mya's devotion to the art of perfume, she often preferred the scent of real life found unaltered in the woods.

Mya smoothed out the rug in her lean-to and then decided to wash off. The nearby creek ran clear with small red crayfish visible on the bottom rocks, and twenty feet downstream the water created a pool three feet deep. As girls she and Lucia had used this spot as their personal swimming hole and preferred it to the murky ponds on their land. Clear waters gave them comfort, and they swam without concern, throwing their bodies against the creek edge and dangling their legs, over the mossy banks. One time Lucia had created a bridge with her legs, and when Mya swam beneath, Lucia peed right on her back. Mya had probably deserved it.

Back then the water had come to their chins, and now it rose to Mya's waist; to submerge her body she had to lie down on the rocks. Fanning out like a starfish, she took up the entire pool like she was floating in a teacup. Mya looked upward to the break in the trees, where clouds passed quickly overhead. One paused, and as Mya watched it formed the shape of an open mouth, not quite human but not quite beast, and then collapsed and moved with the other clouds. A stick popped in the forest, and Mya sat up immediately, held on to a mossy rock, and kept her head low. The sound of feet in the brush neared, and then Luke appeared from behind the lean-to. He peered inside her space and called Mya's name, then straightened up and scanned the trees. Why would he come to her so early? He'd only come if he knew something was wrong with her mother or her sister or the factory.

Mya stood and Luke immediately turned to see her downstream, without her even needing to call his name. He shook his head and hopped over a wall of boulders to come to her. Luke held himself against one of the large rocks, his torso flexed and tight in his white tank top. "Bathtub's broken?" he said.

She wanted to tell him to turn and go, that he shouldn't have come looking for her. Space was important in a relationship, if that's what he wanted to call it. He'd have to learn this at some point. But all she could say was "I slept here." Mya stepped out of the pool and Luke watched her every movement.

"You should've texted me." Luke stepped closer to her.

Mya wiped the water from her face. "I hit a fawn with my truck last night."

"I know; Willow told me," he said. "I wish you would've called, though."

"It happened so fast." She walked past him and back to the shelter to get her clothes. "Sorry if I didn't think to pick up a phone. It's not my first impulse, not like your generation." Did she *really* just use that phrase? How old and crotchety could she be? It was too early for a conversation.

He trailed behind her. "Not just that."

Mya didn't pause as she gathered up her clothes from the leaf mulch outside her tent area.

Luke said, "The flowers."

"What about them?" Mya put on her shirt slowly.

"Johnny Bern overheard Robert talking to one of the floor inspectors about a bad batch and how it might be the whole crop, and they don't know how bad it is. Johnny told his guys at lunch and, you know. My father told me this morning," Luke said. He tossed a stick onto the ground.

Robert shouldn't have been talking so freely about all this. Her mother would have to deal with that, on top of everything else. "Not your business," Mya said. "It's not anyone's business but ours, and no one needs to spread any rumors. You especially." Her tone was hurried and she could hear it, but she couldn't stop it.

"Yes, ma'am," he said.

Mya froze. He'd never treated her like an older woman before. She turned to him and stood in her T-shirt, no pants or shoes, and said, "Is that all?"

"Guess so." He kicked a log into her fire pit. "I just wanted to know if it was true and see if you're all right. But Mya Lenore's always all right. She doesn't need anybody."

Anything she said now would only spur a fight, and that was the last thing she needed.

He began to move, and before he passed her he stopped and said, "The other night at the movies I thought you were so fucking happy, and now you're just bitchy. One minute you're hot, super hot, and then you just shoot me down. I never know what end's up with you."

She tied her hair into a loose bun and put her hands on her hips. "It's who I am," she said. "If you can't handle that, then stop coming after me like some lost damn dog." As soon as it left her mouth, she knew she didn't mean it and wished she could take it back.

He stared at her until she had to look up. Luke laughed once and said, "I don't have that kind of loyalty."

"What's that supposed to mean?"

"I don't need you. I wanted you, but I don't need you. I don't need this shit." His voice was venomous, and she'd never heard him talk with such anger before. He turned his back on her and left. This was a real fight, the first they'd ever had—usually they were so easy together. That's when she knew she didn't want him to go.

"Luke," she called after him, but he didn't stop. "Luke, wait a minute!" As if he couldn't hear her, he moved farther into the maze of trees. He was a farm boy who shot injured animals for work without hesitation. He could leave her here and cut her off for good. Naked from the waist down, she began walking cautiously, but he was gaining speed, and then she sprinted after him, shouting his name and watching his back recede in the distance.

"Damn it, Luke," she said, "I didn't mean it. I'm sorry." A sharp, warm pain spiked in her right shank, and Mya shouted Luke's name. She stopped running, looked down, and saw that bleeding welts had formed into a dark triangle just above her ankle. Her heart sped up, and she immediately scanned the forest floor and saw a gaggle of baby copperhead snakes curled inches away from her feet. Mya hadn't been paying attention, and the snakes were hard to see in the brown leaves. "Fucking shit," she said to herself first, and then she looked up, desperate to see Luke.

He came bounding to her, shouting, "What is it?" before he reached her.

Breathily, Mya said, "There." She stared down at the tan snakes with black markings. She remained as still as their long bodies.

"Are you bit?" he said, and five of the snakes escaped into holes in the forest floor.

She nodded. Luke picked up a nearby stick with a prong at the end. "Hold still now." In one smooth motion, he swept the other snakes at least twenty feet into the distance and then pulled Mya into his arms.

"There's no kit or anything," she said. Her mother always warned her about snakes, but she just didn't listen. Mya's body began to shake, and she tried to control her shock so it wouldn't encourage the venom to spread.

"You need a doctor," Luke said.

They were deep in the woods, at least a forty-minute hike out, not to mention the drive to town. Mya said, "Suck it out. I know they say not to, but just do it."

Luke lifted Mya onto his back and took her to a clearing where soft green grass provided a blanket. He eased her down. Her leg was on fire, and she wanted to put pressure on it or cut it off entirely. Luke took of his tank top, ripped it in half, and made a constriction band above the bite to keep the poison from traveling toward her heart. He pulled out his Buck knife from his pocket and a lighter from his cigarette pack and quickly sterilized the blade. "This'll hurt."

She grabbed a fallen piece of bark and shoved it in her mouth to clamp down on.

He looked up. "Ready?"

Mya closed her eyes, and the hot blade sliced into her skin like it was carving a turkey. Tears ran from the corners of her eyes without her consent, and the blood gushed down to her bare foot. Luke immediately covered the bites with his mouth, sucked hard, spat, and sucked again. He gripped her leg with both hands. He sliced open another set of bites and she shouted, "Mercy!" and then bit down on the bark.

She wanted to wrap him up in her arms, but her body was in too much pain to move. If only she had white willow bark tincture out here to subdue the inflammation. Luke finished and wiped off his mouth, and Mya said, "Get the moonshine."

"Stay put," Luke said, and then he ran to the stream to rinse out his mouth, then disappeared into her lean-to and brought back the flask. He rinsed his lips and mouth with the liquor and spat it out, and then he doused her bites. She reached out for the flask and took a deep gulp.

"Come on." He hoisted her up onto his back again, and she held him tight around the neck.

"Thank you for not leaving," she said.

Luke rubbed her clasped hands and then brought his arms underneath her thighs to support her. He hiked Mya out of the wilderness while the moonshine washed over her pain. Warmth overtook her body like a down blanket sliding up from her feet and over her thighs, and all she could think about was Lucia's cloud. Baby copperheads. Seven, maybe ten, and all at once. She'd played on this property all her life and never come close to being snakebit. That was a punishment from Great-Grandmother Serena. The cloud hadn't come just to warn her about Spots, and just because Lucia couldn't see it anymore didn't mean the curse had disappeared. The cloud would rain down on her, she was sure of it, but how much more?

## CHAPTER 21
## *Curse and Vengeance*

L UCIA FINISHED HER run on the hiking trails just as the sun rose to its noon position. The air had been so clear this morning and the mountains so blue that she'd lost her sense of time and exercised for much longer than she had in months. Her thighs would make her pay for it tomorrow. Lunchtime neared, and Lucia was beginning to worry about her sister; she had hoped to come across her on the trail. That cloud. She couldn't let go of the feeling that the cloud would reappear at any moment. She could almost guarantee it. This was the kind of feeling that her mother and Mya had often referred to during her childhood, feelings Lucia had never known; they had spoken of them as truth and it drove Lucia crazy. She couldn't experience a disappointment or a hope without one of them mentioning it before she did. Sometimes she just wanted the space to feel what she could and the choice to share or not.

But now Lucia understood how urgent those moments must've been for her mother and Mya. These feelings were pushy and didn't want to be kept silent. Thirty-three years. That's all the time it took for them to manifest. Lucia wondered what her life would've been like if it had been as effortless for her as it had been for Mya. Would she have left Quartz Hollow in the first place? Might she be married to Ben? Might her mother have retired already and sought treatment for her memory loss? Might Lucia be president at this point? She'd always believed the gifts had passed her over, a genetic glitch for the Lenore family. In a legacy of talented women, she'd been skipped, only to grow up and be left wondering how it could've been or if it still could be. Suddenly all the choices she'd made prior to this moment felt like a poor investment. Her only consolation was that at least she finally understood her family.

She *had* to tell someone. It was a compulsion without explanation. Technically, the cloud itself had disappeared, but she couldn't shake this sense of distrust. She couldn't tell Mya, not after the fawn and that look of utter relief when Lucia had told her the cloud no longer stalked her.

A dented blue pickup truck that hadn't been there when Lucia left was parked out front. The dragonflies continued to swarm the front porch, so Lucia took off her muddy running shoes by the side door of the cabin and went inside to find her mother. She said "Hello?" as she walked through the empty cabin. Only the noise of cicadas outside responded. Lucia changed into a yellow summer dress she found in her closet, amazed it still fit. A little tight around the hips but doable. Her mother's room was empty, the quilt on the bed perfectly tucked. Lucia peeked behind the curtain of her mother's office, where Willow sat at the desk reading her tablet.

"I can come back later," Lucia said.

"No, no," Willow said, and took off her reading glasses.

Lucia collapsed on the Victorian couch, and it was as hard and uncomfortable as she remembered. Next to her mother's desk, the shredder had the remnants of paper poking from the top. "Were you working?" Lucia said.

Her mother stood, picked up the black can, and put it on top of her desk. "Old files," she said.

"Isn't that Brenda's job?" Lucia said. Brenda came three times a week, sometimes more, to tidy the office.

"Yep," Willow said, and she walked out of the office and returned with a trash bag, into which she dumped the shredded paper. Willow tied the black bag and tossed it by the doorframe. She sat back down and asked, "What's that called again?"

"What?" Lucia said. "The shredder?"

"That's it," her mother said.

"Did Mya come in?"

"Not that I saw." Lucia couldn't stop looking at the bag like some stranger's body was stuffed inside. Not once could Lucia remember her mother actively doing the tasks of an office manager. Maybe she wasn't feeling well today.

"Her boyfriend came over," Willow said. "I sent him to get her, figured they'd be back by now."

"Maybe they're busy."

Willow laughed. "That's all they ever do. Like rabbits."

"God, Mom," Lucia said, but couldn't stop herself from smiling. "How can you stand that?"

"I ignore it. Or I leave. I usually have work to do. You haven't met Luke. He's younger than she is."

This didn't surprise Lucia. "How much younger?"

"Younger than you. Midtwenties I think."

Lucia whistled. "I wouldn't know what to do with one of those."

"He's a nice boy. Hard worker, handsome. I'm sure Ben knows him. Luke's daddy owns a cattle ranch not too far from the Whites," Willow said. "I just worry, he's so young and all. I'd like Mya to find somebody."

"Don't count on it."

Willow shrugged her shoulders, as if to say "You never know."

She joined Lucia on the couch and said, "Last night sounded fun."

"You listened?"

Willow crossed her legs and smoothed her linen dress at the knee. "Not on purpose."

She wondered how often Willow and Mya had had talks just like this during all the years Lucia was away. She had chosen to leave home, but she couldn't help feeling so excluded all the time: excluded from any interest in the business, from the family gifts, from a relationship with her mother and this town. She'd left, yes. At the time she'd felt like she had to. Thinking about all she'd missed made her sad now.

"What about you?" Lucia asked.

"What about me?" Willow straightened her shoulders for the offensive.

"I want you to find somebody too."

"That's sweet. When I retire I can think about all that."

Lucia planted her feet on the floor and rubbed her palms on her thighs. Willow wasn't being subtle anymore about her desire to stop working, but Lucia wasn't ready to make a decision. To stay here for the rest of her life was a lot to ask. It had always been too much to expect but was especially so now, with so much instability in the business. If only her mother could wait until times were better. Unless she wasn't sure times would get better, and in that case, why would she keep the business running?

"Will we see Ben today?" Willow said.

"He said he'd call." Lucia took a deep breath.

"Are you worried?"

"Just in general. Aren't you?" Lucia said.

"Yes." Neither of them spoke for a while. Just a mother and a daughter on the couch. Cue the cello music.

Lucia decided to break the silence: "I know I said the cloud's gone, but it doesn't *feel* gone to me."

"But if it's gone, it's gone," Willow said. "Probably just your nerves. I remember the first time I had a daydream so vivid I thought I was another person. I saw my father's car crushed beneath a rockslide in the mountains, and I was so scared, and I told my mother. She told me he wasn't near the mountains, he'd taken the train for business. Never had I felt such relief before. But he ended up catching a ride and coming back that way, and I never saw him again. I hated those visions so much. Never good things, you know? And it took me years to accept it. I remember too when Mya saw her first clouds form, and she told me the parents of one of her new school friends—they'd just moved to town—would be coming over to talk about Mya's devil storytelling, things about Grandmother Serena and such, which Mya shouldn't have been doing. She was outside and ran inside because she saw her friend and her friend's mother in a cloud. And sure enough, just as she told me, their car crested the driveway. Mya looked so scared, and it took her a long time to appreciate that she sees the world just a little differently. And maybe you just never wanted to be afraid. But I don't doubt how scary it is now, even when you're all grown up."

"You're done?" Lucia said.

"Yes, smarty-pants, I am," Willow said.

"Good," Lucia said. "Because that's not what this is. It does freak me out, I admit that, but that doesn't explain my feeling completely."

The front door opened and Lucia heard a stranger's voice yell, "Anyone home?"

"That's Luke," Willow said. "In the office," she shouted back.

"I need you." Lucia didn't know Luke, but she knew the sound of panic in a person's voice. Willow shot off the couch, and Lucia followed her mother into the kitchen, where a tall, lean, and super-sexy guy with no shirt on stood by the sink pounding glass after glass of water, his body slicked down with sweat. Maybe what her mother had said about Mya and Luke going at it like rabbits was true, and that made Lucia extremely jealous. He could at least not flaunt his body in front of her. Such a young one too—he had to have been in elementary school still when Lucia attended high school, not that it mattered much once everybody in the room was all grown up.

What if, what if, what if, what if?

What a tiny question, and she hated herself for even thinking it. Mya had thought it once before and she had followed her impulse. It would serve her right all these years later, except Luke didn't even notice Lucia, not even a compulsory glance at her breasts, and that simple connection was a necessary one for attraction. Ben and Mya must've had a connection, no matter how small, or she would've never attempted to convince him that he was in love with the wrong Lenore girl, a girl who wouldn't stick around Quartz Hollow, a girl who wouldn't ensure his place as the resident botanist for Lenore Incorporated. A searing-hot hatred for both Ben and her sister traveled the length of Lucia's body like an electromagnetic pulse. *For every action there is an equal and opposite reaction*—she'd been finishing her project on Newton in her senior physics class when it all happened, a mere week before graduation. Newton's third law of motion remained seared in her memory. And what choice did Lucia have but to leave like Mya swore she would? She'd doubted whether her move to the city to pursue acting was the right decision and she hadn't wanted to leave Ben behind. But after what happened, she no longer questioned. She was over this, she told herself, so very, very over this, fifteen years past this.

Luke wiped his brow with a dirty dishrag on the stove and said, "Mya got snakebit."

Willow said, "Where is she?"

Luke chugged one more glass of water and put the glass down in the sink, and then he was the first to go back outside. Mya sat on the front porch steps. Her right ankle was as swollen as an eggplant. Lucia hung back. The black cloud did not appear over her sister's head, but the panic in the depths of Lucia's abdomen was stronger than before.

Willow knelt down next to Mya. "How'd this happen?"

"Copperheads, like a bed of them," Mya said, her voice breathy and quick. "Stepped right on them."

"Barefoot," Luke added.

Her mother's eyes grew large, and Mya nodded. "Half-naked too, so stupid of me."

"You slashed them open?" Willow said, still looking at Luke. "Are you crazy?"

"I told him to," she said. "He got all of it, I think."

"Are you sure?"

His chest rose and fell quickly. "No," he said. Luke stared down at Mya, and the way he looked at her made the tightness inside Lucia's body relax for a moment. She hadn't seen a guy look at her sister like that ever before. Lust, sure, but that wasn't all.

Luke knelt down in front of Mya, put his hand on the back of her neck, and said, "I'll take her to Dr. Kent."

"You sure?" Willow said. "I should go."

Why her mother was worried about Luke, Lucia couldn't understand. He might be younger than Mya, but he loved her; it was as obvious as the blue sky. If anything, her sister would sabotage it because she was too afraid to accept what he had to offer. A small part of Lucia wanted her to, only so she'd know how it felt to lose.

"Mya?" Willow said.

She nodded, sweat dripping from the tip of her nose. She said, "I need water." Luke hustled inside the house and brought her a Mason jar. Her sister only drank a few sips before handing it back.

Mya said, "It's there, isn't it?"

Lucia shook her head.

"It's there, I know it is," Mya insisted. "It's that fucking curse. And it's come just for me. It wants to kill me, I swear it does. It wants me dead."

For all his chiseled muscles and 3 percent body fat, Luke's eyes were sensitive, the kind of eyes an actor needs. Bedroom eyes, Lucia thought. He looked very worried when he said, "She's been talking like that, all the hike back."

Willow looked over at Lucia and then back to Luke. "That's the venom. You just need to get her to town. Call me and let me know if I need to come down there."

"You know I'm right." Mya stared up at them both like a child, her face pale and the circles underneath her eyes swollen and dark. "Lucia, you know I am. Tell her."

"I don't see it," Lucia said, trying to reassure her. "I swear I don't. It's gone."

Willow said, "Luke?"

"I'll call," he said, and lifted Mya so he could secure her in his truck. She let him. She even let him help her with the seat belt. Maybe it was just the poison that made Mya so vulnerable. Luke got in the driver's seat and Mya rested her head on his shoulder. Lucia stood beside her mother as they backed up in the driveway and prepared to turn around. Like a quick blip on a television screen, the black cloud flashed above her sister's head. Lucia raised her hand in the air and sprinted after them, but the truck was out of sight completely, leaving a cloud of Virginia red dust in its wake.

## CHAPTER 22
## *Acceleration*

"THREE THINGS," Dr. Kent said with Mya's chart in his hands. "Have a kit when you're that far out. And don't ever, and I mean *ever*, cut a snakebite and suck out the venom. Promise me?"

Mya nodded. Dr. Kent looked at Luke and waited for him to nod as well.

"And lastly, make sure you get here immediately. Cutting into those bites damaged your tissue, and beyond having a scar, it's likely you'll lose feeling in that area. We'll know in the next few weeks. So make an appointment up front to come see me for a follow-up." Dr. Kent handed Mya her discharge papers. "How does a woodsy woman like you get bit like this?"

Mya gave him a strained smile. "I'm not sure." She had been asking herself the same question. She'd seen copperheads and rattlesnakes before; she'd encountered them many times, but she'd managed to spot them, to sidestep them. This time she didn't even notice, just like she hadn't noticed Spots when she was driving up to the house.

"Just be careful," Dr. Kent said.

"I'll try," Mya said. Dr. Kent's family practice had been a fixture in Mya's memory since she was a little girl. He was the one who first introduced her to Fig Newtons. Though his hair had turned white and the top of his head had begun to bald, he still kept a tray of cookies in the white cabinet above the sink where he stored gauze, tape, and cotton swabs. He patted Mya on her knee like he always had and handed her a cookie.

Dr. Kent checked her wrapped, swollen leg where the nurse had administered the antivenin and tetanus shot. "Looks good," he said, and then he closed the door.

Luke rested his back against a faded red poster of the circulatory system. "I'm sorry," he said.

His face had fallen, and she limped over to him and wrapped her arms around his waist. "You did what I thought was right."

"Still." He refused to look at her.

She took his chin in her hand and directed it toward her. She said, "If you hadn't been there, it would've been hell getting back to the cabin."

"Your leg's real messed up," he said. "I cut too deep."

Mya shrugged her shoulders. "Don't become a surgeon," she said, but he didn't laugh like she expected him to. "What is it? Worried you won't find me attractive anymore?"

"God, no." He squeezed her.

"Then no big deal," she said. "And thank you."

"You're welcome." Luke pulled her into his chest and rested his chin on top of her head. Whenever he did this she felt like the younger one. A nurse knocked on the door and entered, then quickly left, saying, "Sorry."

Luke said, "I love you, Mya."

Without thinking, she tried to pull away, but he wouldn't let her. He said it again: "I love you and you don't have to say anything, I just need you to know that."

No one had confessed love to her in a doctor's office before. She didn't feel well enough to respond. The antivenin had made her exhausted. To respond to Luke now wouldn't be right. Someone knocked on the door again and Mya said, "Coming out, hang on."

Luke opened the door for Mya and supported her as she made her way on crutches to the checkout window. The white halls gleamed from bleach, and the smell of rubbery ACE bandages filled the air. Mya stood behind the glass panel of the checkout counter and waited for the receptionist, Shirley, to finish up a call, her circus-animal scrubs a delightful display of personality in an otherwise sterile environment. Shirley hung up and in a deep Appalachian accent said, "That was your mama. Says your boyfriend didn't call her."

On impulse Mya almost said "Not my boyfriend," but she was able to stop herself.

Luke said, "I forgot."

"You know how she is," Mya said.

Shirley laughed like she knew a long-kept secret about Willow from their school days together. "You're over eighteen, so I couldn't say nothing to her about you visiting here. You call her, will you?"

"First thing," Mya said.

Shirley readjusted herself in her black rolling chair and banged on the antiquated beige keyboard. "Gotta wake it up, hold on."

"Dr. Kent said follow up in two weeks," Mya said.

"Just hang on." Shirley stared at the monitor like she might smack it.

Luke tapped his boot on the floor and Mya looked in his direction, but the flat-screen TV mounted in the corner of the waiting area caught her attention first. The entertainment-channel news had a split screen of Jennifer and Zoe and a headline running beneath them that screamed: BOTH ACTRESSES IN HIDING. WHO WILL PLAY NAUTICA JONES NOW? Mya leaned closer to the glass panel, and the screen changed to a split of Zoe and her longtime boyfriend, the actor/director Clint

Moore, a steamy twenty-first-century version of Paul Newman, a man Mya couldn't stop staring at even when she tried. The headline scrolled: CHEATING MAN, BROKEN HEART: THE REASON ZOE QUIT HER ROLE? "More to come, just after this," said a bouncy blonde with too much cleavage and teeth much too white. A commercial for RingTrue birth control began, and a skinny twentysomething vowed that her partner couldn't feel the insert.

Shirley said, "How's Thursday, July second, at nine?"

"I'm sorry?" Mya said, unable to concentrate and feeling pulled toward the television. She needed to find out if Zoe had already used the formula she sent last night. Mya had never expected that kind of efficacy. She must've used the perfume the moment she received it and applied too much of it in a desperate effort to renew her failing relationship. And her man's cheating revealed today? Could the large dose of perfume cause such a swift rejection? Mya suspected it had this power, but she never expected Zoe to douse herself.

"Does that work?" Shirley asked again.

"I guess so." Mya accepted her appointment card and offered Shirley cash.

"Not that much, child," Shirley said, and handed her back two hundred dollars. "Just a twenty for your copay." Mya didn't keep up with things like health insurance; she rarely went to the doctor.

Luke led Mya away from the desk. He said, "You sure you're fine?"

Mya kept staring at the TV, waiting for the news to continue, but an erectile dysfunction commercial came on next. "Let's go," Luke said. "Your mom's worried."

He pushed open the door. The sunlight flooded the waiting room and Mya covered her eyes. He steadied her on the way to the truck and then opened her door. She said, "Can we stop by the pharmacy? I just need to pick up some ibuprofen."

"Call your mom." He handed her his cell phone, and she dialed her mother as he started the car.

Willow picked up after two rings. "Luke?"

"It's Mya."

"Are you okay?"

"Fine," Mya said. "Got some shots and a scar, but otherwise, fine."

Willow paused, and she heard Lucia say in the background, "Tell her."

"I saw the news," Mya said first.

She heard Willow's steady breathing. "Do you think it's—"

"I do." Mya couldn't help the excitement building in her body. "But I need to make some phone calls."

"Her manager?" Willow said.

"Probably," Mya said.

"Lucia can call."

Luke took a sharp turn off Main Street, the road opening up to rolling green valleys. This was her business, not Lucia's. Why would Lucia make the call? "I can do it," Mya insisted. "I'll be home in less than thirty minutes."

"I want to know now," Willow said.

"Mom!" Mya sounded like she was whining but she didn't know what else to say. Lucia had been home for exactly three days after fifteen years away, and now she was making official business calls.

"And you're ill," Willow added.

"This isn't right," Mya said. "This is my deal, she's my client."

"It's still my business, for now anyway, and she's my client," Willow said. "Lucia's making the call and we'll know something by the time you get here."

Why was she acting like this? What had Mya done to make her mother so indifferent? And what was next? Willow would retire finally and hand over the business to Mya *and* Lucia? Or worse, give the president title to Lucia and let Mya hang on, live at the cabin, maybe oversee the factory and make the same formula over and over again like they had for the past century? Willow couldn't do that to her. Mya had years of experience raising the plants and managing the factory, and Lucia had none.

"Mya, you there?" her mother said.

"Bad reception." Mya hung up on her mother. She handed the phone back to Luke.

Mya stared out at the blur of trees, and the more she thought about it, the more Mya believed her mother capable of changing the entire trajectory of her future. Willow and Lucia did seem closer. Either Mya was ill and paranoid, or she was close to losing future control over Lenore Incorporated. She had stayed in Quartz Hollow her entire life, had cared for the land and the business and their mother while Lucia was away following her selfish passions. Could her mother *honestly* make this decision?

Mya had to know as soon as she arrived home. "Please drive faster." Luke shifted into fifth gear and pressed down hard on the accelerator.

CHAPTER 23

## *Naming the President*

I S SHE OKAY with this?" Lucia said after Willow hung up the receiver.

Willow didn't want to lie to her daughter, but Lucia had work to do and getting her feelings involved would only hamper her. This, above all else, was the most important business skill to master. "She's dazed, and you know how antivenin can be."

"Not really," Lucia said.

Willow didn't have firsthand experience with snakebites either, and Lucia had never spent as much time in the woods as Mya. "You know what I meant," Willow said. "She'll be fine."

"Did you tell her?"

"I decided against it." Willow picked up the phone and handed it to Lucia. "Mya's got enough going on not to have to worry about that cloud. She needs to rest; after that we'll talk to her."

"Do I call now?" Lucia said, and took the phone from Willow.

Willow opened an Excel spreadsheet and scrolled through the names and numbers until she landed on Peter Sable, Zoe's manager.

She highlighted the number. "Here you go," Willow said, and stepped aside so Lucia could stand at the helm of the desk.

Willow sat on her couch. It felt good to be on the other side for once. On many occasions while Lucia was in New York, a bitterness had brewed inside Willow, as if Lucia had purposely stolen the years away, years that she had longed for when her girls were little. She wanted to be near them as they came of age and developed their interests and careers and relationships. Whenever Willow went to the city for meetings, Lucia always seemed busy or only had time for a quick lunch. Jonah rarely came with her. Her own daughter, a mere acquaintance. Certainly she hadn't wanted Lucia to go through the heartache of a divorce, but she had longed for some event to bring Lucia back to the mountains, no matter the cost.

Lucia's long black hair, pale skin as smooth as gardenia petals, big blue eyes, and wide cheekbones mirrored Grandmother Serena's features so much that the daguerreotype of Willow's grandmother on the mantel seemed alive with Lucia standing in front of it. Lucia pinned the receiver in the crook of her neck and said, "No answer."

"Try again," Willow said, and Lucia gave her the same indignant look she used to when Willow asked her to clean the windows of the cabin. Willow valued a clear view.

"Mr. Sable?" Lucia sounded more confident than she had when she first called Jennifer. Willow couldn't be sure, but it seemed like Lucia enjoyed doing this, the way she'd always enjoyed helping Willow dry the dishes. Before she turned thirteen, of course.

"Sir, this is Lucia Lenore calling on behalf of my sister, Mya." Lucia tucked her hair behind one ear, smiled, and said, "Yes. Yes, that's right. Yes, sir, I am. I know, that's what everyone says. I exist, I promise. Born April twenty-seventh. Is that right? How funny. How old is your daughter now? Oh, sixteen's a great time to be a girl. Uh-huh. Right."

Willow leveled her eyes at Lucia, and Lucia held one hand up like she had no idea what was happening. Peter Sable *never* chatted on the phone.

"Sir—okay, Peter," Lucia said. "I'm calling to check in with Zoe. Well, no, not about all that, though we're very worried and hope she resolves her personal problems without much interference from the press. You too, that goes without saying. But Zoe should've received a package from us, last night I believe. Did she mention that? She did? And—is that right? We're so glad to hear it. That *is* high praise from Zoe. I'm so glad we followed up then. Didn't want to bother her, of course, not in these times, but I'm very glad you could spare a few minutes for me and I hope to speak with you again soon. Yes, yes, Peter, I'll tell her, and thank you for being so gracious."

Lucia continued to smile even as she hung up the phone.

What a stunner, her daughter. Peter Sable had always been a hard-ass, but he talked to Lucia like he loved her. Willow said, "That was good, right?"

"Peter told me to tell you that I'm fabulous," Lucia replied, and made a small curtsy.

"You do have something, I'll give you that," Willow said. Lucia cast down her eyes and smiled at the compliment. "You've always had a magical voice."

"And Zoe's using the perfume. 'Adores it,' or so says Peter."

"This'll cheer Mya up."

Lucia sat down at Willow's desk and placed both hands on the top as if she owned it.

"How's that feel?" Willow asked.

Lucia withdrew her hands like she'd been caught trying to steal. She tied her hair into a pile on top of her head and then paused.

"What?" Willow said.

"Are you sure this is right?" Lucia said.

Willow adjusted herself on the couch. She said, "I really have thought this through, and continuing to provide our product to Zoe after the threats she made is a defeat for our company. I'd rather not work with her, honestly. There's no good way to quit a client."

"But why should Zoe be ruined if Mya wasn't clear in the contract?" Lucia said, and tapped her nails on the desk.

"Zoe knew better. This wasn't some innocent mistake, Lucia. It was calculated. The sooner you accept that, the better. Mya didn't put it in writing, but on very select occasions I haven't either; it depends on the client and the industry. With Zoe, considering how immature she is and the competition in music and film, I would've made sure to do it, and it's my fault for not checking the contract, but Zoe knew. It's always made clear in the negotiation, verbally anyway. She just didn't care. What was best for Zoe was all that mattered."

"I understand all that," Lucia said. "You don't want Zoe to get hurt though, right?"

"Of course not."

"But Mya's hair—well, it's her hair. And you let her add it to the formula," Lucia said.

Willow nodded, but what could she say to this point? She would not admit aloud that she wanted Zoe brought down.

Lucia stood from the chair and walked to the window. Willow watched her. A dragonfly landed on the glass panel. Lucia studied it for a moment and then she said, "If this scandal with her boyfriend is a result, it's working fast. Almost too fast."

"That's hard to say."

"You're not concerned? Even a little?"

Willow stared at Lucia. She had a hard time feeling any concern for Zoe Bennett.

"Then I won't worry," Lucia concluded.

"I think that's best."

Lucia sat down on the couch, placed her chin in her hands, and let out a long sigh. "Jonah left me a message."

"Did you listen to it?" Willow rubbed her daughter's back for the first time in years.

"Not yet," Lucia said. "Probably just a thing with the apartment."

"Then why haven't you checked it?"

"I don't know."

"You feel like telling me what happened between you two?" Willow asked softly.

"Not really."

Willow didn't worry about Mya's heart breaking, but she always worried about Lucia. She attached herself too much to goals, plans, places, what people should be like, and what life should look like. Only disappointment came from such high expectations. "I won't miss him," Willow said.

"You hardly knew him," Lucia said defensively.

How irrational even a broken heart could be. Willow'd had one before too. She said, "He didn't want me to know him."

Lucia folded her arms and rested them on her stomach. This was her response, a quiet resignation. Jonah wasn't family and never would be, and Lucia was on the way to accepting it, Willow hoped. If she did, maybe she'd see a different kind of life awaiting her.

A few moments later Mya tossed open the curtain sectioning off the office and limped into the room on crutches. Willow hadn't heard the truck pull up. Luke held her waist to steady her, but she didn't seem to notice him. Her face was red and her blue eyes large.

Lucia stood. "Your leg's so swollen."

"Can we talk?" Mya said.

Willow looked from Mya to her lover boy and back to Mya.

Mya said, "I don't care if he hears."

Luke looked around the room at everything except a Lenore woman.

Willow said, "Maybe you should ask him; maybe he doesn't want to be here to listen."

Mya whipped around. "Luke?"

"Plow needs a new blade."

"See," Willow said.

Luke kissed Mya on her cheek and then said, "I'll call you when I'm done. I love you." And then he vanished behind the curtain.

Mya turned around immediately after he said what Willow thought he said, though she was getting older and perhaps her hearing wasn't so good anymore.

"Did he just say that?" Lucia asked.

"He did," Mya confirmed.

*At least my hearing is still good,* Willow thought with relief.

"How sweet," Lucia said in a taunting voice.

"Shut up." Mya eased herself to the floor and Willow tossed her a pillow. She slid it under her butt.

Willow said, "You seem so—I don't know, harried? Shouldn't you rest or something?"

"Can we get you anything?" Lucia said.

"Stop with this 'we' stuff, please," Mya snapped.

"I meant 'I,'" Lucia said. "Can *I* get you any—"

Mya cut her off. "I need to know something and you're making it harder for me to ask." She pointed her finger at Willow and said, "Are you thinking, at least even a little teensy bit, about appointing Lucia president?"

Lucia coughed, and Willow assumed this gave it away. Mya said, "I knew it, Mom."

"Should I step out?" Lucia said.

"No, obviously not," Mya said. "You should never go, never again, not if you're running things."

"I haven't even—"

"Doesn't matter," Mya said. "It's the principle. She wants someone else to do it because I messed up and she doesn't trust me. You let me change the formula, Mom, and even if I fix the problem, that won't make a difference. That's right, isn't it?"

Willow had hoped to have a separate conversation with Mya about all this, but that black cloud had arrived and there had never seemed to be a right time. "It happened quickly, Mya."

"She's gone fifteen years and then three days she's back and things happen quickly for you? Sorry, I don't get it. It's like you were waiting for her to return."

Mya adjusted the pillow beneath her leg and winced in pain.

"I'm still sitting here, you know," Lucia said. "I can hear you."

"I really don't give a damn," Mya answered. "If you can't handle hearing this, how will you be president? You're too soft."

Lucia stood up like she might leave. In a calm voice, she said, "I'll tell you how, Mya: I don't rush."

Mya's impulsiveness had always made Willow cautious about handing over the business to her. It had weighed on Willow for years, even before the Zoe issue, but she hadn't known how to tell her elder daughter, who had devoted her entire life to the business, that she was in the running for president only by default.

Mya asked her mother, "How do you know she won't get claustrophobic again and split?"

"Sit down," Willow told Lucia, who, after a long silence, obeyed.

"This isn't how I planned to talk to you, Mya, but you brought it up," Willow said. "I've mentioned this to Lucia and she hasn't said a word to me. Not one word in response. Nothing is settled."

Mya stared at Lucia, as if to confirm, and Lucia finally nodded. Mya said, "Why'd you mention it to her first and not me? I've been here the entire time. You owed me that."

Willow stood from the couch without another word, pulled out a drawer from her desk, and presented Zoe's letter to Mya. "This came for you."

Mya read it over once and stared at the paper. She shook her head and rasped, "You shouldn't have opened it."

"But I did," Willow said. "You know, it's one thing to tell me that

I should retire, but to conspire with a client, to plot about getting me to retire early? And for what? I don't even want to know what plans you had."

"I didn't have any plans," Mya said with deep remorse in her voice, so much that Willow almost believed her. "It's just—"

"Just what? Send me out to L.A. for a phony meeting? Push me in a corner to change the formula? Give Zoe the upper hand? Force me to retire? What excuse could you have for going against me like this?"

"You don't seem yourself!" Mya shouted. "For a while you haven't, and I thought it'd be best, but I knew you'd never agree unless you had to."

Willow returned to her place on the couch and said, "I do need to retire. I'm struggling to remember small things and some big things too. I've been trying to carry on and pretend everything's fine, but it's been mounting, and I feel like I'm jeopardizing things by hanging on. But frankly, I haven't sensed that you were ready, Mya."

"What?" Mya slammed her hand on the floor. "I've been ready for the past few years, just waiting for you to give me more responsibility. I can't believe you're telling me this now."

Willow said, "I've seen a spark in Lucia since she's been home; that's the truth. I see it in her and I have to follow my feelings, Mya. So I spoke up exactly when I felt it, and you weren't here."

Mya bowed her head and took a deep breath. Willow watched her chest fill and then fall. "So what's there for me? Travel the world for the rest of my life? Snap photos? Shop? Did it occur to you that I wanted this job more than anything else?"

"It did," Willow said, her entire motherly constitution softening for her daughter. "Of course it did." Mya looked wholly like the toddler she once was, the girl Willow adored who sat at the kitchen table and pretended to play poker against her.

Mya refused to look at Willow anymore, and she couldn't blame her. This was all very difficult. Mya turned her stare to Lucia, and Willow did the same.

"So I can talk now?" Lucia said.

Mya tossed up her hands. "I guess so, you're the boss."

Lucia tightened the corners of her mouth. "I haven't been sure."

This response surprised Willow. "And now?"

"And now I think I want this," Lucia said.

"Well, grand," Mya blurted. "Sure glad you came to a decision. It has to be one of us, and clearly I can't be trusted, even though every single decision I've ever made has been in the interest of the company. Can you say the same for yourself, Lucia?"

Willow said, "The business chooses," before Lucia had to respond.

"What a bunch of bullshit," Mya said, and stood up from the floor. She wobbled when she put pressure on her right leg, then grabbed her crutches. "Maybe it's my time to go. Lucia had her time away, so why not me?"

"Maybe it is," Willow replied, and Mya's face dropped. Some time away would be replenishing for Mya, but it would never happen. She was too attached to home.

"Now, hold on," Lucia said. "You didn't let me finish."

Mya said, "I need a bath." She sounded defeated.

Lucia stood and walked to Mya. "I want to share this with you."

"I don't need your charity."

"That's not how things are done," Willow said. "Too many cooks in the kitchen ruin a soup; that's what my mother always said. That's what Grandmother Serena knew and believed, and you can't just go and change it now."

Lucia faced Willow head-to-head: "Changing the formula isn't the way things are done either, but you agreed to that. And I won't accept the position if I'll be heading it alone."

Willow absolutely shouldn't have given the girls this ammunition against her. And now she fully understood Grandmother Serena's point—change one aspect of the business and the rest is vulnerable. Each president had made the same difficult decision. Serena had chosen Lily because she was the elder, and her younger sister owned a bakery in town and lived close by but didn't work for the business. Iris had too much anxiety about people and decision making to run the business, so their mother had never questioned her choice to appoint Willow. Now, as president of Lenore Incorporated, Willow had the right to choose, and she knew better than to give her daughters equal power over the company—frightful arguments and poor execution would result from that dynamic.

"Mya?" Lucia said.

"I don't know."

"It's that or nothing," Lucia said, and Willow couldn't believe she was being that forceful with her sister. Lucia was president. There wasn't a doubt in Willow's mind anymore. Lucia wouldn't share the job.

Mya turned for the door.

"Creative director," Lucia offered.

Mya limped away on her crutches, and Lucia went to hold the curtain open for her. Clearly Lucia had been thinking about a lot more than she'd let on. One thing seemed certain, something Willow hadn't anticipated: Lucia wanted to see a change in the business. But how big of a change? Willow never intended for a mass overhaul. Mya sometimes mentioned expanding the line of products and becoming more visible as a way to protect the perfume from inquiry. Visibility was not a part of the business plan, only absolute discretion, and Willow had always doubted Mya's ability to adhere to that principle.

Lucia planted herself in Willow's chair behind the desk. Willow said, "Your acting skills come in handy from time to time."

Lucia pursed her lips. "I was going to tell you."

"I bet," Willow said.

"It's for the best," Lucia said, and her energy was so much larger and brighter, as if she were using the family perfume for the first time.

The phone rang. Lucia picked it up without letting it ring twice and without asking Willow if she should answer it in the first place. "Lenore Incorporated," she said, and then her voice softened. "Oh, hey."

"Is it Ben?"

Lucia nodded. "Sure," she said. "See you then." She hung up. "He wants us to come there."

"How's he sound?" Willow asked.

Lucia stood up. "Like Ben."

"What's that sound like?"

"I don't know. Like Ben."

"Like a hurricane or a breezy day?" Willow persisted.

"Let's just go."

"I should change." Willow stood up.

"Why?"

"Look at me," Willow said, and left the office. From behind her, she heard Lucia say, "But I'm driving."

## CHAPTER 24
## *The Infection*

HOW COULD LUCIA explain that she hadn't premeditated accepting the title or offering Mya a new position as creative director? Her decision didn't arrive until she was placed in the spotlight of Mya's anger. Her older sister had always been the better of the two. She was free-spirited, arguably more attractive, more gifted, and better with the flowers and perfumery. The idea that Lucia could be president of Lenore Incorporated was like a little girl's dream of being a princess, a fantasy so false even a three-year-old knows deep down that it's impossible.

Lucia could point to her trip abroad to Grasse and Paris to study perfumery with Mya during their summer break. Lucia had been only a freshman in high school, and Mya far outperformed Lucia in every skill, from the fieldwork, to the extraction, to the creative expression of blending unusual oils together for a scent of paradise. Their mentor, Mr. Dubois, had a passion for talent, and he lavished his attention on Mya. And each time Willow called for a progress report, Mr. Dubois began with Mya, and Lucia could hear her mother's proud voice through the phone. Sometimes Lucia didn't even go to the shop and ended up at a café in town eating too many *pains au chocolat* and drinking her fill of café au lait. Each afternoon Mya returned to their apartment above the House of Dubois smelling like jasmine. She filled the one bedroom of the apartment with the joy of knowing just what she wanted to do for the rest of her life. The scent of her made it difficult for Lucia to sleep during her time in Paris.

Her only fond memory of that time was a weekend in London when she attended a play in a golden baroque theater on the Strand. Mya didn't have the patience for theater, so Lucia decided she could have her own focus. She returned home with the desire to make a life for herself outside of the perfumery. The business was Mya's to inherit. Sure, Lucia assumed the money would be there if she needed it, and it was a relief not to worry about her retirement, especially while she tried to break through as an actress. But maybe that security had hampered her. Often this thought crouched in the back of her mind: she needed to be on the verge of losing everything. The closest she'd come to having nothing was when she landed on the cabin's doorstep a few days ago.

At least, Lucia told herself, she strove for a life of love and passion, just like Great-Grandmother Serena. Even if her attempt was misguided. Even if she eventually failed. Maybe that path had led her directly to this moment. Maybe that was exactly why the business had chosen her.

Willow returned to the office in a belted cobalt-blue dress with a strand of pearls from Paris and a gold cuff bracelet on each wrist, her silver-white hair in a French twist. "You know Ben lives on a farm?" Lucia said, reminding her.

Her mother had outdressed her to go see Lucia's ex-boyfriend. Willow had never cared much for modern appliances or the newest luxury sedan model, but she did spend her money on clothes and accessories and travel. Her closet was a mix of vintage Chanel, Balenciaga, Cardin, and Saint Laurent. She never let Mya and Lucia borrow from her. If the girls had shown any interest in fashion, she would've invested in their wardrobes also, Lucia had no doubt, but they both disappointed her in that way. Neither of them had any sense of style.

"Doesn't hurt to look nice," Willow said. "Makes me feel in control."

Lucia, on the other hand, had changed into a pair of worn-out jeans from high school, one size too small, and a red T-shirt from the Gap. "Should I change back?"

"It's just Ben."

Lucia removed her feet from the ottoman in her mother's office and stood. "You're right. It's a farm."

Willow smiled and said, "Here," and handed Lucia the keys.

They walked through the kitchen and then to the front door. The porch had been abandoned by the dragonflies, at least for the moment. Lucia closed the door behind them. An SUV drove up. Lucia didn't recognize it. Willow walked over to the driver's-side door and hugged the woman who stepped out, then gestured toward Lucia.

Brenda ran over and said, "Oh my goodness, it's been too long. The city girl. Come here, darling, you look so good." Why Lucia had expected everyone to still look the same after all those years, she didn't know, but the wrinkles on Brenda's face, the whitening of her hair, and the pudginess at her waist shocked Lucia. She'd been only forty when Lucia moved away and was an avid hiker and caver. Beauty dwindled so effortlessly.

"I love it," Brenda said, "seeing you two together."

"You'll be seeing more of her," Willow said.

"Best news all year." Brenda shook Lucia's arm. No matter how old she was, Brenda's energy was as high as a teenager's, always had been. Would she become Lucia's assistant when Willow retired, this woman who had babysat Lucia and taught her to braid hair in the second grade? Delegating to her would feel so strange, but she couldn't train someone new. Lucia was the one who needed training, and Brenda could help her.

Brenda held a portfolio underneath her arm. "I can come back," she said.

"Not necessary," Willow said. "Can we do this out here?"

"Sure." Brenda had a knack for making every idea of Willow's sound perfect. Willow walked to the gazebo next to the small lily pond, and Brenda and Lucia followed. They all sat together at a cast-iron table, and Brenda slid the portfolio across to Willow.

"She won't get bored?" Brenda nodded at Lucia.

"I don't think so, do you?" Willow asked.

"Not a bit."

Willow opened the black folder and scanned a printed report. The sun shone through the paper and Lucia could see a lot of numbers spliced with intermittent notes. Not looking up from the paper, Willow said, "Brenda worked up two new contracts for a young model and a brilliant tech entrepreneur. My happy selection." Willow licked her thumb and turned the page as if everything was secure and new clients were a boon. Lucia could tell that Brenda had absolutely no idea what was happening with the flowers, or with Willow's memory.

Brenda turned to Lucia. "Your mom's the best."

"Oh, stop." Willow cast down her eyes. Brenda was the closest thing to a spouse her mother had ever had. "The financing came through?"

"Grace has private cash sources, Texas oil money or something. That's how she started her first Web business, so she's all taken care of," Brenda answered. "But Leya's not in quite the same position."

"Will she accept a loan?" Willow asked.

Her mother's interest rates were significantly lower than the banks', whether she loaned to her community or to a young woman like Leya who didn't have the benefit of being born into wealth. For new clients who needed assistance, she offered an initial loan to begin using the first bottle of perfume, but thereafter most clients could pay biannually or in full. No woman had ever defaulted—no payment meant no more product, and before a client paid her mortgage, she paid Lenore Incorporated. This was a business lesson Willow had drilled into Mya and Lucia.

Brenda swatted at a yellow jacket darting in front of them. "I think so," she said. "It's never a problem."

"Can she handle it?" Willow said.

"Says she can. She's a grown girl, and we can't hold their hands or anything, right? They're lucky to get this opportunity."

Willow was second-guessing in a way that Brenda clearly hadn't expected, and Lucia waited for Brenda to call her on it.

"You're right," Willow said. "You're always right. They never go broke on the product."

"Not a single bankruptcy, Willow, you remember that, okay? It's a good thing you give them." Brenda sounded like a life coach. How many roles could one woman play? "I'm looking at one more contract coming up," she reminded Willow, "but then it's quiet."

Willow organized the papers and slid them back in the portfolio. She tried to hand it back to Brenda, who said, "That's your copy, like always."

"Of course." Willow picked the portfolio up again like she hadn't been confused, but Lucia knew better. "Let's wait though to send out that paperwork until you settle up that last contract, and make sure we have a sit-down before you send all three out."

Lucia tried not to fidget on the wooden bench.

Brenda said, "If that's how you want to do it this time, but I already told the other two girls to expect them tomorrow."

Willow tucked a loose layer of hair behind her ear. "Just tell them we need to review one more thing. They'll understand."

"Sure, that's fine." Brenda's brow furrowed; she clearly knew something was amiss.

"Anything else?" Willow stood to go.

Brenda cleared her throat. "There's one thing, if you have time."

Willow waited.

"I said I'd check on the factory for you," Brenda said, "and Robert pulled me aside before I left and said there's been a lot of talk, rumors and such, about the flowers. Workers want to know if something's wrong, if they'll be out of jobs. Now business owners downtown are starting to worry that your capital won't be there for them next year, and I didn't know what to say. I just felt like I was missing something."

Willow looked at her daughter, and right then Lucia could see her mother's desperation to not be the only person with answers.

Willow said, "I should've told—"

"We should've told you," Lucia said, and placed a hand on her mother's forearm. "But the crop's looking dehydrated and we've got a botanist testing the flowers—we're on the way there now, in fact. It's been really sudden, that's all, or we would've told you sooner."

Brenda looked at Willow. "The whole crop?"

Willow nodded.

"Oh boy," Brenda breathed. "What's in reserve?"

"Not enough," Willow said.

Panic began to spread on Brenda's face, her forehead wrinkles creasing like small valleys. "Let's not go too far here," Lucia said carefully. "The tests aren't back yet and we don't want to worry for nothing."

"But it *is* something, you said it yourself, the crops don't look right," Brenda said. "Willow?"

Lucia intercepted. "Could you ask Robert to make an announcement for us?"

Brenda nodded but looked over at Willow like she wasn't sure who was in charge anymore.

Lucia said, "Have him gather all the employees and announce what I just told you. The flowers are being tested; it seems like a temporary drought issue. There's not been enough rain; everyone will understand that. Assure them it's temporary."

"Is it?" Brenda said.

Willow opened her mouth to speak, but Lucia pounced: "Of course it is, ninety-nine percent sure."

With one hand caressing her neck, Willow looked to the sky. "Might rain today, and that'll help" was all she said.

Brenda said, "I'll head over there right now."

"Great," Lucia said. "And I'll make sure we update you as soon as we know something. Sorry about that."

"That's fine," Brenda said, "I understand how things go." She gave Lucia a hug and then took Willow aside and said, "We should probably talk soon," loud enough for Lucia to overhear.

"I know," Willow said, and waved good-bye to Brenda.

Once they were safely inside the truck, Willow sighed. "Thank you, honey."

Lucia wanted to respond, but she was too struck by the word "honey."

AFTER BEN'S FATHER RETIRED FROM his ob-gyn medical practice, he had become mayor of Quartz Hollow and purchased the two horse farms bordering their property on Highway 221. Lucia assumed Ben had inherited one of those two farms, and when they pulled into the long driveway, she knew she was right. They drove down a poplar-lined driveway and ended up at a large, newly built Craftsman-style house, two stories high, painted a light sage color, with intricate wood detailing on the outside and white eaves. Lucia didn't expect this—a one-room cabin, perhaps, or a tent even, but not such a studied and elegant home. And all just for Ben?

"How nice," Willow said. "I do love bay windows."

Lucia parked the car next to the red barn, and a pack of farm dogs greeted her when she opened the door. They sniffed out her hiking boots and wouldn't let her step down until she heard a sharp whistle.

They scattered, and Lucia looked up to see Ben standing on his wrap-around porch, one arm in the air, his other arm around the shoulders of a girl Lucia hadn't seen before. Willow waved back to him and said, "Who's that?" to Lucia, but Lucia was silent and Willow went ahead without her.

Ben trotted down the long stone staircase to meet them. The girl followed behind him and then stood at his side in a flowing broomstick skirt. She wore a bright paisley scarf wrapped around her head; her wavy espresso-brown hair flowed down her bare shoulders; and her delicate wrists supported chunky wooden bracelets. Lucia couldn't believe how much she looked like she'd just stepped out of a Grateful Dead song.

Lucia tried not to trip on the pebble walkway. Ben wore a pair of jeans and a button-down shirt like a professor; the two of them together seemed so mismatched, and Lucia felt completely self-conscious in her garb. If she could've teleported home and changed into a tank top and skirt, she would've done it.

He said, "Good to see you. Ms. Lenore, Lucia, this is Vista."

"Nice to meet you." A large, beaming smile spread across the girl's face, and her eyes energized Lucia the longer her stare lingered. Lucia imagined her saying phrases that made people feel good, like "the universe listens and responds" and "you must focus on positive energy for positive results."

"You too," Willow said.

"I manage Mya's shop," Vista said, like she needed to remind somebody.

"That's right." Willow nodded. "Good to see you again."

"I've been trying to reach Mya," Vista said. "Could you ask her to call the shop today or tomorrow?"

"I can," Willow said. Vista smiled that smile again at Willow.

"Come inside," Ben said. Vista rubbed Ben's back before she walked to her car, which was parked in his garage.

"I'll call you later," he told her, and then he led the way up the staircase and Lucia reluctantly followed. She had zero desire to tour the gorgeous house Ben shared with Vista. They passed through a heavy oak door, and the inside of the home vaulted up to a stained-glass sky-light in the center of a winding staircase. The house was all wood and tile and Persian rugs and leather furniture. Could this really be Ben's taste? Lucia never knew he cared about interior design. Maybe it was Vista. Maybe he'd developed this interest during Lucia's long absence.

"This is a beautiful home, Ben," Willow said before Lucia had the chance.

"Dad's dream house," Ben said.

"Oh, is that right?"

"Just a couple years too late," Ben replied. "Mom and I chose everything we thought he'd want."

"I was sorry to hear that," Lucia said, and Ben nodded.

"I'm sure he'd love this." Willow looked around her. "He was a good man."

"Thank you," Ben said. "It's good to hear that."

"An awful lot of space for just you," Willow said, as if she'd over-heard Lucia's thoughts.

"That's true. Thought about getting a roommate or two but I keep putting it off. Depends on how long I'll be here."

"I'm sure the space all to yourself is nice though," Lucia offered.

Ben nodded, and Lucia was so relieved she didn't know what to do. He said, "Can I get you a drink or some food?"

"I'm fine," Willow answered. "You?" she asked Lucia.

Lucia said, "No, I'm fine, but thanks."

"This way then," Ben said, and led them through a commercial-grade kitchen with sleek stainless steel appliances. Ben's family had always been well-off, and you could see that in their home and cars. Lucia had always felt like the poor one in the relationship, though technically she knew that wasn't the case, not by a long shot. Yet even now she felt that way. Her mother dressed in couture but mostly drove a truck from the nineties, even though she had a Lexus SUV. People probably assumed her clothes were knockoffs. Willow never seemed to care either way.

Ben led them to a greenhouse with a door that opened on an expansive view of immaculately cut rolling fields with horses standing in the distance, their bodies like toys against the distant mountain range. The room allowed light to filter through, and all along the walls Ben had hung clear vases with cuttings in water, some with roots growing. Orchids of all different shapes and colors stood on one long wooden table against the far wall, and in the center of the room, Ben's workstation was as organized and clean as the rest of his house. He had a large microscope and slides along with goggles, latex gloves, and multiple pads of paper at his workstation, next to field guides for gardenias and rain forest flowers. One wall served as an incubating station with small peat moss containers and lights suspended close above them. Mya had one of those also. Lucia wasn't sure what the metal container was for: it looked like a beer keg with a circular door on the side. "Your personal robot?" Lucia said, and pointed at the silver container.

"An autoclave," he said, and since it was obvious that Lucia had no idea what that meant, he added, "Sterilizes my slides and stuff."

"Oh." This only clarified it a little.

Ben offered Willow a chair and then half seated himself on a metal stool in front of the table. Since there was nowhere else to sit, Lucia stood.

Ben said, "What number am I now among the people lucky enough to see inside this plant?"

"Let's just say you're not alone," Willow said, almost too hurriedly. "My plant guy's in China."

Willow had allowed Ben to put the plant under a microscope their junior year in high school, presuming Lucia would marry Ben, of course. She was going to finance his entire undergraduate and

Ph.D. education, and she still offered to do so even after Lucia broke up with him. Possibly out of guilt for Lucia's breaking his heart. But Ben had refused, and Lucia had been very thankful that Ben chose to disconnect from her family.

"The good news," Ben said, "is that for the most part, isolated from the chlorosis, the cells in the stamen and petals show no signs of collapse. They look healthy."

"That's excellent news," Willow said. "But you don't seem thrilled."

"Because there's bad news."

"You could've started with that," Lucia said.

"I found phytoplasmas in the roots," Ben said, "and I also found a small formation on an auxiliary shoot that will turn into witch's broom. Like a bird's nest on the plant bud. From what I can see, you have a phytoplasmal infection that will result in virescence and phyllody."

"English, please," Willow said.

"These are symptoms that will turn the entire *Gardenia potentiae* flower green and leaflike. It'll look as if no blossoms are on the plant at all."

"No blossoms?" Willow said.

"And no scent?" Lucia added.

"Correct," Ben answered in a calm and steady voice, just like a doctor delivering news about terminal cancer. He picked up a different slide, placed it on the microscope, and flipped on the light at the bottom. He moved out of the way so Willow could bend down and see, and when she finished, Lucia leaned over Ben, his earthy smell distracting her as she stared into the lens, the white light hurting her eyes at first. Once she adjusted, she saw tiny beads clumped together.

When Lucia backed away he said, "So to simplify, normal plant cells look like what you just saw. Do you mind?" He pointed at Willow's pearl necklace and she removed it for him.

"Careful," she said as she handed it over.

He let the pearls settle randomly into his cupped hands. He said,

"Normal, healthy cells look almost like this, and in your plant, they look like this in the stamen but not in the root cells. Those look flattened." Ben placed a new slide under the microscope.

Willow bent down and looked again. "Like pancakes," she said before moving out of the way.

"Almost," Ben said.

Lucia examined the slide. "Will this happen to the stamen and petal cells too?"

He nodded, and Willow sucked in a breath of air so loudly it sounded like a whistle. In a gentle voice Ben said, "I want to go back to the field and look some more. That way I can give you a better sense of how much time before . . ."

Willow placed a hand over her heart. "Before what?"

"Before it can't be stopped," Ben said.

Willow's hand dropped, and Ben reached out and grabbed it for a moment. He did this with such ease—not even Lucia felt comfortable holding her mother's hand like that.

"Could this kill our plant? And I mean totally, no coming back," Lucia said. Her mother bit her lower lip like this was the one question she couldn't bring herself to ask him.

Ben's eyes softened, and that was all Lucia needed to know. "Doesn't look good," he said.

"I need a drink," Willow said.

"Like I said, I want more samples," Ben said, "from the plants closest to the tree line. I didn't go back that far."

"Anything you need. And can I please compensate you?" Willow asked.

"No way," he told her. "After all those pizzas you made me?"

Willow pinched his cheek.

He didn't pull away. "Whatever I can do. Can I swing by tomorrow? Will you be free?" Ben addressed Lucia now, catching her off guard.

"I am," she said.

"Dinner again?" he said. "My treat this time."

She nodded. Would Vista come too? Lucia wanted to know but wasn't sure how to ask without sounding territorial.

Willow stood up and said, "I think I need to go home."

"I understand," he said, and walked them out of the greenhouse and then outside to their truck. Willow put herself in the cab, and he closed her door and then came around to close Lucia's.

"How's five?" Ben said, his voice much cheerier than it had been in his workshop. "We can go to the field and then I can take you to dinner in Quartz Hollow, if you want."

"I don't know," Lucia said.

Willow leaned over to the open window. "She'd love to."

Ben half smiled the way he always had since middle school. "Everybody's got to eat."

"It's a date then," Willow said, and finally Ben looked as uncomfortable as Lucia. She knew her mother would make him uneasy at some point. Willow was a charmer that way.

Lucia said, "I'll see you tomorrow." She pulled her door shut before he could close it.

"You'll marry that one," Willow told her.

"Stop talking crazy," Lucia said, and drove down the driveway.

"Oh stop."

"I mean it, you embarrassed me back there," Lucia said. "Clearly he has a girlfriend and he's happy, so leave it alone. Don't you have other things to worry about?"

"Huge things . . . ," Willow said as her voice tapered off. She turned her head toward the window. "I'm sorry."

Right when her mother had made peace with her retirement, there was a good chance there would be nothing left to give. They couldn't change what Ben had revealed, and it was easier to avoid talking about it for now. "It's okay," Lucia said. She turned up the Nina Simone CD in the player and drove them back to the cabin.

## CHAPTER 25
### *False Calls*

LUKE HAD SAID he loved her, today of all days. Mya believed him the moment he said it, and she also knew she couldn't say it back and might never be able to. The finality of the phrase bothered her, as did its limited scope. Choices, that's what Mya valued, and the phrase that rolled so easily off Luke's tongue had not escaped Mya's mouth for any man thus far. She sighed and raised her head to look above her. She might've ignored the cloud, the fawn, the snakes, Luke's untimely pronouncement, all together in such a short span of time, but now with Lucia taking over the business, Mya understood beyond a doubt that she was cursed. Maybe the black cloud receded until all the terrible events had been carried out. Or the curse stayed from the moment it appeared and into the tortured future, her death the final sign of its disappearance. She should've never sold the perfume to Zoe Bennett in the first place. Or changed the formula for her. Why did she invite this upon herself? She should've done nothing and allowed Zoe to tell the entire world about Lenore Incorporated's product.

Mya pulled up her strapless purple dress and grabbed her crutches, which were leaning against the wooden table in her workshop. She hobbled her way up the stairs and down the hall to Lucia's bedroom, where Lucia's cell phone had been ringing earlier. Her sister's clothes were strewn about the floor and the bed. Mya patted down the covers on the bed as if she'd been authorized to search the place. Finally she felt a lump beneath Lucia's pillow. She'd been sleeping on her phone this whole time.

The greasy fingertip prints on the phone cover presented themselves in the sunlight. Mya wiped the screen on her dress and then tapped the phone awake. It had no lock code. Twenty-two missed calls in three days. Clearly Lucia had neglected her phone since she arrived. She probably knew Jonah had tried to call her many, many times, and she obviously hadn't phoned him back. His urgency made this so much easier. Mya sat down on Lucia's daybed with her crutches beside her and listened for her mother and Lucia, who'd gone out without even telling Mya. They'd cite her injury as the reason, but they left Mya out these days like bullies on the playground.

Silence in the house—she made the call. As the line rang it occurred to Mya that she'd never actually spoken to this guy before and he might not even know that Lucia had a sister. She couldn't be sure what Lucia had divulged about their family history, if anything. Back when Lucia had called out of nowhere to tell them she was getting married, Willow advised Lucia to sign the prenuptial agreement Jonah's parents wanted, but she told Lucia never to expose their business, not even to her "soul mate." That phrase of Lucia's made Mya want to vomit. "Soul sucker" was more accurate.

Mya almost hung up the phone but then she heard static, and Jonah said "Finally," in not the kindest tone. "Where the hell are you?"

"Jonah," Mya said.

"Who is this?" he said, and he sounded pissed.

"This is Lucia's sister."

"Mya?" he asked. So he did know about her. This was not a good sign. Of all the stories Lucia would've told him about her, Mya doubted the kindest versions were at the top of the list. She needed him to trust her. "Is Lucia hurt?"

"No," Mya said.

"Then why are you calling me and not her?"

"She doesn't want to speak to you, that's why." This little jab felt good. She was not so fond of her sister at the moment, but she liked this guy even less.

"Are you calling to harass me?" He told someone in the background to be quiet.

Mya said, "Lucia's here and she's an absolute mess. Refuses to go back to the city. Wants to give up on acting. And there's nothing here for her, you know? She might end up substituting at the local high school and serving as assistant director for the school musicals for the rest of her life, but I think we both know that's not good for her."

"I hate that," Jonah said. "But I can't do anything. We're divorced. I assume you know that."

"I do. You're still friends, though, right? She said so, anyway, and I'd like to think you two are mature enough for that. Between us, she's already met someone here, and they're sleeping together, and I think she'll hitch on to anything at this point because she's so miserable about you. She can't waste away here. It's empty of opportunity for her."

"You two aren't close." Now he sounded suspicious. She'd gone too far.

"Family's family," Mya told him. "She came back here, but I think she needs you more than us right now."

"All right," Jonah said. "Have her call me. Tell her it's about the lease and it's important."

"She needs a reminder of what was good there," Mya said, and all she heard was Jonah's breath in response. "You there?" she said.

"Yeah," he said. "Look, I've got a meeting here. I stepped out for this call, so . . ."

"I'll let you go," Mya said, "just expect a call from us soon." Jonah hung up without a good-bye. Mya slipped Lucia's cell phone into the back pocket of her jeans. She glanced over her shoulder as she left the room, as though she'd burgled the place.

The phone in Willow's office was ringing, and it rang and rang and rang. Mya did her best to rush on her crutches but dropped them in favor of a rapid hop. She pushed back the drapes to the office and caught the phone just before it stopped ringing. "Lenore Incorporated," Mya said, slightly out of breath.

"Is Lucia there?" The unmistakable voice of Jennifer Katz.

"No, but this is Mya Lenore. Can I help you, Miss Katz?"

"Hi, Mya," Jennifer said sweetly, like they'd been best friends in middle school. "Lucia left a message for me, about your perfume for Zoe. I just wanted to tell her I got the message and I'll be placing another year's order for my perfume."

Mya closed her eyes, grateful for this small break. "Glad to hear it," she said.

"Thanks for doing that."

Mya shook her head and massaged her temple. "You're welcome," she said, pushing herself to sound genuine.

"It's just," Jennifer said, "you know, I can't stand her at all, but it's too bad what's happening to her."

"Men suck sometimes," Mya said.

"That," Jennifer said, "but now this other stuff too. It's all so much all of a sudden."

Mya moved the phone to her other ear. "Not boyfriend stuff?"

"No," Jennifer said like she couldn't believe Mya had asked that. "She freaked out on set for that Schol shoot."

"What do you mean 'freaked'?"

"She kept saying everyone hated her and then she just up and quit. It's printed in the *Reporter* and the *Times* this morning. Front page. The studio already called me. But anyway, just pass along my message to Lucia and tell her I'm well."

"Will do." Mya hung up the phone. So now Jennifer Katz and Lucia were best friends. It was like Lucia had come in and usurped her life while Mya had been sleeping.

Mya turned on her mother's laptop and first went to the *Hollywood Gawker* to confirm what Jennifer had said, and there it was on the front page with a huge headline: HOLLYWOOD'S DREAM GIRL BREAKS DOWN.

> *Zoe Bennett, who has won awards for her roles in* Baby Magic, The Terrible, *and* Like Cats and Dogs, *quit her starring role in Nick Schol's* Arrow Heights. *She accused the director and all the staff of sabotaging her because they cut a much-anticipated sex scene from the script. An anonymous source from the set quoted Zoe as saying, "If my audience can't handle that sex scene, then they're immature and ignorant and shouldn't be in the theater in the first place." After her public humiliation with actor/director boyfriend Clint Moore, Zoe has canceled multiple upcoming appearances for fashion and awards shows and refuses to present at the Oscars. Are we watching a star burning out? Only time will tell.*

Mya swallowed and couldn't bring herself to read any more. Hollywood loved a good meltdown. Mya had been so angry with Zoe, even irrationally and temporarily wished her dead while she made the essence from her hair. Now Mya was concerned. Very concerned. Within a day of the perfume's arrival and application to Zoe's skin, her heart had been broken, she'd quit her biggest film yet, and she seemed consumed by paranoia, convinced the world hated her. What could one more application do? An entire bottle? Mya's hair and her intentions—she knew what could come of those. Would Zoe end up in the mental ward? Was that how her career would finish? That outcome was an acceptable one. But could it be much worse? She didn't want the girl to die or to hurt anyone else.

Mya opened her mother's contacts spreadsheet and found the number for Zoe's manager. She called the number and it went straight to voice mail. Mya almost hung up and promised herself she'd have the nerve to call again later, but then she changed her mind and left a message: "This is Mya Lenore from Lenore Incorporated. Considering the recent events, please ask Zoe to stop using the new formula immediately until further notice. There's been a mistake—I mean, I made a mistake, and it could be dangerous. Call if you have any questions." Mya hung up and dropped the phone onto its base like a hot coal. Her mother might disown her for this decision, but whatever came of it was Lucia's problem now, and that might be enough to make her leave.

The office phone rang. "Lenore Incorporated," Mya said, and she braced herself to hear from Zoe's manager.

Lucia said, "Just checking on you."

"I'm fine."

"We're coming back from Ben's."

"Okay."

"See you in a minute." Lucia hung up.

Mya couldn't go into the forest, so she sat on the porch swing and stretched out her bad leg. If only the deer would come back, Mya would feel better, but she hadn't seen the herd since she killed Spots. Nothing made her feel more shunned, not even Lucia's newfound bond with their mother. And she couldn't go search for the herd and ask for forgiveness, not with her leg in this state.

Ivy vines hung down from the ceiling to the floor of the porch, and Mya parted them so she could see the sky. In the distance, thick blue clouds hung above the mountain range, a possible thunderstorm. But ahead of it, the sky was blue with wispy clouds, and Mya stared up. The longer she concentrated, the more the clouds shifted and whirled together to form Zoe Bennett's face stricken by pain, thick tears moving down her cheekbones until the face dissolved almost entirely. Then Zoe vanished, and the clouds thinned to reveal a blue sky once again.

Mya pulled out her cell phone from her pocket and dialed Luke's number just to hear his voice. After a few rings, a young, chipper female voice said, "Luke's phone."

"Hello?" Mya said. "Is Luke there?"

"Hang on." The girl giggled, and then Mya heard a scrambling sound and the line cut off.

"What the hell?" Mya said, and dialed Luke's number again, checking the screen to make sure that his name came up. It did. The line rang and rang, but nobody picked up this time. She hung up and texted him: *I'm trying to call you.* Mya placed the phone on her outstretched leg and tried not to stare at it.

Nothing. He'd always been lightning fast to text her back, even when he was working on the tractor. Maybe that was just one of his little sister's friends. Had to be, Mya told herself. And maybe his phone died. The idea that he had a younger lover on the side was impossible for Mya to imagine. She couldn't be that older woman who obsessed over her younger lover's liaisons. Resisting the urge to call him again would be difficult. She wanted to identify that voice on the other end. Did Mya know her? How much older was Mya? How did Luke meet her? Mya squeezed the phone in her hand like she could make the innards seep out. She considered tossing it into the lily pond—she didn't want another fucking call for the rest of her life.

## CHAPTER 26
# *Burned Brick*

"WHAT'S SHE DOING here?" Lucia said, parking her mother's truck behind a Subaru station wagon, the same one she'd watched Vista reverse out of Ben's garage an hour ago. "Are they friends?" Lucia removed the keys from the ignition and stared out at her sister and Vista talking—or yelling even—with wild gesticulations like they were practicing to be air traffic controllers.

"Isn't that Ben's girlfriend? I can't see."

"That's her," Lucia said.

"She runs Mya's store," Willow said, "but 'friends,' I can't be sure about that."

Without using her crutches, Mya pushed past Vista and limped to the station wagon like the car belonged to her. Lucia tried not to look at Vista directly but found herself drawn to the girl's hippie, casual, artsy beauty: long hair in two braids, chunky wooden bangles, hemp ankle bracelets. Lucia couldn't pull off that earthy look, though she'd tried it out when she first dated Jonah. Vista had no raccoon circles or sad lines around her eyes—she had to be younger than Lucia by a few years. All of this made Lucia want a sip of moonshine. Just a tiny sip. Or another trail run.

Willow said, "What's going on here?" but Mya barely registered the question. "Vista?" Willow said.

Her carefree face finally showed a glimpse of human angst when she squinted her eyes and said, "The store's ablaze."

"Is anyone hurt?"

"Get in," Mya barked at Vista. "Everything's fine," she told Willow.

"Are you headed there now?" Lucia said.

"No, Lucia. I made a spa appointment for a mud facial," Mya said with searing sarcasm. Each day Lucia stayed here, her sister became meaner.

"What about your leg?"

"I don't care if it hurts," Mya said, and she slammed the driver's-side door.

Lucia said, "May I come?"

Vista shrugged and said, "Sure."

She danced around Lucia as they tried to figure out who should be in the front seat. Lucia wanted to be in the back and away from her sister's bad mood, so she said, "It's your car, I'll take the back." Vista appeared dismayed, and Lucia thought the girl would rather be in the back with Lucia. And what did Vista know about Lucia? Had Ben told her anything at all? Did Vista sense right now that the only reason Lucia asked to join was the off chance that Ben would show up at the store to check on her? And he would, of course he would. Ben was one of the good guys.

Mya waved her hands at them and shouted something that sounded like "Hurry up," but Lucia couldn't hear her, sealed as she was inside the vehicle.

Willow said, "I should stay here, just in case someone calls."

Lucia inserted herself into the backseat of Vista's car, and the smell of patchouli and sandalwood incense overwhelmed her immediately. This was the smell Ben inhaled when they had sex. Lucia cracked the window to draw in some much-needed air.

Mya sped down Route 161. Lucia said, "Be careful," and Mya said, "Shut up." Vista glanced back at Lucia but didn't say anything.

"I can't believe this is happening," Mya said, and she glanced over at Vista, who didn't seem to have any plan to respond. "Vista?"

"What?"

"Answer me."

"You didn't *ask* me anything," Vista said with an attitude Lucia hadn't thought her capable of before. This unfortunately made Lucia admire the girl even more. Ben liked spunk.

Lucia watched her sister's head shake back and forth. "How did it happen?" Mya finally asked.

Vista propped two Roman-sandaled feet on the dashboard, her red painted toenails glistening in the sun. She finally said, "The glycerin tinctures. They were going three days and those Crock-Pots were old, I told you that."

"And the extra product, that was still on hand?"

Vista nodded and separated her homemade feather earrings from her hair. "I had them set to ship out to a buyer this afternoon."

Mya turned down the bluegrass music on the local NPR station and said, "Everything of mine, everything I deal with, everything that matters to me, is disappearing." Her eyes flashed in the rearview mirror and connected with Lucia's for a moment. Without words they exchanged the same disturbing thought about the black cloud.

For all the hurt Mya had caused Lucia in the past, Lucia had never once wished her sister to die. She loved her, despite everything, even her attempt to steal Ben away and keep him for the business. Mya had always been a protector. She had the will to protect Lucia, Willow, the business, herself. All of her actions, good and bad, stemmed from this one impulse. When Willow had left town on business trips, Mya took control as mother figure, believing the hired babysitters might mess up. In some ways, Lucia continued to see Mya in that role. No matter what, Lucia didn't want Mya harmed.

As if she too had been thinking about Mya's comment, Vista said, "What's that mean? Everything is disappearing?"

"Nothing," Mya and Lucia said at the same time, but Mya looked at Lucia once more in the mirror as if to say, "You know it's possible."

ALL OF QUARTZ HOLLOW HAD gathered for this fire. Mya parked the car three blocks away from the store. Lucia could see exactly where the store was located, because smoke hovered above that stretch of brick buildings. Lucia scanned the parked cars for Ben's truck, and then she looked at Vista, who was doing the same.

"Watch out," Vista said, and pointed down.

Lucia hopped over a pile of dog excrement on the sidewalk. "Thanks."

"You're welcome."

"So, how long have you and Ben been dating?"

"Not too long, about a month. We're taking our time. There's no need to rush," she answered. "His mom's ill, so, you know, the universe asks us to prioritize."

Lucia had no response for this kind of logic, so she said, "I'm sorry about the store."

"Me too," Vista said. "Negative energy attracts that sort of thing."

The brick walls of the store were already black, and the firemen drained water on the top of the building. The blaze persisted, the flames desperate to reach the sky and consume it also. There must've been a lot of dried tea inside that shop to feed a fire this potent.

"I think I'll need another job," Vista said.

Lucia didn't mean to think it, but the thought came to her anyway: maybe Vista would have to leave Quartz Hollow to find work.

That or she'd move in with Ben officially. If Lucia knew Ben at all, he'd offer, just to be helpful.

Thinking good thoughts about Ben White must've made him manifest (if she used Vista's kind of logic). Ben cut through the crowd and waved his hand, but of course they'd both seen him already. He charged forward and seemed to reach out his arms to both of them, like he was unsure of who to embrace first. Lucia stepped aside.

"This is nuts," he said. Vista nodded and then burst into tears. This startled Lucia. The girl had seemed so put together in the car.

Ben pulled Vista close to him, and Lucia turned away so they could have this moment, but she couldn't miss hearing Vista say, "I called and called and called Mya, and she wouldn't answer, and I had to go all the way out there to get her just to tell her, and I think I waited too long to call the fire people, and look at it now."

Lucia turned back around to tell Vista not to worry or feel guilty, that the fire would've happened no matter what, but Ben was stroking the top of Vista's head and Lucia couldn't speak. And then he caught Lucia staring, and he stared back at her. His eyes seemed somehow less invested in his embrace than they should've been. Maybe he was just in shock like everyone else. Lucia said, "So I think I'm going to check on Mya," and Vista nodded, tears creating the only blemishes on her delicate face. Lucia looked back once with a genuine desire to check on Vista, poor girl, but it was Ben who was still watching Lucia walk away, and this calmed her, if only for a moment.

She waved good-bye to him and he nodded once. Did Lucia detect sadness there, or was she projecting? It wasn't like she could ask him, and what nonsense this all was—he still had his arm around Vista. Plus, Lucia was barely divorced at this point, though she was years separated from satisfying sex and love. Still, she knew she shouldn't bother thinking about anyone else, especially an old boyfriend. She was foolish to think she wouldn't need more time to heal. Being in her thirties should make a girl less naïve, not more.

Her sister stood talking to the chief fireman as close to the building as they could be, the heat extending far from the flames. She turned around as Lucia approached, and Mya's face looked older than it had even yesterday; the wrinkles in her forehead stayed long after her eyebrows stopped moving. "It's burned to shit," she told Lucia.

"I see that."

"Will you call Mom and tell her to come get us?"

"Sure." Lucia patted her pockets. "I don't have my phone. Let me borrow yours."

Mya pulled a phone from her back pocket. The pink case with an Audrey Hepburn sticker definitely did not belong to Mya. She offered Lucia's phone to her but then realized her mistake and tried to take it back. Lucia snagged it before her sister could cover up what she had done and said, "Did you go through my stuff?"

Mya said, "Just call Mom." And then she turned around and did absolutely nothing. She didn't talk to the officers or firemen, she simply stood.

Lucia grabbed Mya's arm and forced her to turn around.

Mya ran her fingers through her sweaty blond hair and said, "I heard it ringing and it wouldn't quit so I answered it. That's all. It was Jonah and I told him you'd call him back."

Lucia dragged her thumb down the screen and saw that the call log did not back her sister's story: "It says *I* called him. Today. There's no way. Did *you* call him?"

"What the hell, Lucia?" Mya shouted, suddenly so defensive that Lucia wasn't sure what to believe. One of the firemen turned around, and his eyebrows leaped on his soot-covered face. Lucia shushed Mya, but it didn't help. Mya said, "I didn't call your fucking ex-husband. He keeps calling you and the noise was pissing me off. Maybe *you* should stop avoiding him."

Who to trust? Her sister or her phone? Jonah had called Lucia obsessively, that much was true, but he hadn't called today, at least not that the phone reported. Lucia checked the volume. It wasn't silenced, but the volume only had one bar. And she'd buried it in her bed. No way the noise disturbed anyone. "Why'd you take my phone?" Lucia pressed.

"This is ridiculous. I have things to deal with right now," Mya said. "I took your phone because I thought you should stop ignoring your life. You did have one before you arrived here, remember? And be glad I did, okay? There's an issue and Jonah needs you to talk to him."

"I didn't realize you cared so much about my affairs, Mya," Lucia said coldly.

"Well, I do," Mya said, and still Lucia couldn't gauge whether she should trust her sister, though some issue, like a problem with the lease, did sound like a plausible reason for why Jonah had called so often.

"Forgive me if that takes me by surprise a little."

"What're you waiting for?"

Lucia crossed her arms and stared at her sister. When would she ever stop bossing her? Becoming the boss might be the only way to change this dynamic.

"Just call Mom," Mya continued.

As Lucia dialed their mother's office number, she forced herself not to look around for Vista and Ben. The compulsion to do so was irritatingly strong, but she couldn't give this small matter away to her sister. Willow answered and said, "Need a ride?" Lucia never had appreciated her mother's intuition as much as she should have. "We do," she said, and Willow said, "On my way."

AFTER A SILENT RIDE HOME, Lucia needed space away from her sister and mother, so she pretended she had a bedroom door to lock and closed the curtain in the frame as fully as she could. If there were a doorknob she'd have hung a Do Not Disturb sign. A stray dragonfly from the front porch flew around her room and then landed on the white post on her bed frame. She cracked the window and said, "Get out while you can." With a sweep of her hand, the dragonfly took flight and escaped. Lucia fell back on her daybed and cradled her cell phone in both hands, and each time she came close to tapping Jonah's name on the screen, she ended up dropping the phone facedown on her chest. She did this over and over until the repetition made her sleepy. Some days, like this one, had a bad habit of feeling much longer than others. Lucia drifted into a nap that accidentally extended past dinner and into a full night's rest.

## CHAPTER 27
### A Visitor

W HAT?" WILLOW SAID to the assistant on the other end of the phone. Her laptop showed it was 6:57 A.M., and as much as she'd wanted to stay in bed and ignore the phone, it wouldn't stop ringing. Lucia pushed the drapes to the side and switched on the office lights. "I just need you to repeat that; it's early."

Lucia slid into the room like a cat and wrapped her arms around herself. "What's going on?" she whispered.

Willow held her hand in the air as Peter Sable's assistant said for the second time, "Zoe's dead. Suicide, possible overdose. Her body was discovered at her home."

Willow covered the speaker of her cell phone and said to Lucia, "Go wake up your sister." To Peter's assistant, she said, "When?" anxiously rubbing her silk nightgown between her fingers.

"Around midnight." The assistant sniffled.

"I appreciate you calling," Willow said. "And I'm so sorry to hear this."

"We received a message from Mya yesterday," the girl said, not at all receptive to Willow's graciousness.

"I don't know anything about that." Willow frowned.

"She asked Zoe to stop using something she sent to her. Said there was a dangerous mistake."

Lucia returned to the office with Mya, who was still wiping the sleep from her eyes. Willow stared at Mya until she had to look her in the eyes, and Willow could see right then that Mya already knew what was happening. "What're you suggesting?" Willow said.

"*I'm* not suggesting anything," the assistant said.

Willow said, "All the world knows what Zoe was going through lately. Let me speak to Peter, right now please."

The girl said, "Zoe's dead; he's too busy to talk right now."

"Then what is this about?"

"He asked me to schedule a time and he'll only speak to Mya," the assistant said.

"If he speaks to anyone, he'll speak to me," Willow said. "You tell him to let the guy, you know, the, the—coroner, yes, let the coroner do his work and determine what happened. He's paranoid—you can tell him I said that too. And tell him for matters like these he'd better be the one to make the call to me."

Mya leaned on Lucia and whispered to her. Lucia nodded.

Willow hung up the phone. They all stood together in the office for an achingly long time, the only sound coming from the percolating coffee in the kitchen.

Mya interrupted the silence. "She's gone, right?"

Willow nodded and said, "I need coffee."

"Come on," Lucia said, and they followed her to the kitchen, where she removed three clay mugs from the cabinet and brought them all fresh cups of coffee.

They sat at the round kitchen table, and Willow had no idea what to say to Mya. She'd left a message for a client and didn't *say* anything to Willow. How many more mistakes could one daughter make?

Mya placed one hand on top of the mug and let the steam escape between her fingers. She said, "I was going to tell you. I thought I had time."

"Tell us what?" Lucia said. "What's going on?" she said to Willow.

"I spoke to Jennifer Katz yesterday, right before I found out about my shop, and she mentioned Zoe's behavior. I just knew it was the perfume. I called her on an impulse; I thought it was the right thing to do. I left a message and told her to stop using the product considering everything she was going through," Mya said.

"I knew it," Lucia said, "I knew you shouldn't have put your hair in it."

Mya's face turned red and she shouted, "Too bad you weren't president at the time, Lucia! Could've saved the day and stopped your sister from another fuckup. That's what you're saying, right?"

"Yes, Mya!" Lucia shouted back. "That's exactly right. You should've found another way, that's what I do know. Not your hair. You killed her. She's dead, don't you understand? She's dead, dead, dead."

"Stop saying that." Mya shoved Lucia so hard she almost tipped backward.

"Stop it," Willow said quietly, but she could tell Mya was about to respond again, so she pounded on the table and yelled, "Stop it, you two!"

They both stared at her.

"Nothing gets solved like this. And keep your hands to yourself."

Mya glared at Lucia. Sometimes they had fought like this as girls, and Willow had just tuned out the noise because the stakes were low: a borrowed purse ruined or a cut in line for the bathroom. She couldn't ignore them now, however. Willow said, "Is it the new formula? Yes or no?"

Mya sipped her black coffee and then paused. "I wanted her to feel irresistible at first, so she wouldn't notice a difference, and then I wanted her to become repulsive. Only to others though, not herself. I had no idea it would turn that way."

"She killed herself," Lucia said. "Except not really. But there's still a mother out there who thinks her daughter was so low that she committed suicide."

"They can't prove anything," Mya said.

"They have the perfume," Willow said, "and your message."

"I didn't spell it out," Mya protested. "If anyone asks, I'll clarify what I meant and say that she'd have a breakout in the sun or something like that."

"Was she on drugs, any that you know of?" Lucia asked. She still hadn't touched her coffee.

"I don't think so," Willow said. Mya shook her head in agreement.

"So what happens if the toxicology report comes back clean?" Lucia's eyes were as large as quarters. "Her manager knows."

"What it did to her can't be traced in her system," Mya answered. "You know that."

They all sat silently for a moment. Mya said, "They'll find a way to charge me."

"Should they?" Willow said.

Mya's mouth dropped and her eyes narrowed. "Let's not forget that *you* told me it was okay to make it. You agreed, no one else, and it was your decision, your business too. You'll go to jail with me."

"Stop being so dramatic," Lucia said. "Mom had no idea what it would do. Only you could've."

"I didn't know it would do that. She must have used too much too fast."

"Can we just figure out what's next, please?" Lucia massaged her left temple.

"Peter Sable will call me," Willow said.

"I just hope they find drugs in her system," Mya said. Lucia looked at her like she'd said something heretical, but Willow actually agreed with Mya on that point: it would make all of this go away without a fuss.

"And until then?" Lucia asked.

"Just wait," Willow said. "We'll hear about it as soon as they know."

"What if Peter exposes us?" Lucia said.

"Might not be much to expose," Mya replied. "With the crop dying and all."

Of all the things Mya could've said, she didn't need to bring that up.

"I never meant for this to happen." Mya sounded as low and guilty as she had when she ran over Spots.

Willow said, "Maybe I didn't like Zoe, but I didn't want her dead." She looked for Mya to agree with this sentiment, but her daughter's face showed little remorse.

"Zoe disappeared," Mya said softly, as if it had just occurred to her, and she looked at Lucia. "I'm next, aren't I?"

"Stop talking like that," Willow said.

"I mean it." Mya sounded desperate. "Great-Grandmother Serena promised this, you know she did. Maybe not this exactly. But this is how badly she didn't want the formula changed."

"She promised grave consequences," Willow said. "She felt she had to protect the formula from anyone who wished to do harm."

Lucia said, "We know the story."

"But exactly how severe are those consequences?" Mya said to Willow. "She left that part out."

"She did," Willow admitted. "Frankly, I never wanted to find out."

"I'm hungry," Lucia said. "Sausage biscuits?"

Mya shrugged and Willow said, "Whatever you want."

Lucia fried sausage patties with extra sage in the cast-iron skillet and baked frozen biscuits in the oven. The fat sizzled, and Lucia slammed drawers and banged plates together.

Willow said, "Look at me." And Mya did. "No matter what happens, you have to promise me, absolutely promise me, to never use hair in another spell ever again, for the rest of your life. Not your hair or anyone's. Will you promise me that?"

Mya nodded and paused before she said, "Could the curse kill me?"

Lucia quieted her movements in the kitchen.

Mya covered her face with her hands and massaged her temples. "It'll drive me away, won't it? I'll end up like Iris."

"I just don't know," Willow said, and she felt heartbroken by this answer. She wished she could promise Mya some other outcome.

Lucia placed a platter of sausage biscuits before Willow and then said, "I'm not hungry. I think I'll shower."

"Go ahead," Willow said.

Lucia returned her clean plate to the cabinet, but before she left the kitchen, she turned and said, "This is serious."

"I'm aware," Willow said. She helped herself to the breakfast Lucia had made without saying another word. Willow willed herself to forget that beautiful girl's dead body on the other side of the country.

Mya said, "It's a moonshine morning."

"What about your snakebites?" Willow said.

"Some things bite worse." Mya opened up the liquor cabinet where they stored the cinnamon-infused moonshine. She brought out the Mason jar, poured some moonshine into her coffee, took a deep gulp, and then tightened her mouth.

Willow nodded at Mya's coffee cup. "Fix me one, will you?"

"Gladly," Mya said, and took Willow's mug to the counter. She watched Mya pour in a generous amount of the clear liquid, leaving little room to top it off with coffee. Her daughter's hands shook; the alcohol spilled down the side of the glass, and she wiped it off with her bare hand. Mya returned the cup to Willow but wouldn't sit down.

"I'm freaking out," Mya said. Willow didn't reply. "*Should* I be freaking out, Mom?"

Willow drank her coffee. It was strong as an unbroken horse. The fire in her throat subsided and Willow again answered "I don't know." What else was there to say? "Just stay close to the house for a while."

"How long?" Mya finally seated herself next to Willow.

Willow said, "Until we know for sure it has all passed."

"That could be the rest of my life," Mya said. "And the way things are going, that might be a very, very short wait."

"Please don't panic." Willow put one hand on her daughter's arm.

"I *mean* it," Mya said. "I'm not being dramatic, I can feel it." She walked to the sink to wash off her hands. Willow waited for her to return to the table, but Mya continued to stare out the window above the sink even after she turned off the water.

"What's wrong?" Willow said.

"It's just . . . ," Mya said, but trailed off.

Willow hurried to the sink and looked over Mya's shoulder to the driveway out front.

A black town car parked in front of the cabin and Mya said, "Is that from Quartz Hollow?"

"Out of town," Willow said, and she waited for it. As soon as the driver opened the back door and one shiny black brogue hit the grass, she knew exactly who'd arrived.

In a sudden panic, Mya said, "Is that a cop?"

"No," Willow said.

"Who the hell, then?"

Willow walked out the front door, coffee mug in hand. Her desire was to speed down the steps to him, but she knew for certain this time that the visit was for business, not pleasure.

Mya came outside on the porch and stood behind Willow like her mother was a human shield. "Mom?" Mya said.

"James Stein." Willow walked down a few steps. "What brings you all this way, and so early?"

James smiled at Willow and pointed a finger at her, his seersucker suit perfectly tailored and without a single wrinkle. His driver brought one small bag to him, and James put one hand on the driver's shoulder and said, "Go back to town and check in, and I'll call you shortly." His driver nodded and returned to the car.

James walked over slowly and stood at the bottom of the steps. Willow met him down there, and he took the coffee from her and said, "You read my mind." She let him taste it, since he was being so forward. Who doesn't call before showing up, at least to give a woman a chance to shower? His mouth twisted and he would've spat it out, she was sure, if Willow and Mya hadn't been standing there.

"You ladies like your coffee with a punch," he said, and he handed the mug back to Willow and wiped his mouth with a white pocket square.

Willow laughed. "It's the mountain way."

"That's new to me, I'll admit," James said.

"It's been that kind of morning."

"That I understand." James leaned to the side to look past Willow.

Willow turned. "This is my older daughter, Mya. Mya, this is James Stein, head of AGM Studios."

"Nice to meet you," James said.

Mya walked down the steps. "Did you know he was coming?"

Willow could tell the truth to Mya and say she had no idea, or she could apologize to James for her daughter being so rude, but neither sounded great. She decided to say nothing at all.

"I don't usually do this, drop in on people," James said.

"Well, now you have," Mya pointed out.

Willow frowned. "Go inside if you can't be pleasant."

"It's not a problem." James placed his black bag on the step. "I believe I've brought something you might want, Mya."

"Me?" Her eyes flared opened and she nudged Willow. Mya leaned over and whispered, "*Do* something." But by that time James had retrieved a small leather box and opened it. Wrapped inside in terry cloth and bubble wrap was the vial of perfume Mya had sent Zoe.

Mya snatched it from his hand. "How'd you get this?"

Willow examined the bottle and saw that her daughter must have been right about Zoe using too much: it was half-empty.

He closed his bag and said, "May I come in first?"

"Yes, of course," Willow said. As she passed by Mya she whispered, "Destroy it."

## CHAPTER 28
### *When One Bedroom Closes*

L UCIA RETURNED TO her bedroom after a scorching-hot shower, so hot her shoulders were still bright red, hot enough to wash away any responsibility she might've had for the death of Zoe Bennett. She had told Mya not to do it. Lucia had protested the decision. But she'd also encouraged her mother to hear Mya's plan, and how could she have known Willow would actually agree to it? Lucia stopped a moment to look at the stickers on her dresser, remnants of who she was in her middle and high school years: J/K, BESTIES, RED HOT CHILI PEPPERS, OASIS, HERBAL ESSENCES. A collection of the trivial things she'd collected and cared about. She pushed her earrings aside to look at a Beatles song lyric she'd written in permanent marker, but she accidentally knocked the jewelry behind the dresser. She pulled out the dresser and found her earrings caught in cobwebs and dirt. She also found a grimy framed photograph of herself and Ben at their junior prom.

She wiped it off with her bath towel. Ben was so much lankier then; his time working in the fields and hiking had filled out his upper body. But his big smile hadn't changed, and the cowlick at the top of his head was still there. He held Lucia like a wind might blow her away, and she looked happy. A big smile to match Ben's. A ridiculous poufy yellow-and-white empire dress she'd never wear again. A single red rose corsage he'd bought for her and placed on her wrist. On this night he'd tell her he loved her for the first time, and she'd say it back without hesitation. Days after this they gave each other their virginities—prom night would've been too clichéd for a love like theirs—and then they couldn't be stopped. They missed school sometimes because they were too impatient. Jonah had been a good partner when their marriage was happy, very giving, very eager to please her, much more experienced than Ben, of course. But now Lucia was experienced too, and she wondered just how different sex would be with Ben all grown up. She positioned the framed picture on top of her dresser, and then she put on a purple broomstick skirt and black tank top and braided her wet hair in one thick rope down her back.

Her cell phone vibrated on the bed. She knew who it was before she even saw his name. She couldn't avoid him any longer.

"Hey," Jonah said, his voice shaky, like he'd just woken up.

"Hi."

"Thanks for finally answering."

"I've been busy." That's all she owed him. She wanted him to wonder. She might not have art openings and meetings with corporate dealers, but she did have stuff to do.

"I saw Nina and she said you never came by, but your stuff was gone. Were you ever planning on calling me?"

"I'm home," Lucia said.

"I know. I talked to Mya."

"She told me. So what do I need to do?"

"What do you mean?"

Jonah always blamed this kind of flightiness on his artistic bent, but it still annoyed Lucia. "The issue. Mya said something about an issue. Do I need to sign something or pay something?"

He remained silent. She listened to his raspy breathing and wondered if he'd started smoking again in her absence.

"You did rent the place, right?" Lucia sat down on her daybed.

"Are you considering coming back?" he asked.

This wasn't his business. Why couldn't she say that to him? "I don't think so." It was the first time she'd affirmed this aloud.

"You're just giving up?" he said. "Shame."

"Excuse me?" She couldn't believe he had the nerve to talk to her like they were still married.

"Don't get mad," he said. "I was just asking."

"You know just like I do that my acting career wasn't working out," she said. And just to spite him she added, "A single girl's gotta eat, Jonah, except, I suppose, the anorexic ones." She pinched her leg for this one; she had promised herself she wouldn't be childish and bitter about their divorce.

"I guess your family's feeding you now," he said, his tone flat.

Now she wanted to hang up on him. She wished she hadn't answered the phone to begin with. "I'm working here," Lucia said.

"In Quartz Hollow?"

"Yes, in Quartz Hollow."

"They've got a good community theater?"

"Don't be an asshole." It officially sounded like they were still married, and that needed to end here. "Just tell me about the apartment."

"A banker and his boyfriend might move in next week."

"Might?" She needed more than this: she needed to know they'd no longer have a reason to communicate. Officially.

"If you don't come back, then yes."

"I'm not coming back," Lucia told him.

"Martin called me," Jonah said, "and I think you should consider taking that role. I know it's television, but it sounds steady."

Lucia laughed out loud. Yesterday had been an absurd day, but now this? "I haven't spoken to Martin in months."

"He mentioned that. You should check your messages. That lead for the kids' show you auditioned for back in November opened up."

*Eco 1-2-3.* An education show for preschoolers about the environment and climate change: nothing she was super passionate about at the time, but she would've taken it on the spot and called her mother to brag about the role she'd landed. It had potential to be long running and had a high pay rate per episode. It would've offered some security and validation. "Are you serious?"

"I won't rent out the place unless you tell me you don't want it."

This wasn't a temptation she needed right now, not with the business in such turmoil. How easy it would be to walk away. Zoe had still had a heartbeat when Lucia agreed to become president. Why should she take over her sister's mess now? But if she left and returned to New York, what her mother and sister said about her always running away would be absolutely true, and she didn't want to be that girl anymore, that same girl Jonah had met and asked to marry, the same girl Mya obviously still hoped Lucia would be.

"Just tell me this: Did Mya call you?"

A long pause gave him away. Was Mya really this desperate to get rid of Lucia?

She wasn't the kind of person to make him suffer, so she said, "I don't think I could live in that apartment anymore. Too many bad memories."

He coughed once. "Have you met someone?"

"What?"

"You heard me."

"But I don't know why you'd ask that," Lucia said. "Mya told you that?"

"You just sound like you've met someone. You sound like you've moved on."

"I moved on before I left New York," she replied, though she was lying and they both knew it, and just like that they'd swerved toward another fight. They had always operated this way, and now it was so easy to see how unhealthy they were together. "Plus, if you recall, you moved on first. That's what matters."

"I fucked up, but that doesn't mean I moved on," Jonah said, and Lucia stopped breathing for a moment.

"You asked for a divorce." Lucia could hear the confusion in her voice.

"You wouldn't look at me," he said hurriedly. "Let alone talk to me. I thought that's what *you* wanted."

Lucia could see him this minute in his studio on Eighth Avenue, the floor strewn with half-used tubes of oil paint and blank or semi-complete canvases lining the bottom of all four walls. The one window letting in a piercing ray of sunlight, and Jonah in the center, staring at it all, the light illuminating him.

"Lucia?"

"What?" she finally said.

"We weren't good married," he said. "You know I know that. But we don't have to be married. We don't have to do it that way again."

Lucia leaned her weight against the dresser and wiped away one more cobweb on her prom picture with Ben. She said, "I want great things for you, Jonah. I always have."

He sniffed and didn't speak.

"My mom's retiring and I'm taking over."

"Wow."

"Wow what?"

"I don't know. Manufacturing?"

"I know, but it's my family."

"But business? Punching numbers? That's not you."

"No?" Lucia said. "Maybe it is; maybe it always was."

"At least call Martin. At least do that. And take care of yourself," he said.

"Same to you." In the past he'd always said he loved her—that was one great thing he'd never failed to do—and she could tell his pause meant the same as hers: How to end it?

"Good luck."

"Bye." She hung up. Lucia gripped the side of the dresser and a deep, rolling feeling like molasses in her veins traveled straight from her feet to her heart. She let out a long breath. She had needed that conversation. She'd underestimated how badly she needed some closure. Why, when everything seemed to be going so wrong for her sister, did so much start going right for Lucia? What had happened to her desire? Shouldn't she be jumping up and down about a leading part, even in a children's show? Days ago she would've. She felt like that life in New York had never happened, as if she had spent all those years in this cabin instead, being prepped by her mother to take over the business, never wanting anything else. Just like Mya.

With her cell phone in hand, Lucia walked out of the bedroom and toward the voices in the kitchen. When she turned right, she first saw a very tall and distinguished older man standing at the island with a cup of coffee. Lucia stopped dead. Was he with the FBI?

Willow glanced over her shoulder and then squared herself to look at Lucia.

"This is James Stein, head of AGM Studios," Willow said, "and, James, this is my younger daughter, Lucia."

A young dragonfly had ridden in on his lapel, and Lucia reached up and gently shooed it away. She said, "Back outside." James widened his eyes for a moment and turned to Willow. "Not you," Lucia explained.

"What a relief." He extended his hand.

Lucia accepted it. "Nice to meet you." This had to be about Zoe, but she'd wait for Willow's cue before she asked questions.

The front door opened, and Mya limped into the room holding a vial of perfume in both hands. The cloud flew in above her like her parole officer escorting her inside. It had grown larger and darker, and Lucia couldn't help gasping.

"I can feel it now. It's heavy, almost like a crown."

Willow looked to Lucia to confirm.

Lucia nodded. She pointed at the bottle. "How'd you get that?"

Mya looked at James and he said, "I paid Zoe a visit."

Willow's hand landed on top of his, and the way he immediately laced his fingers in hers, it was like they were in a relationship. But her mother had never mentioned a man before. She couldn't have forgotten a boyfriend. Her memory wasn't that far gone, was it? Lucia glanced over at Mya, who was also staring at their interlaced fingers. From the way she frowned, clearly she'd never heard of him either.

"Before she, you know . . ." James took a sip of his coffee. "Before she did that, she quit my studio's biggest movie, so I went to see her and I found that vial in her bedroom."

"So you stole it?" Lucia asked.

"Essentially."

"Why'd you do a thing like that?" Mya said.

"What were you doing in her bedroom?" Lucia asked. Willow narrowed her eyes at her, but she hadn't meant to say that. It just came out.

"To the other room," Willow said. "Now."

"Everybody?" James said.

"Oh yes." Willow nodded. "We're all in this together now."

## CHAPTER 29
### *Anywhere but Here*

THEY WERE SEATED in the round room surrounded by the curving floor-to-ceiling bookcases and the overhanging loft where she and Lucia had played as girls, filled now with clutter of all kinds—old expense reports and clothes in transparent tubs labeled with black faded marker that had once clearly said *Donate*. Mya wondered who the hell James Stein was. Who was he to come all the way here unannounced with that bottle? Willow had never mentioned him before, not a single slip about a man on her mind, yet they seemed so familiar, and he knew about the family's business. He knew too much.

Lucia sat on the chaise lounge and stretched out her legs like she was on vacation. In a way she was—free room and board, offered a great job, sister falling apart like on a reality television show. All Lucia needed now was a margarita. Willow moved books off the orange wing-back chair for James, and Mya sat on the cream loveseat, waiting for them to get settled. Willow would not stop shifting items on the coffee table, as if she were making room for the drinks none of them had.

"Mom?" Mya said. "Will you sit?"

"No." She continued stacking the coasters.

James grabbed Willow's hand and said, "It might be better," and just like that, she stopped and eased herself down on the orange ottoman. Zoe's death had shocked Mya, but a man who could penetrate her mother's stubbornness shocked her more at the moment. All three women stared at James. He didn't look surprised, just unprepared. Perhaps he thought Willow's daughters didn't live at home. Perhaps he'd planned only to see Willow and never to meet Lucia and Mya in person.

James propped one ankle on his knee and smoothed his pant leg, then said, "If you need answers, I don't have any."

"Why are you here?" Lucia said.

"To deliver the perfume," he said.

"And?" Lucia prodded.

"And to see your mother," he admitted. "That wasn't clear?"

Willow smiled. How could she be falling in love now, at a time like this? She'd taken away the company from Mya, and the flowers were dying. Zoe was dead. This was no time for love. Yet Willow looked like she couldn't help herself.

"Did the perfume do it?" Lucia said. Everyone became quiet and then slowly turned their attention to Mya, whose face felt hot. Lucia, Willow, and James secretly believed, and always would, that Mya had intentionally killed Zoe Bennett. How would she ever convince them otherwise? Yes, she had ill intent. But not intent to murder.

"Zoe killed herself," James said. "Hanged herself in her home theater. *Why* she did that is up for debate."

"That's not what Peter's assistant told me. Said she overdosed," Willow said.

James coughed, rubbed his chest, and then cleared his throat again. With a scratchy voice he said, "She was in bad shape when I saw her. No shower, seemed very drunk. I didn't think she'd kill herself, but she did make a lot of strange comments about hating herself and being a hack and begged me to forgive her for being such a failure, things Zoe never would've said. She always had the confidence of a redwood."

Lucia sat cross-legged on the chaise lounge. "She was depressed. A broken heart can do that sort of thing."

"But to hate herself was not Zoe's style," James said. "Even if she was sad, she could always manage to love something about herself. When I visited her she despised everything and everyone that had made her so famous. Except the perfume. The only positive thing she talked about was the new perfume, how she'd never stop wearing it."

Willow smoothed her white hair with both hands. "That's not reason enough for you to take the perfume, I wouldn't think."

"You would," he said, "if you had smelled it on her."

At this Mya stood from her chair, but by the way James leveled his stare at her, she saw that he knew exactly what her perfume had been intended to do. Mya couldn't move.

Willow shook her head. "I don't understand."

"Mya does," James said, not once taking his eyes off her.

"Mya?" Willow said.

"I told you already," Mya said, and she began to make her exit from the room.

Willow looked back to James, and he said, "I wanted to eat her because she seemed so delicious, but I also wanted to puke her back up and flush her down the toilet. For thirty minutes I'd never felt anything so strange in my entire life. And *she* was living in it. I told her to return to the studio in the next few weeks or however much time she needed, but she locked herself in her home theater and didn't see me out. I went to her bedroom just to find that smell, and the bottle was open on her vanity. Half-empty, as you can see."

Willow closed her eyes like she'd just been told of women and children dying in some mass genocide in a faraway country.

"She used too much," Mya told him. "It's not like the usage rules had changed. But you're right about everything else, about the smell."

"But why?" James asked, like he couldn't believe her.

Sometimes that question had no place in a conversation.

Lucia said, "Look, Zoe's dead, and it was nice that you brought it back, but it could make us look guilty, right? I mean, if she was bragging about the perfume to *you*, who else heard about it? Her manager knows."

"That occurred to me," James said, "and I still took it."

"So you think we're guilty?" Willow said.

He rested his hands in his lap. "Do you think you're guilty?"

Willow shook her head and then looked at Mya. Mya said, "Someone else might've made a different decision, given the same perfume. She didn't have to kill herself."

"That's true," James said, "but did you consider what kind of personality you were dealing with before you made it?"

Mya shifted in her chair. Attention-obsessed Hollywood narcissist. Of course she'd thought about it. James Stein didn't think Mya was innocent; there wasn't even a sliver of hope. He'd turn her in. That's the kind of man her mother was attracted to, apparently, and it was sickening. He had no loyalty to the business or to her family. Mya said defiantly, "She made a choice and I won't be made to feel guilty about it."

"Let's say she didn't kill herself. Your plan was to make a perfume, take a large amount of Zoe's money for it, and kill her career at the same time?" James said. "That's ethical to you?"

Mya nodded.

"But *you* selected her," James said.

"Now, hold on," Willow protested.

"No." Mya stood up. "He's right. Revenge isn't ethical, but neither is greed. Zoe made the first mistake here. She should've stayed where she belonged. Cameo roles are one thing, but she had to climb and she knew it was wrong. That's why she didn't tell us about Schol's film. She deserved a consequence."

Lucia said, "She deserved to die?"

"I didn't want her to die. I just didn't want her career to ruin Jennifer Katz. I mean, that's not ethical either, right? Not on Zoe's part, not on our part."

James looked at the ceiling, and Mya followed his gaze there but found nothing but the same old skylight.

Lucia said, "You could've accepted the consequences of your contract mistake."

"And let Zoe ruin the business?" Willow finally stepped in to defend Mya. It was about time. "That wasn't a decision I could make, and you wouldn't have either. You either, James, so nobody start in with the high and mighty today."

"I would've called Zoe's bluff," Lucia said. This made Mya want to toss a book at her sister. "She needed us more than we needed her; she would've quickly figured that out."

"After she did some damage," James agreed. "She was impulsive." Again he looked right at Mya. Why did he keep doing that?

"So what?" Lucia said. "It would've been a glitch in the business. Not a tragedy, not like this."

Finally, her mother's face pinched with annoyance. Willow said, "I'm sorry you weren't the one to make all the decisions."

"You honestly think that was the best decision?" Lucia asked.

"I did."

"It doesn't matter now," Mya told them. "It's over."

"I hope the report comes back inconclusive." James stood up from his chair. "But I wouldn't want to live with that."

"Well," Mya said, "you won't have to." She didn't like this man at all. And he did not like Mya. It was palpable in the room. He didn't seem to like Lucia much either, so that helped Mya a little.

Willow stood with him. "Take a walk with me?"

"I should go," he said.

"Just a short one, while you wait for your driver."

"Nice to meet you two." He walked out of the round room and back through the kitchen to the front door. Willow said nothing and followed him out.

Mya picked at her cuticles and waited for the front door to shut before she said, "Bastard."

"He did us a favor," Lucia said. "I think."

"Are you my sister?" Mya said, looking directly at Lucia.

"What's that supposed to mean?"

"What I said."

"Yes. Obviously, I'm your sister."

"Then act like it for a change."

"Fine," Lucia said, "act like this is a big deal and I will."

"I'm terrified. How can you not see that?"

"You're scared that you might die." It pained Mya to hear this confirmed. "Not about Zoe and what this means for us."

The phone rang in the office and Mya's heart pounded faster with each ring. "You know what it is," Mya said.

"Should I answer it? Or get Mom?"

Mya and Lucia hurried to the office, and Lucia stared at the phone like it might go up in smoke. "Pick it up," Mya said.

Lucia snatched the phone and said, "Lenore Incorporated—no, this is Lucia Lenore, that's right . . . No, she's not here . . . Now, hold on, Peter, you can talk to me about that . . . I don't think that's a good idea—hold on, let me ask her, but I doubt it."

Mya chewed her fingernails. She *hated* listening to other people's telephone conversations, especially when she happened to be the subject.

Lucia put him on hold and dropped the phone on the desk. "He's so pissed, oh my God."

"Tell me." Mya stood right next to her at the table.

"He's accusing you of crazy things, of killing her on purpose, of getting rid of evidence. He wants to press charges but can't."

A wave of relief swept over Mya. "Why not?"

"The report came back. She had trace amounts of prescription drugs in her blood but that was it. Normally not fatal, but that's what they're blaming it on, saying she was sensitive to it. Peter swears he knows it's not true and all the papers are writing about Zoe's drug problem. He's weeping. Just weeping and screaming and wants to speak to you and only you. Breathe."

Mya hadn't noticed she'd stopped until Lucia pointed it out, and she finally inhaled, her lungs burning. She said, "What should I do?" She wanted Lucia to say, "Don't speak to anyone," but instead her sister shrugged and offered up the phone to Mya.

"You decide," Lucia said.

Mya accepted the receiver and Lucia pushed the button. "This is Mya Lenore," she said.

Peter Sable, who was a legendary entertainment-industry hard-ass, remained silent on the other end of the line. Mya almost hung up until she heard him cough.

"Peter?" she said softly.

"I don't even know what to say," he said in a voice so low and so hoarse that she almost didn't recognize it.

"How about you call back later then?"

He grew louder as he said, "But I know what you did. No one can prove it, but I know that it was here and what it did to her. I watched her use it and saw how much she changed. As soon as it touched her skin she turned into someone else, someone deluded and angry and sad and ill, and now it's just gone. How'd you get your hands on it? Where is it?"

"Peter," Mya said, "I have no idea what you're talking about."

"Sure you don't. Not on the phone you don't."

"Is that all?" She scratched her snakebite bandage with her nails.

"You watch out," Peter said. "You hear me? You think you can't be touched?"

"Excuse me?"

"You heard me, I know you did," Peter spat, and hung up.

Mya's mouth remained open as she handed the phone back to Lucia. "What happened?"

Mya dropped onto the couch and put her head between her legs, taking deep breaths to curb the oncoming panic. The other side of the couch dipped and Mya felt Lucia rubbing her back. Lucia asked, "Seriously, what just happened?"

She couldn't talk. Where was her breath?

"Mya," Lucia pleaded. "Talk to me."

She shook her head back and forth.

Lucia said, "Are they pressing charges or something?"

Mya continued to shake her head, and she squeezed her eyes shut tight. She'd never meant to hurt Zoe, not like this. But no one would believe her. She gripped her hair and finally found her voice: "He told me to watch out."

"For what?" Lucia said naïvely.

Mya finally sat up and laughed at how childish her sister could be sometimes. "For whatever's coming."

"He threatened you?"

"I'm pretty sure," Mya said.

"You think he meant it, or he was just upset?" Lucia kept her hand resting on Mya's back. They'd lost this kind of affection so many years ago that it felt foreign to Mya now, but it brought her comfort and she was grateful.

"He meant it," Mya said. "This is it, I told you."

Lucia moved to the edge of the couch and put her hands together. She said, "Then you need to go. You can't stay here."

Mya shook her head. "I won't feel safe anywhere but here."

"You'll need to go somewhere until we hear from him again. I don't think you did it on purpose, but I do think you've always been reckless, and that's why we've come to this."

Mya wanted to respond with some forceful comeback, but her entire body felt like a dried leaf crumbled beneath a boot. It was true, what her sister said. Why did her actions have such permanent results? Other people seemed to make mistakes that worked out just fine in the end. She couldn't stand being Mya Lenore sometimes, and she had no idea how to fix herself.

## CHAPTER 30
## *Experiments*

F ROM THE WAY Mya stared at the slow spin of the ceiling fan and refused to speak, Lucia could tell that her sister didn't want company, at least not Lucia's, so when Mya called Luke to come pick her up, Lucia slipped out of the office with her mother's laptop and went to the kitchen. Lucia searched Zoe's name. She needed proof of her death.

Zoe's movies still played. Her red carpet appearances streamed on YouTube with millions of viewers, more now than ever before. Her name appeared on page after page of Google hits that heralded her overdose. She lived; at least that's how it felt. All over the world people blogged with sad messages for a woman they felt they knew but never had the chance to meet, hope of that day dying along with her. The world loved her, apparently, and had lost her and grieved her. It was as if Mya had bestowed on Zoe the exact amount of attention she'd always wanted.

Lucia closed out the browser and shut her mother's laptop. Too much was happening now. She drummed her fingers on the black machine and wondered if she was foolish to stick around and take on not just a failing company but a compromised one. No sane person would do that. She had a job waiting for her, a paid apartment, maybe even regular sex with her ex-husband. All she had to do was make the call to her agent.

Except she couldn't *feel* the desire. Just *poof*—no longer there. Lucia had been defined by doubt her entire life: she doubted her family gifts, and they never presented themselves; she doubted her marriage, and it ended; she doubted her acting skills, and her career never took off. Now she doubted what felt like her last option in the world, one that, for whatever reason, she believed could work. A storm was brewing all around Lucia here at home, and at any point a lightning bolt might strike her. She needed more than ever to trust that she could handle this. That she might even be the one to help.

Lucia's phone buzzed as Mya walked past her at the table. Without stopping she said, "Luke's here, we're going for a drive." Lucia turned around to ask her when she'd be back but she'd already shut the door.

Ben had sent Lucia a text message: *Can I come by now instead of tonite?* She texted: *That's fine.* He wrote back, *See u soon,* and Lucia cradled the phone between her palms.

LUCIA CLEANED UP THE MORNING dishes but couldn't handle the quiet in the cabin. She walked outside and sat in the gazebo to listen to the stream passing underneath. The tall meadow grass moved so fluidly that at first Lucia hadn't noticed the small breeze. She took a deep breath, hoping to smell the family flower, just as she had for so many years as a girl, but now the scent no longer hung over her like a cloak. She ached for its sweet, pungent return. To lose the flower would be like losing a mother or a father, and they couldn't afford to lose another family member. Not that she had any memories of her father. She did have memories of the flower, and as such, it would be a much greater loss. How was it that she still had time to sit at a place like this alone and hear the water pass, the crickets chirp in the grass, and the wind maneuver through the leaves all around as if a client hadn't died that morning, as if the world around her wasn't in chaos?

Ben's truck moved up the driveway. Lucia wasn't sure what she would do with more quiet without answers, so the sound of his door opening was a welcome one. Ben didn't see her at the gazebo at first and she watched him pull out his bag, his biceps like one of the smooth stones from the creek below. His T-shirt hugged his chest as he stretched over his truck bed to shut a storage unit. He smiled as he made his way toward the cabin.

"Ben!" Lucia called, and he glanced around to find her. She waved, and he finally spotted her and walked up the few steps into the gazebo. "Missed you there," he said.

"Sorry," Lucia said. "I needed some air and the porch swing's taken." She pointed toward the cabin, where dragonflies continued to zip vertically, freeze, and disappear, able to change direction so swiftly that Lucia could stay outside all day long and watch them.

"Still here?" he asked, and at first Lucia thought he was referring to her. Lucia's extended stay in New York City had made her forget how long the dragonfly season lasted, but as much as she tried, she couldn't remember a time when there were so many, and so close to the cabin.

Ben dropped his heavy bag on the table. "Appreciate you letting me come early."

"It's fine," she said. "We appreciate you coming at all." He must have made a date for the evening with Vista, and this interrupted their schedule, so that's why he couldn't come at five. "And don't worry about dinner," she added.

"About that . . ." Ben wiped his brow with the back of his hand.

"It's okay, really," Lucia said. "Another time."

"No," he said, and Lucia's face grew hot. That was a rather blunt rejection. "Not like that," he said. "I meant no about canceling dinner. I was just hoping you'd come to my place early tonight and let me cook for you this time."

"Really?" she said. Technically, she was aware that there were men in the world who cooked for women (often she viewed them chopping and mixing and kneading on culinary shows), but she'd never met one before. She thought about how she and Jonah had been experts at dining out, and then she stopped herself. Would there ever be a time when she didn't compare her life now as single Lucia to her life then as miserably married Lucia? This state of limbo could not make for a happy life.

Ben appeared embarrassed by her surprise. "I like showing off the kitchen."

"Oh, if that's all," Lucia said. "In that case . . ."

"I just want to hang out with you like old times," he said. "We can ride over after this."

How had she forgotten what to do when a boy said something like this? Flip her hair? Bat her eyes? Purse her lips? Stare in a cold and unforgiving way just to make him sweat? Why be compelled to do anything at all? Instead laughter exploded from deep inside her and his face fell. She waved her hand and said, "I really want to, I swear."

"But?"

"No but," Lucia said. "I want to."

"Roast okay?"

"Perfect."

"Ready?" Ben said, and picked up his bag and hung it on one shoulder, then left the gazebo.

She followed him down the stairs. "We can go around that way." Lucia pointed toward the cherry trees and they began their walk to the flowers. Just as they rounded the cabin, her mother and James were making their way back, hand in hand.

"Who's that?" Ben said, and stopped.

"I guess he's my mother's boyfriend, I don't really know. I'd never heard about him until this morning." Lucia squinted at them in the distance.

"Why's he here?" Ben suddenly sounded protective. Back in high school he'd been the only man regularly around the house.

"Long story," Lucia said.

Willow and James walked directly to them, and Willow first gave Ben a hug and then introduced him to James.

Lucia said, "Mya's out with Luke."

"But at breakfast I told her not to leave."

Lucia shrugged. "She's with Luke and I'm sure it's fine, and we're going to Ben's after we look at the fields."

"We'll just stay here then and wait for Mya," Willow said to James, and he nodded. Lucia didn't want to think about what might go on in the empty house. She should tell Willow about Peter Sable's phone call, but it could wait. No reason to ruin this moment for her mother.

Willow turned to Ben. "Let me know as soon as you find something."

"I will," Ben said. James took Willow's arm and they continued walking. Lucia watched them as they headed back to the cabin. No space was visible between their bodies, and Lucia didn't know what to say. Her mother could be so secretive sometimes. She'd fallen in love and told no one.

"James seems like a good guy," Ben said as they continued their walk.

"How do you know? He didn't speak."

"I just know," Ben said.

They crested the hill, and Lucia caught sight of hedges that should have had blossoms white and grand, just like a bride. Yet here at the top of the hill those blossoms were choking with green. The tips of the flowers were still white, but that was all, like fingertips poking from a green sinkhole. "This isn't right."

"It looks much worse," Ben said. "Your mother didn't say anything about that."

"I can't figure her out," Lucia told him. "Seriously, it's like she's just given up. I'm worried."

"Let's just see." Ben led Lucia down the rows. She stared at the dying flowers as she passed and thought about her great-grandmother Serena and all the years of successful business. These fields looked like some alien species. This couldn't be their family's flower. Her family's flower could not be weakened, let alone wiped out.

They neared the end of the shrubs, and wilderness stretched for many miles beyond that. Ben placed his hand on Lucia's shoulder and said, "You can come help me if you want." It was like asking if she wanted to apply makeup to her mother's corpse.

"That's okay," she said, demurring. "I'll wait here."

Lucia found a boulder near the tree line and climbed up. She rested supine on the flat top, draped one arm over her eyes to shield them from the sun, and held her breath as she waited for Ben to finish his work. But she could hear him nearby—the snip of his scissors, the yank of a hedge from the ground, the shake of the dirt from the roots—and it was all too much like an autopsy.

Eventually, she heard his boots in the grass and then felt his hand tugging on her overhanging foot. Lucia propped herself up on the boulder and looked down at him.

"Just like those blueberry fields," he said, and smiled at her with all the knowing of the teenage boy he once was. She wasn't expecting this from him, more like "The flower's completely dead. Your family's business is finished." But this? No matter how preoccupied she was, she could remember how she never picked the blueberries because she liked watching his back muscles contract as he bent over and stripped the bushes of their bounty. He would bring those ripe, warm berries to her mouth and feed her, and when they kissed it tasted of summer juice. The blueberry field was one of their favorite places to make love. She might've forgotten some moments they shared, but not that. Obviously, he still remembered too. They stared at each other's sunlit faces. It had been ages since she'd had sex, and all Lucia wanted to do was wrap her legs around him and hang on. *To hell with Vista*, she thought, though instantly this made her feel bad—but he'd mentioned the blueberries for a reason.

He anxiously looked through his work bag and said, "I left something, I'll be back." He set down the hedge sample he'd uprooted, the stems slightly flaccid, and turned to walk back to the rows from which he came. That's when Lucia saw it, and it made her whip her head around in disbelief—the green flowers leaned after him like children reaching out for a parent. She wasn't imagining anything. Lucia hopped down next to the hedge sample. The flowers leaned in Lucia's direction now. Their roots were no longer in the ground; they moved. They absolutely moved. She bent down next to a flower and held out her hand, and the green, dying blossom stretched out to meet her and rested in the palm of her hand. She'd heard the stories. Her mother made this happen when they were girls, but the flowers had never moved for Lucia or Mya. Ben had to witness this or her mother wouldn't believe her—the flowers couldn't be dying if they were still moving. She stared after him, at his tan neck and the buzzed hair on his head.

Lucia called, "Ben, wait up," and ran after him. He stopped and turned, waiting with a confused and frightened look on his face, like some disaster had occurred. She had every intention of stopping and speaking and telling him to come back to the flowers and see, he had to see what they were doing—this was what she willed—but she couldn't stop running; she had no control. Ben held out both arms, and Lucia put both of her arms around his strong neck and felt his soft hair underneath her fingertips, and before she could kiss him first his mouth was already on hers and her body exploded with warmth. They kissed and stroked each other; Lucia kept her eyes closed, but then she felt him watching her and she opened them. His eyes wrinkled at the sides as he smiled. She smiled back, and out of the corner of her eye she saw something move like the flight of a dragonfly.

"Did you see that?" Lucia said, and Ben looked over, then shook his head and brought Lucia's mouth back to his. She kissed him again but still stared over at the flowers. He followed her eyes over, and then they both pulled away from each other.

"Did they just do that?" Ben asked incredulously.

"I think so." Lucia didn't know what to do. She wanted to kiss him again because it felt so good after so long, but she also wanted to test the flowers. But he went first and kissed her with more passion than he had before. He stopped only when the flowers closest to them leaned over and brushed against their legs.

He jerked away and said, "Holy shit," and the flowers immediately retracted.

Lucia was too elated to feel scared, but Ben looked frightened. "Lucia," he said quietly, like the flowers might hear him.

She moved away from him and said, "I know." She bent down to touch the flowers and they didn't move, but then she reached out for Ben's hand and he interlaced his fingers with hers. When she reached out again, the woody stems bent like rainbows, and the green petals lifted to Lucia. Ben squeezed Lucia's hand, and the flower continued to rise. The green on the petals began to recede just slightly, and the scent emerged.

"This can't be explained." Ben looked up like he needed an escape route. "No rational answer, not a single one."

Lucia stood up from the flower and it moved back; the leaves began to turn green and thick again, and the smell vanished. Lucia reached out to Ben, put her hand on one of his cheeks, and kissed him again lightly, then let her hands move under his shirt and up to his smooth, contoured chest. He kissed her back.

"Like an experiment." Lucia cast her eyes down to the grass.

"You mean . . . ?"

Lucia nodded.

"Right here?"

"Here," she said, and Ben kissed her neck and then her collarbone and quickly lifted her shirt off her body like all he'd needed was her permission. He removed her bra and kissed each breast softly, cupping them in his hands. Lucia closed her eyes in deep pleasure and guided his body to the ground.

## CHAPTER 31
## *Onset and Past*

JAMES HELD HER hand on the walk but didn't try to kiss or hug her, and Willow refused to be the one to initiate it after the night they'd spent together in the L.A. hotel room, a night she had been sure she wouldn't forget for as long as she lived, like some smitten schoolgirl. But now she couldn't remember if she'd kissed him first, if he'd asked to stay or if she'd asked him. It had been only a few days, but she couldn't remember, and this made her too anxious to concentrate on romance.

Instead, they talked. About the flowers and Willow's grandmother Serena and how she discovered the plant that first time in Borneo and how deeply in love she had been with her husband, and about Willow's mother, who'd died widowed but still very much in love with Willow's father. The word "love" kept coming up in every context except between Willow and James. Yet she felt a deep urge for James, like she had when she first met him. Now her knees ached, and she mourned all those youthful years when she could've been in love with James and had a successful relationship like her mother and Grandmother Serena had.

When they returned to the cabin, Willow knocked the mud off her hiking boots against the bottom porch step. James copied her even though he had opted not to step in the mud at the bank of the pond, a place he insisted he wanted to see rather than the fields of flowers. Willow hadn't been in the mood to see the flowers either. Before stepping into the cabin James said, "I don't think your daughters approve of me."

Willow laughed. Perhaps returning to the house reminded him of the girls; he hadn't mentioned them once during the walk, not even when they passed Lucia and Ben. "They're not sure what to think of you."

"My mother never was either," he said. "The loud one, that's how she thought of me."

This was the first time he'd mentioned his childhood. "I was the reliable one," Willow said.

James took Willow by the arm as they entered through the red door, the wrens shooting out of their nest of eucalyptus branches. James ducked out of their way. "Do they do that every time?"

"Almost," Willow said. "But only if they like you."

James slowly inched his way around the door like more might fly out if they spotted his movement.

"Want some tea?" Willow said, and left him at the doorway peering into the empty nest. Willow removed the loose-leaf green tea from the cabinet and kept an eye on James as she prepared their cups, but he didn't notice, as he was too busy inspecting the framed pressed-flower arrangements decorating the walls.

"It's quiet," James said. "No daggers in the room."

"I'm sure they think you're my boyfriend," Willow said as she filled the kettle at the sink, "and they're mad I didn't tell them. I know my girls."

"Is that far off?" James pulled out one of the wooden chairs at the table and sat down.

"About as far off as China." Willow flashed a small smile at him. "I don't date."

"Me either," he said. "Too busy."

"Exactly." She secured the top on the kettle and lit the stove.

"But then there's you," James said, "and the whole not being able to stop wondering what you're doing or where you are. And now I know. This place is beautiful, Willow. I see why you hate coming to L.A. The land rolls on like a woman's curves."

Willow said, "I might not've described it that way, but I've always loved it." The teakettle boiled and began to whistle, so Willow pulled it off the stove and filled her white porcelain teapot. Sharing space with James felt natural to Willow, as if they'd carried out this morning routine before.

Willow offered a teacup to James and placed the pot in the center of the table.

"And when you retire, will you stay?" James said.

She sat down next to him. "Who made up that fantasy?"

"It'll happen," he said. "Maybe you don't want to retire."

Willow tried not to stare at his mouth as he talked. She couldn't help wondering about those lips and wanting to feel them against her mouth again, but she didn't want to let on. She said, "Maybe I'll buy an island, just a small one."

James laughed. "Move-in ready, complete with a landing strip?"

"Nothing else will do," she said.

"I want to hire a captain for my yacht and just go."

"That sounds fun too." Willow checked the teapot to see if the leaves had finished steeping. As she poured his cup she said, "You can sail over to my island and visit."

"Thank you." James brought the tea to his mouth, took a small sip, and put the cup down. "But what if I want more?"

"There should be more in the pot," Willow said, peering into the teapot and checking the level once more. "There's still some." She took her first bitter sip and then squeezed a lemon slice and dropped it into her cup.

James laughed and placed his hand on top of Willow's, and it was so warm and so large that she couldn't see her hand anymore. "I meant with you."

"Oh," Willow said. "Oh."

"Oh, no? Or oh, yes?"

"Oh, I don't know."

"What good will retirement be without companionship?"

She paused for a moment. "I've been with people for as long as I can remember. Mya's never left home. Some time alone might be nice."

"Maybe for a year or two, but then what?" James wouldn't let her hand go.

Willow didn't know why she was arguing for something she didn't really believe. She didn't want to be alone, yet his offer had come so suddenly and so directly that she didn't know how to respond except to push him away. A little bit of romance would've been nice. This felt more like a negotiation. "You hardly know me," she said.

"Not true," he said. "I know the younger you, and that's how we'll live in retirement."

"I don't even know if you have kids."

"Catching up gives us something to do while we sail," James joked, but Willow shook her head, because this wasn't good enough.

"I hate sailing," she said.

He rested against the chair back. "Two kids, five grandkids, two ex-wives," he said, like he was listing off his résumé.

"Really?" she said. "You must be difficult to live with."

"I am," he said. "But I'm good at other things that they didn't appreciate."

"That's a worn-out excuse." Willow finished her cup of tea.

"How about I show you and we can discuss this more later?" James moved his hand now to Willow's thigh, and this made her cough. She wiped some tea from her lips and said, "James?" her southern accent so suddenly prominent that even Willow noticed it.

"May we go to your room?" he said.

"But you haven't finished your tea." Willow's heart felt like a drum tattooing in her chest.

"Willow," he said flatly.

"What?" she said in a panicky voice.

"Show me your room." James stood up with his hand outstretched for her to take.

The girls could walk in at any moment and hear them, and she'd be mortified, and then there was the issue of her not having had regular sex for the past ten years. All this caused Willow to hesitate. She felt palpitations like the kind leading to a heart attack. What if she forgot what to do? She wasn't flexible anymore. What if her thighs seized up with cramps and she cried out and had to stop? Or what if her vagina simply didn't work anymore? Too dry, maybe, and she hadn't planned this, so she didn't have any coconut oil to assist them. Didn't she worry about all of this that night in L.A., or was she so drunk that it never occurred to her? Why couldn't she remember?

When she didn't take his hand, he finally let it fall on her head; he stroked her hair and she leaned into his pant leg. "We can just nap," he said. And the more he stroked her head, the deeper she moved against his body, and the smell of his skin and the bergamot and oakmoss and lingering neroli from his cologne made Willow's body warm to him. She breathed deeper and took him in and had no idea what was happening to her. This man she'd known for such a short amount of time felt so much like the man she was always meant to love. Immediate. Undisputed. Outrageous. And he seemed to feel the exact same way about her. She rolled her cheek against his leg and then looked up at him, and he cupped her chin in his hand and she said, "I'm not too tired."

"You're not?" he said.

She said, "My room's got the best bed in the house." She stood up and kissed him on the mouth, then said, "I'd like to show you."

TUCKED TIGHTLY BENEATH THE COVERS, Willow's body felt drugged and buoyant, like a leaf floating in a pond. She'd awoken to the sound of a tree branch tapping at her window. James slept beside her, snoring lightly and with a small dribble of drool on the pillow. She'd lived alone for so long that a sight like that would've been reason enough to make her turn away from anyone else but him. She kept her arms by her sides and rested there, motionless, afraid to move for fear of rousing him. She hoped he'd want to have sex again, because she couldn't believe what she'd been missing out on all these years. It's not like she hadn't had good sex before, but she'd forgotten, and not because her memory was bad. Too long without a good thing, even just a few days, apparently, makes anyone forget. She'd forgotten like she might a cholesterol pill—missed one and didn't even realize it.

James's deep breathing made one stray hair on his pronounced forehead fly up and then back down, and the longer she watched this the more convinced she became that she wanted to see this exact peaceful sight each day when she woke up for as long as she had good health. She reached over to move the hair away from his brow, and the moment her skin touched his, his eyes opened. "It's okay," Willow said softly. "Go back to sleep."

He said, "Can't," and pulled her closer to him. She snuggled against his warm body and put her head on his soft patch of chest hair.

"That's what I needed," he said, and played with her earlobe.

She kissed his rib. "Let's go."

He said, "Just need a minute."

Willow said, "I mean let's travel together. Retire and roam the world. Twice. Three times over."

James swept Willow's hair to the side so he could look in her eyes and said, "Serious?"

"Very," she said, and nothing had ever made her feel sixteen again quite like this. It was like she had another stretch of youth before her.

"Think about it, if you need time."

"I have," Willow said. "I've thought about it for years. I just needed you to come along."

He squeezed her.

"Plus, I have so much money that I never spend," Willow said. "It seems shameful, really. Some economy could use it."

His stomach caved in when he laughed. "How much is so much?"

"You can't imagine how much," Willow said. "That much."

"So you'll be my sugar mama?"

"Guess so," Willow said.

James tickled her hip.

"But there's one thing." She needed to tell him. Had to tell him. It was only fair.

James readjusted the pillows behind him and sat up. "I'm joking. I've got my own funds, don't worry."

"No," Willow said, "nothing like that. It's just . . . Well—I think you should know that the only reason I'm retiring right now is a problem I'm having."

"Come here." James draped an arm around Willow's bare shoulders and pulled her closer. Her instinct was to be on the farthest side of the bed while she told him. "What's that mean?"

"Some days are okay," she said. "When I've rested enough and don't have a lot of stress to deal with. I've had a good stretch recently since Lucia came home and agreed to take over the business, but for the past few years I've been forgetting things."

"I forget things too."

"But not like this," Willow said. "I forget names all the time. I sometimes forget where I'm going when I'm driving, like to town or somewhere familiar with a set destination in mind, and suddenly a place I've seen my whole life looks totally foreign and it takes me a long time, hours sometimes, to figure out how to get home, and I panic and I weep. I hadn't told anyone until it happened at night after I went to see a movie in town and I couldn't remember how to get home. I had to pull over and sleep in the truck. A police officer who I've known since he was a boy found me. It was utterly humiliating. I've told my assistant."

James held her tighter. "But not Mya?"

Willow shook her head. "Mya and Lucia are both suspicious. I haven't told them how bad it is yet. But I feel like you should know before you really decide to be with me." James began to shake his head but Willow said, "I mean it, I don't know how long we'll have, and I could end up forgetting you altogether. Maybe soon, maybe not. I forgot the first time we met, and I'm so scared that'll happen again. That I'll forget everyone I love and it'll hurt."

James didn't move and he didn't protest. "You've seen a doctor?"

Willow nodded. "Months ago. It's early-onset Alzheimer's." She covered her mouth. "That's the first time I've said it."

James leaned over to look Willow in the eyes. "Is it recommended you stay here where you can see your doctor regularly?"

"I haven't broached that topic yet," she said. "But I want some freedom to enjoy my life without concern, even if it's just for six months. I know that's irresponsible, but I can't help it."

James remained silent and Willow said, "You're having second thoughts; I understand that completely."

Willow used to believe consciousness and the spirit existed after the body, but now, piece by piece, who she was died with every word forgotten, every malfunction of her brain. She'd changed her mind about all this in this last stretch to the finish of her life. The account doesn't function if there's no manager watching over it, and without awareness of a self, no self existed. She wanted to enjoy her body and be aware of her mind for as long as she had left.

James took her chin in his hand. "I support what you think's best. You want to go, that's your choice. A personal doctor can travel with us—whatever it takes. I fell in love with you the first time I met you and I never forgot it, so you won't either. What I want now is time with you, as soon as I can have it." He kissed her gently, stroked her hair, and held her for a long time.

Willow had almost fallen asleep when he said, "Excuse me." He rolled out of bed, his bare ass strong and high, his calf muscles defined. He entered her bathroom, and it was an odd sight, a man in there. He called, "Anywhere good to dine in Quartz Knot?"

"Quartz Hollow," she said, and heard him say, "Oh yeah," to himself. *He likes to talk while he's in the bathroom. Can you deal with that?* the single woman inside Willow asked, and the single woman decided she could, but that she also needed to keep a tally of his strange behaviors and check in with herself regularly to make sure she could accept them. No point in going it alone this long just to sacrifice her peace at the end. They would not marry, she was convinced of that, but still, cohabitation required commitment, and commitment required practice, and she'd been out of practice in that area too. She'd have to compromise.

Willow waited for the door to open and for him to reappear before she said, "There's a farm-to-table place I think you'll like."

He climbed on top of her and put his full weight on her body before he kissed her, then rolled back to his side and buried himself under the covers.

"What about your girls?" he said.

"What about them?" Willow covered her breasts with the cotton sheet.

"Will they come?"

"Are you joking?"

"I wasn't, no."

"That's about the last thing I think they'd want to do, especially

Mya. She's not happy that I've asked Lucia to be president. And now Zoe," Willow said. "I think we can plan on just the two of us."

"And Mya?" James asked. "What will she do now?"

"That I don't know. Once Lucia left home I always expected Mya to take over. But you can't force what's not right—I learned that with their father, in fact."

"You haven't mentioned him before." James readjusted his back so he was sitting up against the leather headboard.

"Such a long time ago, really, it feels like an unrelated life." Willow snuggled closer against James. His skin radiated so much heat that a blanket wasn't necessary. "Mya had the most time with him and looks the most like him, but Lucia never met him. He did have charm like her though. He was a jazz musician. I met him a few years after I'd graduated from high school, on a trip to San Francisco. I was supposed to take over the business for my mother soon after my trip. I went out there for fun and shopped for vintage couture. I stopped at a bar one night in the Haight and he was playing. I danced and he bought me a drink after, at least I think that's how it happened. Either way, that's where I met him. My sister had already moved away from home and I was the only one to be chosen. I liked the work, but I was scared and wasn't ready for that life of responsibility. A lot like Lucia and Mya, I guess, though I was much younger. I met a mysterious guy, and he was a sure way out. I stayed out there with him and spent my early twenties going to bars and watching him play, until I got pregnant with Mya. We lived together north of San Francisco, in a cabin in the redwoods. He skipped out when I was pregnant with Lucia."

"What was his name?" James said.

"Michael." Willow laughed. "I haven't said his name aloud in a very long time."

"Do the girls ever see him?"

"No," Willow said. "They never saw him again. And you can

imagine how mad my mother was when I finally returned to take over and I was saddled with two small children."

James held Willow's hand and she had nothing left to say. She rested her head on his bare stomach and he continued to stroke her hair. The perfume can't prevent a family death; that's what Willow had thought as her mother lay ill with pneumonia in this exact room. With her white curly hair spread across the pillow in the room with a window looking out on the hills, she had taken Willow's smooth hand (the wrinkles she had now were so distant then) and said, "Pass it on when you no longer love it." A young and grieving twenty-nine-year-old Willow thought that could never happen. How could she ever fall out of love with the family business? For years now she'd imagined herself working until the day she dropped dead of a stroke, just like her own sister, but now she knew she'd likely die of something less immediate. She could live a very long life but die without a clue of her whereabouts or her own history.

If she didn't pass the business on to a Lenore woman, no one else could make the flowers grow. And God help her, she had two healthy daughters who seemed far less capable of what Willow's mother had asked of her when she was seven years younger than Mya and a mother of two young children. Willow often thought it had something to do with their father's genetic material. She didn't allow herself to think of Michael very often, though one glance at Mya and she couldn't help but remember him. She had his sly mouth and sandy blond hair. No one falls in love with a musician and doesn't know on some level that he might go. But love never guaranteed longevity. Neither did vows, which Lucia had now discovered.

Michael had left without leaving a note to tell her where he went or why. She suspected the stress of never securing steady work broke him, but she didn't know for certain. Had she been more mature, she might not have cursed him by taking their courthouse wedding photo and poking out his eyes with a rabbit's rib bone. She sealed the mouth, hands, and feet of his image with red wax, then placed the photo before a black candle that burned to the bottom of its wick, banishing him from their lives. She was protecting her girls from a man like that, someone so undependable.

She had loved Michael, the way his hands curved around the guitar, and she hated him for leaving, and that kind of passionate anger fills the body and invades everyone nearby until no one knows what's normal anymore. She couldn't deny, however, that Mya and Lucia were a part of him, and certainly some of their behavior could be attributed to Michael. Like Mya's not telling Willow that she planned to leave the house with Luke, despite her mother's warning. Though she had always been quick to dismiss it, Willow had wondered from time to time if their father's being absent might've hurt the girls more than she'd like to admit. Neither girl had managed to have a successful relationship, and Willow felt guilty about it all.

She glanced up at James, who was staring out the window. She wanted an excuse to stop thinking about the past. She narrowed her eyes in what she hoped was a sultry manner and said, "Again?"

He rubbed his lips together and nodded, and she opened her arms to invite him, grateful for her bed being so fully occupied after all these years, grateful for a chance to shut out the world and forget everyone but James and herself.

## CHAPTER 32
### *Paranoia*

MYA DIDN'T HAVE the energy to ask Luke about the girl who'd answered his phone, but she had to or she wouldn't be able to concentrate. She went ahead and assumed he was fucking her on the side and told herself that was okay. He said he loved Mya. So what, right? She didn't say it back and never intended to, so she couldn't expect him to stick around as her recreational entertainment. She thought he was satisfied in that area of their arrangement, but if he wasn't, she couldn't hold it against him. He was young. She was not. He wanted commitment. She did not. Why, then, did it piss her off to the tenth degree?

She needed to drive, to feel in control, despite her swollen leg. Mya loved Luke's burly truck. The deeper she drove into the Blue Ridge Parkway, the more the roads curved, the larger the overlooks became, and the more altitude they gained, the closer Mya came to asking him, mostly because he wasn't asking her much of anything, not even why she was being so quiet. Soon they had passed Crooked Overlook, the blue mountain peaks stacked against one another like folding triangles and the clouds motionless in the valley like a blanket of floating snow. Mya couldn't handle the stillness anymore.

"So who was she?" she asked. And never before had Mya felt so old.

"She?" Luke said.

Mya gripped the tattered steering wheel cover.

"You know what I'm talking about," Mya said, and the mountain walls blurred as they accelerated by. "Don't act like you don't know."

"Just one of Jena's friends." Luke tried to hold Mya's free hand but she slid it beneath her thigh.

"She didn't sound sixteen."

"Maybe she's fifteen, I don't know, all my sister's friends look fifteen." Luke looked genuinely mystified. "Why?"

Why? That was a really good question. *Why* did this matter to Mya?

Luke nudged her thigh. "Seriously, why'd you ask?"

"No reason."

"Jealous." He smiled like a little boy, his one dimple exposed.

"Don't get a hard-on." And then Mya looked over at him, taking her eyes off the winding mountain roads that she knew by heart. He wouldn't stop staring until she relented and smiled. "Maybe a little jealous," she confessed.

"Good," he said. "Mya Lenore is a normal girl."

"Normal" was not how you described a woman who made suicide spells by accident. "Normal" had never been a word Mya used to describe herself. She was not normal. Dangerous, careless, foolish, but certainly not normal. And why, of all feelings, would jealousy seem normal to anyone?

"So then you do love me?" Luke asked.

Mya turned her face away like he'd splattered grease on her. A buck stood at the edge of the road ahead of them. "Watch that," he said, and she said, "I see him."

"Don't avoid the subject," he pressed.

"I'm not." They passed the buck and he stared at their truck, then they passed a soapstone wall with a sign that read, BEWARE OF FALLING ROCKS. She'd passed the sign many times and never paid attention to it, but today it felt ominous.

"How much farther?" she said. She hadn't visited the Cascades in a few years, preferred the pond on her land to the small, cold pool at the bottom of the waterfall, but it was a nice secluded place with few visitors. A protected place. When Luke suggested it, she'd accepted like no other idea would do, but she didn't tell him about Peter Sable. Mya'd never been threatened before, and she wasn't quite sure what to do. Peter was raging, and probably she was nervous for nothing—it was absurd to think he'd come after her physically; he wasn't the Hells Angels of movie star managers—but still, the mountains and Luke were the only things that made her feel secure.

"Not far," he said. At the upcoming bend in the road, Mya spotted another herd of deer, five of them and a fawn, but Luke didn't say anything this time.

Luke changed the radio station to Rock 95.3 and the eerie sounds of Pink Floyd's "The Wall" grew louder in the cab. "You love me," Luke said. "I know you do. Mya Lenore, you love me."

She wished he'd stop talking. Perhaps he thought that if he tortured her she'd finally acquiesce. When you'd hurt and driven away as many people as Mya had, you never wanted to reveal anything again, not even the most essential of feelings. Not even love. Not even to yourself.

"You love me like your deer," Luke told her. "Admit it."

"I do not."

"But you *do*. Why's that so hard?"

"Because I don't know how, that's why," Mya said. Her body felt like it was filled with buzzing bees, and she kept her vision fixated on the deer, their bodies frozen but at any moment prepared to leap.

He reached over and squeezed her arm. "Promise me you'll try."

But before she could respond, Luke said, "Watch them," and pointed to the deer just ten feet ahead of them.

Mya peered into her rearview mirror and said, "This guy."

"What?" Luke said, and looked into his side mirror.

The driver had come out of nowhere since she last looked behind her, but that was normal on the parkway. Locals sped, the roads were windy, tourists drove slowly. Luke said, "Make him tail you, he'll get it."

"He's on my ass," Mya said, and instead of slowing down, she sped up. "He wants to pass, that fucking asshole."

"Just let him go."

Mya eased her foot off the gas and they decelerated, the herd of deer now visible in Mya's mirror. As the SUV came up on the left, Mya glimpsed a bald man in a white collared shirt and black sunglasses looking directly into their truck just as Luke said in a bewildered voice, "What the fuck's he looking at?" The SUV slowed down just ahead of them in the passing lane and didn't move over, and Mya's heart began to beat three times too fast. Luke said, "What's he doing?"

Luke reached over and blasted the car horn, which made Mya even more alarmed. This was some kind of hit man sent from L.A. because she'd killed Zoe, she knew it. The end had come for her, and she'd take Luke with her. Her arms shook and she began to make a noise like a cross between a hum and a shout, and Luke said, "Calm down," but he sounded unsure too. A sign for their turnoff to the Cascades was on the right side of the road, along with the sign for the Cascades Overlook. Just as she approached the opening on the right for the overlook parking, the SUV swerved in front of Luke's truck, cutting them off and nearly clipping the headlights. The SUV hit its brakes to handle the curve and Luke shouted, "Oh shit," as Mya tried to gain control of the wheel, and all she could see was the deep vertical drop from the overlook into the mountains below, and she wanted to close her eyes but she absolutely couldn't. Mya overcorrected to the left but slowed down to avoid rear-ending the guy, and she felt the truck trying to fishtail, but she held on to the wheel. The SUV pulled into the semicircle turnoff for the overlook, its reflection growing farther away in her side mirror. Peter Sable's hit man was not chasing her to avenge Zoe Bennett's death—and for the first time all day Mya felt relieved and happy and absolutely ridiculous for almost wrecking Luke's truck and possibly their lives because of her paranoia.

CHAPTER 33

## *Intertwined*

THE CLOUD COVER broke and freed the sunlight, but it wasn't the brightness that woke her. The scent of the flowers enveloped them like a blanket. Lucia opened her eyes and squinted until she no longer saw black spots. Her arm had intertwined with Ben's as they slept, their naked bodies attached at the hip, their clothes tossed all around them. Lucia squeezed Ben's arm and he woke to the same image: the hedge nearest them had stretched and constructed a canopy over Lucia and Ben. The hedges were taller than Lucia had ever seen them before, and the flowers were a healthy white again. Except when she propped herself up on her elbows and detached herself from Ben, the plants pulled away and the flowers began to turn green. Ben sat next to Lucia, hip to hip, and the blossoms that had been in the process of hardening and turning green were once again softening, succulent, and white as an angel.

Ben gripped her hand hard before he whispered, "It's like they healed because we . . ." But he wouldn't finish his thought.

"We what?" Lucia said, and looked over at his naked torso, the defined muscles in his abdomen, and the strength in his arms. He was better than she remembered. Much better. Enthusiastic but in control. Lucia had never had an orgasm with him all those years ago, and if it took different lovers for her to come back to Ben and be in sync with him, then she'd made the right choice. Emotionally it was like they'd never parted.

"It's too insane." He pulled his clothes over and covered his exposed lap.

"Say it."

Ben put on his shirt and stood to put on his boxers, and the flowers straightened, just like him. He stepped away from them and hurried his tasks. "Like they grew because we, you know, because."

"Had sex?" Lucia laughed, still seated in the grass.

"Exactly."

Lucia hugged her knees to her bare chest. Being naked in this field with this man—she could do this all day long. "It's not crazy."

"But it's impossible," Ben said.

"Suppose it isn't." Lucia stood up before him, and he darted his eyes away from her body but then immediately looked back.

Ben threw his hands in the air. "So they want you to have sex, that's what you think?"

"They're not perverted." Lucia put her hands on his chest. "It's not like that."

"They won't procreate unless you do?" His face turned from tight disapproval to a state of shock.

Lucia hugged him, let her ear fall against his chest, and listened to his breath. She laughed once and then again, and more, until she couldn't control herself. "That's exactly it, I think."

"No way," Ben said softly, as if he'd just found out he was having twins. "They're not flowers. They look like flowers and smell like flowers, but they're not flowers at all."

Lucia held him for fear that he might start running.

"Like they're your biological clock or something."

"People still use that phrase?"

"I don't know." Ben finally let his arms relax around her.

Lucia said, "Mom needs to retire, and soon, and Mya and I, well, we're just not in that part of our lives. I thought I was, but it didn't happen with Jonah and I never thought I'd come back anyway, even if I had kids. Figured Mya would have the babies my mother wanted. My mother and her mother and her mother's mother, they all had daughters before they were thirty. Why didn't I think about this? I don't know."

Ben was listening carefully, she could tell, but he wouldn't look at Lucia. He stared at his bare feet buried in the grass. Finally he crossed his arms and went into professor mode: "Let me, just for a moment, let me straighten this out, okay? You're telling me that I have to go see your mother, who's expecting a reason and a solution for these acres of dying plants, the very bedrock of your family's money, and I have to tell her the only way I can save the flower is to fuck her daughter?"

"'Fuck' might not be the best word." Lucia put her clothes back on. "I can tell her, don't worry. I'll just say I have to find someone and fall in love and have a baby. Or Mya does. But maybe just me, who knows?" She took a deep breath and felt a flash of heat in her body from all the responsibility that thought entailed. "Just those small things. No need for you to confirm it."

Ben didn't respond at first, and then he said, "You think it takes love to make the flowers move like that?"

"Did I say that?"

"You did," he said.

A baby alone could save the flowers. Maybe. But the past usually held the answers, and if the past was anything to go by, then Lucia knew she had to be inexplicably, vulnerably in love to fulfill the expectation. She had to love like Great-Grandmother Serena had loved her husband. Love the way Grandmother Lily had loved her husband. The way Willow must've loved Lucia's father at some point, but definitely the way she loved Mya and Lucia. To risk for love. And to sacrifice. Serena couldn't have foreseen this loveless, childless generation of Lenore women; she probably never considered that rotting fruit can hang on a healthy vine.

Lucia reached out her hand for Ben to hold. "I think I did say that."

"I can't see your mother now," Ben said, gesturing to his rumpled, grass-stained clothes.

"I understand."

"Can we go to my house? And talk about this over dinner?"

"Are you upset?" Lucia dropped his hand to give him space, but then he took it back and pulled her close.

"Terrified," Ben said, and he kissed her like fear was a necessary evil.

PART THREE

# THE DRY DOWN

## CHAPTER 34
### *Glass*

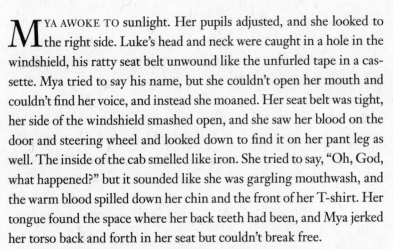

MYA AWOKE TO sunlight. Her pupils adjusted, and she looked to the right side. Luke's head and neck were caught in a hole in the windshield, his ratty seat belt unwound like the unfurled tape in a cassette. Mya tried to say his name, but she couldn't open her mouth and couldn't find her voice, and instead she moaned. Her seat belt was tight, her side of the windshield smashed open, and she saw her blood on the door and steering wheel and looked down to find it on her pant leg as well. The inside of the cab smelled like iron. She tried to say, "Oh, God, what happened?" but it sounded like she was gargling mouthwash, and the warm blood spilled down her chin and the front of her T-shirt. Her tongue found the space where her back teeth had been, and Mya jerked her torso back and forth in her seat but couldn't break free.

Her neck wouldn't move, but she could turn her eyes to the left, and she looked into the aching blue sky. So perfect, not a bad thing could go wrong beneath it. "Help me," Mya tried to say. "Somebody help." She hurriedly scanned around and noticed the trunk of a small sedan hanging over a mangled and badly bent guardrail. She began to cry. She didn't know how much blood they'd lost, but her body felt lighter and unburdened. What had she done?

Luke was right here, and she loved him, and he had to know that. "I love you," she said, and it came out as a grunt, but his body still didn't move. She squeezed her eyes, looked back out into the sky, and searched for clouds that would move for her, to show her what was to come. Not a single cloud moved, and she wanted to scream just to feel less alone. She looked back up and said, "I'll never ask to see another vision ever again, I'll never do another thing wrong. Strip me of it all, I swear, strip it, just take it away. But send someone for us. Please, God, I don't want us to die right here."

Mya felt a weight move above her, like a bird's nest being lifted from the crown of her head, and for the first time she witnessed the cloud, darker than a ripe blackberry, more frightening than a gathering tornado, like deep space or a black hole or just an endless nothing. It moved out through the broken windshield. Her heart rate quickened. She wanted to touch it, but it moved steadily away from her and across the road and up, like a helium balloon disconnected from a child's wrist. She watched it fly away, and then she wanted it to come back, because at least when it was with her she was still alive. She didn't know if this meant she would now pass into whatever came next, a "whatever" she wasn't prepared for. "Come back," she said, but it moved up faster, and a single white cloud in the sky broke open and swallowed the blip of black. Mya waited, for the world to go blank before her, for her thoughts to cease streaming, as they might have already for Luke, whose blood trailed down the hood of his truck. She was Zoe, just dying, all the same no matter how it comes, no matter who you are. She deserved this little death, all alone. Why wasn't it here, why wouldn't it come? She wished to go now, not to prolong it anymore. At least then she would've made up for all the wrong. But Luke was good, had always been so good, and it wasn't right for him to die too. Mya closed her eyes for death to come and settle, and she said, "Just me, strip me of all my power. But leave Luke behind; please don't take him too."

# CHAPTER 35
## An Irrational Leap

LUCIA DIDN'T PANIC as they hiked out of the fields, or as they snuck past the cabin, or as they loaded Ben's truck and sped out of the driveway, or as they drove through the town of Quartz Hollow to reach Ben's house. Only after they pulled into his driveway did panic settle in her chest like a thousand pounds of dirt. The dirt packed down even harder when his house came into view. She rolled down the passenger-side window to breathe and tried to push the air down farther in her abdomen, but still it was shallow. *Will I live here? In this house with Ben for the rest of my life?* Lucia asked herself this over and over again, and it shortened her already rapid breath. The future had never felt so close, yet she wasn't sure what Ben wanted. They were first loves. But a lifelong commitment? She thought he must regret running into her at the farmer's market.

"Are you okay?" Ben asked after he turned off the ignition. Lucia hadn't noticed that they'd stopped moving. Inside she couldn't slow down.

"Maybe I'm spacing out a little." She massaged her knees.

He dropped back against the headrest, and his hands held the steering wheel like he was still driving. Ben said, "Let's just have dinner and some beer and relax a minute."

"Beer won't help."

"You're right. Tequila's better."

They exited the truck, and Lucia walked beside Ben to the porch. The front door wasn't locked, and as soon as they entered, Ben dropped his work bag in the foyer. Lucia smelled beef roast and rosemary. Ben led her to his kitchen, and she took a seat at the tan-and-brown granite bar, where a Crock-Pot sat. He opened it up and ladled au jus onto the roast, then cut off the heat. He retrieved hummus and carrots from the refrigerator for appetizers.

"I can't believe how good that smells," Lucia said. Ben smiled and then retrieved a bottle of Jose Cuervo and a salt shaker from the liquor cabinet and a lime from a basket next to the phone. He brought out a knife to slice it. Lucia said, "You weren't joking."

"I don't joke about tequila," Ben said.

"The one-two," Lucia said, and he handed her a shot glass and a lime.

"You remember."

"I do." They had spent many summer days at the Cascades taking two back-to-back body shots and then swimming in the frigid pool at the bottom of the waterfall and making love on the moss-covered rocks. Too many afternoons to count. Of course she remembered. Of all the memories she'd wished she could forget, the ones with Ben were the ones that haunted her. Even on her wedding day with Jonah at the courthouse. Jonah wore jeans, sneakers, and a button-up shirt, and they had walked in together like they were purchasing tickets at the movies. Lucia wore a secondhand dress that she'd given back to charity shortly thereafter. They were low-key people. Who needed the fuss? She'd said these very words, yet as she stood before the judge who instructed them as if he were reading her rights, her arms down by her sides, her shoulder touching Jonah's, she wondered about Ben and what he was up to and if her wedding day could've been different with a different kind of man.

Ben held out his hand, and she offered her wrist. He kissed and then licked it and dashed a bit of salt there. His warm tongue gently removed it, and then he swallowed a shot and Lucia placed a lime in her mouth so he could take it from her. And then he did it again. "Your turn," he said. She stood up and picked her favorite spot on his neck where his collarbone dipped, and he said, "Really?" She nodded with a sly smile. He had to bend his knees so she could reach it. The tequila burned and calmed her, and then she took her second one off the spot between his thumb and pointer finger. The liquor did its job quickly and Ben said, "Don't you feel better?"

Since the tequila made her instantly loose, she had the courage to say, "You and my sister never did anything like that, even after I left, right? I know it's stupid but I just need to know."

Ben's shoulders slumped. "She tried to kiss me just that once, and I've regretted that day since. You didn't forgive me, but I swear nothing happened. Mya was just jealous of you."

"Of me?" Lucia said incredulously.

Ben gave her a look like she should've known better. "If you've forgiven me after all these years, you should probably forgive her too."

"I know you're right," Lucia said, and dipped a carrot in Ben's homemade hummus—anything to chase down the liquor. "And Vista? I feel bad about how this all happened."

"I broke up with Vista. I didn't get the chance to tell you out at the fields."

"But you were with her at the fire," Lucia said, and sucked on a lime just because.

"When I saw Vista standing beside you, I knew I didn't feel for her the same way she did for me. Last night I told her. We'd talked about needing space before, but it was time."

"I see," Lucia said, and then they were quiet.

Ben washed his hands in the sink. "Do you remember that time we took our sleeping bags up Buffalo Mountain and stayed up all night and waited to see the meteor shower?"

"I do," Lucia said, and ate another carrot.

"And we wanted to close our eyes and go to sleep, but we knew that if we did, we'd miss that window of ten minutes when the sky would light up like snow flurries. It was a long shot and it was freezing. We didn't think we'd see it; I know I didn't. It took hours, but it did happen, and we felt like the luckiest people in the world." He turned off the sink, dried his hands, and stared at her.

For some reason this memory made her anxious, and she didn't know how to add to his story. "You hungry?" she finally said.

"Not really," he said, and he pulled her close.

"I thought we'd talk and eat or eat and talk about all that; wasn't this your idea?" she said.

"It was," Ben said. "But now I have another idea." From Lucia's short distance, his mouth smelled like citrus, and she wanted to lick his lips.

He swept the hair from her forehead, looked her in the eyes, and said, "The entire drive, it's all I thought about."

"You could've shared with me," she said.

"I couldn't," he said. "Too nervous."

Lucia said, "Hence the tequila."

"Lucia," Ben said, and his voice became so controlled and serious that she stopped smiling and stared up at him. "You left me; that was your choice."

"I know. And I'm sorry."

"That's not what I mean." He sat down at the bar so they could be at eye level with each other, and he pulled her to him. "It hurt like hell when you got married. I moved on. What choice did I have? Met other women and had good relationships but nothing deep. And then you showed up again. I never pretended for a moment that I stopped loving you. I wanted to. But I never did."

"I feel awful," Lucia said. She'd been so selfish for so many years. Only her own path had mattered to her during her twenties. Other people's desires and feelings had been second to her own.

He raised her chin with his hand and said, "You had to go. I hated that, but I accepted it."

"You don't hate me now, not even a little bit?" she blurted out, a question only the tequila would've let her ask.

"I did," he said, and put both of his hands on her hips. "I let that go the moment I saw you at the market. A life with you is what I want. Always have."

Lucia caressed one of his cheeks and smoothed down his hair. She had let him go back then to love him better now. She loved him. She couldn't deny it. "Make a baby with me," Lucia said, but it barely came out.

He tilted his head to the side. "What's that?"

She leaned in, put her cheek to his cheek, and whispered in his ear. He pulled her back just enough to look her in the eyes. "Okay, but after we eat," he joked.

Lucia laughed and pinched his side, and then he stood without warning, took her hand, led her away to the staircase, and then lifted her up and carried her up the stairs slowly, kissing her in a different place with each step he took. At the top of the staircase he put her down and they went side by side into Ben's bedroom, where Lucia closed the door.

## CHAPTER 36
### *Memory of a Rose*

WILLOW GAVE JAMES a tour of Main Street at dusk, the sun closing in on the mountain line beyond them, the sky a bruised purple and a thousand shades of orange and yellow. James especially liked Willard's Hat Shop, established 1937, and promised to stop there before he left town. Willow took pride in this town and the way James enjoyed Garden 2.0; he was shocked by the quality of the grass-fed venison roast with a currant and coffee sauce, as if only large cities could have that kind of artistry in the kitchen. Of all the businesses she'd loaned start-up money to, Garden 2.0 was one of her favorites. The chef had started a sustainable-food movement in Charleston, South Carolina, and believed he could start a trend in Quartz Hollow too, attracting locals and tourists alike. His restaurant turned the biggest profit of all the businesses she'd helped and continued to grow. He'd be opening another restaurant in Charlottesville soon. These were the offshoot achievements of Lenore Incorporated. Willow felt a greater sense of purpose when she supported local entrepreneurs. What would become of them if Lenore Incorporated faltered?

Quartz Hollow could dry up like a lonely western town after the gold rush, and she'd be to blame.

James slapped a blue mailbox on the corner of Main Street and Laurel Lane and said, "It's like the world doesn't happen here."

No cars passed by, it was true. Traffic almost ceased altogether around eight P.M. "I like it like this," Willow said.

"Reminds me of being a boy in Brooklyn and walking with my mother to pick up my father's suits at the tailor," James said.

"What else don't I know about you?" Willow asked, stopping to pick up a stray candy bar wrapper and toss it in a trash can. "Or is that a question for our pending retirement?"

They continued walking to Willow's truck. James said, "It was so long ago—I talk about other things now."

"We don't have to," Willow said.

"There's no legend to it," James said. "My mother taught pre-school and my father sold bonds, but he wasn't very good at it. We never had much, me and my three brothers."

"Where are they now?" Willow said.

"Two are dead and one is an art director in Ontario. Don't see him much," James said, and shook his head. "All I wanted was to leave Brooklyn and make a lot of money—I didn't know how I would, but I decided I would. Hollywood was the only place where I didn't need a plan to do that. That's what I believed anyway, and somehow it worked. I wanted to take care of my mother, but she died before I had a chance."

"I don't want you to talk about these things if it hurts too much," Willow said.

He shrugged. "You smother some things too long and they don't define you anymore."

"My sister's dead too, and I miss her. She died completely alone. It took days for a neighbor to check on her, and I've never forgiven myself for not being there. She didn't want me in her life, but the guilt doesn't go away. It's strange to be the only one left of a generation."

James moved to the side to allow Mrs. Parks and her Westie to pass by. Mrs. Parks glanced at Willow and stopped. "Good to see you out, Willow dear."

"Thanks, Mrs. Parks," Willow said, and as soon as she passed, Willow explained, "She read for story time at the library when I was a girl and her husband ran the hardware store just back that way. My mother loved them."

"You've stayed here all your life?"

"I've traveled a great deal; my mother made sure of that. I always loved Paris the most, but wherever we'd gone—Morocco, Thailand, Borneo, you name it—I was never happier than when we drove back to Quartz Hollow."

They continued walking, and James stopped in front of the drugstore and said, "Let me drop in here a moment."

Willow sat down on the bench outside and waited until James returned with a single red rose wrapped in plastic. He said, "Thank you for waiting."

"The most beautiful flower I've ever smelled." Willow laughed.

"You don't remember." James looked dismayed. "I bought you a gas station rose many years ago after our walk on the beach."

"I don't remember," Willow said, and she was tired of feeling guilty each time she said this. "I can't promise I won't forget this one either, but right now, in this moment, I love it. So thank you, and keep them coming."

"Shall we?" He offered Willow his arm, which she used to stand up from the bench. Her white truck was only a few feet away. "Could I drive? It's been so long."

"Know how to drive a stick?" Willow dangled the keys before him.

"I think so." He opened the door for Willow. "Fasten your seat belt, just in case."

"Oh, goodness," Willow said, strapping herself in. "The first of our many adventures."

"Exactly." He hopped into the driver's seat. "I've never driven a truck before. Always wanted to."

He put the keys in the ignition and he looked like he was ten years old. This both charmed and bothered Willow. He could run them off the road. "Now it's in neutral, you know that?" she said gently.

"I knew that. Who doesn't know that?" But he continued to wiggle the stick shift in search of first gear, and Willow heard the transmission grate. "I keep hearing that, what is it?"

"Metal?"

"A buzzing. I heard it during dinner and now here. Is it your phone?" He stopped talking and looked around at the seats. Willow strained to hear what he did, but she couldn't.

"There," he said. He picked up her purse and said, "Hear it?"

Willow blushed. She only heard it after she unzipped her purse. "I never have it on vibrate," she said, as if this should make up for her bad hearing. Some strange number with a Quartz Hollow area code came up on the screen. And she'd missed the call six times already. "Hang on." She dialed the number.

An automated voice said, "Virginia Presbyterian Hospital, if you know your party's extension, please dial it now, otherwise wait for an operator."

Willow put her hand over the phone and said, "It's the hospital," to James. He killed the engine and stared over at her as she began to talk to the operator who asked how to direct her call: "Yes, this is Willow Lenore, I've missed six calls from here and—yes. I will." She looked over at James. "I'm on hold."

Another voice answered from the emergency department: "Willow Lenore?"

"Yes, I'm here." Her forehead began to sweat. *Lucia, Mya, Mya, Lucia.*

"Your daughter's been in a severe accident," the woman said.

Willow clutched her throat. "Mya?"

"Mya Lenore and Luke Hanson."

Willow cupped her mouth and then said, "Are they . . . ?"

"They're in the ICU. I advise you to come as soon as you can."

"I will," Willow said, and she hung up and dropped her phone in her purse. "It's Mya," she said. "She's in the ICU. Can you make it around the corner?"

James turned the truck back on and said, "Just show me the way." He had no trouble finding first gear on his second try.

This was the kind of thing that had kept her awake at night when the girls were teenagers. She hated for them to be driving around with friends doing who knows what, especially on these curvy mountain roads. She'd assumed those nights of agitated half-sleep, night sweats, and leaping from the bed at the phantom sounds of the phone ringing or the front door opening were behind her. Back then all she wanted was a partner in her worry, someone in bed beside her to tell her everything was fine and to listen out for the sounds of her daughters arriving home on a Saturday night. She weathered those days and hardened, like a pioneer woman. It should have been Willow in the driver's seat speeding to the hospital—that's what her racing heart and blood pressure told her—but it was James who drove fast and with a solemn face, just like a father might.

"THEY WERE WHAT?"

"Speeding near the Cascades turnoff, head-on collision," Donald told Willow, his face pink and his breath shallow. Willow knew his daddy. He'd retired from her factory five years ago but couldn't get his son to follow his career path. Now here he was, the town sheriff and a boy she remembered from birth, telling Willow that her daughter might die.

"I need to see her," Willow insisted, her arms crossed. No one came to her side. "I want to see her right now!" she shouted.

A nurse ran over. "In just a minute, Ms. Lenore, I promise."

James came over and wrapped one arm around Willow, and she buried her face in the crook of his shoulder and let out a bitter cry. Hadn't she always worried this would happen to Mya? That she would die before Willow? Mya lived as if planning didn't exist. Not a day had gone by since Willow watched Mya fall off the monkey bars at the park, the horse in her riding lessons, or down the front porch stairs for no apparent reason that Willow didn't wonder if she'd lose her daughter first. Mya had stayed out of trouble in her thirties, and Willow thought she'd made it past the point of concern. Then the cloud had emerged.

"Mom," Lucia called from behind her. Willow turned away from James and there was Lucia running to her. Ben trailed behind her. Lucia gave her mother a hug. James shook hands with Ben and took him to the side to get a cup of coffee.

Lucia began to cry and kept saying, "It's all my fault, I told her to go. I insisted and now she's in the hospital."

Willow stroked her daughter's hair. She had actually forgotten how it felt like corn silk and smelled like rain. "Can't think like that now. At least she's here and not at the morgue."

Lucia tried to get control of herself, but it was clear to Willow that Lucia couldn't stop shaking. She whispered into Willow's ear: "I know who did this, I swear I do. Peter Sable threatened Mya this morning when you'd gone out."

Willow jerked away from Lucia and held her at arm's length: "Why am I just finding out about this?"

Lucia wiped the tears from her cheeks. "Is she going to die, Mom?"

"I don't know."

"I didn't really believe him but this just seems too, you know, coincidental," Lucia said, her voice bitter now.

The same quiet nurse came to Willow and said, "You can see her now. But just immediate family."

Willow and Lucia held hands, and James and Ben sat down together. Willow was following the nurse out of the lobby when Luke's father pushed through the doors of the waiting room.

Willow stopped. "Hang on," she told Lucia, and walked over to him. "Randy, I'm so, so sorry."

Luke's mother came from behind Randy, her face red like a hot candy. She placed her arms around her husband and said, "Come now."

He tightened his mouth and then pointed at Willow. "Your girl's nothing but trouble, Willow Lenore. Nothing but . . . I want her away from my boy. If he makes it through, you see to that, you hear me?"

"Calm down, Randy," Willow said, forcing herself not to cry as the other people in the waiting room broke off their conversations and stared at Willow.

"He's a good boy." Randy rubbed his knuckles in his open palm like a mortar in a pestle. "And he might not walk again, have they told you that?" Willow shook her head, her ears on fire. "Why's she got to ruin good boys?"

"Don't you say that, don't you dare say that," Willow said.

Lucia came over, took Willow by the arm, and said, "Come on, Mom." She looked over her shoulder and called, "We're so sorry," to Luke's parents, but they didn't respond.

Mya had broken many hearts since middle school, never once allowing her own heart to break. She'd caused many local boys to move out of town, Willow knew; some even moved out of state. "Was he right?" Willow asked, her voice cracking as Lucia forced her down the hall. But before Lucia could respond, they arrived at the glass window of Mya's room, and there she lay, tubes in both arms and her nose, her hair matted with blood, her face swollen to five times its normal size. Her eyes were open, and Willow stared at her daughter as if she didn't know her. Had she ever hurt any of those boys on purpose? Is that what the town thought? Had Mya known what might happen to Zoe?

Lucia pulled her mother's hand and led the way into the room. Mya's eyes were bloodshot, but as soon as they landed on Willow, they closed like someone had blown hot air into them. "Mom," Mya said with purple lips.

A young female doctor whom Willow didn't recognize knocked on the door. "I'm Dr. McNeil. Can I come in?"

"Sure."

Willow sat down in the chair next to Mya's bed.

Dr. McNeil held her clipboard. "She's a lucky girl."

"Really?" Lucia's voice brightened. She put one hand on Mya's blanketed foot. "That's such good news."

"The crash should've been fatal for both of them," Dr. McNeil said.

Willow thought about Randy and Janet in the waiting room, and she hoped this would relieve them.

Dr. McNeil nodded her head. "Mya woke up from surgery a few hours ago and everything went well. She had a moderate fracture in her jaw, but we didn't need to wire it shut. It may take her a few days to feel comfortable enough to talk. She also experienced a serious head injury we're monitoring, but we're certain she's lost her sense of smell and taste, and she'll need physical therapy to fully regain her balance. We reset her shoulder, so she's in a lot of pain. She's had a few hours to digest this news, but it would be good to talk with her about it when she's ready."

Mya began to whimper and Lucia shushed her as Mya tried to shake her head.

"And Luke?" Lucia asked. This question seemed to calm Mya.

"It's wait and see. He's still in surgery," Dr. McNeil said. "If you have any other questions, just call the nurse and she'll get me."

"And the other car?"

"A single driver," the doctor said. "In surgery too. We'll let you know as soon as we know."

Dr. McNeil left, and Lucia turned to Mya and hugged her legs. Tears rolled down Mya's face. Lucia held on to the white blanket draped on Mya's legs, and Mya placed one hand on Lucia's head. It was a tenderness Willow hadn't seen between them in so long, not since they were little girls, and Willow felt gratitude to see her two daughters acting like sisters once again.

Mya made a guttural noise and Lucia looked up. "You need to say something?"

Mya nodded and wiggled her fingers for Lucia to come closer, but neither Willow nor Lucia could understand her.

"Write it down." Willow handed her a pad of paper from the bedside table, but Mya shook her head.

"Her shoulder might hurt too much," Lucia said.

Mya closed her eyes and turned her face away from them.

## CHAPTER 37
### *Newborn*

HOW COULD MYA express that knowing she'd never smell again felt like the apocalypse? She had been given what she asked for, and now, four days later, she wasn't dead. For that Mya was thankful. But the deep smells of garlic and celery and green peppers and onions sautéing in olive oil filled Mya with so much pleasure. She could recall it so vividly, the way the vegetables glossed in oil gave up their will and collapsed in the pan, saying, "Take me now, before I burn, succulent as I am." Now she couldn't remember the smells from those many nights in the kitchen. One smack to the head and countless nights of pleasure were forever lost, never to be experienced again. Just like that. It was her atonement for changing the formula. The cloud had lifted and disappeared, only to leave Mya behind with this lifelong loss.

And her days, she'd lost those too, since they had been taken up with mixing the finest oils in the world into new and unusual scents. The warm sensation that overcame her when she smelled musk, she could feel it still, but not a single trace lingered in her nose. Vanilla pleased her, she remembered, jasmine and ylang-ylang more. Soon after she'd awoken from surgery on the day of the accident, the doctor had informed her of the consequences. Willow had insisted on an extended stay at the hospital while Mya's jaw healed. She believed it was the safest place for Mya. Mya's body was bloated from painkillers and Jell-O. During this time, she had begun to substitute color for scent—white for chicken broth, purple for coffee, and burgundy for her family's perfume. The colors of her memories spread before her like a collection of paint samples, and the world became a two-dimensional experience all at once.

What would hiking be without the smell of composted leaves on the forest floor? And sex too. It was Luke's scent of fresh cut grass and rich Virginia soil blended with ocean-salt sweat that filled her body with lust. Was it possible that she'd never feel aroused again? Sex was all that had made her feel fully alive. With scent went taste, she knew. Everything that she'd lived for had been removed when the crown of her head busted through Luke's windshield. Ninety-five stitches, plus all that Mya considered important.

She should be dead, or so said the emergency team that came to the scene.

Mya remembered only one thing before the crash: that last paranoid look into the rearview mirror to make sure the SUV was still parked at the overlook, and of course it was, of course. All it took were those few seconds, and the other car approached around the bend and Mya was in the wrong lane. She remembered little else: white sunlight, perhaps, her plea and the floating cloud, and then waking up in a gurney. She still had her body, but she had to live with no sense of smell for the rest of her life.

Lucia waited for Mya to speak for the first time in days, while their mother sat in a chair with a vacant look on her face, like a porcelain doll. Lucia sniffled for Mya, and Mya wanted to cry for Luke. Loving her was his only mistake. The other driver had to live, Luke had to walk again; she couldn't accept any other result. They had to come out of this alive and strong. Mya loved Luke, and she hadn't had the chance to tell him when he could hear her. She was frightened of love and commitment, and that was her excuse. She regretted very few things in her life more than this.

Lucia knelt by the side of the bed and rested her head on Mya's arm. Each time Mya tried to talk, her throat began to burn, a result of the injury or her pride, she couldn't quite tell. She would now depend on Lucia to mix the oils in her workshop, and she'd have to muster the humility to ask Lucia to do this for her. Lucia hadn't committed to the study of the family trade, but now she had no other choice. Mya needed her sister. Her mother had long since lost her touch or interest or both. But still Mya couldn't make her voice come. The idea that Mya would need someone else to smell for her—it was a grief she hadn't yet fathomed.

"What is it?" Lucia put her cheek next to Mya's face.

"A favor."

"Anything," Lucia said.

"Is it there?" Mya said, her voice raspy, her jaw aching.

Lucia stood and leaned closer to Mya's mouth, and Mya repeated herself. At first Lucia tilted her head, but then she followed Mya's gaze and said, "Oh—no, it's gone. I haven't seen it since you've been here."

Mya took a deep breath. "I watched it go."

"That's good news, right?"

"Don't trust it," Mya managed to say. "Wasn't Peter."

Lucia grabbed Mya's hands. "It's fine now, it can't get worse." The heat in Lucia's hands pulsated into Mya's.

Mya squeezed Lucia's hands. "It'll kill me next."

Lucia bit her lip.

"I need you," Mya said, and Lucia's false optimism fell from her face, her cheeks no longer high and round. "A spell."

Lucia laughed in disbelief. "I can't do that stuff," she said.

"Now," Mya said.

Willow stood from her chair and walked over to the bed. Mya was relieved to see her mother in motion. Her silence since she'd arrived unnerved Mya more than anything else. Willow said, "What're you asking her to do?" Willow petted Mya's head. When was the last time she'd done that?

Mya said, "Protect me."

Lucia pushed away from the bed and put one hand on her forehead. She said, "I can be president, I think. I can try at least, but not this. This is sort of ridiculous. I was never good at it then, even in make-believe on the playground, and I just wanted away from it all. And now you're telling me I need to do it or else you'll die?"

Mya looked to their mother.

"Let me help you," Willow said.

"Oh no," Lucia said. "You agree with her? Really? With all that pain medication? You know under normal circumstances she'd never let me into her workshop. She used to tackle me to the ground to get me out."

This was true, unfortunately. Mya had tried locking the door, but Lucia could pick it. She tried shouting, but Lucia wouldn't budge, impervious to her anger. Mya couldn't concentrate with Lucia in the room studying her every move, and a few times she'd tackled her to the floor in order to remove her. "Sorry," Mya said, even though she knew it was twenty-five years too late.

"I can't," Lucia said, her hands on her hips. "I come home, the business is going bust, you want me in as president, and I said yes. To help the family and try to save this big mess Mya and you made." Mya looked over at her mother, whose face was as alert as an owl's. But Lucia continued. "And the damn flowers could die. Really die. Like not come back, ever, die."

Willow put her hand up like a stop sign.

Lucia continued on: "And I never asked much about the flowers growing up I guess, but they're the weirdest damn flowers in the entire world. You know that, right? They're totally voyeuristic. Ben and I figured that out. Alone. On our own. Get what I'm saying?"

Willow said, "Not really," but Lucia kept rolling, her gaze fixed on the floor. "And I had really amazing news for you guys and couldn't wait to see you."

Willow said, "What?"

"I wanted to explain the day Ben and I figured it out and I wanted to tell you both in person. But then I got the phone call and Mya was in the hospital." She stretched her arms out to the ceiling like she was praising God and said, "Who gives a damn if I know how to save them? Who gives a damn if I'm having a baby and that it's the only way to save the flowers? Already—go out to the field and see for yourself—the scent's back, I swear it. That's how I know I'm pregnant. No test required. But on top of all that, I need to go home and make a protection spell for Mya? It's too much for one visit home." And with that Lucia left the room and slammed the door, and Mya watched as two ICU nurses followed after her with shushing fingers held to their lips.

Willow sat back down and rested her hands in her lap. "I don't remember hormones working that fast," she said.

Mya's little sister would have a baby before her. Lucia was the one the flowers had chosen; the business and everything else belonged to her.

"And how did the flowers . . . ?" Willow asked, talking to herself, "Oh," she answered. "Oh. How strange."

"Mom," Mya tried to say, but her mother drowned her out with a long hum.

"A granddaughter." Willow's face brightened. "That Bennie, I knew it."

Mya grabbed an empty plastic cup from her tray and tossed it at her mother. Willow gave a little shout. Tears streamed down Mya's face, and Willow stood up and embraced her.

"Oh, honey," she said.

Only one sister had an heir. Only one daughter could become president. After all these years of Mya's tending to the flowers and the business, the flowers wanted Lucia—this was the final blow. Mya wanted some love to call her own. She'd concentrated on herself so long that all she had expected to come to her had passed her by, and she had nothing now. Unless Luke still loved her. And why would he? She had almost killed him, and he might never be able to work the farm again.

Mya let her mother hold her hand for a long time, both of them quiet with understanding. Lucia returned to the room ten minutes later. Mya couldn't look at her, but she could feel her standing there.

Lucia finally said, "I shouldn't have told you like that."

Willow held out an arm for Lucia, inviting her in for a hug. Lucia came to her and Willow said, "We're happy for you, make no mistake about that."

Mya wished she could be happy for Lucia and the flowers and the family business, but she just wasn't ready.

"I'll try, Mya," Lucia said. "If you want me to."

What *did* Mya want now? She'd been stripped of her power, just like she'd asked for prior to blacking out, but what was she left with? Luke was on another floor, knocked out in surgery for the third time. And no one would tell her what this one was for. Mya might make it through all of this with him and he might love her still. That small possibility was all she had left.

"Should I do it?" Lucia said.

Mya turned her face away from her mother and sister and nodded. For the first time in her life she could imagine having a child, but now she'd never have the chance to smell the scent of a newborn. Mya had never tried to make anything from pure love before, and she was certain she was too broken to try. She couldn't have made a protection spell even if she were well.

## CHAPTER 38
## *Oil Drops*

L UCIA'S HOPE OF having a child had died during her marriage. Jonah had made it clear he was more concerned with art than creating a family. And she'd accepted his answer as her own: she too was trying to be an artist and had no time for motherhood. Plus, babies were thieves. They stole dinners out and hours of sleep. Lucia had no time for it, just like Jonah. She pushed those feelings away and down so deep that the idea of a celebration had never occurred to her. But now she wanted a party. Yellow balloons and flower-printed paper cups. Cake. Presents. Congratulations, at the very least. So far, none of that had happened.

Just four days after Lucia made love to Ben, she and Willow stood at the edge of a healthy mid-June crop of *Gardenia potentiae* flowers, their lovely white petals reaching upward to the exposed sun, their scent ready for harvest.

Willow said, "You're certain?"

Lucia nodded. Of course she was certain: Wasn't the field evidence? Lucia wouldn't need a pregnancy test to know it was true. It had been sealed with her intent.

Willow bent over, placed her palms on the ground, and said, "Best news in months."

A party wasn't necessary, but why did it feel so much like a transaction? Fertilize an egg, business as usual.

James approached them from farther down the field. Willow stood to watch him come near and said, "He's handsome, isn't he?"

Lucia always preferred men her own age. Also, she didn't know how to comment on her mother's boyfriend's good looks, so she opted to say nothing.

Willow said, "Will you two get married?"

"Me and Ben?"

"Who else?" Willow said, and wrapped one arm around Lucia's shoulders. She patted Lucia's belly with her other hand.

With Mya's accident and Zoe's death, no one, not even Lucia, was prepared for this kind of news. She wanted to feel happy about it, but marriage hadn't occurred to her, not once. "I don't think so," Lucia said.

"How come?" Willow held her hand out to the flowers. One section of the hedge moved to her without hesitation, and she plucked one flower from the bush and inserted it behind her ear.

Lucia had a million reasons, but the most obvious one was Ben hadn't suggested it and neither had Lucia. "I've done married before. Didn't turn out so well."

Willow pulled her close. "Don't judge your future by your past."

"That's wise and all," Lucia agreed. "But the flowers are thriving. What more is necessary? Maybe you never needed to get married, maybe Grandmother Lily didn't need to either, if love was the only requirement."

"That wasn't an option for me, I guess." Willow dropped her arm from around Lucia's waist and walked forward to the edge of the flowers. She bent down once more and the flowers lifted to meet her delicate nose. In that moment Lucia found the little girl her mother once was, a girl Lucia would never meet, except, perhaps, in her own daughter. Willow said, "They smell like they always have. Maybe better." She snapped off another flower at the top of the stem and turned to face Lucia. Willow fastened the flower in her silver bun, but her smile faded, and right then Lucia understood how lonely she must've been all these years. Working hard and without a lover, yet never talking about it, never complaining, never having time to share her burden.

James came to them and said, "That's lovely," and leaned over to smell the flower in Willow's hair.

"Thanks."

"Ben's coming by later to sample the flowers once more," Lucia said. "Just so you know."

James smiled. "I like that kid."

Lucia smiled back at James. "Me too." She continued to stare at him, wondering who he would become in her mother's life. A husband? It was so hard to imagine her mother married after all this time. Lucia appreciated his calm, steady presence. More than anything, he seemed to love her mother and make her happy, and it was about time. She'd always hoped for a James for Willow.

Lucia looked out to the fields once more; the rolling hedges of white were stable and unmoving. "Should we go?"

"The sooner, the better," Willow answered.

MYA'S WORKSHOP FELT SO DESERTED, as if the vials of oil and the spiders suspended in the corners knew it was not Mya who entered this space. Very little sunlight filtered through the slats of the bamboo blinds. Lucia walked to the windows. Willow and James followed.

Willow sealed the door behind her and then lit the candles. She gathered droppers and cloths and large glass bottles of essential oils from Mya's cabinets. Lucia and James watched as Willow fluttered around Mya's room, so frantic that she knocked over a bottle of geranium oil. It shattered on the ground and filled the room with the scent of a second-rate rose. She quickly grabbed the broom and began sweeping the oily glass into the dust pan. James tried to go to her, but Lucia grabbed the back of his shirt and he stood still. Willow stood and braced herself on Mya's table.

"Mom?" Lucia said softly.

"What's wrong with your sister?" Finally Willow looked up and over at Lucia like she might have an answer.

"Calm down." Lucia wasn't sure why her mother was acting so strange. She'd seemed fine when they were in the fields.

Willow said, "There's always something more with Mya. She knew what she was doing when she made that scent for Zoe. Let's just admit that it was no accident. How could my own daughter be capable of a thing like that?"

"You have to believe her. She didn't mean to."

"The outcome doesn't change based on intent," James said, and both Willow and Lucia looked at him.

Willow stopped staring at James. "Yes, that's true."

"She didn't mean to," Lucia pressed. "She's just reckless."

"Doesn't make it right." Willow's voice was flat.

No one answered.

"But she's family," Willow said. "For God's sake, I made her."

Lucia placed her hands on her stomach and a sudden terror overtook her body—she had no way to control who she would birth into the world or what would happen to her, for good or for ill.

"She's family," Willow repeated. "I just don't know if I should protect her like this. I'm not even sure she deserves it."

Lucia had never thought her mother would talk this way about either of them. Mya didn't have malicious intent. She'd never been good at dealing with her problems. She always went for the easiest way and she didn't learn from her mistakes, even when she was the one who ended up being hurt. But her sister wasn't a murderer. Lucia said, "I don't think you should."

"I can't do it." Willow began gathering the supplies to return them to the cabinet.

Lucia laid one hand on her mother's. "Mya asked me, not you, and I want to try."

Willow continued to stack the bottles where she first found them. "I can't let you."

"I think she wants to be forgiven," Lucia said.

Willow paused.

"Please just let me try. I'm going for something longer lasting. Something committed."

"We'll step out then." Willow and James walked out of the workshop, and Lucia commandeered Mya's stool.

How many times she'd wanted to be the one front and center. But Mya defended her space. Lucia had hated her for it—white, jealous hatred. But it was Mya's one thing, this space. It was what she loved. Protecting that was all she had. Lucia didn't agree with her sister all the time, but Mya was family, and Lucia wanted her to be alive and well. Motherhood might be the last grace available to Mya, to sacrifice and put another person's needs before her own. This was the pinnacle experience that Mya needed in order to change, and Lucia had to bottle it somehow.

Lucia glanced at the vials her mother had first arranged on the table: orange blossom, clove, civet, *Gardenia potentiae*, bergamot, vanilla, and ambergris. *Too complicated*, Lucia thought as she stared at the line of bottles, and she returned all but her family's essence to the shelves. Stored high up, perhaps as a way to restrict its use, Mya kept a bottle of attar of roses and oud oil, two of the most expensive essential oils in the world, scents that she'd first encountered in Paris on their very first summer trip to the Dubois shop. The richest of experiences needed the richest of scents. Lucia found a stool and used it to reach the bottles. She eased each one off the shelf.

Willow walked into the workshop holding a small wooden box and placed it on the table.

Lucia climbed down and said, "What's that?"

"Something you left behind." Willow smiled and then pointed to the bottles. "Interesting choices."

Inside the box were old handwritten letters from high school. Some from her classmates, but most of the letters were from Ben. "Where were these?" Lucia asked in surprise.

"Kept them in the office," Willow told her. "I had a hunch you might want them someday."

The house had always been cluttered from her mother's little intuitions, just like this one. "Thanks."

"We're heading back to the hospital now."

"Ben's coming over and we'll be there soon."

"You can do this," Willow assured her.

Lucia hoped for that to be true. She'd had one vision, the first one in her entire life, but that didn't guarantee she could blend a protection spell.

James appeared in the doorway. "Can I drive again?" He jingled the keys.

Willow said, "I suppose," as if she were put out, but Lucia could tell her mother loved his playfulness.

Once they left, Lucia opened the box and unfolded a stack of notebook paper filled with Ben's handwriting. Skinny letters leaning up and to the right. She scanned through pages and pages of letters detailing his days with intermittent declarations of his love. Lucia stopped when she came across a passage about the parkway on her eighteenth birthday—it was the first thunderstorm of the spring season and the first time she knew for sure she was leaving him for New York City, and she didn't know how to tell him.

*I was thinking about your birthday, how the roads were winding through a foggy mist and flashes of lightning filled the valley below us for seconds, illuminating the vastness before turning black again, and when the rain finally stopped we pulled over on the side of the road. You got out first and began to walk ahead of me and I was worried something was wrong that you weren't sharing, but then you stopped and we stood in the middle of a cloud, and I asked you to dance with me and told you I wished it could always be this way between us, but you didn't say anything. I'll never forget that day for as long as I live. I've never loved anyone or anything like I love you and I always will. I promise you that, no matter what happens.*

Lucia remembered that foggy night, and she remembered thinking how many other places and other people she needed to meet. So much to do and accomplish. What a scared and immature girl she'd been not to tell him what she was thinking. He knew anyway. He knew she'd leave him, but he kept writing anyway. Ben had loved her all these years, just like this letter promised he would, and he had a compelling love to offer, a kind that can only be sustained by the faithful. It was her turn to learn this kind of love. And Mya's turn too.

She smoothed his letter on the table like a place mat and put the glass vial on top. She released thirty-six drops of the attar of roses for Mya, thirty-three drops of oud oil for herself, and then four drops of their family's oil for the mother-and-child unions to come. She closed her eyes and recalled her acting classes in small studios in Union Square and how she learned to access sadness to call forth genuine tears. Lucia took this letter, her absent father, her divorce from Jonah, and all her handicaps along the way, and she shoved them aside and wrapped her arms around her belly, soon to swell with a love unlike any before, and from that place she brought forth tears and caught one in the vial. She capped the bottle and shook it to blend the oils together, then placed it back on Ben's letter. Flanking the vial with both of her hands and with all the love she could possibly imagine, Lucia activated the energy in her palms. The vial shook in the center, and Lucia kept her love pouring forth from her hands. Lucia wrapped it in a purple cloth, swirled the liquid together once more, and said, "For Mya and Luke and a child, to protect them in love forevermore."

## CHAPTER 39
### *Anointment*

W E SHOULD GRAB some lunch and a drink maybe," James said as they stood in Mya's room, watching her sleep. His phone rang and he said, "Hang on," and walked out of the room and back to the lobby.

The swelling in Mya's face had gone down, but she still had the puffiness of a newborn in her cheeks and neck. Willow's grown daughter looked like her baby. They'd lived together for so long that Willow no longer noticed Mya's upturned nose, her pouty lips, and the exquisite jawline so many boys had fallen for, the same features as her father. Willow had been proud of her daughter's arresting beauty, which never failed to make strangers stop and say, "Oh, she's stunning." The longer they'd lived together, the less Mya had seemed a daughter and the more she'd become a roommate and difficult friend. For all their intimacy, Willow didn't feel close to Mya like she should have. Lucia's long absence had stunted her as a teenager in Willow's memory, the intervening years unable to shape what Willow's imagination had sealed. She didn't have the same experience with Mya. For the sake of their relationship, Mya should've left home, and Lucia and Willow should've pushed her to do so.

*That's it, then.* Willow stroked the light hairs on Mya's arm and pushed down the loose tape holding in her IV. So that's why James had finally come to Willow, to help Mya feel like she didn't have to stay in Quartz Hollow to act as her guardian any longer. She'd always been the protective one. For so long Willow had focused on Mya's anger and her mistakes, but not this part of her daughter, the part that was good. "I'm sorry, sweetie," Willow said softly. So many times she'd felt like such an awful, humbled human being because of motherhood.

Willow turned because she could feel James approaching. He opened the glass door. "Work." He waved his phone in the air like evidence.

"You need to go?" She hadn't let herself think about his pending departure. The idea that the two of them might retire right here in Quartz Hollow and have the cabin all to themselves was just fine by Willow.

"Zoe's funeral, lots of press," James said, "and the director postponed shooting but wants Jennifer back in the film. My assistants are overwhelmed. And the LAPD left a message. Want to know if I know anything about a missing perfume. They say Zoe's manager won't stop yammering about it. I called the chief back and it appears they aren't putting much stock in Peter's claims. The final cause of death is the hanging, but they say they needed to follow up, for procedure."

Willow looked around Mya's room to make sure no one was near. "Do you know anything?"

"I have no idea about any perfume," James said.

"You told him that?" As much as Willow wanted to sound playful, she couldn't. She had never asked him to cover for her or her daughter, nor had she asked him to stay here while Mya recovered. But he had chosen to, and that was out of Willow's control.

James said, "How about that drink?"

Willow nodded and patted Mya's arm once more. A nurse in teddy-bear-print scrubs passing by Willow in the long white hall said, "She's doing good, Ms. Lenore," and flashed a big smile. Willow thanked her and right then remembered the woman's mother, who had the same wide smile. Lenore Incorporated had financed her business, Joanne's Salon on Main Street. "How's your mom?" Willow asked, and the nurse stopped, her white shoes squeaking on the waxed floor.

"She's good," she said. "Business is good. I'll tell her you say hello."

"Please. And tell her I'm due for a trim."

"Will do."

They stepped into the elevator and James said, "Everyone's so nice."

"It's the mountains," Willow told him, pushing the "G" button.

"I always thought it was the South." James adjusted his collar in his reflection in the metal doors.

"That too." The elevator began to descend. "Do you think I see my daughters too much?" She looked over at him.

"Distance makes the heart grow fonder." He took her hand.

"You believe that?"

"I have to," James answered. "I'm leaving tomorrow."

"Oh yes," Willow said, but she'd forgotten, perhaps by choice. The doors opened on the ground floor. A piano in the lobby played Chopin by itself next to a large planting of fake bamboo. The nurse at the front desk looked like she might take a nap. Dark clouds filled the windows.

James asked, "Should we drive?"

"Storm's coming," Willow said, and James seemed very pleased with himself, like he had wished for a storm just so they couldn't walk. Driving a stick shift in the mountains was his new favorite activity. She handed him the keys.

"Right this way." James took her by the arm, and just as they pushed through the revolving door, Willow saw Ben and Lucia coming toward the main entrance.

Willow waved; Ben saw her first and they trotted over. "You're leaving?" Lucia said. "In this?"

"Mya's asleep. James is leaving tomorrow."

"I'm sorry to hear that." Ben shook James's hand. "It was good to meet you. Your studio produces the best stuff."

"Thanks," James said. "I like to think so, but it's good to hear."

"Big fan of *The Memory Makers*. Easton's best," Ben said.

"I agree," Lucia added.

"You two should come out to L.A. soon, before I retire," James said. "I'll show you around."

"Can I come?" Willow asked.

James stepped away from her. "Truth?"

She wasn't ready for this. And in front of the children? He was breaking up with her? "No," she started to say, but he began at the same time: "I want you to go back with me tomorrow."

Lucia smiled and then realized James was serious. "She can't," Lucia answered for her.

"I know," James said. "But I want her to."

Willow's face flushed; Ben noticed and smiled. She gave Ben a hug. "Congratulations. It was meant to be this way." Willow wanted those two married. She wanted Ben as an official son.

"That's a lovely necklace, Lucia," James said. Lucia immediately clasped the pendant resting on her breastbone. Willow hadn't even noticed.

"Ben gave it to me," Lucia said.

"May I see?" Willow said, and Lucia offered up the sterling silver chain. The sparkling blue dragonfly with silver-outlined wings and two ruby eyes landed squarely in Willow's palm. "Gorgeous. From Sarah's shop, I imagine. Is that right?"

"You're right," Ben said.

Willow did like his taste: Sarah's glass jewelry business was one venture Willow had been especially eager to support. She knew it would be a big hit with the hikers seeking a talisman for the trail. "This will do," Willow said, "until you find a proper ring."

At this Lucia's eyes flared, just like Willow knew they would. "Can I talk to you?" Lucia said. "Over there." She pointed to a bench.

Willow nodded and sat down.

Lucia pulled out a small purple cloth from her purse and said, "Ben's mother isn't feeling well today and he wants us to go to her house to share the news with her, to cheer her up. If Mya's sleeping I was hoping you could do this." Lucia handed the bottle to Willow.

"But you made it," Willow said.

"I know," Lucia said, "but I need you to finish it." Willow didn't trust Lucia's story. She wanted Willow to be part of this. Even as a little girl Lucia had a mischievous way about her. If she wanted something from Willow, she found an indirect way to get it. And this time, she was doing it for the sake of Willow's relationship with Mya. Willow accepted the bottle from her.

"The sooner the better," Lucia added. "And Luke too."

"Luke?" Willow said. "I don't know how to see him."

"They'll let you in," Lucia assured her.

Willow remained seated and Lucia stood.

"This is the right thing to do," Lucia said before waving good-bye.

James came over and sat down next to Willow as she watched Ben and Lucia retreat to his truck. Willow opened the top of the bottle but left it wrapped so no one could see. She inhaled deeply and couldn't believe what a simple mix Lucia had made. It wasn't a scent at all, not really. Their family's flower was never a base note, but Lucia made it one. How strange. Plus, there wasn't a top note that Willow could detect. Lucia might not have been the perfumer in the family, but she'd trained enough to know a scent needed a top note. Willow smelled again, searching for it, and smelled nothing . . . but then something, there it was. She looked at James; he raised his eyebrows, she leaned over and kissed him, and he kissed her back. "I love you," she said. Her body filled with her need for him. Love in her toes and her fingertips and her cheeks. She pulled away from him and stared into his gold-flecked irises.

"That scent," he said. "It's overwhelming."

She capped the bottle and wrapped it back up.

He ran his fingers through the loose hair on her neck and said, "You know, there's never going to be a right time."

"I know." She rested her head on his shoulder.

"And we can put it off and put it off and work and work until we think it's the right time, and then we'll see the right time pass."

"I want to be here for the birth," Willow said.

"We can come back for that," James said. "For as long as you want."

"Give me two months," Willow said.

James shifted against the wooden back of the bench. "That long?"

"Mya will need support as she recovers, and Lucia needs training."

"I guess I could use that time too. I'll oversee the start of the production with Jennifer, and it'll give me enough time to broker a real estate deal."

"You'll sell your house first?"

"I'm looking to buy." He shifted his weight to the side to access his pocket and pulled out his phone.

"But why? Right when we're retiring?"

James tapped the screen and pulled up a document. He then maximized it and handed Willow the phone.

"What's this?"

"Our retirement." James put both hands behind his head and watched her.

On the screen stood a two-story white stucco home with a clay roof, open marble patios, multiple infinity pools, two tennis courts, and a greenhouse. It had generators and water-treatment plants, all it needed to self-sustain. It was move-in ready with a landing strip. Just Willow and James on a property that promised a little over thirty acres and the gift of a second life.

"It's an island near Belize," James said. "But my agent's still browsing."

Willow handed him back the phone. "You're serious?"

"Quite."

"I can't let you buy that."

"A minor concern." He put his phone back in his pocket. "What I need to know is that in two months you'll be with me on my yacht and packed and ready to go to this place. I need a promise."

A streak of lightning illuminated the ridges of the storm clouds heading toward them. "I think we should go inside now."

He grabbed her hand. "Willow, I need to know."

She leaned over and kissed him again, his skin smooth and scented with clove from his aftershave. Willow said, "Don't you know already?"

"So I'll call my agent then?"

Willow stood and thunder crashed in the distance. "I'll start shopping for a bikini."

He laughed and slapped both of his thighs before standing up. "Your girls will be surprised."

"It won't be much of a shock, I don't think." Raindrops began to fall, and the leaves on the nearby maple trees trembled. "I need to go see Mya once more. It won't take long. You can wait in the lobby and then we'll get lunch, I promise."

"How come I'm always waiting for you?" James said as they began to run back to the entrance, a wall of rain falling behind them.

Back inside, Willow wiped the water from her face and said, "Because I've waited so long for you, since Sunset Beach."

"I've waited just as long." He caressed her cheek with his thumb and sat down in a leather chair. "I'll be waiting right here." James picked up *Entertainment Weekly.* Zoe's face, lush like cream, her bright auburn hair cascading in curls down her shoulders, took up the entire cover.

Willow placed one hand on his shoulder. "She really was beautiful."

"More beautiful now than ever before." He began to flip through the magazine.

Up and off the elevator once more, Willow drew in a deep breath and walked to the front desk. She asked to see Joanne's daughter, who graciously directed her to Luke's room as long as she promised to be just a few minutes. He was still recovering.

"And the other driver?" Willow said.

"Still recovering," the nurse told her, "but on the mend."

Inside room 302, Luke slept alone, his face bruised and stitched, a black patch over his left eye. The monitor tracked his heartbeat with green lines. There was a tray of untouched hospital food. *His parents must be out to lunch,* Willow thought. She glanced over her shoulder and out the glass windows and waited for the hall to be clear of passersby before she opened the bottle. His fingers twitched. Using the dropper Lucia had wrapped with the bottle, Willow anointed him from toes to heel to ankle to calf to thigh to hand to wrist to arm to shoulder to neck to ear to eye on his left side, the center of his forehead, then back down his right side. He didn't move once, but the room filled with Lucia's scent, and all Willow could think about was James and that island and the ballooning of love she felt for him. She loved this hurt boy before her, and she loved her daughter on the floor below, and her daughter in the truck with Ben, and the little child forming in Lucia's uterus. She loved and loved as she walked out of Luke's room unnoticed, took the elevator down to Mya's room, and double-anointed her from head to toe.

## CHAPTER 40
### *Sealed*

SOMEONE WAS NEAR, seated in the chair next to her, or closer even, like a cat on her chest. Mya lifted her head off the hospital pillow and glanced around the room, but no one was around. The morphine drip helped relieve the pain in her jaw, and after she hit the button she reached for the remote to the television. Settling back into her inclined bed, she wondered when her mother and sister would return. She needed an update on Luke, and if they didn't come back in the next twenty minutes, she'd find a way to go to the nurses' station and ask. But for the first time since the accident, she felt zero panic.

Mya turned to channel 36 and waited out a commercial for Premier Mortgage Lending. No scams. No down payment. No closing costs. All the convenience you could imagine: A Best Fit for the American Consumer. She muted the television. A large golden E spun around the screen, and then a picture of Jennifer Katz, with her hair curled, her blue eyes lined and dazzling, appeared on the flat-screen. She escaped into a limousine after a *Vogue* fund-raising event, smiling and waving at the paparazzi. A dark-haired guy with a neon-blue streak in his hair and impossibly tan skin said, "And Miss Katz is back from her long vacation in Hawaii. Welcome back, darling."

A picture of Jennifer at a press conference took over the screen. She was dressed in all black. In a mournful voice she said, "I'm so sad about Zoe Bennett. It was a tragic loss for Hollywood and I want to do justice to her in this role. I hope that my performance will live up to what she would've expected from herself. She had high standards, and I can't believe she's gone."

The entertainment host returned, the diamonds in both of his ears flashing: "There you have it, folks. That's why she's America's sweetheart. Such grace. Such compassion. We love you, Jennifer. And for all of you watching, until next time, be fierce, be glamorous." And the signature bouncing music ushered the host's image away.

Wasn't this what Mya had wanted, for Jennifer to be back on top without having to worry about Zoe anymore? Mya had wanted to put Zoe in her place for breaking their agreement, but not to put her in an early grave. It was this she'd have to live with for the rest of her life.

Jennifer had received what she wanted. The contract was fixed. And Mya could still die because of it. Perhaps the family business was never meant for Mya, despite her devotion. This should have made her devastated, depressed. Where were those feelings now? "You aren't who you were anymore," she repeated to herself. Each time she said it, she expected to feel crushed. Instead, each time she felt lighter. Who she'd become wasn't who she was meant to be. Ever. After thirty-six years, she needed to start over.

She pointed the remote at the television to turn it off. Mya watched her right arm like the stiff limb belonged to someone else. An iridescent sheen flashed in the sunlight. She swiped it with her other hand and lifted it to her nose, for a brief moment forgetting she couldn't smell. Absence—that's what she smelled, an immense clarity in her nose. She let her arm collapse to her side. She thought it might be an antibiotic cream, but then she saw the sheen on her other arm and her hands, and she ripped back the blanket and saw it on her legs. She was filled with a swooning feeling, and she loved it. It had to be the morphine.

She glanced at the clock. Only ten minutes had passed. Mya ripped the fluid IV from her arm and walked right out of her hospital room, her gown open in the back and flapping. Luke was upstairs, she knew that, but she didn't want to stop and ask for directions. The nurses would hurry her back to her room. She pushed the elevator button over and over, and when it wouldn't open, she took the exit and hustled up the gray stairwell. People stared at her in the third-floor waiting area, but she walked straight through and past the nurses' station, a woman calling, "Miss?" to her back. They were following her at this point, she was sure, but she searched every room in the hallway until she glanced through a window and saw Luke's father, with black hair covering him like a bear, standing there with his arms crossed.

Mya opened the door without knocking and there he was, awake, with a black patch over his left eye.

Luke's father uncrossed his arms. "What're you—"

"It's okay, Dad," Luke said, "I want to see her."

Three nurses barged into the room. "Miss Lenore, you can't be up here."

"I have to." She moved away from them and went to Luke's bedside, opposite his father.

"Sir?" one of the nurses said to his father.

His large hands scratched his forehead. He finally looked at Mya. She said, "You have no idea how sorry I am. I love your son and never wanted to hurt him."

Luke coughed and turned his head to Mya. She placed her fingers in his open palm. She bent down to Luke and stared into his one tired eye. "I mean it. I love you so much, and I should've told you earlier. Before all this. I've loved you this entire time." Mya dropped her forehead to his blanketed chest and tried to smell him, because she always had, and not being able to made her feel a hundred feet away from him.

His father nodded at the nurses, and they left the room. "I'll give you some time." He squeezed Luke on the shoulder. He didn't smile at Mya, but he didn't scowl anymore either.

Once the door closed, Luke caressed Mya's head. "Just in time."

"For what?"

"Doctor just came in."

"Oh no," Mya said.

"Lost vision in my left eye."

"No, no, no."

"But I can walk," Luke said. "I feel like I've been given another life. I don't care about the eye."

"You're not upset with me?" He shook his head, and she leaned into him and kissed him softly. Her jaw ached but she didn't care.

Luke took a deep breath through his nose. "I woke up and the room smelled like flowers. I still smell it, but I don't see any." He laughed. She hadn't seen him this happy in a long time. Maybe never.

"The accident," Mya said, "was my fault. Took my eyes off the road."

"What about the other driver?"

"She's okay," Mya said.

"That's good, then."

Mya gave him a weak smile, and she noticed the same shimmering oil on his body. "I came up here to tell you I love you. And I don't expect you to still love me anymore or want to be with me. I just needed you to know. I hate that I almost lost the chance to tell you. You have no idea how sorry I'll always be that you got hurt."

He remained silent, and she backed away from the bed. She was suddenly aware of how little her gown covered, how exposed she was. It was hard to watch him in the bed, so weak. He was her mountain man and she had permanently injured him. Mya walked to the door.

He said, "I've only been to two states. Did you know that? Down to North Carolina for a beach trip once and then back home."

"I didn't know," she said.

"I want to go to Disney World and Thailand."

Mya smiled. "You should do that, all of it."

He took a sip of water from a small white cup on his table. "I never thought about it much before."

Luke was too young *not* to travel. He would meet good people and beautiful women his age who would fall for him as easily as Mya had. Quartz Hollow shouldn't be his only place. "I think you'd love it. And you can always come home."

"Yeah, that's what my mom said."

So he was serious. Mya knew she'd have to let him go, but to have his plans be so final so soon made her chest burn. All she could say was, "Good," and she opened the door to go.

"But I can't go," Luke said, "if you stay. I need a tour guide."

The places on her body where she'd been rubbed with the oil warmed instantly. Luke looked down at his own arm and touched a spot.

"Do you feel that?" she said.

His eye widened and he looked startled. "I've got these warm spots all over." He pointed to a few others. "How'd you know?"

She returned to his bed and lifted up her arm for him. Luke examined her skin and then smelled it. "That's it," he said, like he'd solved a Rubik's Cube, and then he smelled his own arm.

"My sister did this," Mya said, "to protect us from further harm."

Luke said, "Oh," like he needed no other explanation, and she loved this most about him. He laced his hand in hers. "I'm serious, Mya. Go with me."

She shook her head. "My sister's pregnant."

"You're shitting me," he said. "Whose?"

"Ben's," Mya said.

"Damn, that was fast. An accident?"

"Planned, I think," Mya said.

"Old Bennie," he said. "That bastard. I had plans." A small smile appeared on his face.

"To impregnate my sister?" Mya said.

"Don't be stupid. I wanted to be the first to knock up a Lenore girl. I've sure been trying my hardest."

Mya said, "How romantic."

Luke put his hand on her shoulder and forced her to lean down closer. "You know I mean it," he said.

"I believe you," Mya said. She couldn't stop herself as she closed the blinds to Luke's room and locked the door. She climbed onto the hospital bed with him and he was ready for her. He lifted the sheet and she climbed underneath, keeping her weight off him as best she could in case he was sore. All the more reason they shouldn't do this right here, right now, but Mya couldn't stop. "I love you," Luke said in her ear, and she whispered, "I love you too," before sealing his mouth with hers.

## CHAPTER 41
# *Success Reigns*

S O WE'LL BEGIN production on that when, again?" Lucia scrolled down the November calendar. "Three weeks from now?"

Brenda said, "Right before Thanksgiving," with her notebook open in her hand. Lucia wasn't sure how Brenda kept up with everything in one tiny notebook and without an electronic device, but Willow had promised Lucia she could, and she was right.

Robert scratched his beard and said, "It'll increase winter productivity at least forty percent, and we won't cut the workforce this season."

"It's a good deal." Lucia smiled as she marked the date, then saved it and closed the laptop. She dropped both hands on top of the smooth metal and said, "I think that's it for today."

Robert and Brenda stood and gathered their coats. Robert helped Lucia put on her red pea coat and she buttoned the front; it was still large enough to cover her second-trimester baby bump. "Feeling well?" Robert said.

Lucia nodded. "Too good. Can't stop eating." She finished her sixth chocolate chip granola bar of the day.

They walked into the kitchen, and Lucia looked out the window above the sink at the world outside. It had already started to darken, as it did too soon in the autumn months. The leaves were golden, ruby, and orange and fell with the large wind gusts. The grass had already begun to disappear beneath the blanket of leaves.

"Want me to wait?" Brenda said.

"No, I'll close up," Lucia said, and opened the refrigerator. The shelves were bare except for diet ginger ales and juices. "Thanks, both of you, for coming."

"Tell your mother hello when she calls," Robert said.

Lucia laughed. "If she ever does."

"She's having too much fun." Brenda wrapped a blue scarf around her neck.

"Too much sun." Robert opened the door and a wren flew into the house. Brenda waved her hands and said, "Shoo," but it landed on top of the kitchen table. Robert and Brenda left the cabin and waved good-bye.

"Every time," Lucia said to herself, but then she grew quiet thinking about Mya and how long it had been since she'd called home too. Lucia missed them both. The cabin was just an office space now, uncluttered and hollow. No books out, stacks of paper, or piles of laundry, and no bird's nests, antlers, snakeskins, or whatever else Mya brought in from the woods.

Mya and her mother had probably felt the same way about Lucia while she had been away in that other life with Jonah. She had rarely thought about them then, and she hoped her mother and Mya were too wrapped up in their lives to think about her now. They'd both promised to be home for the birth, and Lucia could wait five more months. If only they'd check in once in a while . . . but now she sounded like her mother.

Lucia turned out the lights in the kitchen, and when she opened the front door, the wren dashed over the top of her head and went out to the porch. She locked up, a habit she couldn't let go from her days in the city. She stopped to watch the fading golden light of the sun pushing through the bright yellow leaves on the maple tree next to the house. A herd of deer came from behind the cabin and stopped at the bottom of the steps.

"Hi there," Lucia said. They looked at her sideways and circled her. "Should I come with you?" she said to them. They continued moving to the side of the house and then back toward the fields. Lucia wasn't a great substitute for Mya, but lately the deer had been hanging around the cabin when she came over for work. She spent so much time at the factory working on the expansion of Lenore Incorporated's new line of organic goat's milk beauty products and mineral cosmetics, all formulated from local ingredients. The endeavor brought all of Quartz Hollow together and stabilized employment even more. She tried to have meetings with Brenda here once a week or so, and she always put out corn and carrots for the deer. Before Mya and Luke left for Sweden to volunteer as reindeer trackers, Lucia had promised to give attention to the deer Mya was leaving behind.

Tonight the herd just wanted some company. They walked slowly up the hill, and Lucia trailed them. Hiking felt good after a long day of conference calls. It was a two hundred e-mail kind of day, but the highlight was talking to Jennifer Katz after lunchtime. Oscar buzz circulated like a honeybee swarm around Jennifer's most recent film, in which she'd nailed the part of a mother who willingly gives up custody of her children because she wants to be a musician. Jennifer didn't want to have children, but after making this film, she said she sometimes looked for toys in her house and bought kids' things when she shopped, all of which she promised to send to Lucia. They never talked about Zoe. Or Mya. Just the Oscar and how Lucia's daughter would be born in the season of the awards.

Once Lucia crested the hill with the deer, they trotted quickly and paused at the edge of the woods. Lucia couldn't keep going. Her feet were swollen and tired, and it was too dark to go deep into the land with them. She half expected to find her dragonflies hovering there, but they'd been gone for months, and with winter nearing, the deer would soon stop coming around regularly. The fields were flat, the flowers picked. The shrubs were green and woody and waiting for spring.

Maintenance workers had aerated the land this past week and dug out a trench around the fields to fill with wooden beams to protect the plants from runoff. All Ben's idea. He was the director now. Soon they'd add organic matter and a thick layer of fallen leaves. The adjacent trees would provide what they needed. Lucia placed her hands on her belly and rubbed it. She imagined patting her daughter's head when Grace finally came into the world. The deer stood still, watching her, and she felt like she was missing something. She turned around, but nothing was out there with them, save the rustling leaves that had already fallen and the grass, turned pale for the season. Darkness would descend soon, once the sun fell beneath the tree line. It was time for Lucia to go home and have cast-iron roasted chicken and herbed risotto with Ben.

The deer remained like a still life against the trees in the distance, the mountains beyond patched where some trees had shed to their winter bareness. Lucia inhaled a deep breath of burning wood. The deer had revealed absolutely nothing, except what the season of her life looked like now: quiet but altered. She'd spent the summer learning what it meant to be pregnant and how to run a business: morning sickness and a job to do and learning from her mother how to manage employees, build their trust, and delegate duties to an assistant. She had so many names to learn. Conducting interviews with Willow had been easy, and she'd quickly memorized the contract, but she wouldn't begin movement on anything new until after Grace's birth. Willow and James would be here when Lucia took her first business trip to New York, and as long as her mother's health was good, she might come with her. During all of this training, she'd even moved into Ben's house, and together they'd prepared the nursery. Ben's mother, who finally agreed to move in with them, had died suddenly on the Friday the baby furniture was delivered, and the funeral took place a few days later. The transition into autumn had been an arduous one.

Lucia walked back to the cabin and reminded herself to grab the folder of account summaries for the upcoming year. She returned to the office, so much Willow's room still. Same furniture, same lamps, same rug, same books. Lucia liked to pretend she didn't have enough time to change it. Both Brenda and Robert assumed the familiarity brought Lucia comfort, and that was fine. Feeling her mother's presence in the room made being alone in the cabin much easier to tolerate. One immediate change, however, had been the clutter. Lucia couldn't work in it. She could now use the desk drawers to store important folders—like the one that she couldn't seem to find now. She opened each and every drawer and then repeated the process. During the more stressful parts of her day she'd made a habit of holding the dragonfly pendant and sailing it back and forth on the chain as if it were flying. The rhythm helped her to concentrate. The golden light thinned and warned of the setting sun. Lucia stopped moving the dragonfly and retraced her steps: *e-mails, meetings, phone calls, spreadsheets, business proposals*. All activities she'd completed at the desk.

But then Jennifer had called, and that wasn't about business. They had chatted, and Lucia always paced around the office when she spoke on the phone for pleasure. There on the towering corner bookcase was the cream folder she needed. She'd slipped it in between a couple of old books to keep it steady. The folder was stuck, so she removed the oversize book titled *Rain Forests* along with her folder, and an item slipped to the floor. Lucia opened her folder to see what she'd lost, but she'd clipped everything together.

She bent down to find a warped picture of Great-Grandmother Serena resting against her shoe: Serena's hair was in a messy pile on her head (Lucia's hair responded to humidity just like that), her sleeves cut off, her pregnant stomach bulging over her pants. Serena stood next to Great-Grandfather Alex as he hugged her. A large palm tree trunk towered in the background. Lucia flipped over the photograph and saw that Serena had scrawled, *Much in love, forever and always, Borneo, 1927.* Serena had not yet discovered *Gardenia potentiae.* She had her entire life ahead of her. Lucia flipped it back over. That could've been Lucia in the rain forest, it looked so much like her.

She wondered if Willow had ever seen this picture before. Lucia opened her folder and clipped the picture on top of the business documents so she could show her mother when she and James visited. Lucia turned off all the lights in the cabin and lifted her purse and leather satchel from the kitchen table, then deposited it all into her Volvo station wagon, which was parked outside. She'd just begun heading down the driveway when her cell phone rang. She rarely stayed this late at the cabin and Ben was probably worried. She fumbled for the phone in her coat pocket. A restricted number.

"Hello?" she said.

"It's me."

"Finally." Lucia drove slowly down the gravel drive.

Mya sounded like she was smiling when she said, "I've got news."

"Coming home?"

"We are," Mya said. "How'd you know?"

"Lucky guess."

Mya laughed.

"I still need a creative director." Lucia turned right on Highway 221 to go home to Ben. "Got a big project ahead, if you're interested."

As if she hadn't heard her, Mya said, "I can't wait to see you."

"Me too. And Mom? Have you heard from her?"

"She'll be there before you know it." Mya's voice was breaking up. All Lucia caught was "Coming for Thanksgiving."

"Of course you are," Lucia said. "Because you know I can't cook."

"Lucia."

"You're breaking up."

"Can you hear me?"

"Now I can."

"I've got another reason."

"Oh yeah?"

"I'm coming back so I can birth him at the cabin."

Lucia wasn't sure she'd heard her right. "Him?"

"That's right."

Lucia placed one hand on her belly and Grace began to kick, finishing with one swift jab beneath a rib. Lucia adjusted herself in the driver's seat and said, "Get home soon then."

"We're in transit."

Lucia heard static and called out for her sister, then the line went dead and she dropped the phone in the seat next to her. All those crushed rose petals Mya and Lucia had rained down had pieced themselves together. Lucia switched on her headlights to help her navigate in the dark. Of all the lives she could've had, this was the only one she wanted.

# *Acknowledgments*

Many thanks to the following:

Alexandra Machinist, for discovering me in the slush pile and following your intuition. Rachel Kahan, editor extraordinaire. I can't imagine this novel without your suggestions. And Laura Cherkas, for your keen eye. I am indebted to all of you, and to everyone at William Morrow.

My colleagues at Queens University of Charlotte, especially Charles Israel, Julie Funderburk, Mike Kobre, and Melissa Bashor for reading drafts of this novel (and others) and supporting me. Boris Vinatzer, associate professor of Plant Pathology, Physiology, and Weed Science at Virginia Tech, for answering all of my questions about plant science.

All my dearest friends, especially Megan Ihlefeld, Matthew Lee, and Jennifer McGroarty, for leading lives of adventure and sharing those stories with me. Nina de Gramont and David Gessner, for showing me what it means to live and love as writers.

My mother, Chareatha Franklin, and my sister, Rachel Ripley, for being first readers and never doubting what I hoped to achieve. My daughters, Mimi Creech and Hattie Creech, for understanding why I spend so much time in front of my laptop.

And my husband, Morri Creech, for promising.

## About the author

## About the book

Insights,
Interviews
& More . . .

## Read on

# Meet Sarah Creech

Magen Portanova

SARAH CREECH was born and raised in Lynchburg, Virginia, a small city in the foothills of the Blue Ridge Mountains, and she grew up in a house full of women who told stories about black cloud visions and other premonitions. She attended the University of North Carolina, Wilmington's undergraduate creative writing program and went on to receive an MFA in fiction from McNeese State University in Lake Charles, Louisiana. Her work has appeared in various literary journals, such as *storySouth* and *Literary Mama*. She currently lives in North Carolina with her two children and her husband, the poet Morri Creech, and she teaches English and creative writing at Queens University of Charlotte. When she's not writing, she spends her time gardening, cooking, and mothering. ∾

# On Inspiration

I'M DRAWN TO PEOPLE who seek adventure. I pull from the richness of their stories once they've returned from their journeys. As it happened, a dear friend of mine traveled to the rain forests of Borneo in the South China Sea to study orangutans at Camp Leakey, a refuge and rehabilitation center established by Birute Galdikas. I couldn't go with my friend, even though I was desperate for a trip. I had a two-year-old daughter and a job, so I went along in spirit by reading Birute's accounts of her time in Borneo, from the moment she arrived to the moment she left.

I was most moved by her memoir, titled *Reflections of Eden*. I'm inspired by the fearless spirit of women like her, and Jane Goodall and Dian Fossey, to name but a few powerful female scientists. I wanted a character to go to that mysterious and beautiful place like Birute did and find self-affirmation. What my character Serena finds is the magical flower at the base of the perfume in my novel *Season of the Dragonflies*. The perfume Serena develops guarantees any woman who wears it extreme success in the career she most desires. And that's how my writing process began, with Serena Lenore traveling to the South China Sea at the turn of the twentieth century. From there, the novel is about Serena's heirs and what they do with the business she created.

American women are more powerful

now than they have ever been. Soon women will make up more than half of all physicians, and that's just one field in a steady trend. With the Lenore family perfume I wanted to create a product that mirrored the growing influence of women in our culture. More and more women are given conflicting messages about our roles as mothers and workers. We are told to lean in, which we can control, or that we can't have it all, which is out of our control because of our biological clocks. I wanted my novel to explore the tension between these two messages through the Lenore family, who are trying to help other women by taking away the glass ceiling, by streamlining and accelerating success. I also wanted to explore the possible consequences of this effort. What do the Lenore women sacrifice in their lives in order to provide this perfume to others? ∽

# Lost in the Stacks

BECOMING LOST IN THE STACKS at
the library became my precursor for
becoming lost in the pages of a novel.
I visited the small public library on
Memorial Avenue in Lynchburg,
Virginia, with my single mother.
We went multiple times a week.
While she searched the stacks for
the ten or more books she'd check
out that day (by nightfall they'd be
strewn about her bed and on the floor
like jacks) I had no choice but to play
in the nearby stacks, touching the
rough spines of adult books I was
not allowed to read. Someday, though,
I would be able to, my mother promised
me, and maybe even write novels once
I grew up.

My habit of running my palms
along the spines of books and stopping
wherever I had the impulse to stop
followed me through all of my adolescent
years, as I haunted the middle school
and high school libraries. I discovered
*A Raisin in the Sun* with this tactic,
along with Fitzgerald and Henry James.
I continued to let my hands guide me in
the stacks during my college years, when
I could drink a cappuccino—nobody
seemed to care about those café noises
inside the library—and walk through
the stacks in a languorous manner,
letting my fingertips touch the spines
of the titles. I found Faulkner, Welty, the
Brontës, Richard Yates, the screenplay
for *Pretty Woman* (the original does not
have a happy ending), and other oddities

this way. It's that sense of suspense and surprise that I desire when I read novels. Libraries taught me this feeling first, however, by allowing me to discover books curated by someone else. What world would I find on the top, middle, or bottom shelf? Each trip to the library with my mother felt like a vacation we couldn't otherwise afford.

I'm all grown up now and with a daughter of my own who's about to turn five. She loves libraries, too, but she's growing up in a much different environment than I did. She lives in a big city compared to my hometown. We have twenty public library locations in Charlotte, North Carolina, compared to the two I grew up with in Lynchburg. My daughter has access to Imaginon, a large library facility devoted to children's and young adult's books. They have children's yoga on Saturdays, a large train to climb on, a theater for seeing plays, and rotating installations for imaginary play. Right now they have a fairy tales exhibit where children can make shoes like the elves and try on slippers like Cinderella. They can dine like kings and queens. And when they're done with all that fun, they can race past shelves of books on their way to other rooms in the library where iPads are attached to desks with learning games available at their fingertips. The resources at this library astound me. It's a requirement that we read books when we go to this library, but that activity competes with a tremendous number of stimuli. My daughter doesn't get lost in the library stacks. She's in a ▶

playground amid the books, but books are no longer the playground.

Just to make sure she receives the old-fashioned library experience, I take my daughter to the library at Queens University of Charlotte, where I teach. Recently, they moved the entire collection of books to the basement, in an effort to decrease the stacks and move to more digitized information. This frees up much-needed space in a small library. North Carolina State University uses the bookBot robotic book retrieval system so that no stacks are visible. Books are kept in a climate-controlled storage facility. A robot retrieves a book for the reader within minutes, and the entire system uses a fraction of the space as traditional shelves. I understand the appeal. I wish our library had more books, as it is my main resource for researching the novels I want to write. However, I have a very hard time imagining a library where I couldn't search for the books the best way I know how: browsing in person. Sometimes I don't look up titles. I disappear into the stacks and let my intuition guide me. I found a Coco Chanel biography this way, and that text became an important resource for my novel *Season of the Dragonflies*.

I plop my daughter down in front of the small collection of children's books, and she browses, too. She comes away with books about geometric solids and African American spirituals. It is this freedom to roam the books that made me love books and the place that housed.

I hope my daughter will carry into her future the strong sensory memories of being at Queens, with the smell of dusty books and the quiet of a basement. I hope she'll remember our time there together as playful, even though the book selection was small and the toys nonexistent.

I'm told by my librarian friends that going digital (and stackless) is the future of library spaces. I hope the American spirit of innovation will find a way to re-create the anticipatory feeling of browsing. Perhaps a 3-D image of the stacks, one in which a reader can scroll with her finger as if she's touching the spines along the shelf? Whatever happens, I hope my daughter will remember this feeling of chance and possibility whenever she enters that ever-sacred space known as the library. ᴄᴡ

# Reading Group Guide

1. Did Serena earn the unique gardenia and its potent gifts? Is the flower truly inherited wealth for her descendants or do they too have to find a way to earn its magic?

2. What prompted Serena to curse any variation of her perfume's formula? Do you think her concerns were justified?

3. Serena becomes a mother at a young age and then later a businesswoman, as does Willow. Lucia and Mya are in their thirties when motherhood and business become important factors in their lives. How does this prolonged adolescence affect Lucia and Mya?

4. Choices and consequences are major themes in the novel. How many of Mya's choices are prompted by anger or selfishness? Does she deserve the consequences?

5. Zoe Bennett blackmails the Lenore family and is viewed as a villain by Mya and Willow. Did Zoe have a legitimate grievance with the Lenore family? Was Mya right to take action against her?

6. The Lenore family business is essentially a black-market operation with little oversight. Do they abuse their wealth and power? Is their scent always a force for good?

7. Discuss Lucia's role within the Lenore family. Why did her gifts remain dormant for so long? What brings them to the fore?

8. "Willow didn't want to lie to her daughter, but Lucia had work to do, and getting her feelings involved would only hamper her. This above all else, was the most important business skill to master." Do you agree? How has this business skill affected Willow's relationship with her daughters over the years?

9. How are the men in the book—Alex, Luke, James, Ben—a part of the flower's complex relationship with the Lenore women? Is the gardenia truly a woman's flower or do the men also play a role?

10. What is the future of the Lenore women and their perfume? Will the company change under Lucia's leadership? What will Mya's role be now that her sense of smell is gone? How will their stewardship of the company differ from their mother's?

11. How does fragrance affect your life? Is there a special perfume or scent that reflects your identity? What fragrances instantly evoke emotion or memories for you? ❧